THE POT

LEGAC

PART ONE:
DOMUS MUNDI

BY

CHARLES DAY

ANCIENT TIMES

PROLOGUE

Master Ourea was trying to do four things at once. None of them well. He tried smiling to himself, but it didn't work. Tension spread across his shoulders forcing blood through his veins.

"All life involves risk," he murmured. "Our life depends on it." Damp crimson hair dropped over his face. He swept it back. His eyes ached. He knew they'd be spiked with fire.

Calm down. Breathe

He pulled his hood over his head.

One thing at a time. Concentrate. Slow down...

He reached into the leather bag hooked over his shoulder. First one hand, then the other.

Using his fingertips, he pulled the bundle out.

"Shhhhh... Quiet now..."

Wrapped in hessian cloth, he set the bundle down next to a polished, silver stone.

"Argentum Metallicum," he murmured. He closed his eyes. Breathed in. "This is the right thing to do," He opened his eyes again. "Then do it, you old fool!"

He glanced over his shoulder. Still no sign of Dominus Hephaestus. "Nice and steady. As we've practised."

He scraped away the bark, leaves, and gravel uncovering the granite rock beneath. He took another look over his shoulder, took a step back from the silver rock and fired up his atomic plasma cutter. Lines he'd cut before threw thin shadows in the dusk. Dismissing his usual finesse, he wielded the cutter more like a novice than a surgeon and cut a rectangular hole through the granite.

"Half-way there..." He turned his plasma cutter off, rotated the tool in his hand, pointed the opposite end at the granite block and switched the tool back on again. A tractor beam reached out, gripped electric fingers around the rock and heaved it out, leaving a hole big enough for him and the bundle to squeeze through. He paused. Silence. "20 minutes. That's all I've got." He peered into the hole. The sun took its final rays over the hill. Fumbling through his pockets, Ourea took out a small, powerful torch. He tossed it into the dark. "Perfect," he muttered.

He picked up the bundle, cradled it in his cloak, stepped into the hole and climbed down the stairs he'd first carved a year ago. "Whatever you do, don't slip."

Fourteen steps later, he reached the bottom of the cavern. Ignoring the body on the floor, he rushed over to the smaller of the two pearl stasis cots. Placing the bundle on the ground, hands disappearing into the hessian, he brought out a six-month-old baby girl.

"Don't look at me, sweet child." Ourea squeezed his eyes. The baby blinked. She gazed at Ourea and smiled. "Don't waver now. You have come this far – this is the right thing to do." The baby didn't make a sound as Ourea strapped her into the cot, her eyes following his every move. She reached up and grabbed his finger. "Don't look." Ourea wiped tears from his cheeks. "Whatever you do, don't look."

Trusting eyes stared back at him as he closed and sealed the pearlescent cot. Ourea's finger caressed the power button. "Do it," he whispers. His trembling finger pressed the button. At once, tremors rippled through the child's body as her eyes closed. The cot beeped confirmation that all bodily functions had ceased.

Ourea fell to the floor, wrapped his arms across his chest and squeezed his fists tight. Almost without his permission, one hand darted back to the controls. He pulled it back.

"Don't stop now. Get on with it."

Turning his back on the child, Ourea rummaged around in his cape, his guilty fingers found what he was looking for. He crawled over to the body lying between the two cots, carefully chose one of three syringes, bent over the body, and injected its contents into a cavity just behind its right ear. With shaking hands, he selected a second, smaller syringe. Bile rose in his gut. He placed the tip of the syringe millimetres from the centre of his right eye. He took one deep breath, then pushed the needle straight in. He kept pushing until he felt resistance. The resistance that triggered the syringe to automatically inject half of its contents into the vitreous body, deep within his eye.

The syringe, not caring for its patient, beeped softly, telling Ourea to remove the needle. He obliged. Breathing hard, he paused a moment, wiped sweat from his brow, and in one swift moment he repeated the process, injecting the remaining half into his left eye. Dropping the syringe on the floor, he had just enough time to put on soft leather gloves before the agony started. First, his right, and then his left eye. He rolled to the floor, pressing the gloves to his eyes, stopping his nails from ripping them out. Seconds before insanity kicked in, the pain ebbed away. Ourea stood up, straightened his cloak, dusted his gloves, blinked, and tapped the child's cot. "Now." He cleared his throat. "That wasn't so bad was it?"

Extinguishing the torch, he hobbled up the granite steps, paused at the top to look and listen. Satisfied he was still alone, he clambered out of the cavern.

Scurrying over to some bushes, he found the planks of wood he had prepared earlier and placed them over the entrance to the cavern. Ourea then covered the planks with leaves, mud, and twigs. All the time mumbling to himself. "Come on, come on, nearly there." With the cavern hidden from view, he sat. "First stage complete," he whispered and smiled for the first time in days. "Where was Hephaestus?" Ourea had less than 60 minutes to accomplish the next phase and that phase couldn't start until Hephaestus arrived.

"Patience," he said to the trees. "Pompous Hephaestus may be bombastic, certainly, punctual, always." His hair on the verge of turning red now reverted to flaxen. His eyes calm. His pulse controlled. Sure enough, moments later Hephaestus burst into view, shattering the quiet and solitude as he huffed and puffed into sight. "Ah, Ourea, there you are," he boomed. "I have been all over Saxa Antiquis looking for you!"

A blatant lie, Ourea thought. All you had to do was switch on your portal tablet, insert my cluster and my exact location would have appeared on the screen.

"Well, Dominus Hephaestus, you have found me now," replied Ourea turning to look at the citizen before him. What he saw was more or less an image of himself, and indeed every other one of the male species of his kind. A strikingly beautiful biped of average height, 2m 50cms, with long, lean legs. Two long and extremely powerful arms and hands. A powerful chest, lean stomach, and hips. A head in proportion to the massive body. The skin, smooth and translucent, and as perfect and as beautiful as Italian white statuary marble. Like Ourea, the hair had no set colour. It changed shade to reflect the natural surroundings and emotional state. The individual had no control, other than to fight the emotions that drove the change.

Ourea leaned back, took a breath, and smiled. His hair tinted red for a moment and settled back to gold as he looked into Hephaestus' eyes which were, by far the most startling, frightening, hypnotic and beautiful thing about these individuals. They were black. So black they seemed to absorb all light, with no reflectance whatsoever. The iris, pupil, and sclera were indistinguishable. Yet within the depths of this utter blackness were specks of pure gold. The specks of gold made indiscriminate patterns within the pure black of the eyes. Yet these patterns were as unique to the individual as fingerprints are to humans. But, unlike fingerprints, the gold patterns were a true measure of the temperament of the individual. The more tranquil, the more indistinct the colour became. The more passionate, the fiercer and brighter they burned.

Hephaestus' eyes were incandescent, yet his hair was a beautiful yellow, telling Ourea that Hephaestus was full of passion and excitement, rather than anger and hostility.

"You've finished!" bellowed Hephaestus, as he tripped over his voluminous cape.

"Yes, Hephaestus," replied Ourea. "The final circulus, Saxa Antiquis, is complete. The work on this alien world is almost done. One task is all that remains."

Hephaestus could barely contain himself. "Saxa Antiquis," he sighed. "A sight to behold." He reached out and stroked the cold granite of the great stone circle. "Thirty megaliths," he beamed at Ourea. "They said it wasn't possible!" He stared up at the megalith capped lintels forming a continuous ring and stepped inside. He ran his hand across the stones of the smaller inner circle. "Sixty standing stones?"

Ourea nodded. "All there."

In the centre of the standing stones loomed five great stone arches or trilithons, arranged in the shape of a horseshoe. Inside the horseshoe were 19 solitary obelisk-like standing stones, mirroring the horseshoe shape.

"The pièce de résistance," Hephaestus clapped his hands. "Argentum Metallicum. Will anyone ever appreciate this exceptional metallic rock? They will never know it crossed galaxies to be here."

Hephaestus couldn't take his eyes off Saxa Antiquis. "This is the key," he shouted. "Linking all the other monuments together. Argentum Metallicum." He stared at the gleaming silver slab. "The heart, the brain, the life of not only Saxa Antiquis, but all the other monuments on this world." Hephaestus threw his arms in the air. "Saxa Antiquis will bring the whole chain to life!" Eyes blazing, hair a deep crimson, he turned to Ourea and nodded.

"Get on with it, then."

Ourea reached into his cape and brought out two leather containers, one red and one green. Unimpressive and unassuming, and quite, quite dead.

Stage two, Ourea thought.

He approached the central trilithon, standing greater in height and width to its four brothers. Ourea went first to the left leg, the atomic plasma cutter in hand. This time, much more deftly, he cut a rectangular, but shallow hole into the slab. Nodding his approval, he went to the right leg and cut a parallel duplicate. Taking his gloves off, Ourea used fingertips to open the green leather container, reached in and carefully withdrew a transparent obelisk containing deep in its core, a clear, almost transparent plasma.

"Don't drop it!" Hephaestus leaned forward but plunged his hands into his cloak.

Ourea flexed his fingers, still tingling from touching the clear, ironstone obelisk. He put the gloves back on and lowered it into the recently excavated hole. Once the green obelisk had been installed, Ourea offered up a silent prayer to his Gods that the injections into his eyes had worked. He then cleared his mind and gazed intently at the obelisk. Locked in a hunched position, Ourea remained completely still. He didn't move, didn't waver. He stared. After a few minutes, the obelisk glowed. Very slowly the plasma turned a brilliant white, then got darker until it was as black as Ourea's eyes. Still, Ourea didn't move. Still, Ourea stared at the obelisk. Then, within the utter blackness, pinpricks of tiny gold began to appear. Slowly, the dots grew larger and more substantial, moving and changing shape as they did. Finally, the dots configured themselves into a replica of the gold dots in Ourea's eyes, they then faded to dark bronze and froze. The obelisk pulsed and Saxa Antiquis began to vibrate.

"It's working!" Hephaestus rocked on his heels.

Ourea looked up for a moment and rubbed his eyes. Ignoring the searing pain in the back of his head, he rose and went to the red leather container and retrieved the second obelisk. He walked calmly to the second hole, hunched down, and repeated the process. Again, as soon as the golden dots inside the plasma configured themselves into a replica of Ourea's eyes, the dots faded to dark bronze and froze. Ourea trembled. Fear? Excitement? Both? A palpable sense of life and purpose swelled from the stones. Saxa Antiquis was alive and it was communicating. For the last time, Ourea switched on his plasma cutter and using the same tenderness he gave to the child, he heated the slab. As he did, the slab changed phase from solid to liquid and began to flow. The liquid rushed into the hole and surrounded the obelisk. Ourea switched off the plasma cutter and watched as the liquid solidified, leaving a seamless, unblemished surface without a hint that the surface had ever been touched. The plasma obelisks were hidden for all eternity.

Now, standing in this immense structure, Ourea felt a little afraid, reflecting on what he... they had done. Throughout this land, they had built a network of over 1,500 of these stone monuments, Saxa Antiquis being the Holy Grail. It had taken time. Even with all the technology that they had available to them. It had still taken fifteen complete rotations around this planet's star to accomplish this. But they had done it. All of these monuments, except for Saxa Antiquis were listening stations. They were placed to record what happened on these lands, to transmit the data to Saxa Antiquis, and Saxa Antiquis would relay the information back to Domus Mundi.

"Are you sure Saxa Antiquis is properly aligned." queried Hephaestus somewhat pompously.

"Of course," responded Ourea placidly, as if lecturing a child. "Saxa Antiquis has a permanent line of site to Domus Mundi... Furthermore, Argentum Metallicum will, if correctly operated, act as a portal allowing immediate transportation back to Domus Mundi."

"The Rursum-Alium Bridge?" Hephaestus whispered, inflected with fear and awe.

Ourea merely nodded. "Yes, the Wormhole."

A dark silence descended between the two citizens as they contemplated the enormity of what they had just said. Hephaestus shook himself. "Wormholes indeed, the stuff of fantasies and nonsense," he said aloud, trying very hard to cover his fear. "It's a spaceship for us. We will be home in a year! You coming, Ourea?" he boomed.

"In a while." Ourea dropped his hands to his side. "You go ahead. I'll be along shortly."

"Don't be long then. Blast off for Domus Mundi tomorrow – early start."

"Yes, yes, soon." With that, Hephaestus crashed through the undergrowth on his way back to the shuttle. Ourea watched him go. Pompous as he was, Ourea was going to miss him. He was going to miss a lot. But he had work to do.

Stage 3, nearly there, he thought to himself.

Glancing over his shoulder he watched the single moon rising. A beautiful full moon in a uniquely cloudless sky. Strange, he thought, there seemed to have been a full moon quite recently. He shifted his gaze so that he was looking straight along the axis of Saxa Antiquis, his back to the large central trilithon and looked along the two sitting stones and waited… and hoped. His eyes ached. "Let me see it. Just one last time," he prayed aloud. There! Yes, there it was… Home.

He could just make out the twinkling of his home planet's sun. One last time, he thought. The light hitting the back of his eye had started its journey to this planet some 200 years ago. People he knew and loved had yet to be born. But he didn't care. Comforted and revived, he got back to work.

He went back to the grand arch of the central trilithon and studied the two standing stones that made up each side of the arch. He chose the left standing stone. Examining it closely, with one eye turned to the moon, he selected two points approximately 1.5m above ground level. Rummaging in a pouch in his voluminous cape, he withdrew two items and placed them on the grass. Using his plasma cutter, he cut into the rock, the flame danced like a firefly on a summer's evening. Ourea cut two parallel cavities into the rock, and once completed, he inserted the two packages into each of the cavities before imperfectly resealing the excavated hole. Work done. He waited a little longer. Looking up, he saw that the moon was just about to pass exactly over the siting stones, along the central axis of the open end of the horseshoe directly onto the central trilithon, reflecting beautifully off the central slab. This is what he'd been waiting for. The edge of the moon's reflection fell just a little higher than the site where the top of the newly installed packages lay. Quickly gathering his plasma cutter, the fireflies danced again. He carved three words, along the edge of the moonlight exactly over the area where he had placed the two packages. The letters of the words reflected in the moonlight. The words he carved were: Vica σώσε μας (Vica save us).

The moon marched on its endless journey, and soon the words were invisible. Even when Ourea shone his torch on the place where he'd carved the words, he couldn't make them out.

He looked one last time at his work. Satisfied that there were no traces of what he had done, he packed up his tools and hurried back to the entrance of the cavern.

Stage 4. The final stage.

He cleared away the debris, moved the planks of wood and climbed down the steps. His eyes fully accustomed to the dark, he didn't need a light. He hurried over to the larger stasis cot and picked up the final syringe, moved over to the inert body on the floor and injected the cadaver, this time through the ear and directly into the brain. He stood back and waited. He stared at the hands. That would be the first sig. The fingers twitched. Ourea leaned against the stasis cot and breathed out. The limbs twitched, the body shook, the hair a cascade of rainbow colours. The body sat up, raised its head, and slowly turned towards Ourea. He had braced himself for this moment, but he started when he found himself looking at... himself!

Ourea watched as the clone's eyes cleared and focussed on him. Unlike Ourea, the clone wasn't surprised to see itself staring back at him.

"Hello, Ourea. I'm fully functional and understand exactly what must be done. I will leave you now and attend to my duties."

"Ah. Good. Right. Of course," Ourea removed his cloak.

The clone took the cape and the tools and stared at Ourea. "Is everything alright?"

Ourea nodded. "Fine. Absolutely..."

The clone donned the cape, ascended the stairs, and left the cavern. Ourea waited until he heard the granite slab scrape along the ground, saw it silhouetted in the night sky as it was gently lowered into place. Through the seams around the hole, he watched as the slab was atomised into place. The cavern was sealed. Ourea was alone with the inert baby on this alien planet. He went over to his stasis cot, secured himself in, and did a systems test. Programming the computer, he sealed himself in. One last look at the walls around him and the baby, he hit the button. Milliseconds later – oblivion.

PRESENT DAY
CHAPTER ONE

Thundering hooves of a thousand horses galloped through V's mind. The pain. The fourth night running. She knew before her blurred eyes focused on her bedside alarm clock that it would be 04:15 am. As it had been for the past three mornings. Her eyes glared at the red glowing numbers. They gleamed malevolently back... "Shit. I need sleeeeeeeeeeeep!" Thumping in her head told her that wasn't going to happen. She shut her eyes. The pain in her head intensified.

Winning the fight with her bedclothes at last, she sat up. The thudding of horses' hooves muted. The pain was gone. She knew that if she lay down again, the pain would return just as quickly as it had vanished. She felt brave enough to open her eyes again. As she did, a shaft of bright sunlight pierced them, searing her brain. She grabbed a pillow and buried her head in it, hoping by some miracle that that would help. It didn't. She turned around and was again hit by a thin sliver of blinding light. No matter where she moved on the bed, the beam of sunlight followed her. She checked her watch.

"04:17!" she screamed. What is it about this time in the morning? Four times now she had been forced awake by the pain in her head.

It's no good.

Giving up any hope of getting back to sleep, she tossed back the bed covers, stumbled into her slippers, grabbed her dressing gown, and slammed her bedroom door behind her. Now she was up and, on the landing, she paused for a moment as she wondered what to do next. Just as she was about to head for the stairs, a tall, striking man emerged from a door at the end of the corridor. Big-boned, large featured, trim giving way to a few extra pounds, with hair sticking up at all angles. The colour of that hair - well, V was never very sure. Sometimes blonde, sometimes white, sometimes grey. On this occasion, it seemed to be... orange? Must be the light, V thought. Uncle Peter. Her guardian and the man V loved and respected above all others.

V fell against him and wrapped her arms around his waist. The smell of wax, polish and old books bloomed off him. Not a patient man by nature, he exercised the most extraordinary

patience with her. He was supremely intelligent if a little eccentric - She had learned so much from him.

"Morning V," he said, somewhat blearily. "Heard you get up. I just wondered if all was well?" He managed to say all of this and navigate his way down the long hallway, with his eyes tightly closed. Just as he had finished speaking, a large and ominous crash, followed by a few choice words, emanated from the direction of the kitchen.

"Ah," Uncle Peter kept walking, eyes still tightly closed. "I do believe Mrs. Campbell is up...breakfast? Or is it too early? No," he said decisively. "Never too early for breakfast.... What do you say, V?"

But, just at that moment, V 0couldn't say anything. She grabbed Uncle Peter's hand and pulled him back from the top of the stairs. Uncle Peter's eyes flashed open, frowned at the stairs, and grinned at her. V looked into his eyes and once again felt herself drowning in Uncle Peter's most captivating feature. His eyes were the deepest, darkest, bluest eyes she had ever seen. They were so blue, they were almost black. Indiscriminately scattered within them were small, very fine specks of gold. But it wasn't so much the colour of his eyes that drew her in, it was how he looked at her. Sometimes, when he turned those magnificent eyes on V, she would feel like nothing in the universe could touch her. At other times they terrified her. They can see right through me, she thought. Never lie to Uncle Peter. No point.

"Oh, yes breakfast would be wonderful, thank you," replied V.

"Good Oh... Mrs. C, breakfast for two please," bellowed Uncle Peter, as hand in hand V navigated Uncle Peter down the long, imperious staircase.

Just as they reached the bottom of the stairs, a beautiful, melodic, serene voice that never needed to shout, yet could always be heard, sung out, "Is this a private breakfast, or is anyone invited?"

Uncle Peter and V turned and stared at the woman at the top of the landing – Aunt Izzy, Uncle Peter's wife. Beautiful, ageless, skin like porcelain. Aunt Izzy was tall, with a willowy, athletic, and strong figure. Her features were perfect, some may say elfin-like, but in perfect proportion to her build. Her smile was like the rising of the sun on a cold, bleak winter's day. Her hair a golden blonde colour, long and beautiful. Her eyes dark, soft and kind. Charming, intelligent and unpredictable. Always poking fun at Uncle Peter and his rather stiff and formal ways. If he was in a mood, she would tease him out of it in no time.

"Of course, my darling... Make that breakfast for three," Uncle Peter bellowed again, as they waited for Aunt Izzy to join them. Aunt Izzy, impeccable despite the early hour, glided down the stairs. In comparison, V felt like a bag of unwashed, un-ironed laundry. None of which was true. Despite her age, V cut a striking figure. Unusually tall, her hair was black, and long, hanging down to her hips. Her skin was flawless and white. The contrast between the black of her hair and the paleness of her skin made the gold flecks in her black eyes shine. When she wanted to, she had a beautiful yet gentle demeanour about her. But usually, she was strong-willed, stubborn and Mrs. Campbell would say, obstinate. Grabbing hold of V's other hand, the three of them strode off to the kitchen. Aunt Izzy looking long and hard at V; she tried to evade the stare, Uncle Peter was oblivious to it all.

Moments later they were in the kitchen. Huge, comfortable, warm and the "property" of the redoubtable Mrs. Campbell. V had to do a double take; Mrs. Campbell was usually primly and quite properly attired in a Victorian sort of way. Yet here she was, in an orange and yellow striped dressing gown, complete with hairnet struggling to keep her long and luxuriant snowy white hair in place. Pince-nez glasses on the edge of her nose, threatening to fall into whatever it was that she was creating on the Aga, and slippers – well V felt quite jealous of those slippers. They were grey with hippo heads where her toes were. This was a Mrs. Campbell that V had never seen before. The usual Mrs. Campbell came across as your archetypal Victorian grandmother: Full-bosomed, portly, short, wireframe glasses, a gentle nature, tinged with steel.

She must have once been young and beautiful thought V, but then again, as far as V was concerned, she had always been just as she is now: a mature lady, slightly bent but most definitely not broken. Always there for a cuddle, a comforting word, a word of advice, or a word of warning. Somebody V could always turn to if she ever needed to. Mrs. Campbell would always be there with a smile, a welcome and something tasty that would usually put V's weird world to rights.

Mrs. Campbell took Uncle Peter and Aunt Izzy by surprise as well. They stopped talking and stared at this strange apparition in their kitchen. Mrs. Campbell stopped what she was doing, turned around, summoned what dignity she could and stared back at the three of them. "What do you expect for 04:30 in the morning?" she asked, not unreasonably, before turning back and resuming her work at the Aga. Uncle Peter, Aunt Izzy, and V just looked at each other, looked at Mrs. Campbell and burst into laughter.

Mrs. Campbell smiled to herself, did an invisible jig and thought mission accomplished.

Once these three started it was almost impossible to get them to stop talking. They chattered away about anything and everything, only stopping to take a bite of food or a drink. Completely oblivious to what it was they were eating; they were so engrossed in each other. Mrs. Campbell's heart fairly sang with joy. She had been watching V very closely, as she had always done. She was aware that over the past few mornings something hadn't been quite right. She expected that this morning would be no different... She suspected that Aunt Izzy and Uncle Peter were also aware of what was happening to V, or at the very least, knew what was disrupting the girl's sleep. Nevertheless, Mrs. Campbell had her suspicions but was determined not to give in to them, so had devised this little plan and ridiculous wardrobe to try and lighten the moment, deflect whatever it was away from V, if only fleetingly. So far, so good, thought Mrs. Campbell again, quietly congratulating herself.

Breakfast done, V declared that she was going to change and go out for a walk, to clear her head before she started on her schoolwork. Besides, she added, the ponies need feeding.

"Your Aunt Izzy and I have to fly into town this morning. Be gone for a few days. Leaving at 9 am. Try to be back to see us off, eh?" bellowed Uncle Peter – he never did anything quietly. Mrs. Campbell froze at the kitchen sink. She slowly turned around and stared at Uncle Peter with a worried, questioning look in her eyes. He just looked back at her, the golden specks burning. Mrs. Campbell paled, her knees giving way, she collapsed into a chair. Oh God, she thought. Now? So soon?

V, oblivious to the sudden change in atmosphere knew that a request from Uncle Peter was really an order. "Absolutely! See you at 9!" V shouted as she dashed to her room.

Mrs. Campbell, a picture of abject misery, watched her go... Uncle Peter got up from his chair, went over to Mrs. Campbell and gently squeezed her shoulder before he left the kitchen. Mrs. Campbell's pleading eyes turned to Aunt Izzy who simply smiled, bent down, kissed her on the forehead and whispered, "We have no choice." Then she too was gone.

Lost in her thoughts, Mrs. Campbell just sat on her chair, her shoulders shook, her hands hanging low, making no attempt to conceal or even wipe away the tears as they streamed down her cheeks.

Startled by a door slamming and footsteps approaching at a rapid rate, Mrs. Campbell wiped her eyes, got up and went to the kitchen sink, ensuring her back was towards the door as V rushed in. "Don't be late," Mrs. Campbell shouted, just before the back door slammed shut.

V sighed with relief. Never happier than when she was outside, letting the free spirit within off the leash. The sun shone brightly, the sky was a beautiful blue, and the early morning dew was already burning off the grass.

In the distance, she could hear the boom of the waves as they crashed into the rocks and cliff faces to the west of her, a testament to the storm that passed through here a day or two ago.

She loved this place. This place was an island off the west coast of Scotland, very close to the Inner Hebrides called Udal Cuain (Scottish Gaelic for "to be tossed around by the Ocean"). The island had been the property of her guardian's family for centuries – going as far back as the 1500s. Uncle Peter had told her, with great pride, that the island had been gifted to them for faithful and loyal services by King James IV of Scotland, shortly before his death in 1513. The idyllic Island of Udal Cuain, is the westernmost of the Small Isles archipelago, in the Scottish Inner Hebrides. The closest neighbouring island is a twenty-minute ride by motorboat. The island is 7km long and 2km wide. The island's orientation is exactly north, south. The only buildings on the island are the huge manor house in which V and her guardians lived, plus various outbuildings, one of which had been converted to a house for Mr. and Mrs. Campbell. Electricity was provided by diesel generators; however, two large wind turbines had since been built and provided ample energy. Telephony, television, and access to the internet were provided by satellite as no telephone cables had been laid. Bizarrely, there was a helipad and a helicopter on the island very close to the house. V's uncle flew to the mainland as was necessary – for business reasons or shopping. Shopping she thought with a giggle. Most people go to the supermarket by car or bus or simply walk. But not Uncle Peter! Good old Uncle Peter has to go by helicopter!

There was a large bird population on the island comprising not only guillemots and razorbills but also sea eagles, golden eagles, and puffins. In the nearby waters dolphins usually played and occasionally smaller whales could be seen. For some unexplained reason, about 20 ponies were living on this island. How they got there, no one seemed to know – the only reasonable explanation was that many years ago an old, eccentric relative of V's uncle had them shipped over. The hardy beasts have existed and thrived ever since. The ponies were tame and could often be tempted to come over and have a nuzzle in exchange for an apple or a polo mint. V often thought they were strange beasts but couldn't quite put her finger on why. Still, she knew and loved them all. The coastline comprised striking basalt cliffs, with basalt pillars rising over the western part of the island and sea cliffs which dominated the northern part. To the south and eastern ends of the island are secluded sandy beaches, which were usually sheltered from the prevailing stormy weather conditions. One other unique feature of this island was Compass Hill. Not very tall, only 139 m above mean sea level, it sits on the eastern edge of the island. It was made of volcanic rock called tuff, but what made this hill unique was its huge iron content, so high that the compass of nearby ships were distorted, pointing to the hill rather than magnetic north. Somewhat wickedly, V had always thought that good old Compass Hill had been responsible for many a panic offshore and that some of those panics had resulted in a few necessary changes in underwear for some of those poor unsuspecting seamen! She glanced at the hill to her right and giggled at the thought.

But what made Udal Cuain special was the feature at the northernmost end of the island. It was this feature that constantly drew V. In all the years she had lived at Udal Cuain, she barely visited any other part of the island. Not out of choice, it seemed. She was pulled there. Always had been.

By now, V was approaching the Orchard. She could hear the soft, contented whinnying of the ponies. The whinnying getting louder the closer she approached. They know I'm here, she thought, and sure enough, the bigger pony, which she called Mr. Marmaduke, for no other reason than she liked the movie, came trotting over and nuzzled her for food. Expecting this, V dug into the bag she had brought and out came some bananas and raisins. She noticed that only five other ponies were with Mr. Marmaduke. So she shared out the remainder of the treats.

Once fed and petted, V resumed her journey to the northern end of the island. This time accompanied by Mr. Marmaduke and the five other ponies. Mr. Marmaduke walking along next to her, the other ponies ambling along behind her.

The closer she got to her destination, the faster her heart beat. Breath caught in her throat and butterflies erupted in her stomach... Her legs, on autopilot, knew exactly where they were going. Interaction with the brain wasn't necessary, which was just as well, because V's brain wasn't engaged on anything, other than taking in the landscape and willing her body to climb this last, steep rise.

Eventually, she crested the hill and sat. Not only to let her body recover but also to absorb the sight before her. Remarkable. So remarkable that it was, she felt sure, a complete secret from the rest of the world. It had to be. If anyone else knew this was here, Udal Cuain would drown in tourists. What was even more peculiar, was that she could find no record of this structure at all. She'd spent hours on the internet. Nothing. Even searching on Google maps revealed nothing at all. Oh,

Udal Cuain was there alright; the manor house, outbuildings, even the helipad, but where the structure was, showed up as nothing but grass and woodland. When she mentioned this oddity to Uncle Peter, he merely shrugged his broad shoulders and said, "Technology. You can't trust it," and ambled away, with what she thought was a weird, but kind of humorous look in his eyes.

This structure was magnificent. It comprised of enormous stones standing strong in a circular arrangement. The structure, which she called Pétalo, comprised an outer circle of thirty capped standing stones. The capped, standing stones surrounded five huge stone arches, which were in a horseshoe shape, all perfectly in place. There were also two circles made of smaller stones – one inside the outer circle and one inside the horseshoe. The entire site was surrounded by a circular ditch and bank, although V wasn't sure if the ditch and bank were connected to the standing stones, or whether this was a pre-existing structure, or whether this was just a coincidence. Despite its age, which, according to Uncle Peter was around 4,000 years, the structure was nearly flawless. The joins seamless, barely discernible. If it wasn't for the obvious weathering on the rock faces, then this structure could have been built yesterday.

However, what never failed to make her heart miss a beat was the large slab of what she could only describe as a silvery metallic rock which lay flat on the ground inside the inner horseshoe formation, a few meters in front of the central stone arch within the horseshoe. Despite its considerable age, the stone was flawless. It showed no sign of weathering, was smooth and metallic and glinted blindingly whenever the sun shone. This is where she would sit. No matter the time, the weather or the season, this stone was always warm – never cold and never hot. Just warm. And, to her, always seemed somehow vibrant and alive.

She settled herself comfortably. Mr. Marmaduke who had kept her company now wandered off a little way to feed on the lush grass which grew around the stones. The other ponies had disappeared.

V idly watched Mr. Marmaduke eating the grass and wondered why this place was never overgrown. It was always pristine. Everything about this place was pristine. She was never as peaceful or as content as when she was here. But she always felt a little afraid. Because despite the sense of peace, the perfection, the contentment, there was also the sense of unbridled power, just waiting to be unleashed.

Despite the still early hour, the morning was getting hotter. Feeling a little drowsy, V settled herself down on the silver metallic slab. The slab was far from uncomfortable and seemed to mould itself around her. She put her arms behind her head and gazed into the heavens, feeling not a little tired from her lack of sleep. She unshackled the reins of her mind and let it roam freely. At times like this, her mind did what it always did. It conjured up blurred pictures of her early childhood, of which she could remember very little. She tried so hard to grasp and hold onto those blurred images, to try and make sense out of her early childhood. But, just as the fingers of her mind were about to tighten their grip on those memories, they would immediately fade and then vanish.

Her earliest memory was, she guessed when she was about five or six years old. She was frightened, terrified. She had no idea where she was, except for the fact that she was on a bed – at least she thinks it was a bed. It was dark. She had never since been in such a dark place. She couldn't move. She thinks she was restrained somehow, because every time she tried to move, she would be gently pushed back into the bed. She remembered it was so quiet. Silent – which made it even more frightening for her. She didn't know how long she lay like that. In the silence. In the dark. Scared and afraid. It could have been days, it could have been hours, it could have been seconds. Then she became aware of a slight lightening, the dark wasn't so dark anymore. Slowly, the dark began to be replaced by a soft yellow light. The light seemed to come from everywhere at once, gradually pushing back the shadows. Her fear subsided, just a little. V became aware of sounds. And movement. The silence wasn't so silent any longer. The place that she was in wasn't so still and desolate. She wasn't sure what she heard or what she felt, but she knew it wasn't anything to concern her. Then slowly, her peripheral vision caught movement. She became aware of a shape, no, two shapes approaching her, then bending over her. Those shapes she later came to know as the faces of Uncle Peter and Aunt Izzy. She could remember looking into their eyes. Nothing was said. No words uttered. Her fear went, her uncertainties vanished. All those negative feelings replaced by warmth, love, and security. Two more shapes then approached and bent over her. The shapes that she came to know and love as Mr. and Mrs. Campbell. As V gazed into their eyes, time seemed to stand still. V's eyes became heavier and heavier. At last, they closed and she drifted off into a deep, dreamless sleep.

V's next clear memories of her childhood were when she was eight years old. She knew that for a fact because it was her eighth birthday. As far as her memories were concerned. One minute she was five or six years old, the next it was her eighth birthday. In those intervening years, she had no recollection of anything. Nothing. Just a blank. As if all of those memories had been wiped clean. Or, if she had never lived those years. She had asked Uncle Peter about it one day a few years ago. His response was quite typical: cryptic… He simply said, "V, my darling. The mind is both strange and powerful. Nobody understands how it works. Your brain has all the power connections, wiring, storage, memory, and processing power you need to function as a human being. If your brain is the hardware, then your mind is the software. It's the operating system that gathers, stores and manages information, using the massive processing resources of your brain."

"Yes, Uncle Peter, I see that. But this still doesn't explain why I have no memories of my childhood before I was five or six years old. And then only a fleeting memory of seeing you when I was in a cold, dark, lonely, scary place. Then nothing until I fell out of bed on the morning of my eighth birthday!!"

Uncle Peter said with a chuckle, "Yes, my love. I can remember that. You gave your Aunt and me quite a start. One-minute peace and quiet, the next, thud, followed by language your aunt and I were shocked you knew!" And with that he roared with laughter and disappeared into his study, slamming the door behind him.

To this day, V has no satisfactory explanation for the memory gaps. She settled deeper into the metallic slab as she thought about what little of her childhood she could remember. In fact. She was almost positive that from the moment she fell out of bed on her eighth birthday, she could pretty well remember everything that had ever happened to her, had been said to her, she had felt, she had experienced - up to and including this very day. Nothing left out. No blanks. Complete and uninterrupted memory.

She remembers an idyllic life on the island, with just her guardians for company. Uncle Peter and Aunt Izzy teaching her everything she needed to know from growing carrots to the theory of relativity. She often felt that she had done it all before. Everything was there in her mind. She just had to have someone remind her that it was there. Then she understood instantly.

She remembers every single day of the two years she spent at boarding school in Edinburgh. Academically, no one at the school even came close to V's ability. V tried to pass herself off as a normal kid who happened to pick things up quickly. In reality, everyone knew this wasn't the case. She was in no way challenged. It didn't matter what the subject was, or the degree of difficulty, she just understood what was being taught to her.

Unfortunately for V, all this positivity and excellence didn't translate well through her peers. She didn't have enemies, but she also had no friends. V wasn't seen as cool, nor was she seen as particularly likable. In fact, her peers were a little afraid of her. She wasn't bullied or taunted by the other girls; she was pretty much ignored. The girls left her alone. They would be polite and speak to her if they had to, they would put up with her. But, collectively, they refused to befriend her. They didn't bully her, so the teachers had no real power to do anything but watch V become more and more of a loner, an outsider. V's behaviour didn't change as a result. She was just as deferent, just as polite, and when needed, just as helpful to others. She seemed happy enough. The teachers felt she was just incredibly lonely.

In fact, nothing could be further from the truth. V was very happy to be left alone. She was happy to be cast out from the crowd; free to do her own things, go where she pleased, and not be beholden to anyone. She was often seen walking the grounds by herself, either holding a book, or just looking around with those hauntingly beautiful eyes, and a look of abject pleasure on her face. Or, she would be visiting the school menagerie. The animals had no prejudices, they were glad to see her. There she would sit for hours at a time, surrounded by them, happy in their company, with her own thoughts. The animals strangely calm and content As V thought about her time at boarding school, then her time at the island since boarding school, the day slowly got hotter. She became drowsy and drifted deeper into memories of Mrs. Campbell laughing and crying again, the day she returned to the island.

CHAPTER TWO

Uncle Peter's helicopter thundered metres overhead. V jumped up, paused for a moment as she tried to pull herself together. As she gathered her wits, she caught a glimpse of something odd a little way off in the distance. At first sight, it appeared to be a very large, old, odd-shaped coarse blanket propped up on sticks. She did a double-take and gazed at the strange object.

That's no blanket, she thought. That looks like an animal. A horse? A large, odd-looking and extremely dishevelled horse at that... "How the hell did that get here?" V asked herself.

By the time the thunder of rotors had settled into a dull roar, then to a distant rumble far over to the southeast, V became aware of someone yelling her name. She knew that voice only too well.

Shit, Shit, Shit, she thought to herself as she dragged her eyes away from the strange beast and turned them towards the bellow. As V did so, a huffing and puffing Mrs. Campbell crested the rise. Her face a mottled red, perspiration glinting from her top lip.

"There you are young lady. Do you know what time it is? You were supposed to be back in time to see your aunt and uncle off."

"Oh... sorry. I lost all track of time." V stole another glance in the direction where she had last seen the...apparition? Nothing. Whatever it was had gone. Had she imagined it? No.

"It's no good apologising to me, young lady. You promised to be back by nine to see your guardians off. No. I don't want to hear it. I have to get back to check on Mr. Campbell... You get yourself back to the house and get on with your studies. I'll check on you later,"

Without waiting for the now scrambling V, Mrs. Campbell turned and headed off in the direction from which she came. "I'm too old to be running around the countryside after your shenanigans!" She muttered as she went.

V smiled. Mrs. C would be out of the house for at least an hour? Maybe more? I wonder V thought. Do I have time?

V headed back to the house – leaving the elderly lady in her wake – which only helped fan Mrs. Campbell's temper.

Three miles of fast jogging later, V let herself into the house and found herself outside Uncle Peter's study. His inner sanctum, his Holy of Holies. She had only ever been inside twice. Only when invited and only when Uncle Peter was there. She looked at the door. What was usually an uninspiring and normal door, suddenly became a huge terrifying barrier guarding whatever was behind it. V was rooted to the spot. I shouldn't be doing this. Then something pushed her, urged her on. Someone or something was overriding her brain and forcing her to do the things she was about to do.

Of its own accord, V's hand reached out towards the doorknob. It felt cool to the touch. Her wrist twisted to the left. The knob turned effortlessly. She gave a gentle push, and the door swung open on silent hinges. She stood and looked around the room. V sensed that the study seemed to be aware of itself, of the history that echoed within its walls. An aroma that was somehow woody, smoky and earthy all rolled into one, permeated the space. No doubt from the shelves upon shelves and rows upon rows of books that fully occupied two walls. A ladder on wheels was connected to the wall and could move between the two walls, allowing access to every book, no matter which shelf or how high. The third wall was covered in nine flat-screen computer monitors - three rows of three.

In the centre of the room was Uncle Peter's desk. It owned the room. It was huge and seemed to be as old as time itself. The dark mahogany wood waxed to perfection shone and glinted in the sunlight, which streamed through two wall-to-ceiling windows that looked out onto the paddock. Behind the desk was a large, comfortable chair. In front of it, was a huge leather couch with a patina that would have taken hundreds of years to develop. In fact, other than the gleaming computer and the banks of monitors, the room seemed ancient. Wherever there was space, hung a picture or a painting. All of them old and most of them of people. One caught her eye – it was a picture of Pétalo. But Pétalo depicted in a way that she had never seen before. Almost like a building site, completely devoid of natural vegetation.

Something pressed against the small of her back, V fell into the room. She regained her balance and spun round – no one there. The door closed behind her, seemingly of its own volition. She was in. An uninvited guest in what appeared to be a very strange world. She continued studying the room. There were old sea chests neatly stacked in one corner of the room. Each chest secured with brass or copper bands and old steel padlocks. There was a whiteboard behind the desk, between the two windows. It was full of drawings, letters, symbols and writing in a language that she had never seen before. V stared at the huge whiteboard, trying to make sense of what she saw. She shrugged her shoulders, gave up, took another look around the room and paused. She almost missed it. In one of the walls of books, there appeared to be a door.

She sidled over to the door. It was smaller than a normal door and given Uncle Peter's size, she wondered how he managed to squeeze through it. She reached out to where the doorknob should be, only to brush against books. No doorknob. She looked at the door. From afar, it appeared to be a doorway, but now that she was up close, she wasn't so sure. Still, she tried to find a way in. She pushed and pulled, prodded and poked all to no avail. She looked at the books, looked at the shelves, ran her fingers along the shelves. Nothing. No push pad, no buttons. Frustrated, she sat on the floor opposite the door and stared at it.

There were no carpets on the floor, just ancient oak floorboards. She studied the floor more closely. One part of one floorboard, just by the skirting board appeared, to be much darker than its adjacent sisters.

It was darker and smoother. V had to look closely. Yes, there was definitely a difference. She reached out and touched the wood. The wood was invitingly warm and very smooth. Whilst trying to figure out what to do next, she idly rubbed her forefinger along the smooth groove in the floorboard,

V squealed in pain and jolted her finger away from the wood. A spot of blood bloomed on her fingertip. More than a spot of blood, she was leaking the stuff. She sucked her finger. Must have snagged it on a splinter, she thought. Just as she was thinking that thought, she felt herself sinking, or the room rising. Before she knew it, her eyes were level with the floorboards, yet she kept descending. She wondered if she was hallucinating. She was now below the level of the floorboards and still descending into what? She had no idea, it was pitch black.

As she came to a halt, bright yellow lights lit the void. It was a huge cellar. Looking up, she could see Uncle

Peter's study, through a hole in the floor. Looking down, she was still sitting on the floorboards that were connected into some sort of pulley mechanism that allowed the section of the floor to be lowered and raised. What was the trigger? Weight? Friction? Did I knock something? V sucked her finger. Maybe my blood? V chuckled – DNA? If the blood type matched, then the pulley mechanism started, and you were lowered into the cellar. That would explain why that part of the wooden floor was smoother and darker. Smoother from years of fingers brushing over that part of the floor and darker due to the blood that had been spilled - blood that was the key to operating the mechanism.

Puzzled she looked about her. She was in a cellar. She tried to superimpose the house over the cellar and gave up. This cellar must be under Uncle Peter's study, under a good part of the hallway and the lounge. It was high enough for even him to walk without having to stoop. Going off at various angles from the cellar were walkways, she could see the light disappearing up the tunnels. She had no idea where these walkways went and right now wasn't the time to find out. Another day, she promised herself.

The cellar was far from empty. It was full of "stuff," Some of this stuff was very old and quite visible, swords, suits of armour for people, and suits of armour for horses, old flags and banners, muskets and guns. An arsenal that seemed to start hundreds of years ago, right up to fairly modern, Second World War stuff. Some of the suits of armour had clearly seen better days, with obvious dents and dings and even the odd hole. There were numerous chests and crates dotted about the place. Neatly piled against one side of the room were what looked like... two capsules? She wandered over. One was very large, about three metres in length, the other about two metres. There were all sorts of instrumentation inside as well as straps and what looked to be an exceedingly comfortable bed or mattress. Next to them was machinery the likes of which she had never seen before but seemed oddly familiar.

"Where to start?" she asked herself, turning a full circle, acutely aware that it would not be long before the very angry Mrs. Campbell returned.

On the other side of the cellar were a dozen sea chests - two were open. That she thought would be as good a place as any. She ran over, heaved open the first chest, sneezed on the dust and jumped as a lifelike painting of somebody that could have been Uncle Peter's twin brother stared back at her. The closer she looked at the painting, the more this person resembled Uncle Peter. The clothes were different – hundreds of years old. She stared at the face. Just under the chin, a recent wound newly scabbed over. A deep diagonal cut about two inches long that started from below his bottom lip, running down towards the bottom of his chin. An injury that closely resembled a much-faded scar that Uncle Peter had today. Coincidence? she thought. It must be. She put the picture to one side. rummaged a little bit further and found nothing of particular interest. She went over to the next chest and heaved it open. V pulled out a couple of parchments. She opened one, it showed a coat of arms. She dug a little deeper into the crate and pulled out another parchment – this comprised a lot of unintelligible written words and a couple of large red wax seals over some faded signatures. She put these next to the painting. She closed the second crate. Stood up and had a quick look around. Her eyes fell on the capsules. She spotted a leather case poking out from beneath the smaller one. She ran over and picked it up... The leather was old, yet supple. Knowing that Mrs. Campbell would soon be checking in on her, she stuffed the parchments into the leather case and ran back to the floorboard pulley system. She sat down...Nothing happened.

Shit, she thought, how does the bloody thing work from this end? She looked around. Could see nothing obvious. Calm down, think this through. There must be another mechanism for the return trip, and seeing as the machine had already descended, it must be a simple matter to make it ascend. She looked at the pulley mechanism, felt around. Nothing. Then she spotted it. Immediately under the pulley mechanism was a dark, shallow incline in the granite. She rubbed her injured finger in the groove and moments later, she started to rise. In no time at all, she was back in Uncle Peter's study. The floorboards seamlessly back together, she got up, grabbed the leather bag, ran over to the door, stopped, and listened. Satisfied, she carefully opened the door and glanced up and down the corridor. Nobody around. Carefully and quietly she left Uncle Peter's study, closed the door behind her and started to make her way to her bedroom. She was at the foot of the stairs when she heard Mrs. Campbell opening the kitchen door. Stealth gave way to haste as V shot up the stairs, ran along the hallway and crashed into her room. No sooner had she stuffed the items under her bed than she heard a light knocking at her door.

Calming herself down, she walked slowly to the door, grabbing a book on the way. V opened the door and saw Mrs. Campbell standing there with a weird look in her eyes.

"Everything alright?" she asked.

"Yes, thank you, Mrs. C. How's Mr. C?"

"Better, I think another day in bed and he will be fine. I, um, I didn't expect to find you here, I thought you'd be downstairs in your den working on your studies. Are you quite alright?" She asked, again with a strange look in her eyes, as she glanced around her room. Mrs. Campbell's eyes fell on her cut finger and then her rumpled bed...then carefully studied V's eyes.

V, pushed past Mrs. Campbell, ensuring she shut the door firmly behind her. "Yes. I'm fine thanks. Just came up for a book – which she thrust in her direction as evidence. I'm headed downstairs now. Unless there's anything you would like me to help you with?"

"That's very kind, but no thanks. Not just now. There are, however, one or two things that I have to take care of. For Mr. C you understand. I'm afraid lunch will be a little late today."

"Oh, don't worry about that. I'll be fine," and with that, V headed for the stairs and seemingly to her den.

But V had no intention of going to her den, at least not just yet. She wanted to have a closer look at the items she had liberated from Uncle Peter's cellar. V waited for Mrs. Campbell to come down the stairs and leave.

As soon as the back door had closed, V ran back upstairs to her room, dived under her bed and got the items she had shoved there moments before. Finally reaching the privacy of her den, she spread the parchment with the coat of arms out in front of her. It seemed familiar. She looked at the Motto: "In my defens," She racked her brains, history never being her strong point. This was a truncated version of the only motto associated with Scotland Royal Arms: "In my defens God defend me," Then, the penny dropped. King James IV of Scotland truncated the original motto for his coat of arms. So, she thought to herself, this is the

Royal Coat of arms for James IV? She went over to her computer and Googled James IV.

"I thought so," she mumbled, the motto was correct. However, according to V's suspicions, now corroborated by Google and an embroidery of King James IV Royal Coat of Arms hanging in the Great Hall of Stirling Castle, the crown above a shield with a picture of a rampant red lion, should have on either side, two white unicorns standing on their hind legs. The Royal Coat of Arms that the parchment depicted was identical in every way, save one fundamental difference. No white unicorns were standing on their hind legs, rather two huge black, horses. Well, they resembled horses, yet somehow weren't. The depicted beasts were massive. Bigger than any horses she had ever seen – maybe twice as big. Their backs were different, with lumps and bumps where there should have been none. Muscles upon muscles glistened through the yellowed parchment. Magnificent tails, which were startlingly white, as were the horse's manes. Yet it was the eyes, even in this old and yellowing parchment that stood out. They were very large, very brown, yet brimming with intelligence, love, and wisdom.

V shrugged her shoulders and thought that maybe this Coat of Arms wasn't connected to James IV at all.

She turned her attention to the document. This made no sense to her. The only thing she could pick out were some figures, which she assumed was a date – 1510. Three years before the death of James IV. She carefully laid this to one side and looked at the leather case.

V's clumsy, uncoordinated yet determined fingers fiddled with the straps and brass catches. The case fell open and something fell face down on the floor. She looked inside the case. Nothing else, empty. As she reached out for the document, her hands started shaking and she felt terribly cold. Her fingers touched the document, which felt like a piece of rigid canvas. She turned it over, gasped and dropped it. Steeling herself, she picked up the canvas and deliberately turned it over and looked at it.

Looking back at her was a painting of five figures. One of the figures was of Uncle Peter's double, complete with a scar on his chin which still hadn't healed. Next to him was a smaller man, wearing a hat that resembled, slightly, a modern-day beret, with long brown hair, nut brown eyes and a very intelligent face, with all sorts of gold and finery draped around and on him. Next was the face of that huge animal, with the hauntingly beautiful eyes that towered over everyone in the picture. Next to the animal was a petite woman, slight of frame, with long brown hair and a regal appearance again, bedecked in fine clothes, gold, and wearing the most exquisite jewels. Standing next to this petite yet grand lady was an extremely tall person. V couldn't tell if the person was male or female. The chest was deep, the shoulders broad. The face was startlingly beautiful, yet sexless. The skin strikingly white, like porcelain. The eyes captivated her. They were black, blacker than anything she had ever seen, yet within those black, almond-shaped eyes were fine specks of gold. She gasped at the hair, she wasn't sure if the colour was to do with a reaction to pigment within the parchment, but the hair looked to be yellow and pale blue. This person was holding a huge wooden stake, at least four metres high. Placed atop the stake was an enormous Coat of Arms - the same coat of arms that was in the parchment. But it was the picture's background that shook V. For in the background was undoubtedly and unquestionably V's favourite place in the world: Pétalo.

This is too much. V closed her eyes and pressed her palms into her face. No sleep for four or five nights was catching up. Then the mysterious sighting near Pétalo earlier this morning, coupled with the intrigue of Uncle Peter's study and now this picture. A man that to all intents and purposes was Uncle Peter, except that's ridiculous because the picture is at least 500 years old. The other man and lady, clearly regal figures. Could they be King James IV of Scotland and his wife, Mary Tudor? That animal and that very strange looking person. Suddenly it all became too much for her. "If I could just get an hour's sleep," she said to herself, "then maybe I can start making sense of all of this."

Her eyelids drooped. The warmth of the sun pressing against her skin rocked her into the arms of sleep.

Just as she was beginning to nod off, her subconscious heard the word "Lunch" bellowed by Mrs. Campbell.

V's stomach knotted. Food was the last thing she needed, but it gave her an excuse to leave the house, get some air, and try to sort her head out.

V stumbled into the kitchen, stammered "I'm not hungry, thank you. Back later," and promptly left through the back door. V failed to notice Mr. Campbell now fully recovered sitting in the kitchen eating his lunch. Mrs. Campbell just looked at him. They gave each other a knowing look and then went about their duties.

V had no idea where she was going. She found herself at the entrance to the barn. Then she heard the soothing word Pétalo in the back of her mind. At once, she felt better. Too tired to walk, she trotted into the barn and over to the quad bikes. There were five of them. All parked line abreast, all the same make, power, and colour. She chose the nearest bike, checked it over (As Uncle Peter had told her a thousand times), ensured there was sufficient fuel, the brakes worked, etc. Satisfied that all was in order, she grabbed a radio, checked it, put on her crash helmet, chugged out of the barn, and then accelerated off towards Pétalo.

As she rode, a plan developed in her mind. As hard as it was, she had decided to ignore the parchments and paintings - at least for now - and concentrate on the strange horse-like apparition she had seen earlier that morning. She was convinced that everything she was experiencing now was connected to that. Find that and she hoped she would begin to find the answers to the mountain of questions she had.

The feeling of apprehension, which had been simmering in her stomach all morning, grew with each turn of the quad's wheels. Ten minutes later, she crested the rise and promptly forgot everything else as she gazed in awe at Pétalo... It was stunning, especially at this time of the day.

V didn't have the strength to get off her bike, she just about managed to remove her crash helmet. Then, she simply sat where she was, drinking in the sight before her. She didn't know how long she sat there. Ten minutes, fifteen. She felt completely relaxed. She turned towards the sun and closed her eyes. A shadow drifted across her face; then it was gone. The shadow came back. She waited for it to move on, for the wind to blow the cloud away. It didn't. The shadow stayed where it was. She gave up and opened her eyes, then fell off the quad in fright and stumbled back a few steps. Still scrambling away, she looked up into a pair of large brown eyes. The eyes never wavered. Whatever it was that those eyes belonged to just stood there. Didn't move. Just stared at her, into her, to her very soul. They were dark and huge. In contrast to the remainder of the beast, they were quite beautiful. The eyes were patient, kind and understanding. V began to feel a little unsettled by the unwavering scrutiny of those eyes. She had never seen anything like them before – or had she. But where?

The eyes reflected both wisdom and intelligence yet were somehow haunted. Eyes that had seen suffering and hardship, yet despite this had managed to retain their humility and kindness.

With a huge effort, she managed to drag her eyes away from the penetrating stare and looked at the rest of the beast. It most closely resembled a horse. A large horse say maybe 25 hands in height. In its prime, it must have been a striking animal. Huge and powerful. But now it was wretched, dirty and pitiful. To say it was dishevelled was an understatement. The coat appeared to be black, but she wasn't sure if the colour was real or just dirt. The animal was ulcerated in places, open sores oozed pus along its back, flanks, and croup. The tail was knotted and covered in grime. The mane was non-existent. Stubble where hair should have been. Its ears, although pricked forward, were missing chunks of skin. "Ah, it's a male horse" she said to herself, "a stallion," The legs were strong and sturdy, but again evidence of hardship was to be seen along the forearm, knee, and cannon on the front legs and gaskin, hock and fetlock on the rear legs. Cuts and abrasions were numerous and clearly painful. Spots of blood evident. However, where this horse-like animal differed from every other horse she had ever seen, wasn't only its size but in the shape of its back, loin, croup, and flanks. They were not streamlined and sleek like a normal horse but bulged ingeniously in places. It's as if something had been there before and ought to be there now, but has since been, for whatever reason, by design or disaster, removed. This horse, because that is what V had decided it was, must be in absolute agony, she thought. Yet it just stood there patiently watching her, with no outward signs of distress.

"And, where the hell did you come from?" She rubbed a grazed elbow... "I wasn't asleep. Granted my eyes were closed. But I heard absolutely nothing. Nothing at all. Yet here you are."

Still sitting where she had fallen, she surveyed the area around the horse and was surprised to see the entire population of the island ponies surrounding her and the beast. The ponies were not in the least alarmed – in fact, V felt that they revered the animal and stood a respectful distance away to show it, seemingly curious about how she was going to handle the situation.

In her shock, V had forgotten how to move. She was beginning to feel uncomfortable with cramp setting in. The last thing she wanted to do was to spring up and start hopping about like an idiot. I've got to move she thought. She looked up into the horse's eyes and spoke very softly saying, "Hey boy. I'm just going to stand up. Ok? Ready? Here I go." She slowly and awkwardly got on her hands and knees, paused, and finally hefted herself onto her feet.

During all her exertions, the horse didn't move. Didn't make a sound. When V was finally standing and stable, she again looked into the horse's eyes. She was almost convinced that there was a look of amusement there, which she dismissed as nonsense.

Having pulled herself together, she was undecided as to what to do next. Here they were, several metres apart, just standing looking at each other. "Nothing for it," she said to herself.

"Now boy, I mean you no harm." She rooted around in her pocket and brought out an apple. "I have this beautiful, juicy apple for you. Can I bring it over?" she said in a soft, calm measured voice.

The horse didn't move. It didn't look at the apple but continued to look into V's eyes. Hesitantly, V took a couple of steps forward. The horse remained passive, showing no signs of stress or fear. It completely ignored the apple that V waved around in front of her as if she was trying to shoo away a pesky fly. The horse merely continued to stare straight into V's eyes.

V got to within a couple of metres of the horse and stopped. Waited for a few moments to make sure all was well, before resuming the longest journey she had ever taken in her life. Those few meters seemed like ten thousand kilometres.

"Ok. Here goes." And with that, she took one confident step forward, stopped, took the step back, paused, had a strong word with herself, took two steps forward, and stopped again.

This is impossible, she thought. As she walked towards the horse, all the early morning noises of nature – the singing of the birds, the sighing of the breeze, the bumble of the odd bee, leaves rustling in the wind – all those noises seemed to fade. But, even more disconcerting, the colours around her faded too. As soon as she started retreating from the animal, the colours resumed their normal hues and brightness and the noises around her resumed their chaotic choruses.

I must be imagining things, she thought to herself. Throughout all her comings and goings, the horse remained absolutely calm. Had not moved, but also hadn't taken his eyes away from hers. She felt those eyes had begun to tease her. "Well, here goes," she said once more and stepped forward. As she had experienced before the early morning sounds disappeared and all the colours in the world drained away. Finally, she stood within inches of the horse's muzzle.

Complete silence engulfed her. No noise whatsoever. Although she was aware of birds flying around, she heard nothing. She could see the grass bending slightly in the breeze, she could feel the breeze on her cheeks, yet she could hear nothing. A fly flitted past, in absolute silence. She looked away from the horse's eyes and the world around her was in shades of black, whites and greys. No colour. She looked at her blue jeans. Grey. Her arms, a slightly paler shade of grey. The horse was black, but then it had always been black. Startlingly white clouds against a backdrop of grey sky. It's like living in a black and white silent movie she thought. All fear gone, replaced by curiosity and wonder.

The horse continued to look down at her. Up close, he was bigger than she first thought! But seemed so intelligent. The eyes wise and patient, kind and gentle. She still couldn't bring herself to touch him. She just needed to satisfy herself that the noiseless and colourless environment she now found herself in wasn't permanent. So, she whispered "Just a second" and slowly moved away from the horse. The horse simply watched her go. "It's as if he knows what I'm thinking," she said to herself.

As she continued to move away from the horse, so the familiar afternoon country sounds returned, as did the colourful world that she was used to.

She didn't know what she should be afraid of, but she was suddenly scared. More scared than she had ever been in her life. She reached out and touched the horse – needing comfort. As her fingers brushed the horse's hair, so she felt calmed. All traces of fear was gone. Not only that, but something quite peculiar also happened. So startling, 000that it caused V to immediately withdraw her hand. There was no bolt of electricity that shot from the horse through her hand and into her body. There was no pain. No. For that brief millisecond of contact, immediate understanding flooded her body. She seemed to have seen into the animal's soul. She felt tremendous hardship and sorrow. She knew exactly what the horse was thinking and feeling. As soon as she withdrew her hand, contact broke and all feeling and understanding left her body.

She again approached the horse and offered him the apple. The horse gently lowered its head, sniffed, took the apple, and ate it.

CHAPTER THREE

Nox boomed into V's mind. She steadied her hand on the beast's muzzle and looked around her.

"Where did that come from?"

Nox blinked. V turned around and looked behind her. The ponies stared back.

V shrugged.

Nox flooded her mind again. Nox, that is my name.

She looked into the animal's eyes.

"Nox?" she repeated...

The animal nodded.

V took a step back. The animal followed her and pressed his muzzle against her arm.

"You can hear me when we touch."

V pulled her arm away, then reached out and touched the beast's flank.

"You can talk to me." The voice was soft and warm, calm and serene. "I can understand everything you say, but I can only communicate with you through your mind."

"I umm, I see," stammered V. "My name is V," she said. Lame.

"Yes V, I know."

V looked into Nox's eyes. "Who are you? Where do you come from and why are you here?"

"My name is Nox. I have no idea where I come from. I'm here to watch over you, protect you, mentor you and to help you. Although you have not known it, I have been with you your whole life. Your constant companion. By your side as you grew, as you were prepared to undertake the challenges that lie ahead," said Nox. "A life that you have yet to fully understand.

A life that will soon become very different from the one you have known."

"Well, that's nonsense." A laugh escaped V's throat. She swallowed it whole. "You've been watching over me my entire life? Why am I only seeing you today? Why is my life so different?"

Nox's baritone voice slowed her mind.

"You needed time to grow. But time has run out."

"Run out for what? And what happened to you? And does that mean that you can read my mind? When I'm not talking to you?"

"No," replied Nox. "I will only be in your mind when invited, when called. Just as you will be in my mind when I invite you."

"Have you been in an accident? And why does the world turn black and white when I'm close to you, and all of nature's noises disappear, only to return when I walk away from you?"

Nox's eyes gleamed. "So many questions, V. I will answer what I can. The rest you will discover as we travel…"

"Travel where? I'm not going anywhere."

Nox kept talking as though V had said nothing. "I understand I must look a terrible sight, but I'm fine. My physical appearance is a consequence of my getting here and to what is happening in your world."

"My world? This is my world," said V. "It's not perfect. Far from it. What's happening here to cause you to look like you do?"

"This world we are in at the moment is the world that you remember. It's the world you have shared with your guardians and the Campbell's. But it is not your world, V. It's not where you were born. This place you call home, is simply your lifeboat. It's a place of safety.

Your guardians and the Campbell's are your protectors. Their work is done. Now I'm to assume that role. "

Nox paused for a moment and looked deep into V's eyes. "I see you don't believe me. That's fine. But before you dismiss out of hand what I have just told you, answer me this. Have you ever really looked at yourself V? Have you ever asked any questions about yourself?"

V looked into Nox's eyes. They were bright and alive.

"Well?" Nox pushed quietly, patiently.

"No," answered V, almost in a whisper.

"Ah," said Nox. "So you have. You have wondered at your physical appearance. Yes? Your physique, your hair, the colour of your skin. Your eyes, yes. Those eyes of yours. Have you never wondered about those? Yes. I see you have. Your intelligence. How you were treated at boarding school. Yes. I was there. I was with you the whole time. There is nobody in this world that can come close to you. Not even Uncle Peter. Have you never wondered why this island is so close to you? Or why Pétalo is so important to you? Why you are always drawn to it? It's because you are connected to them. Udal Cuain, Pétalo they are in your DNA. Just as I am."

V wrapped her hands around her head, pulling herself into a tight, safe ball away from Nox. "I don't know what you're talking about."

"Look inside, V. Deep down."

"I always tried to fit in."

Nox shook his head. "You know that's not true."

Nox watched her. He said nothing.

V stared up at him. "Are you reading my mind now? Get out!"

Nox stepped back.

Are you there? she thought. Can you hear me?

Yes, I'm here, call me when you're ready.

V breathed in, then let it all out. She stretched her fingertips over her face and rubbed. Blood flowed to her skin. She squeezed her eyes shut, then opened them again. Nox was still there. Watching her. Strangely comforting.

Pétalo had always called to her. Like she belonged there. Being honest with herself, she realised that it wasn't the house that was home, nor even Udal Cuain – the island she adored so much. No, it was Pétalo that was really home to her. But why? She asked herself.

Having recovered a little, but still feeling very fragile, she called Nox over. He stopped what he was doing and softly, soundlessly walked over to her. He knew what she wanted before she spoke. He lowered his head and she clung to him. And for the first time in her life; she cried. The tears rolling down her cheeks. Nox stood there, doing what he could to ease her pain.

Eventually, the tears ran dry, the dry wracking sobs stopped. V stood back from Nox, wiped her eyes and looked at him.

"I often felt I was living someone else' life," she said to him. "It was a happy life… Just not mine."

"I understand," she felt Nox say. "The life you have lead has been necessary. It has been your life; it's prepared you for what must come next. This is why I'm here," Nox said. "I will help you as much as I can and I'll always be at your side. But you must lead, you must find the way, you must get us back and you must save us."

"Back? Save us? Back to where? Save us from what?" she asked, panic rising in her voice. "This is my home. This is where I belong. There is nothing threatening or dangerous here."

"No," said Nox. "Whilst it's true that Udal Cuain has been your safe haven for as long as you can remember.

Udal Cuain is not your home and it's now no longer safe for you to stay here. One day, you may choose to come back here if you so wish, but it's not where your destiny lies. To stay here will destroy everything you know and love. Your destiny lies far away from here. In a different part of the universe on a world not unlike Terra. Domus Mundi, the world where you were born."

"But here it's safe." V said earnestly, trying to get Nox to understand.

"No," said Nox. "They're coming for you. Your guardians were able to fight them off this time, but it's getting harder."

"WHAT.........!" Shouted V "That's nonsense. Uncle Peter and Aunt Izzy are on the mainland, in Edinburgh. Uncle Peter is attending to business matters and Aunt Izzy, well she went on a shopping trip. The only fighting they are likely to have done was with the crowds and tourists on Prince's Street!"

"No, that's not true." said Nox. "That is what your guardians want you to believe, but it's not what's happening, nor was it the reason for their trip to the mainland. Your guardians are constantly fighting the evil forces coming for you. This time it took all their powers to stop them. Despite what they told you this morning, they'll have to stay away from Udal Cuain for a few days to heal and recover. We've got to get to Domus Mundi, and we have to be there within the next 36 hours."

"Why?" asked V. "I thought you said Uncle Peter and Aunt Izzy had fought off the enemy."

"No," replied Nox. "They merely brought us time and only a little. The enemy are, as we speak, regrouping and will be ready for another onslaught within the next twelve Earth hours."

"To keep all those you love safe, you have to get away from here. You have to draw the enemy's attention away from Udal Cuain, away from your loved ones. That's the only way they will be safe. At least for the time being."

Leaning against Nox, V felt her mind reach overload. Too fast. Everything was happening way too fast. This morning she had pancakes for breakfast, and now she's responsible for saving everyone and everything she knows and loves.

She stepped back from Nox. "All this seems too fantastic to be real. But... although I don't understand why, I believe you. Why do I believe you?"

Nox didn't move. He stared at V with his deep, calm eyes that seemed filled with an eternity of truth and knowledge.

"Who are the enemy?" V asked. "Why are they after me? Where is my home and how am I going to get there?" Panic bloomed in the pit of V's stomach. Nausea swept through her gut into her throat. "What do I do?" she asked Nox softly. "I don't know where to start?" For the first time in V's life, she had no answers to any of the questions she was asking. "Where do you come from? How did you get here? Where do you go when I'm not with you? How long have you been here?"

"I have been to Udal Cuian several times over the last half millennia. I come when I'm needed and I serve those that need me, for as long as they need me, then I go to the next place that I can be of service."

"But for the last eight years, and to the end of my days, my destiny lies only with you."

"Eight years?"

"Yes." Nox went on. "This journey was different."

"I don't remember anything before I was eight."

"I know. In the past, I have recovered from the journey very quickly. Without the need of assistance. But on this last occasion, I couldn't move, my body was too broken. Your guardians knew I would be coming."

"You arrived on my birthday?"

"Yes. Your Uncle Peter found me. He came to Pétalo. He came and gave me food and water and he injected me with something. He spoke three phrases to me, looked deep into my eyes and left. I ate, drank and then fell asleep. I slept for two days. When I awoke, I felt much better mentally. I didn't hurt so much physically. I tried to stand. But couldn't. More food and water had appeared. I assume from Peter. I slept again. I don't know how long I slept. But when I awoke the second time, I felt much stronger. More food and water had appeared. I ate and drank my fill, then with a tremendous effort, I was able to stand. Once mobile, I headed towards your house and waited patiently until I saw you. From that moment on, I have never been very far away from you. Despite our long association over centuries, I haven't spoken to Peter since the day I arrived. I have seen him of course, from a distance, when he was with you. But he has chosen not to see me or communicate with me again. His time is over, now it's your time."

V thought about what Nox had said. "What did Uncle Peter say to you? And what do you mean his time is over?" she asked.

"Illam vehementissime amamus. Refer illam, confide nemini nullique rei," Said Nox.

V thought for a moment: "We love her very much. Bring her home, and trust nothing and no-one," she said.

"Yes," said Nox.

"Why is his time over, Nox. Is he going to die?" Panic causing her voice to rise.

"Don't worry," said Nox. "He is not going to die. His time with me is over. Our communications, tenuous at the best of times, are now terminated. My time, my destiny now lies with you – as it has been ordained, from the beginning of time."

"Oh, I see," said V, not really seeing at all.

Silence descended. Suddenly V's eyes opened wide and she blurted out "Centuries!" a lot louder than she had meant. "You said you had known Uncle Peter for centuries. How is this possible? He is only in his late forties now."

Nox tilted his head and studied V. "Come on now, think."

"It was you," V said quietly, thoughtfully. "You were with me earlier today when I went into Uncle Peter's study. It was you that made me open the door. It was you that shoved me in the back and made me fall into Uncle Peter's study…"

Nox looked at V, with that glint in his eye "Why? Why did you make me go in?"

"Because," said Nox, "you need to know I'm telling you the truth."

"The pictures I found," said V. "The face. It was Uncle Peter wasn't it. And the horse. Was that you? And the Coat of Arms on the parchment, was that you as well? How could it be? That was at least 500 years ago. "

"Yes indeed," said Nox. "They were pictures of your Uncle Peter and yes, myself – in my younger days. I was a juvenile in those pictures. The white mane and tail are a sign that I hadn't yet reached adulthood. I'm now, in your terminology, a young, mature adult that has just reached its prime."

V looked at Nox "Did you say in your prime? Forgive me Nox but look at you. You still haven't explained how it's possible, but you look like you've been around for centuries."

Nox chose to ignore her remark and avoided answering her questions directly. He simply, but forcefully said "V, we really don't have time for full explanations right now. We need to leave Udal Cuain and we need to leave quickly. I promise, when I can, I will answer your questions as fully as I'm able. But we have to get away from here, and we have to do this NOW. "

Nox watched V. He saw and recognised that look in her eye so he relented a little. "All I will say is this, then we must move. You have heard of your great theoretical physicist Albert Einstein. And you will have heard of his theory of relativity?"

V nodded.

"Alright" said Nox. "Well, the essence of the theory is that the faster you move through space, the slower you move through time." V just started back at Nox, realisation dawning on her face.

"Yes V, Uncle Peter must have travelled somewhere away from Earth at considerable speeds, perhaps approaching the speed of light, so that for him, time would slow down considerably in comparison to Earth where time moved on at its normal pace. Therefore, Uncle Peter aged far less quickly than people here, and as I was his companion, just as I'm now yours, then time slowed down for me as well. Now V, we must move."

"Why can't anyone else see you like I can?"

Nox, getting more than a little exasperated tried to balance the need for answers to her torrent of questions against the pressing need for action and urgency. The answer to this question was twofold, both explanations were long and difficult and required an understanding of brainwaves, particularly beta brain waves, and how they can be calibrated, aligned so as to match ... mine. That part of the explanation could wait. Taking a deep, impatient breath, Nox replied "Because over millennia, our species has adapted. Through our brainwave pathways we can automatically deflect the light around us so that an eye, adapted to be able to see in white light, will not be able to see us. It's a protection mechanism. Rather like a chameleon can blend in with their surroundings, so I can deflect the light around me to make me invisible to the naked eye. A very advanced stealth mechanism. So, I'm physically here – you can kick, touch, smell me, but you can't see me with your human eye, because I have deflected the light around me so that the receptors in your eyes don't focus on me, but on the light around me. You have the capacity to do this, I just have to teach you how."

"Unlike a chameleon who can change colour to blend in with his surroundings, I can't switch this off. I was rewired before I came here, making this phenomenon permanent. The procedure can be reversed when I get back to Domus Mundi. But for now, you can only see me through the merging of our brain pathways. I have managed to recalibrate and strengthen your beta brain waves and have merged our brain pathways. You, your guardians and the Campbells are the only people on this planet that that can see me."

"Understood," said V. Although she didn't at all. "What now?"

Relief at last, now we can concentrate on getting away from here.

"Now we need to find out how I got here so we can leave."

"You woke up on the metallic slab in what I call Pétalo?"

"Yes V, that is quite correct," responded Nox.

"And you are quite sure that you didn't land anywhere else first?"

"As far as I remember," Nox replied. "I was in such bad shape that I'm not sure I could have gone anywhere else first. I was quite unable to stand up for several days, so I'm pretty sure the metallic slab is exactly where I arrived."

"Ok," said V. "If that's where you arrived, it will almost certainly be a point of departure as well. That will be our starting point in trying to figure out a way back to Domus Mundi."

Starting at the metallic slab, she looked carefully around her. At each of the stones in turn. Working her way to the outer stone circle. Running her hands over the stones, as high as she could reach. On all sides.

"I can't see any way to make this thing do the things it did for you"

"Well, we must make it work. We can't stay here any longer."

V was just about to ask another question when she was disturbed by the ponies. Or rather, the ponies, especially Mr. Marmaduke appeared to be disturbed by something. His head pointed to the South; his ears pricked as he softly whinnied to his herd. The herd immediately stopped what they were doing and listened. One of the younger ponies galloped off in the direction in which the rest were now looking. On alert, they fanned out in a large circle, keeping Nox and V in the centre.

V listened. She heard nothing but the sighing wind and the gentle rustle of the leaves in the trees.

A moment later, the younger pony came back and whinnied at Mr Marmaduke. The herd relaxed. V didn't. She finally heard what sounded like an angry bee trapped in a turbine. The sound got louder and stronger until some minutes later Mr. and Mrs. Campbell appeared over the crest gripping onto a quad that looked determined to toss them both into the mud. The quad stopped inches from V. Mr. Campbell switched off the vehicle leaving silence except for the soft ticking of the cooling engine and huffs and puffs of Mrs. Campbell as she tried to dismount the quad with as much dignity as she could muster.

Mr. Campbell looked at V with sad, baleful eyes as Mrs. Campbell approached V, with a look on her face that V had never seen before.

"What's wrong?"

Mrs. Campbell stopped a foot in front of V and looked around her. As she did so, her eyes fell on Nox. "Nox, it's good to see you again."

"Domina Altrix, it gives me great joy to see you and to see you looking so well." Mrs. Campbell studied Nox – took in his terrible appearance and simply said "Look after her, Nox. Peter sends his deepest affections and sends this message: Illam vehementissime amamus. Refer illam, confide nemini nullique rei,"

Nox merely nodded at Mrs. Campbell and said: Vica est anima mea antequam - sicut semper.(My life before Vica's – as always)"

She nodded and mouthed the words "Thank you"

Mrs. Campbell then looked at V, tears in her eyes, pulled her in for a hug and stroked her hair. Then she gently pushed V away and looked deep into her eyes. "Uncle Peter called. Both he and Aunt Izzy are ok. They are hurt, but only superficially. Uncle Peter has done all he can to protect you and the island. Unfortunately, it's not enough. The Ostium has broken through and will be here in a matter of hours – a day, maybe 36 hours at most. There are still a few friends that can help delay The Ostium, but it is now just a matter of hours before they will be here. You V, you MUST be gone. You are our last hope. If you are here on the island when The Ostium invade, then Domus Mundi is lost, Earth will very quickly follow. From there, who knows? I don't have time to answer any questions, mainly because I don't know the answers. Uncle Peter wanted to explain all this to you. He was planning on doing so on his return. But he hadn't realised how bad things were, how strong The Ostium had become. We are truly sorry V, to have so little to tell you. I can't advise you, I can't help you. Nox is your best hope but despite his many, many abilities even he doesn't have all the answers. Trust him, V. Trust what he says."

Mrs. Campbell went to the back of the quad where a package was secured to the carrier rack. She gave the package to V. "You were supposed to find this in Uncle Peter's study."

V blushed.

"Don't worry dear, you were supposed to get access into Uncle Peter's study today – it was all he could do to help you. Uncle Peter and Aunt Izzy send their love. They are so proud of you, of the person you have become. It has been their pleasure to watch over you, love you and nurture you over these many, many years. Now they must let you fly."

Mrs. Campbell rushed up and gave V another huge hug. Kissed her forehand and clambered back aboard the quad. With a last, long look at Nox, Mrs. Campbell then thumped her husband on the shoulder and without another word, the quad turned and disappeared back in the direction from which it came.

V stood where she was, cradling the package that Mrs. Campbell had given her. She felt abandoned, she felt alone but above all she felt absolutely terrified.

CHAPTER FOUR

Pulling herself together, V looked down at the surprisingly light package that Mrs. Campbell had flung into her hands. V carefully opened the package and smiled, as the first thing she came across was food, the package also contained a book, a cape, a small but powerful magnifying glass, a map of the night sky and something that she had no idea what it was. It was as smooth as polished glass. Silver in colour and exquisitely made.

She looked at the book; old – ancient. It was bound in something that resembled leather, but far more supple, softer and stronger. Red in colour with gold text emblazoned on both covers and the spine. A golden clasp secured both covers, protecting the book from falling open and damaging the pages. V didn't understand the text on the cover, the spine and the back of the book. Clicking open the golden clasp, the book fell open. The pages were in immaculate condition. Although the book felt ancient, it looked brand new. The pages were not yellowed, or dry, or cracked. But fresh, malleable and dazzlingly white. The colours of the text were clear and sharp. The pages were full of exquisite drawings. Beautiful in their detail. The text was handwritten in a language she didn't understand. The handwriting was so neat, it was almost musical.

A cacophony of uncoordinated, haphazard noise filled her head. She closed the book and the sounds subsided. She put the book aside.

Next she unfolded the cape. The material was light and opaque yet seemed to be as strong as chainmail. The cape could be folded into such a tiny package that it would easily fit into a pocket. Yet, when fully opened, it was big enough to cover her from head to foot - and probably Nox as well. The clasp at the throat of the cape was silver in colour. V rolled it over in her hands. One minute it was pliable, the next solid. In fact there were several of these silver clasp like things, at strategic places along the cape. She had no idea why, because it seemed like it should be worn like a poncho. V slipped it over her head. As soon as she put it on, it automatically moulded itself to her body. A perfect fit. She took it off and it reverted to its original size. *Amazing* she thought to herself.

Next, she picked up the magnifying glass. Made of a silver metallic material, the tool culminated in a convex lens, only 5cm in diameter, but superbly engineered. When she looked through the lens, she was amazed at the clarity and detail of what she saw. *This was no ordinary magnifying glass* she thought to herself. There were all sorts of accoutrements in and around the handle. What they were for, she had no idea. *Best to leave those alone* she thought.

Next, the map of the night sky. Unremarkable sprung to mind. It unfolded to the size of a poster. Reasonably large and greatly detailed. The material was like canvas rather than paper. It was strong and pliable, but didn't crease, and when laid out became quite rigid. On one side of the map, the constellations were familiar to her. On the other, the constellations were, unrecognizable. All text was written in the same way as the book and when she studied the shapes, music flooded her mind. She could barely discern the constellations they were so dimly printed on the map. *Odd*, she thought. *Everything else in the package was so precise, so well made, and so clear. Yet this single chart, containing two maps of the night sky were barely visible.* She wondered what use they would be.

Finally she withdrew the silver tube. It was metallic, the same material as the handle and frame of the magnifying glass. It was smooth, like polished glass. Shaped like a…torpedo… about 30cms in length. And that was pretty much it. No buttons to push. It had no bumps or cavities. Completely smooth. *Oh well*, she thought, *perhaps Nox knows what this is.*

She had another look at the parcel packaging. Simple brown paper. No name, no identifying marks. She wondered how Uncle Peter had come by this. An Uncle Peter who was clearly very different from the guardian she thought she knew and who she loved so much.

V looked around her. Nox was standing a little off to her left, he seemed very curious about the package and its contents. The ponies were still there. Mr Marmaduke, as ever, seemed to be on look out. The younger and fittest of the ponies standing next to Mr. Marmaduke awaiting orders. The remaining ponies were standing in a loose circle with V and Nox in the centre.

V's eyes swung back to Nox. "Well, what do you think? A book written in a language I can't understand, a cape that seems to shrink and expand at will, a star chart that is barely readable with constellations I have never seen, a magnifying glass and a long silver tube. Important no doubt. But I have no idea how, or in what context. Any ideas?"

Nox was silent for a moment. "I knew there was a package for you, but I had no idea what it would contain. All I do know is that these items were carefully chosen by your ancient ancestor, Ourea. He went to great lengths to ensure they were passed down to you. Perhaps the book will provide the answers you are looking for."

"But I can't understand the words. I have no idea how to read the book," moaned V.

"I think you understand how the language works. You just have to try and tune yourself in. Listen to the words. You don't read them like you do in the languages you are familiar with. Let the words speak to you. They can do this in a number of ways. Whichever way they choose, you will understand. Just open your mind to them. The words were written for you and only you by your ancient forefathers. Only your mind can free them."

V looked at Nox to see if he had any more advice to offer. Nox simply stared back. "Apparently not" she muttered and turned her attention back to the book lying innocently on her lap.

Written for me, huh? She thought. *If this was written for me by my ancient forefathers, how old is it and how could they possibly know about me? I was goodness knows how many generations away from being born. There is so much I don't understand. One day I may get all the answers. But for now, I need only one answer. How can I get myself and Nox to Domus Mundi? The instructions are here, the tools are here. I just need to put the two together and I have less than 24 hours to do it.*

Tapping hooves from Mr. Marmaduke forced V's attention away from the book. Nox was alert. The veins bulging in his neck, his ears pricked, standing still, not a flicker of movement. Total concentration.

" Please gather up your possessions and come to me," No panic just commanding. V quickly did as she was told. "What is it Nox?" she asked.

"Climb aboard," said Nox, as he bent down to try and assist her as best he could. V paused for a moment, she looked at his bleeding and suppurating back "Are you sure?"

"Please. Get on. Now!" rumbled Nox in a voice that wasn't to be argued with. V did as she was told, but it was no easy task. She'd forgotten how huge Nox was. But with a nudge from him, she finally sat tall. Once aboard, V was astonished to feel his back move and shift until she felt wrapped in a comfortable saddle. It actually changed shape. Nox's back moulded itself around her. A hand grip appeared on Nox's withers, made entirely from bunched flesh, muscle and coarse hair. She jumped as she felt something curl around her legs and feet. She looked down and was astonished to see growths appear from Nox's flank that bound her legs and feet to his side. She was now absolutely secure. Once Nox was happy that V was safe, he waited.

What is it Nox? she thought. Silence. V could tell he was tuned into her mind; he was just concentrating on the sounds and smells in the air. Nox stood absolutely still for what must have been a minute or so. Then he seemed to relax a little. Mr. Marmaduke, whinnied to Nox, and then he too seemed to relax, just a little. Yet V could tell that both Nox and Mr. Marmaduke were on high alert.

Suddenly, Nox neighed softly. The noise startled V. This was the first time she had heard him make any noise at all!

"What is it Nox? What's out there?" she asked with a slight quiver in her voice.

Nox remained silent, but she could sense that although he was tense, he wasn't overly worried or concerned. That appeased her fears – but only a bit.

Nox whinnied again. V couldn't hold herself back any longer.

"For God's sake Nox, what the hell is going on?" she blurted, unnecessarily loud.

Nox's calm voice flooded her mind. "V. Please. All is well. Just be quiet, or he'll take flight and we'll never get to hear what he has to say."

He? Who is he? V thought back at Nox. But again, Nox remained stubbornly quiet. V gave up, trusted in Nox, kept her eyes firmly shut and gripped onto him for all she was worth.

Nox remained absolutely still. His head, slightly raised, as if he was smelling the air, and slowly moved from side to side, scanning the horizon. His ears were pricked and occasional whinnies and neighs emanated from him. Their tone and volume changing.

V's ears then sensed a pressure difference in the air around her. The leaves rustled in the breeze, branches swayed, the trees themselves started to move. She felt the breeze against her cheek strengthen and increase in temperature. Dust billowed about them, moving in little eddies across the grass and paths. Visibility decreased. The strength of the wind freshened; her clothes whipped around her. The temperature continued to increase. The sand and grit that moments before were playful eddies were now like little wasps, stinging her bare skin. She screwed up her eyes to see. Tears wetting her cheeks. Still the intensity of the wind increased. The trees rocked, throwing up small twigs as well as sand and grit. The wind screamed in her ears. Visibility was zero.

Nox's voice filled her mind. "Don't be afraid – this is a friend"

"A friend?" queried V, not sure what Nox was referring to but *with friends like this, who needs enemies,* she thought.

Just as V thought the wind couldn't possibly get any stronger or louder; the noise was suddenly shattered by absolute silence. Absolute peace and tranquillity. Not a breath of wind, not a movement.

V opened her eyes and could see absolutely nothing out of the ordinary. She was used to the fact that whilst she was in very close proximity to Nox, the whole world was black, white and grey. In fact she thought nothing of it now. But other than that particular oddity, everything else seemed exactly as it was before. There was no damage done by the terrible wind, no evidence of the detritus that it had blown about. Everything was calm and serene.

For a moment V thought she had imagined it all. She was about to mention the same to Nox when a voice that came from everywhere at once boomed "Greetings Nox."

"Greetings Ventus," Nox's voice flooded her mind. "Quite an entrance," Nox went on.

"Yes. Sorry about that," laughed Ventus. A laugh like thunder. "So," boomed the voice. "What is this you have on your back?"

"You are not sorry," Nox admonished Ventus and then went on to introduce V.

"V!" boomed Ventus. "No... Means nothing to me I'm afraid. I'll settle on "Pulax" ... Yes. Very apt."

"Flea! Flea!" bellowed V. A combination of relief and anger just increasing her ferocity.

"I'm no flea. My name is V," she bellowed indignantly. "And who or what are you, Ventus? In fact, where are you?" V heard a chuckle in her mind. "And that's quite enough from you, Nox" she added.

"Spirited one this," boomed Ventus, liking what he saw. "I'm here, I'm all around you," boomed Ventus. "I'm the wind on your face, the breeze that tickles your cheeks, that plays with your hair. I'm the storm that frightens you. I can cool you on a summer's day, or I can blow your house down. I can be the sailor's friend, or his worst enemy. I can cause floods, tempests and mayhem. I'm Ventus, the wind. You can never see me, but you can feel me. You can hear me. I can soothe you to sleep, or I can have you quaking with fear. I go where I please, when I please."

"One thing I can't do, is to help you in your quest. I can't stop what is coming, but I can try to assist you where I can. I bring a message from your guardians. The enemy is close. Chaos looms. Your guardians are now powerless to hinder its progress. The only one capable of preventing catastrophe is you, V. You have to get away from Udal Cuain immediately. Without delay. The Ostium knows your abilities V; they know you are their greatest threat. Be warned. They will follow you. They will hunt you down. They will not stop until they have you in their power. I will do what I can to delay them. I will try and buy you extra time. But I make no promises"

"Farewell Nox, old friend. Travel well and travel safely. I know not whether we shall meet again."

With that, the storm unleashed itself and Ventus was gone.

V's thoughts floated on a raging sea of chaos. Nox's voice flooded her mind, soothing her. "One step at a time. Concentrate on the task at hand. Ventus is a canny old soul, he will find a way to delay The Ostium. Your immediate task is to get us to Domus Mundi. Accomplish this, and you will have bought Earth valuable time, as the enemy will follow us there. Together we can do this V. This is your destiny. This is what you were ordained to do. This is why you have been so protected. Your forefathers believed in you. Your guardians believe in you. I believe in you."

Nox turned to look at Mr Marmaduke and whinnied something to him. Mr Marmaduke neighed in response, then seemed to call to the ponies and with that, they galloped off. Some to the North, some to the south. Nox then readjusted his body to allow V to dismount.

Getting off, was a lot easier than getting on. She turned to look at Nox. She could see his back was redder, the sores bleeding where her jeans had chafed his skin.

"Are you quite alright?" she asked, concern in her voice. He nuzzled her shoulder in response.

"How come your skin and coat are in such poor condition?"

"It's to do with this planet and what is going on, on Domus Mundi. On Earth, there are microbes in the air that are slowly destroying the outer layer of my skin, the epidermis. However, the main problem is that the epidermis harbours defensive Langerhans cells. These cells alert the body's immune system to viruses and other infectious agents. Unfortunately microbes in your Earth's atmosphere attack my epidermis, kill off the Langerhans cells and leave my skin open to infection. The protein keratin is also compromised, which is why I have no mane, my tail is shrinking and why my hooves are in such bad condition. As I said to you, some work was done to me, prior to leaving Domus Mundi. It seems that whilst undergoing these procedures in order to prepare me for the journey here, some Ostium agents managed to compromise some of the drugs used on me. They either injected me, or caused me to be injected with something that reacted with my epidermis and over time caused it to become susceptible to the microbes in this world's air and to subsequently fail. I was supposed to have succumbed to this condition long before meeting you. But The Ostium underestimated the strength of my body. I have been able to fight off the microbes and infections. But my ability to do this is getting weaker. About one year ago my skin started to show the effects of the illness. It is now progressing rapidly. I estimate that without treatment, I have around four months before the illness becomes irreversible and two months to live thereafter." Nox said all this quite matter-of-factly. As if he were discussing the weather. "Then we have to get you to Domus Mundi. We have to get you treated!"

Nox just looked at her. "Yes," he said simply."

Crushing the panic rising in her stomach, V sat down and turned her attention to the book. It was large, about the size of an A4 sheet of paper. It was thick, around 10 cm thick and crammed with maybe 1000 pages of text and drawings. But it weighed nothing. Well, V thought to herself. From what I have experienced over the last two days it seems like strange, unexplainable and weird are becoming the norm. And that normality is indeed becoming weird, unexplainable and strange!

She pressed on the golden clasp and the book fell open at a random page. As her eyes fell on the text, so music began playing in her head. This time the music didn't seem so random, so chaotic. If she concentrated hard, she could make out some sort of logical melody. She closed the book, the music stopped.

She looked at the title of the book. Two brief notes played in her mind which she understood as "Vica Pota," This made no sense to her. She looked at the book's title again, and again the same words musically appeared in her mind "Vica Pota,"

Well, thought V, *I'm making progress. I don't understand what Vica Pota is, but at least I understand something of what the book appears to be playing to me. Perhaps I need to start at the beginning to make sense of the music. Perhaps it's impossible to start anywhere else. You have to start from the first "word" and work your way methodically to the last "word" to make any sense at all out of what the book is trying to tell me. Perhaps, starting on a random page is impossible in this language.*

V put this theory to the test. She chose a page at random and again music filled her mind. Unintelligible. A vague sense of rhythm but nothing that spoke to her. She then flicked to page one. At once the music started to make sense to her. Through the music, she saw words that she could understand.

I'm reading the index! There were a lot of words she could see clearly through the music but didn't understand what they meant.

Then something weird happened. The music kept playing one phrase to her. No matter where she looked in the book, the book would only play this one phrase. 'Saxa Antiquis' All she could see in her mind no matter where she looked in the book, were the words 'Saxa Antiquis'. She looked at the book's title and the words 'Saxa Antiquis' appeared in her mind and not the phrase "Vica Pota," *Was the book trying to tell me something? Trying to guide me?*

She tried to flick through the pages. Nothing. This time they were stuck fast. It was as if the other pages had been glued together. The book had decided that the only page V could read was the index. *Very well,* thought V, *if you want me to read the index, I'll read the index.*

As she cast her eyes to the top of the index page. All music stopped. She couldn't understand anything at all!

Stick with it, she thought. *The book seems to know what it wants me to do.*

She continued to scan the index word by word, phrase by phrase, line by line. She must have got to the fifth or sixth line when the music bellowed the phrase 'Saxa Antiquis' in her mind and, at the same time, the book took on a life of its own as it tried to flick through the pages to the correct place. Correct chapter. She was so startled; she dropped the book to the floor. Fortunately, it fell the right way up and V looked in open mouthed astonishment as the pages, of their own accord, flicked through until they came to the correct chapter. For there, as her eyes fell to the top of the page, the musical words 'Saxa

Antiquis' imprinted themselves on her mind. "This is where the book wants me to start reading." She murmured, wondering why 'Saxa Antiquis' was so important, and at the same time wondering what this book actually was!

She began to listen to the symphony the music was playing to her as her eyes moved along the text. Saxa Antiquis is the correct name for her beloved Pétalo. She understood who built it, when it was built and why it was built. She became familiar with the names Dominus Ingeniarius Hephaestus and Dominus Cæmentarius Ourea. She came to understand the importance of "Argentum Metallicum," the metallic stone slab. She read about the cuts Ourea made into the stone in front of the central trilithon and the packages left by him. She wondered why Ourea gazed at the two obelisks but took note that he did so.

The music shifted. "Petra Circumdatos" played repeatedly in her head. The music stopped and once again the book went through its ritual of flicking through the pages back to the index. In silence, her eyes scanned the index, further and further down the page she went. Two lines from the bottom, "Petra Circumdatos" screamed in her mind. This time V knew what to expect. Letting go of the book, the pages flicked through until they came to the chapter entitled "Petra Circumdatos," The text was accompanied by schematics and drawings. From the drawings, she recognised the torpedo-shaped tool that accompanied the book in the parcel. She bent down and picked it up. Yes, she said to herself. This is "Petra Circumdatos" whatever that is.

V got up and walked over to the silvery metal slab. She sat down, with the book on her lap, tool in hand and focussed on the text in front of her.

At once, music filled her mind. Petra Circumdatos was a hand-held masonry or rock cutting tool. V looked at the tool and could see no obvious means of turning it on or off, or regulating the power of the unit or, for that matter, where the actual beam, or whatever it was, actually left the tool.

Turning her gaze back to the book, music again filled her mind and with the combination of the text and diagrams, so she came to understand the tool.

Ok, Ok thought V as she focused on the book. As she tried to read past the point that she last got to, so the music stopped. As she started to backtrack through the text she had read, so the music started again, albeit softly. So softly she could barely see it with her mind's eye. The further back her eyes went along the text, the louder the music got, reached a peak and as she continued retracing her steps, so the music started to die again. She focused on the text where the music was loudest. Nothing was coming to her mind. Just loud music. She continued to look. Slowly almost imperceptibly a diagram was forming over the words. Before she could stop it, her finger touched the area on the page where the diagram was beginning to take shape. The music in her mind reached a crescendo, and immediately a 3D life sized hologram of the rock cutting tool appeared before her eyes. It was crystal clear. An exact, life sized, virtual replica of the tool she was holding in her hand. It was hanging there in space. Right in front of her. Slowly spinning on its central axis.

Slowly she reached out towards the hologram. She found she could orientate the

hologram any which way she wanted. She also
learned that touching a particular area on the
hologram, expanded that area showing her greater
detail. Explanations of what each part did and how to
operate it would follow. Rather like an inset on a
terrestrial nautical chart or geographical map.

She learned that each individual Petra
Circumdatos was coded to its one and only operator.
If you picked up a tool that wasn't coded to you, then
it simply would not work.

What sort of code? she wondered. *DNA?
Brain waves?* She read on. Almost immediately, she
found the answer. *No. Nothing as basic as DNA, or
Brain waves but retinal scans. All you had to do was
to stare at one particular place near the thinly
tapered end for "dýo defterólepta,* She had no idea
how long this was, because whatever units they had
for time, had no meaning to her.

V assumed that this unit was coded with her
retinal scan, otherwise why else would it be here?
How it came to be coded with her retinal scan, she
had absolutely no idea.

But, thought V, *assumption is not good
enough. I need to know whether I can operate this
unit or not.*

She turned to the hologram, zoomed in on
the thinly tapered end of the virtual image of the tool,
and found what she was looking for. It seems there
should be five very discrete and very small linear
rectangles cut very carefully into the tool. She picked
up the tool and looked closely but could see nothing.
Read invisible for discrete she thought to herself. She
ran her fingers very gently along the tool, but could
feel absolutely nothing. *What am I supposed to do
now?* she thought.

Nox's voice boomed in her head. "Did you not mention something about a magnifying glass?" He said, then promptly tuned out of her mind.

That animal is stalking me, she thought, with a smile. *Magnifying glass. Of course.*

V rummaged around in the package until her fingers touched the cold, hard material of the magnifying glass. She brought the glass up to her eye and looked through it at Petra Circumdatos. She marvelled at the finish of the rock cutter, even though the magnifying glass it was faultless. She looked at the area on the rock cutter where the hologram indicated the five linear rectangles should be. Nothing. *Surely, I must be able to see it with this,* she thought. She tried again. She picked up the glass and stared through it at the rock cutter. Then a strange thing happened. The magnifying glass clicked, and by itself, changed focus…

There they were. Five linear rectangles, exactly where they should be. She looked at them in relation to the orientation of the tool and noticed that the tool wasn't circular, but the side along which the rectangles were carved into the handle (at least she assumed it was the handle) was flat. She thought the tool slightly resembled a semi cylinder, but the flat edge was much smaller, and rather than bisecting the circle in the middle, bisected the circle 95% from the circle's completion. So the straight edge was barely discernible. But it could just be seen with the naked eye and felt by touch.

She removed the magnifying glass and stared at the tool where the now invisible rectangles were. Nothing. Then, just as she was about to look away, a piercing green light flashed into her eyes. She blinked in surprise, the light went out and the tool remained absolutely inert. *Ok*, she thought to herself. *Maybe that was supposed to happen. Let's try that again.*

Steeling herself this time, and determined not to blink if the green light appeared, she looked at the same spot on the rock cutter. Sure enough, 5 seconds later the same green light flashed into her eyes. This time she didn't blink. The green light filled her eyes for about 2 seconds. As it went out, the rock cutter vibrated in her hands. The metal warmed up and reached a comfortable temperature. She could also see five red, rectangular pin pricks of light where the rectangles were, which changed to amber, then green. The lights remained green and the rock cutter gently pulsed in her hand.

"Well, it must be on and I assume ready to work. But how do I make it cut? And more to the point, how do I switch it off?"

She turned her attention to the hologram and continued to examine the rock cutter in great detail. V learned that there were pressure sensors in the surface of the metal, which started about 6cm and 10cm from the tapered end of the tool, which was the cutting end – being the opposite end to where the rectangles were. It was here that the rock cutter was gripped, between thumb and index finger – rather like holding a terrestrial pen. Squeezing gently started the plasma beam flowing and the harder you squeezed, the hotter and more intense the beam became. Moving your index finger up and down the tool would affect the diameter of the beam. The closer your index finger moved towards the cutting end of the tool, the narrower and more focussed the beam became, covering a very, very small surface area. The higher up the cutter your index finger moved, the wider and greater the surface area the beam covered.

"Right. Got it." And as she said this, the rock cutter softly beeped at her, stopped pulsing and the lights went out. It at once went cold.

I hope it has switched itself off and not run out of power. V thought

To reassure herself, she went through the process of powering up the tool, then counting the seconds before the tool self-powered down. "Ok. Got it. 240 seconds. Now, I need to see how it works." V made sure everything, except the rock cutter was packed away in her backpack. She then moved 400m away from Saxa Antiquis, a distance that she thought was reasonably safe, and rummaged around on the ground until she found some granite that resembled the trilithon granite.

Nox had been nothing more than a silent, curious spectator to all of this. He did however wander over to V's new location, stand a respectful distance away and resumed his watchful, if impatient vigil.

Satisfied that her granite specimens were safely secured, and pointing away from Saxa Antiquis, V powered up the cutter. Holding the rock cutter between thumb and index finger, with the tip of the tool about 3cm from the granite specimens, she gently squeezed her thumb and index finger. A plasma beam shot out of the end of the tool, went straight through the granite slab specimen, straight through the granite pillar the specimen was leaning against and caused a granite boulder, two meters behind the pillar, to shatter. All of this in a fraction of a second. All of this before V had quite realised what was happening. Releasing her grip, the beam

vanished . She gazed at the tool in horror. "My God."
She stared at Nox. "I barely squeezed and look what
the tool did. It passed through all that rock like it
wasn't there!"

She dove into her backpack and pulled the
book out. As if reading her mind, the book flipped to
the appropriate page. V tapped the text, the hologram
appeared. She studied it intensely and reread the
instructions. This time, the music took her to a section
of text that she felt sure she hadn't read.

According to this new piece of information,
the five rectangular lights served several purposes.
They informed the user that the tool was powered up,
the status of the tool and also indicated the rock
cutters power settings, each green light an order of
magnitude more powerful than the preceding light. So
five green lights meant that the plasma blade would
be 10,000 times stronger than if the tool was only
showing one green light. V had inadvertently been
using the rock cutter on the most powerful setting!

Following the instructions, V powered up
the tool and set about testing the various power
settings. She soon found the unit easy and safe to
operate. Even at its least powerful setting, the plasma
cutter was able to surgically cut through the granite,
rather than simply blast a hole through it! She also
learned how to change the power of the plasma beam
by widening and narrowing the surface area the beam
covered. At its narrowest setting, the cut in the rock
was so fine, it was barely discernible, at its widest
and with a combination of power levels, it was
possible to melt rock, and with a bit of practice,
seamlessly fill in previously cut holes. Satisfied. She
got up, put everything away, and with a huge smile
on her face, looked at Nox. "We're ready."

CHAPTER FIVE

V gathered up her bits and pieces, glanced back at the shattered rock, and made her way back to Argentum Metallicum. She dug into her backpack, got the blanket out and spread it out on the ground next to the metallic slab. Next she reached in for the book, the magnifying glass and the rock cutter, placing them neatly on the blanket. Book in hand, V collapsed onto the blanket - trying to quell the fear that was welling up inside her. The fear that was clawing at her insides as thoughts of The Ostium, her aunt and uncle and the words of Ventus crowded her mind. She closed her eyes, got her breathing under control, and said to herself, "Forget The Ostium; time is the real killer. It would be time that would kill everything she loved and cared for. Time is the real enemy right now. Concentrate, girl. Concentrate on the task at hand."

V opened the book, pictured the musical words, Saxa Antiquis in her mind and at once, opened to the correct chapter. Calming, almost hypnotic music filled her ears, a symphony of words flooded into her mind. She at once felt the fear and panic subside. She closed her eyes and concentrated.

Nox had taken the opportunity of having a quick look around. Satisfied that there was no immediate threat, he quietly wandered over to V, lay down next to her and closed his eyes. His ear's ever twitching. His eyes might have been closed, but his mind active and his senses very much on the alert.

V wanted to be sure of the exact location on the slab where Ourea had carved the two parallel holes. She also wanted to remind herself exactly what

Ourea did to the obelisks he had placed inside the newly created holes.

Her eyes flew open as a thought struck her. She wondered if it was possible to get a holographic image of the exact locations of where these holes were cut. She looked long and hard at various places in the text where it seemed obvious to her that a drawing or schematic would have accompanied the descriptive in the text. But nothing materialised. No shimmering images appeared over the text.

V wasn't deterred by this. She was beginning to understand what she was now growing to accept were her "people," her forefathers, her family. She just knew that this book not only contained everything she needed to know, but also contained everything it possibly could to help her succeed on this quest.

Whilst she was thinking these thoughts, her eyes had drifted to the top of the page and rested on the title of this particular chapter. As her eyes lingered so a blurred image seemed to glow from the chapter's title: Saxa Antiquis.

"Of course"she shouted! Startled, Nox immediately raised his head off the blanket, opened one eye and gave her a look. Satisfied that she was alright, he settled himself back down again.

Sorry boy. No reply. Nox maintained a dignified silence.

It makes perfect sense, she thought. Holographic images associated with the title. As you read the chapter, you can refer to the image any time you like! "Obvious, really," she said to herself. Feeling a little embarrassed that once again, it had taken the book to show her, rather than finding these things out for herself.

This time, quite deliberately, she reached out and touched the blurred image. A perfect 3D holographic image of Saxa Antiquis appeared before her very eyes. Quietly rotating in space about its central axis.

She rotated the image until she found the area she was looking for. Zoomed in to the central trilithon and focussed on the stone slab directly in front of it.

V was still having difficulty with Domus Mundi's context for time and measurement. The text told her that Ourea cut two parallel rectangular holes. It even gave the dimensions, but the dimensions were meaningless. She knew there must be an answer. The book? She went to the index and thought *conversions*. Nothing. *Appendices*, she thought. Nothing.

She closed the book and looked at the other tools lying next to her on the blanket. Anything here? She picked up the magnifying glass and looked at the tools it had in its handle. She didn't understand what they were for. They all seemed to be tools to be used physically, rather than as a form of reference. No joy there. Feeling deflated, she got up and marched around, thinking hard.

As she got up, she disturbed Nox. Nox sensed the frustration in her mind. "Are you alright?" he asked

"No." she replied hotly. "No. I'm not alright. In fact, I'm very, very not alright." Nox had to work that one out for a second. When she thought at him, he understood every word she said to him perfectly, no matter what she said, or how she said it. But, when V spoke to him, he sometimes had difficulty in understanding what she said, especially when the language she used was somewhat colloquial! When she spoke to him, Nox had to mentally translate what she was saying, into his language and, well some of the words she came out with, and some of the phrases she used simply didn't fully translate. As was the case now. In cases like this, he had to try and fill in the gaps!

"What seems to be the problem" Nox asked in a calm and understanding voice. "Perhaps I can help…,"

Well, she thought back at him – Nox gave a mental sigh of relief. V chose to think at him rather than speak to him. At least he would fully understand!

The book tells me everything I need to know, when I need to know it. It taught me how to use the rock cutter and it told me a lot about Saxa Antiquis. It told me where cuts were made into the rock and why. It even gave me the dimensions of the incisions into the rock. And that's the problem. All dimensions used, I'm unfamiliar with. So, as an example, if the book says "a cut was made triánta dýo defteróleptaI," I have no idea what this translates or converts to in the measurement systems that I'm used to dealing with. Until I understand, then I can't proceed

"1,371.6 centimetres" responded Nox.

V stopped and stared at Nox in open-mouthed amazement. "What?" she demanded. "What did you say??"

"Your question" responded Nox. "Triánta dýo defteróleptaI in your measurement system is 1,371.6 centimetres, or 13.716 metres, or 0.013716 kilometres." he responded around a mouth full of grass.

V just stared at him. Still not fully convinced. "How do you know?" she asked.

"As you know, I have been coming and going to Udal Cuain over many centuries. Over this time I have had a fairly good grounding of your language and measurement units, which changed over time. Before I left Domus Mundi, for this trip, my mental programming was upgraded so that I could understand the more modern version of your language. In fact, I can now understand most of the languages spoken on this planet. Part of the programming included the metric system and how to convert from the Domus Mundi measurement system into your Earth metric system. I admit the programming wasn't 100% successful, but it was good enough, at least to start with. Remember, I have been here since your eighth birthday. I have had plenty of time and opportunity to observe you and everyone you have come into contact with. I even sat in on some of your lessons when you had them outside. This gave me time to hone and refine the understanding of your language. Understanding of your language is now 100%, along with your numeracy system,"

"I do still have a problem with some of the things you say. But everything you think at me, when I'm in your mind, I understand perfectly."

"Oh," was all she had to say. "Well, whilst we are on the subject" she went on "Is there anything else you think I ought to know, or anything else about you and your abilities that I should be made aware of. Because now would be a very good time to tell me…"

"No. Not really" said Nox. "What you see, is what you get…" he said somewhat haughtily and wandered off a little, found a comfortable place and settled himself down in preparation for a doze.

Closing his eyes, he thought at V "Oh," he said. "It'll be moonrise shortly, I believe this is important, although I don't know why. We really do need to start making progress before then."

She looked at him whilst he settled himself comfortably on the soft grass, with his eyes drooping. "We?" she said in surprise… "We must make progress?" "Since when was "We" singular," she asked. "The only person working around here is me!!"

His voice low and sleepy. "Anything you need, just ask" and with that he tuned out.

V simply gave him a look, winced again at the state of his body. Now that she had been in his company for a couple of days, she could see how quickly his condition was deteriorating.

He must be in absolute agony, she thought. *But he doesn't show it. Even when I'm in his mind, I can't sense any distress…The sooner we get away from here and get him some help, the better.* All thoughts of The Ostium were, for now, out of her mind. Her sole driver was getting Nox the medical treatment he so desperately needed. With that, she turned back to the book and to Saxa Antiquis.

As she did so, Nox opened his eyes, which were very keen and alert, watched her for a moment, smiled to himself and closed them again. Nox was far from sleeping. He was on high alert. Constantly scanning the horizon with his mind, sensing the ground for the slightest tremor with his body, tasting the air for any hint of a threat, his ears sensing subtle air pressure differences. He also had part of his mind constantly tuned into V's. *She was good*, he thought, *very good. But she still had a long way to go.* Part of his mind was always tuned into V's. She thought he had tuned out. At least, that was the impression he gave. But that wasn't the case. He was with her. Always. Not to pry. Not to snoop. But to protect, to help and when necessary, to enter into her subconscious to help her sleep, to calm her down, to give her resolve. Nox never fully slept. Ever. He couldn't afford to.

V rummaged in her pocket and dug out the notebook and pencil that always accompanied her and found the appropriate page in Vica Pota. She looked at Nox and called out the dimensions that sang into her mind. Nox wasn't in the least fazed, he simply thought back to her: "1.5m in length, and 0.75m in width and 40 cm in depth. The second hole has to be exactly parallel to the first but separated by 0.5m"

V thanked Nox and duly noted the figures down. *Hmm,* she thought to herself, *where precisely on the slab were these holes initially excavated? At the top? Bottom? Mid way?* She had no idea, and the book was of no help. "Always, always, one step forwards and two steps backwards," she muttered. "Let's think about this a little more. Ourea was tall around "2m 50 cm,"

"Ok, 2m 50cm. I'm 1m 90cm, so 60cm difference, around 2 ft." She sketched a scale drawing of Ourea in her notebook, together with a scale drawing of the central slab – using a maximum height of 3m for the slab. She doubted that he would have worked at head height. The book said he approached the slab, which means, she reasoned, that he didn't kneel and didn't stand on anything. So, 3m max height for the slab was a reasonable assumption. He must have worked at a comfortable height. She sketched a picture of herself, to scale, again using a 3m slab height. She picked up the rock cutter, and moved towards the appropriate stone slab, positioned the rock cutter comfortably and held it as if she was about to start cutting. She made allowances for the dimensions to be cut and experimented with different cutting positions. Finally, she came up with the position that she felt was the most appropriate. Made marks on the slab, measured them, scaled them up to account for the height difference between herself and Ourea and marked what she had calculated to be the actual cutting locations on the stone slab.

"Well, this may have been a comfortable cutting position for Ourea, but for little old me, it's quite a stretch." She looked around her, found a suitable rock and tried to shift it towards the stone slab. No matter how hard she tried, she couldn't shift it.

Nox heaved himself up, walked over to her and asked if he could help. V showed him what she was trying to do and asked if he had any ideas. With that, Nox simply nodded and with his leg, quite easily and effortlessly, rolled the stone to where it needed to be. V climbed on top, satisfied with the positioning, thanked Nox, again marvelling at his strength. That rock must have weighed in at over two tons and it was half buried in the ground. He merely thought *You're welcome* and went back to his new favourite place, settled down and went back into listening mode.

Right. Nearly ready, V thought to herself. *Just need to practise using the cutter on the granite first; to ensure I have the correct settings. I don't want to blast a hole into whatever is hidden in the rock.*

She found some odd bits of granite on the ground and set to work with the cutter. Very quickly she felt confident that she had the correct settings and that she could cut accurately enough.

One more try on the actual slab may be best she thought. Just to be sure. She went to the slab, selected a location well away from the prime area, in fact the area she chose was at ground level and started cutting. Or tried to. The rock cutter refused to work.

"What now," she said. "Why can't anything ever run smoothly?"

She pulled the rock cutter away from the slab, went back to her test piece and, sure enough the rock cutter worked perfectly. Puzzled, she went back to the stone slab, knelt down and tried cutting. Nothing. The tool refused to work. Completely flummoxed, she sat down and grabbed hold of the book to see if there were any clues there. Nothing. Nothing sang to her that would help. Fed up of sitting down, she jumped up and decided to see if the rock cutter would work anywhere else on the slab. Maybe it was just the location she was trying. She was grasping at straws, and she knew it. But she also knew the tool was here. It had been left to her. It must have a purpose. It must.

V walked resolutely and determinedly back to the slab. She put the beam on the lowest possible power setting, but also ensured the beam itself was at its maximum width so that when the tool did spark into life, if it sparked into life, she could at once shut the beam down without incurring any accidental damage.

V methodically ran the tool over the slab. Starting at the bottom, moving the beam horizontally along the slab. From one side to the other. She then raised the tool slightly higher and worked her way back. She continued in this way, slowly working her way up the slab, but also ensuring that every part of the slab had been covered.

Nothing. She was fast approaching the area she had calculated where Ourea would have cut, but so far nothing. The cutter remained on, but stubbornly refused to work.

Well, I've come this far, I must carry on she thought as she climbed onto the rock.

Once settled, she resumed the arduous task of running the rock cutter backwards and forwards across the slab.

With her mind wondering what to do next if the cutter refused to work, she very nearly missed it, the beam pulsed. Just for the briefest of moments. It pulsed. It was so quick, V asked herself whether she had imagined it, or whether it had really happened.

Checking to make sure the cutter was on its lowest settings she very slowly and very carefully worked her way back. There it was again. A slightly longer, but still very brief flare of the beam. Going back to where the beam flashed. She tried again but keeping the cutter perfectly still. The beam flashed and started to slowly cut into the granite. She stopped. A small hole had appeared, about 1mm in diameter and a couple of millimetres deep. She fiddled with the settings. Still keeping the power on its lowest setting, but this time narrowing the beam so that it was at its absolute smallest, smaller than the width of a human hair. She reasoned that the only direction to go was up, in a straight line from the pin prick she had just carved into the granite. She went back to the marker, switched on the beam and sure enough, the beam flared at the granite. Keeping her hand as steady as she could, she slowly moved the cutter upwards. Sure enough, the beam continued to cut. Higher she went.

The beam continued cutting. Her arm moved; she went offline. The cutter immediately shut down.

It seems like I have to trace the ancient cut. As long as I stay within the track of the ancient cut, the cutter will work. As soon as I stray, or go offline, even slightly, the cutter shuts down. It must be a failsafe system. This slab must be very special and cutting anywhere but over Ourea's original cut could damage something crucial within this slab thought V. *This is why there was no indication of where to cut. The rock cutter would find its own way and would be able to cut in the appropriate area*

Again, she marvelled at this ancient technology. Many thousands of years old, but so far advanced of anything she had ever come across on Earth.

She went back to work, cutting a line in the granite, following the ancient cut. She didn't cut deeply, just deep enough to see it clearly, so that once the outline of the two areas to be cut had been completed, she could then go back and cut to the proper depth.

Within a few minutes, she had the outline of the first rectangular hole. She felt really connected with Saxa Antiquis. To think, she was retracing the steps of her forefathers. Ourea had stood here, all those millennia ago, doing exactly what she was doing now – only doing it so much better. This was the closest she had come to her forefathers. V felt quite emotional. *No time for this* she thought to herself. *I have work to do.*

With that, she got out her tape measure and measured exactly 25 cm from the inner edge of the first rectangular hole, to what should be where the inner edge of the second rectangular hole should be.

She marked the spot with a little chalk and drew a straight line towards the bottom of the stone slab of 0.75m length. She got the rock cutter out, fired it up and sure enough it worked. V then set to work making a shallow incision, following the ancient cuts of the second rectangular hole.

Finished, she stepped back to admire her work. There, on the face of the stone slab, were two identical, parallel rectangular outlines carved into the rock.

V paused a moment and checked the time. *Moonrise still an hour away,* she thought to herself, *plus it's a full moon tonight. In fact, she reminded herself, it's a blue moon – not because the moon will appear blue in colour, although this can happen. No, in this instance, it's when a second full moon occurs within the same calendar month. There was a full moon at the beginning of the month, and here we are 29 odd days later, having a second full moon within the same month.*

She had a quick glance at Nox. He hadn't moved. *Still resting peacefully,* she thought.

She went to the first template, keeping the tool on a moderate power setting, but with a very fine, narrow beam she was about to begin cutting, then stopped. *How can I gauge the depth to be cut? I must not guess 40cm, I must know it's exactly 40cm.* she asked herself. She knew she must not damage the slab in any way – clearly this was a very special stone slab. Unique, irreplaceable in fact. *I feel like a surgeon who was just about to perform his first open heart surgery.* She thought to herself. *If the surgeon made a mistake the patient is dead. Well, if I make a mistake, I am stranded here, the enemy will capture me, Earth will fall just as Domus Mundi fell, and there will be absolutely no hope.*

She felt tears of frustration welling in her eyes. Also, not a little self-pity. "Why me? Why is this left to me?" she moaned aloud.

"Because you can do it and you will do it and you will do it correctly." Nox's voice flooded her mind. "Just stop and think clearly – you know the answer. It's obvious – take a minute. Get yourself a drink and think. The answer is there "

V didn't respond to Nox, but immediately felt better, calmer, more relaxed. She went to her back pack and stopped dead. "Of course!" she said. "The answer was so simple, right in front of me all the time - literally! Nox, how did you know?"

Nox merely lay where he was and said nothing,

V hurried back to the stone slab and to the cutter. *It was so simple,* she said to herself. *The slab protects itself. It would not let the rock cutter fire up anywhere except where Ourea's ancient cuts were. If I moved 1mm offline, the cutter shut down. It stands to reason that if I cut along the ancient lines, the slab will prevent the cutter from cutting any deeper than 40cm. It's impossible for me to damage the slab or the entombed material. The slab will not let the cutter inflict any damage on it at all. Wow,* she thought, looking at this stone slab in amazement. *What are you?* she wondered.

With renewed confidence, she picked up the rock cutter. Standing on her stone, and with a steady hand she proceeded to cut into the granite. Sure enough, once at target depth, the cutter cut out. In no time she cut to a depth of 40cm around the first and second rectangles. Now to liquefy and remove the granite. *What am I supposed to do with the liquefied granite?* she asked herself. *I can't just let it drop to the floor. I must collect it in something. And that something has to be able to withstand temperatures of between 1,215 °C – 1,260 °C, the melting point of dry granite at ambient pressure.*

Actually, V said to herself, *I really don't care what happens to the molten granite. The objective is to get away and if Saxa Antiquis is the tool to do that, and cuts need to be made into parts of Saxa Antiquis in order to do what's necessary then so be it.*

With that, she adjusted the setting on the cutter to maximum power and maximum beam width. And set to work.

It didn't take long for the granite within the rectangular area start to glow, then to melt.

During the past few days, V had been exposed to so many unexplainable marvels – from Nox, an alien with whom she can communicate telepathically, to books that have a mind of their own. V really had thought she had seen everything. Far from it. What she saw now caused her to pause in her work and wonder at her forefather's technological ability.

V had automatically assumed that once the granite had become molten, it would flow and that gravity would take over and cause the molten granite to flow down, towards the ground. What was actually happening was that the molten granite was indeed flowing away from the cuts she was making, but flowing horizontally; horizontally away from the slab, to a distance of perhaps 2 to 3 feet (1m) slowly congealing as it cooled, into a ball. The granite ball, like the holograms she had seen before, just floated, in space, slowly rotating on its axis. As she melted more magma away from the slab, so it streamed away, horizontally, and joined the ever expanding solidifying granite ball. Which continued to hover in space a few feet away from the slab and from her. As she moved, so the ball moved, the flow of molten granite adjusting to compensate for V's movements. Thus she never got closer or further away from the slowly solidifying ball of granite. Not one drop of molten granite dripped to the floor, or was lost. How this was happening, V had no idea, and frankly didn't have time to think about it. V was beginning to accept the fact that her forefather's technology was so far advanced, that defying the laws of terrestrial physics and the universal law of gravity were a mere stroll in the park for them. She pushed the why's and wherefores to the back of her mind and just concentrated on the task at hand.

Within a matter of minutes all of the granite had been removed and had flowed away, joining the granite ball now just hovering in space, slowly rotating on its axis.

She then went over to the second area to be cut. Exactly the same thing happened. The molten granite just flowed horizontally away from the slab, forming a second granite ball that sat, suspended in space, slowly rotating on its central axis, exactly parallel to the first granite ball.

Having excavated the granite, the contents of the cavities were exposed. She peered inside one cavity and then the other. She didn't know what she expected to see. What she saw, left her a little nonplussed. All she saw were two very large tubes that fit perfectly into the cavities cut for them. One tube had red banding at the top, the other, green banding. Inside the tubes was a clear looking liquid – well she didn't know if liquid was the right term; a clear looking material that she assumed was in a liquid phase. The tubes were made of a clear, glass like material. V doubted it was glass because the material was totally resistant to the rock cutter, totally resistant to molten granite and was able to cope with being totally entombed in a large quantity of solid granite.

She sat back and looked at the two obelisks. For some inexplicable reason, the longer she looked at them the more frightened she became. They seemed completely inert, lifeless. Yet they seemed to exude tremendous, unimaginable power.

V shook herself, went back to the blanket, sat down and opened the book. She knew what she had to do next, she was just trying to delay the moment, because she was terrified of taking the next step. "It's an easy step to take," she said to herself. "All I have to do is stare into the green obelisk first and wait for something to happen. Then I do the same to the red obelisk. It was the "something to happen bit" that terrifies me." She was terrified on two counts.

Firstly, she was terrified that nothing would happen – and if nothing happened, then she assumed that that was it. Saxa Antiquis was dead and she would be marooned on Earth, to await the terrible fate that seemed to be gathering.

Secondly, she was terrified that something would happen – and if something did happen what sort of power would she be unleashing? How would it manifest itself? But, more than anything else, what really terrified her in this instance was that a functional Saxa Antiquis meant that she would have to follow her destiny to Domus Mundi.

"Well," she said to herself as she picked up the book, then promptly put it down again.

"I'm terrified either way. No point in delaying. Let's just get on with it,"

With that. She went back to the green obelisk, chose a spot and just focussed on it. And waited. And waited.

Then…She became aware of an effervescence. The obelisk seemed to boil, then glow. Very slowly it turned a brilliant white, then started to get darker and darker until it was black, a depth of blackness that V had never experienced before. She instinctively knew whatever was happening wasn't over. She continued to remain absolutely still and stare into the obelisk. She became aware of Nox in her mind. Steadying her, giving her the confidence to stay where she was. Slowly, V became aware of small pin pricks appearing in the utter blackness. Tiny golden dots started appearing. Very slowly, the dots became larger and more substantial. They seemed to move and to change shape. The golden spots gravitated to the area within the obelisk into which V was looking.

V became aware of a dull throb in her eyes, the dull throb grew and grew and soon became tremendous, unrelenting pain, agony. Just as she was about to pull away, in awful pain. Nox's voice flooded her mind. "V, concentrate on the obelisk. Ignore the pain. It won't last long. Just concentrate on my voice and don't take your eyes away from the obelisk. It will be fine. No harm will come to you,"

She just about heard Nox reassuring, voice through the intense pain. She trusted in him completely. So despite the agony, she hung in there. Never before had she known such pain. She felt sure she would be blinded by this experience. So intense was the pain.

Slowly, the pain started to ease, leaving a nagging ache behind her eyeballs. The pain though was quite tolerable.

She was now able to concentrate on what was happening in the green obelisk. The golden spots, which, whilst she was suffering the terrible pain in her eyes, had been gently moving in a haphazard manner; they now coalesced together and then, with seeming purpose moved to preordained positions. As soon as the golden dots within the blackness of the obelisk stopped and settled into their final position, they glowed with amazing brightness, the glow faded and the golden spots disappeared. Just as they disappeared, the obelisk started to pulse rhythmically. *It seemed to pulse in time with my heart,* she thought. Then she felt Saxa Antiquis …quiver. Deep inside her, she felt Saxa Antiquis waken and start to come alive.

Nox voice boomed into V's head. "Well done V. You may leave that obelisk. Please proceed to the red obelisk and do exactly the same thing"

V broke contact with the green obelisk, moved over to the red obelisk, selected a spot and just stared. Exactly the same thing happened. The substance within the obelisk effervesced, changed colour to white, then black. Golden dots appeared. This time V experienced no pain. The golden dots immediately configured themselves into shape, flared and disappeared. The red obelisk started to pulse, the pulses synchronised exactly to the green obelisk pulses and to V's heartbeat.

This time, V sensed a definite, palpable sense of life and purpose within Saxa Antiquis. Saxa Antiquis was awake, it was alive. It had purpose. It was waiting.

V moved away from the obelisks feeling quite drained. She sat on the blanket and closed her still throbbing eyes and promptly fell asleep.

Nox, was more aware than ever of the time pressure. He could sense foreboding, he could sense The Ostium, he could nearly smell them. But he had no choice. He moved over to V and lay down beside her. After what she had gone through and what was now happening to her before his very eyes, sleep wasn't just necessary, it was crucial. But how long. That was the question he was wrestling with. He could see and sense changes coming over the girl. The changes were accelerating. He came to a decision. *Twenty terrestrial minutes. That's all I can allow her. I hope it's enough.* He could sense the physical and mental changes taking place. This wasn't the V of only seconds ago. That V was gone forever. What sort of V would replace her? That was the question...

Nox kept to his self-imposed timetable and on the stroke of the twentieth minute he gently woke V. He watched her closely and furtively examined her. V's eyes had gone completely black. Her pupils were indistinguishable from her irises, which in turn were indistinguishable from the sclera, all completely black. The blackest black he had ever seen. However her irises, which were deep, deep black now contained golden flecks and spots; all of various shapes and sizes. Her hair had also changed. It was multi coloured. The blackness now gone. Her hair displayed a rainbow of colours. Even as he looked at her hair, he could see the colours changing. Her whole stature had changed. She now had a sense of self. A sense of pride, certainty and confidence about who she was and where she had come from. Her figure had filled out and she had grown taller, he thought to himself. The name of a person, long since dead, came to mind - Ourea. *Yes* Nox thought. *If Ourea had had a daughter, this is what she would have looked like,*" Mentally, he could sense changes in the way V's brain functioned. Parts of the brain had been "woken up." If she was smart before, when she had learned to control and utilize these parts, she would be quite brilliant he thought to himself and a lot more perceptive.

Nox also felt different. He felt stronger and more alive than he had done in years. He didn't hurt as much. In fact the pain he had had for so long, that had become such a large part of his life was mostly gone. He actually missed it. Where V was lying against his flanks, trying hard to wake up, the pain too had gone. Her body no longer irritated his skin.

Nox looked at V. She was still half asleep. Then V's mind opened to him. He was able to see. Wonder and awe filled his mind. He had always known V was special, but now he understood. He now knew who this person was. Where she had come from. Where her heritage lay. He was shocked. How had they managed to do this? How had they managed to shelter her? Keep her safe? How had they managed to keep her alive? For the only time in his life, Nox was afraid. Not afraid of the person that was struggling to wake up next to him. But what she represented to both Domus Mundi and to Earth. He knew with absolute certainty that the enemy would shift heaven and earth to get this girl, and that's what frightened him. They would stop at nothing. They would not stop until this girl was dead and her body consigned to the depths of Ostium hell. She was the one person, the only person that could stop them. Defeat them – destroy them forever.

Nox wasn't sure if the enemy yet really understood who she was and what she represented. He somehow knew they had a pretty good idea but were not 100% certain. Still, that was enough. Their uncertainty would mean that she would be killed if they caught her. But before killing her, in order to be sure, they would torture her thoroughly and terribly.

CHAPTER SIX

V slowly came to. She was aware of the dull ache behind her eyes and the ravaging pain in her body. Then everything came flooding back. She was reluctant to open her eyes.

They must be damaged, she thought, the pain had been so intense.

But, very slowly she opened them and marvelled. Her vision, which had always been good, was now so much better. But what she found even more peculiar was how her eyes worked. On the one hand, they seemed to work much, much better than they did before. The vision was so much sharper, the colours so much clearer. *Colours!* she thought, *I'm lying next to Nox and I can see in colour,* she wondered to herself... *Where has the black and white word gone?* On the other hand,... They felt so different, they didn't feel normal at all. She couldn't put into words how her eyes felt. *Well,* she reasoned to herself, *so long as I can see, that's all that matters.*

Her body ached horribly. She knew she had changed. She felt so strong, so confident, so alive. Her mind seemed to be working on a different level. And working so much faster. She felt she could do absolutely anything. All the self-pity, the concern, the doubt, that had all gone.

Her clothes felt extremely uncomfortable. She looked down at herself and was amazed to see how her clothes had shrunk. "How could this have happened?"

Nox could sense everything that was going on in the girl's mind. He didn't interfere, he let her come to terms with it in her own time. He also sensed that her mind remained partially closed. Her mind wasn't operating at its full potential, as it had done before she awoke. *Whatever happened to her mind before she awoke, had now closed itself off. She has to learn how to use her mind to its full potential, to control her mind when conscious and fully awake* he thought. *I can't teach her how to do this. This must come from her. She is not yet aware of her heritage, her background. Her true capabilities.* Nox thought to himself.

V's eyes fell on the red and green obelisks, she immediately felt tuned into them. She could sense that they were now operating as they should and would continue to do so for all eternity. Why they had stopped she wasn't sure. But it was clear that something had caused them to stop working. She looked at them a little harder. The pulses quickened, they seemed to be communicating with her. Then, V understood. They stopped working to protect her. Had Saxa Antiquis been left working, over the intervening millennia, the enemy would have learned to sense the presence of the obelisks and eventually to have located them and of course Saxa Antiquis. Had Saxa Antiquis remained fully operational not only would the enemy be alerted to its presence, but would have eventually provided a direct pathway to Udal Cuain and subsequently, when they finally learned of V's existence and her importance, directly to her. So, all those thousands of years ago, when Domus Mundi was fighting a losing battle against The Ostium, one of the last orders given before final capitulation, was to shut down Saxa Antiquis and to wipe anything to do with Saxa Antiquis from all records and all minds associated with the project. Within Domus, everything to do with Saxa Antiquis had been destroyed and anyone associated with the project, no matter how remotely or how fleetingly, had Saxa Antiquis wiped completely from their minds. In fact, the elite group of scientists went one step further and ensured the entire population's minds were wiped clean. To the people of Domus Mundi, Saxa Antiquis no longer existed. It never did. Since then, Saxa Antiquis had remained dormant, alone, neglected and quite forgotten. Waiting for the day when it would be reawakened.

V let this information sink in for a moment, then struggled up.

"Jesus, my body hurts," she groaned out loud. She looked at Nox and marvelled at him. "Well, boy," she said to him. "You are looking a lot better. Your sores are not ulcerating quite so much."

Nox, true to form, said nothing. But she sensed that he was really pleased with how he was feeling. She smiled to herself and got back to work.

That was to be her immediate intention before she realised just how uncomfortable she was in the clothes she was wearing. *Unless I want to walk around naked, there is not much I can do about that.*

"Are you not forgetting something?" Nox's voice boomed in her mind. It seemed extraordinarily loud.

"No" replied V. "I don't think so,"

"The cape," Nox said. "Try the cape,"

"The cape" V retorted. "That's a cape. I need clothes"

"V, we really don't have time to debate this. Please, just humour me and go try on the cape,"

"Oh very well" grumbled V. She went to her backpack, which now seemed incredibly small rummaged around, found the cape, went behind the central trilithon, struggled out of her clothes and put on the cape. Within seconds the cape not only shrunk to her size but also morphed into a one-piece trouser suit. "Wow," she said to herself. "All I need now is the cape and I could be superwoman," she chuckled, but at the same time marvelled at the clothes she now wore. They fit her perfectly, they moved when she did, they were incredibly warm and extremely comfortable to wear. The colour seemed to change with her environment. *Perfectly camouflaged as well,* she thought to herself.

Then she stopped dead in her tracks.

"Colour," she repeated to herself. She went back to her backpack and bent down. Colour. Her hair.....

"What the hell has happened to my hair?" she shouted at nobody in particular. She grabbed a handful and looked at it. Her hair was now a fiery red and seemed to be getting darker and brighter all at the same time. "Nox!" she yelled. Immediately Nox came trotting over.

"Is there anything different about me?" she asked, her hair now changing from red to purple.

"Well," said Nox, not quite sure how to answer this question. "Your hair seems to have changed a bit. It seems to have many more shades to it and those shades seem to change as your mood changes. It's not completely black anymore" V had quite forgotten that Nox could only see in black and white. "And" Nox went on "You seem taller and fuller and your eyes have changed"

"My eyes!" she shouted and ran to her backpack and rummaged around until she found what she was looking for. A small compact mirror. She opened the mirror and nearly dropped it out of sheer horror. She didn't recognise the person looking back at her. Quite apart from the hair, which was now a multitude of colours, were those eyes. Where she had had beautiful black eyes before, they were now completely black. Pupil, iris, sclera – all completely black. Not only black but the blackest, darkest black she had ever seen. Except... Except for some golden flecks of various shapes and sizes that were sprinkled haphazardly within what would have been her iris. The shape and positions of the golden flecks rang a bell. "This was the shape the golden flecks in the obelisks manoeuvred themselves into before they flared and died and the obelisk started pulsing," she said to herself. The exact image of the golden flecks in my eyes. This she couldn't explain. She turned to Nox. He just looked at her. No help there. Then she looked at Nox again. He was still massive, huge. Even though he seemed more massive, impressive than he did just a few short moments ago, it's just well, I don't seem to have to look up quite so much into his eyes

"Have you shrunk?" she asked. Nox bridled at that.

"No," he said haughtily, "In case you have not noticed, you have grown, by I would say a good half meter,"

"Nonsense," V retorted.

"Really?" responded Nox, "Then how do you account for the sudden shrinking of your clothes? Why are you standing next to me at least a head taller than you were?"

V had no answer to that.

V glanced back into her mirror. Her skin, it had paled considerably and now appeared to be translucent and featureless. The characteristic creases in her skin had vanished... She looked up at Nox.

Complete bewilderment and incomprehension written all over her now beautiful and ageless face.

"V, I understand a lot has happened over the last half hour or so. Things have happened to you and to me that I can't explain. But we must be getting on. The moon has risen. For some reason that I'm not totally clear about, the moon is very important to us this evening." Nox said in a calm yet persuasive voice.

"Yes, Nox. You are quite right. Explanations can wait. At least for now. The changes to me have made me feel a better, stronger person. I can only assume it's the same for you. These changes will not hurt us, but I assume, will continue to strengthen us"

With that, she turned, collected the rock cutter and headed towards the green obelisk and the now rapidly cooling granite ball that was still patiently hovering and rotating in space.

She knew exactly what to do. Completely at home with the rock cutter now. She automatically set the power and beam width settings she flared the cutter to the hovering, rotating granite ball. The cutter danced, the granite melted and flowed horizontally back towards the green obelisk. It took no time at all to completely re-entomb the obelisk and smooth over the surface of the granite so as to ensure the cut completely merged with its surroundings. She did the same for the red obelisk and in no time the red obelisk was also entombed.

She stood back and admired her work. She went back to the blanket, gathered up all the bits and pieces and returned them to her backpack. Satisfied that nothing had been left behind, she turned and looked at Nox.

"Well?" she said… "What now? Saxa Antiquis has been restarted. I can feel her life within me. She is content and working perfectly. What happens next?"

"All I know V is that when I arrived on this planet, I arrived on the silver metallic slab, just over there. I was barely conscious and barely alive. I have no recollection of the trip, or how I got here. One minute I was on Domus Mundi, the next here, near-death and in tremendous pain. The one conclusion I can draw from that is, that if I arrived on the metallic slab, then it stands to reason that that is where we depart. How it works, I have no idea,"

"Well. At least that gives us somewhere to start," she said to herself. She left Nox where he was and marched over towards the metallic slab – or *Argentum Metallicum* – to give it its proper name, she thought to herself.

"Ok, Argentum Metallicum. There is no doubting your beauty. Your perfect symmetry." she said to the slab. "But you are where it all happens" she went on. "But, what happens? How does it happen? How do you work? What secrets are you keeping from me and how can I tease those secrets out of you?"

She circumnavigated the silver stone, then chose a spot right in the middle of the slab, facing the central trilithon. She sat down, closed her eyes and didn't move, didn't make a sound. She just sat and concentrated. She listened to Saxa Antiquis, she felt Saxa Antiquis in her body, she could sense its presence, its power, she felt part of the great stone circle. Would it talk to her? Would it connect with her?

She just sat there. Nox watching her. He understood what was going on. He made no sound. The moon continued its relentless march across the northern hemisphere sky, its reflectance gaining in intensity as it did so. . Still, V made no sound, she didn't move. But sat perfectly still. Her mind now connected to Saxa Antiquis, seeking a way to make it work. To get them back to Domus Mundi. Although she was gaining some understanding, Saxa Antiquis wasn't giving up its secrets on how it worked. It just worked.

Her subconscious mind caught it. But only just. Her subconscious mind broke into V's conscious mind – alerted her. V brought the rest of her mind to bear on what her subconscious thought it had heard. She blanked everything else out and listened with the full power of her mind. Concentrating so hard. For a moment nothing.'.. Then, there it was. Extremely faint the quietest of whispers, she heard the phrase "Vica Pota σώσε μας," She knew exactly what this phrase meant. It meant "Vica Pota Save us," This phrase was now repeating itself over and over in her mind. "Vica Pota Save us," "Vica Pota Save us," "Vica Pota Save us," Now she was tuned in, the sound was soft but clear. Spoken in a rich, deep baritone voice.

V opened her eyes and looked towards the central trilithon. The voice remorseless in her mind. "Vica Pota Save us," She rose effortlessly into a standing position and slowly started to walk towards the central trilithon. The closer she got, the louder and clearer the phrase became.

Nox, watched her go. He could sense she was concentrating, using her full conscious mind on something. He didn't interfere, he didn't intrude.

Merely watched her. On high alert, ready to leap into action should the situation demand. But for now, he stood, looked, watched and waited.

The closer V got to the central trilithon, so the voice got louder and clearer. The voice was acting like a homing beacon, trying to guide V to its source. V didn't rush, she took her time. She knew this was a pivotal moment. She got to within 1m of the central trilithon. The voice was loud, but not deafening. It was definitely coming from the central trilithon. But where she thought. This was a huge structure.

It had to be one of the two standing stones and not the lintel she thought. She veered off to her left and headed towards the central trilithon's right standing stone. The voice in her head immediately decreased in volume. The closer she got to the right standing stone, so the quieter the voice became. "Not this one," she said to herself. She pivoted and walked towards the left standing stone. Immediately the voice increased in volume and continued to do so until she got right up to the stone. "It's coming from here," she said to herself. "The voice is originating from, on or in this standing stone." She said to herself with absolute certainty. And, as if in confirmation, she could sense Saxa Antiquis become even more powerful. More threatening. She shuddered. "Just how powerful is this stone circle" she wondered.

She tried to look over the standing stone but could see very little. "Damn it," she said to herself. "It's getting dark," As she glanced over her shoulder, she could see the moon flexing its muscles. She bent down to the slab again.

"Nope. Can't see a thing. But, it should not be too long before the moon's reflectance will be of advantage,"

Backpack, she thought. *Tools.* With that, she got up and promptly fell to the ground again... A sharp pain in her head, dizzy and seeing stars. She looked up. Nox was standing over her with her backpack in his mouth.

"Damn it Nox," she said. Rubbing the sore part of her head that had collided with the bottom of his jaw. "Can you at least give me some warning that you are here – a polite cough or something?" She removed her bag from his mouth, and muttered "Thanks"

"I don't cough," said Nox. "Perhaps I should sneeze instead," he said as he headed back to his makeshift bed.

"Whatever," responded V, subject and pain forgotten as she rummaged in her backpack for a torch.

Finding what she was looking for, she went over to the left slab from 3m above the ground – she found she could comfortably reach 3m height now, down to ground level. Nothing. The moon was ascending quite quickly now. V paused in her work to marvel at the moon. It looked huge and full and beautiful.

"Enough daydreaming" she said to herself and was about to bend back to her task when she noticed, for the first time, the astronomical alignment of the central trilithon. It seemed that the full moon would pass in exact alignment over what she now knew were the siting stones, along the central axis of the open end of the horseshoe directly onto the central trilithon. "This phenomenon would happen in only a few minutes" she said to herself. So she paused from her work, to watch.

Sure enough, a few moments later, the moon passed exactly where she thought it would, in exact alignment with the siting stones, horseshoe central axis and central trilithon. However, what she hadn't expected was the way the moon's light reflected and shined off Argentum Metallicum. and hit the central trilithon, lighting part of the stone slab. She cast her eyes over the stone slab. Saw her shadow, moved a little so her shadow no longer blocked the reflected light and she gasped in amazement. For there, at the edge of the reflected moonlight, she saw four words carved into the slab: "Vica Pota σώσε μας" – "Vica Pota Save Us"

As the moon continued its walk along the night sky, so the reflected light got brighter and the words became clearer, then started to dim as the moon's reflected light started to move away. V realised that as soon as the reflected light moved away from the words, the words would become invisible. Quickly, V rummaged in her backpack, found her chalk and marked where the words were. She tried filling in the cuts with her chalk, so she could read the chalked letters, and she succeeded to a certain degree. Certainly, enough for her to know where the words were. The moon moved on, the shadows dulled and faded and soon there wasn't anything to see in the ambient moonlight. But there, still visible were the chalked letters spelling "Vica Pota σώσε μας,"

The voice in her head went silent – which was just as well thought V because if it had carried on much longer she would have gone stark staring mad.

Just then, V jumped as a strange noise shrieked in her ear, followed by a soaking. Rain sprang to mind. Quickly followed by, "Can't be.

Impossible," She touched the wetness on her cheek and clothes, "hmm, seems a little more viscous than water," she turned around and there was Nox with her backpack in mouth, slurring the words "I sneezed as instructed" he said, gave her the bag and strutted of back to his roost.

If looks could kill, Nox would have dropped dead there and then. As it was he settled himself comfortably. Looked at V and deliberately put his head down and closed his eyes. V then dissolved into fits of laughter. She laughed and giggled for a good minute or two before coming back to her senses.

Having got that out of her system, and dried herself off as best she could, she went back to the slab. Looked at the chalk marks and studied the rock surrounding the carved marks. Despite being a full moon, it wasn't quite bright enough for her to see clearly. So she donned a head torch and looked at the magnifying glass and thought, *Why not.*

Dropping the backpack, switching on the head torch she looked carefully at the rock surrounding the words Vica Pota σώσε μας. No. The torch didn't help, too many reflections from the silica and mica crystals in the granite. She switched it off, waited for her night vision to return and studied the rocks again.

She sensed that something wasn't quite right. She couldn't see it, but her subconscious eye could. She concentrated harder and looked again. There, yes and there. Something has cut into this rock and it has not been resealed properly. Some of the patterns in the granite don't quite match.
Here…and… here… and here.

With that, she used a straight line and with her chalk, joined up the "dots," What she saw was a straight horizontal line of about 1m width that underlined the words Vica Pota σώσε μας; with the words Vica Pota σώσε μας right in the middle of the chalked line.

She then went to the right end of the chalked line and started to look vertically down the slab. More blemishes she said to herself. She again joined up the vertical dots, producing a vertical line of about 1.5m in length. She quickly figured out this was another rectangular. Found the remaining blemishes, chalked them out, joined them up and she did indeed chalk out a perfect rectangle.

Rock cutter. She had to trust that the cutter would, of its own volition follow the ancient cut, because she knew without a shadow of a doubt that Ourea had cut out this rectangle and had deliberately resealed it all be it badly, so as to leave clues as to where the ancient cut was. These cuts, this rectangle, was meant to be found and opened. She doubted this was critical to the operation of Saxa Antiquis because she could sense that Saxa Antiquis was purring away quite happily. She knew that the contents within this rectangle were critical. But critical why? How?

Ensuring the rock cutter was set appropriately, she began to cut. As she looked at the slab, she started to cut at the top left corner and worked her way horizontally across the slab to the top right corner. She estimated the rock cutter penetrated the slab to a depth of half a metre before cutting out. Having successfully cut along the first line, she then proceeded to cut the right-hand vertical line, from top to bottom. She continued proceeding around the rectangle in a clockwise direction until all four cuts had been made, each to a depth of half a metre.

Fiddling with the rock cutter's settings, she then set about removing the 0.75 cubic metres of granite. This took no more than a minute or two. Once again the molten granite flowed away from the slab in a horizontal direction, about a metre or so away from the slab, where it slowly cooled and coalesced into a granite ball, hovering and rotating slowly in the air.

Switching off the rock cutter, she stood back to admire her work. Lying in the cavity was amongst other things a metal box. She stopped for a moment. Rummaged in her backpack, found the blanket, laid it out on the floor, and then went back to the cavity. She removed the box, opened it and found neatly folded material inside, which weighed almost nothing. Removing this from the box, she placed both the material and the now empty box on the blanket. Turning back to the cavity she saw something metallic reflecting blindingly in the torchlight. She reached in. Her fingers brushed against it. It was cold to the touch. Nearly as cold as ice. It was smooth, she could feel no blemishes in the material at all. She found some of her now useless old clothes, shredded her shirt into rags, wrapped the rags around her hands and fingers and brought the metallic object out of the cavity. And nearly dropped it. It was heavy. It was physically small, about the size of a large coffee mug, but incredibly heavy. She reckoned it must have weighed around 100 kg. Once prepared for the weight, she was surprised at how easily she managed to lift it and carry it. She placed the object on the blanket and looked at it. It resembled a four-leaf clover.

From the metallic objects centre point, each of the four leaves measured 10cm in length and were

9cm in width at their widest point. The stem measured around 17cm in length and around 7 millimetres in width. The object had an overall thickness of 8cm, that shimmered a silvery green in the moonlight.

She went back to the cavity to see if there was anything else. There was. A small schematic of Argentum Metallicum that appeared to be made out of the same material as the star map she found in the parcel Mrs Campbell had given her. *Was that only earlier today - it seems like years ago,* she thought. She put that on the blanket and returned once again to the cavity. She felt around and touched another metallic-like object. She withdrew this and looked at it. It was a silver, rectangular box measuring about 15cm x 5cm. It had no visible buttons to push or parts that opened. Another puzzle, she said to herself. Time for that later. The box too went on the blanket. Finally, she brought out two, well they looked like small, metallic thermos flasks. She shook them and could hear liquid sloshing around inside. Those also went on the blanket. And that was it. Nothing else.

Carefully checking one last time, and still finding nothing, she picked up the rock cutter and quickly resealed the cavity. The job she did, she thought, was nominally better than Ourea's she said to herself, more than a little pleased.

Going back to the blanket she sat herself down and studied the bits and pieces that she had recovered from the cavity.

She selected the schematic of Argentum Metallicum and was pouring over this. The music spoke to her and she was able to clearly understand the schematic. She knew where to go and where to touch to release the holographic images.

V was so absorbed in what she was doing that she didn't notice Nox's head shoot bolt upright, his ears twitching, sniffing, and tasting the air. He stood up and started pacing. Trying to identify and pinpoint something. His movements caught V's eye. She looked up for a moment, then returned to what she had been doing whilst muttering "Everything alright?"

Nox wandered off a little way, but still remained within sight of V, he ensured he could see her at all times. He had now pinpointed the source of the trouble and was staring into the distance, trying to see the perceived threat.

V slowly became aware of vibrations through the ground. Startled, because she had never felt anything like this before, she stopped what she was doing and looked up. Saw Nox was about 50m away, standing very still, looking in one direction. His voice filled her mind.

"Please put everything away into your backpack and stay where you are. Something is headed this way. I don't believe it to be a threat, but in these difficult times, I need to be sure."

V didn't reply, she simply did as instructed. Stayed where she was and also tried to concentrate her mind on the incoming threat.

The vibrations became severe, the ground visibly shaking. And, deep within the pit of her stomach, she could feel the thud, thud, thud of the low-frequency vibrations. Then she heard the noise. The frequency of the vibrations and the noises she now heard were vaguely familiar. Then a wave of relief flooded her mind – emanating from Nox.

"Most definitely friends," he thought at her and asked V to come to him. He bent to accommodate her, and she jumped on his back. His body immediately accommodated and secured her. "You are definitely bigger than you were, "Nox said to V. "Your mass has definitely increased by at least 20 kg," he thought at her.

Now she fully understood what the noise was. It was the thundering of hooves. Like stampeding cattle. Headed right for them. She didn't sense any aggression or panic coming from the minds that commanded those hooves, she felt a sense of urgency, but no panic, and certainly no aggression. In fact, she felt a little panic rise in the pit of her stomach.

"Shouldn't we move, sort of get out of the way?" she asked Nox.

"No," said Nox. "They know where we are. I have spoken to them, they will be slowing down in a few seconds and should be here within less than a minute" And no sooner had Nox stopped thinking those thoughts, than the noise decreased, the thudding of hooves dulled. The vibrations in the pit of her stomach ceased. And sure enough, moments later, 20 ponies, with Mr Marmaduke at the front, trotted into view.

They stopped and then did the most peculiar thing. They all lined up behind Mr Marmaduke and in perfect unison, they all bowed their heads at Nox, then turned to look at V and bowed their heads at V. Nox returned their bow. Then...nothing. Everyone seemed to have paused...nothing happened.

V... Nox's voice boomed into her mind. *Oh, Oh yes of course,* she thought back whilst at the same time bowing courteously back at the ponies.

Time unfroze. "Greetings Dominus Nox."
Said Mr Marmaduke – V now understanding every
word.

"Greetings Speculor, What news?" Nox
replied

"Dominus…? "V queried at Nox. "Shh"
responded Nox "Later"

"We have news from mare germen radicum
eius. "

"The sea watcher? What does he have to say
for himself" demanded Nox. V had never heard this
imperious, unchallengeable tone in his voice before.

"The Ostium are approaching the mainland
coast. It is very nearly at the Isle of Skye. Ventus has
been trying to delay them by blowing down power
lines, but they got wise to this and are now infiltrating
through subTerranean power lines. The Ostium are
headed for Talisker. From there they will then have to
cross the sea of the Hebrides to get to Udal Cuain.
There are no subsea power cables that run between
Skye and Udal Cuain, so The Ostium will be delayed
until they find a suitable routing. But they will find
one and they will be here, within hours. But given the
lack of suitable technology between Talisker and
Udal Cuain and on Udal Cuain itself, progress may
well be slower than that. Nevertheless, The Ostium
are relentless. Doubly so as they know Vica Pota is
here on the island." As Speculor said the name Vica
Pota, so they turned as one and solemnly bowed at V.
She returned the bow, puzzled by what was going on.

"As they know Vica Pota is here" went on
Speculor, "And they know that Vica Pota may be the
one, they will not stop, they will find a way – as you
know they can adapt and change. Getting here is not
in any doubt. The question is when? Minimum 6,

maximum 12 hours the sea watcher estimated. He too
will do what he can to delay. But he can only do so
much. The Ostium will get here, and when they do, if
Vica Pota is here, they will take her. Then all hope
will be lost. Forever."

"We will resume our duties. We'll split up
and stand guard around the circumference of the
island. We will keep watch. Should The Ostium
come, we will do what we can. We will give you as
much warning as we can. We will be unable to stop it,
we will try to delay it," Speculor finished.

"Thank you, "said Nox. "You have been
valuable allies and friends. I hope we will be gone
before The Ostium gets here – just before we leave, I
shall wipe your memories of our ever having been
here and of you watching over Vica Pota for all these
years. In your mind, it will be as if we and Domus
Mundi never existed. In that way, I'm sure you will
be mistaken for wild terrestrial ponies and as such,
absolutely no threat and you will be left alone.
Protected."

"We thank you Dominus Nox"

Turning to V, Speculor went on to say
"Domina Vica Pota. It has been our privilege to
watch over you these last years. Stop The Ostium.
Save Domus Mundi. Protect this world. We will do
what we can to delay The Ostium"

With that Speculor bellowed and the horses
charged off, their stampeding hooves gradually fading
from sound.

"Vica Pota, Dominus Nox. Who is Vica Pota
…?"

"You are Vica Pota," said Nox. "On Domus
Mundi, that is how you were known, that is your birth
name. On Earth, you are known as V"

"The Book," said V, "I thought the book was called Vica Pota...."

"No," said Nox "It is your book. It was written for you by your forefathers. The book will not work, will not open for anyone else but you. Neither will any of the other equipment you have found. They all sense your DNA through your fingers, and have the ability to scan your iris and only when the two match the data logged within the equipment or book or maps memory, will they open or operate and divulge their contents or secrets. The book was instructed to help you. To take you step by step through the processes you need to know. The book is your mentor and guide. Prepared for you by your forefathers all those millennia ago. Your forefathers knew a day would come when The Ostium would take control of Domus Mundi. Unfortunately, not many people listened or believed that it would be possible for Domus Mundi to be overrun. But a few, Ourea being one, they knew. They also knew you would be coming. They knew Domus Mundi, its ways and its technologies would be alien to you. They knew you would not have a guide to instruct you on Domus Mundi technology. So, before The Ostium conquered Domus, this book was written and hidden to teach you and to guide you. The other items left behind, the rock cutter, the glass, the cape, the star map. Also tools left behind to help you find your way home. The items Ourea left for you that you have just uncovered. Those were not recorded – it seems Ourea took it upon himself to help you further."

"So, who am I" Asked V quietly. "Really. Who am I?"

"You are Vica Pota. That is your real name. You are descended from the oldest, most respected house on Domus Mundi. Your parents were visionaries. They were the most eminent, the most respected scientists and thinkers on your home planet. They were known everywhere, loved by everyone. They foresaw the end of Domus Mundi. They knew that life on your home world couldn't go on as it was. Your parents went to the authorities to the seats of governments and pleaded with them to start the changes necessary to rescue your planet from its eventual decline and demise. But despite your parent's great standing and respect they were ignored. The Government, the seats of power within the various zonal authorities listened politely because your parents deserved that respect. But were effectively humoured and totally ignored. The Governments, the seats of authority, could simply not believe anything was powerful enough to overrun Domus Mundi. Unfortunately, and despite your parent's warnings, the seats of power's eyes were very much focused on being invaded from other worlds – and indeed, there were no other worlds that were powerful enough to conquer your planet. Unfortunately, it wasn't from without where danger lurked. It was from within. This your parents foresaw. Your parents knew that the current lifestyles on your home planet were unsustainable. Would eventually, corrupt, decline and be overrun. They knew that without change, Domus Mundi would die."

"So, your parents got together with likeminded people. Scientists, physicists, bio technicians, cryogenicists, engineers. They needed a plan to safeguard Domus Mundi, or at least to give it a chance of eventual survival. They knew they were too late to stop what was about to occur. The time for action, for change was long gone. Events would run their inevitable, yet lethal course. But, they could put in place a plan that would eventually, many millennia in the future, give your Home World one final chance to recover. That final chance was you."

"Your parents knew Ourea, who in Terran terms, is your mother's brother – your uncle, was shortly to be leaving for this new world "Terra" that had been discovered. His task was to establish a chain of listening temples over the Northern hemisphere of the world, Saxa Antiquis being the key. That he would be gone from Domus Mundi for nearly 20 Terran years. This was an ideal opportunity to put their plan, a desperate, incredible and dangerous almost hopeless plan, into action. And to safeguard you. Get you off-planet to somewhere that was safe, secure, somewhere to hide you. The scientists got to work creating all the tools that they thought you would need. The book, the tools, the maps, the cape. The bio technicians got to work building stasis cots, one for you and one for Ourea. A stasis cot that, in your case, would grow as you grew. Stasis cots that could sustain you and Ourea for thousands of years. The bio technicians also got to work on refining and simplifying cloning technology. Your parents got to work making the tools necessary to drip-feed knowledge in your brain. As you grew, as your brain enlarged, so more and more knowledge would be fed into your brain. Into your subconscious. These tools were incorporated into your stasis cot. You have been absorbing this information for many thousands of years. You have all the knowledge of your home world as it was before The Ostium destroyed it. Certainly, all the knowledge you will need to retake Domus Mundi from The Ostium. This knowledge has been slowly teased out as you grew and as you became educated here. There is still much you must learn. And you will. But the plan was for you to have all the knowledge of your home world, transferred into your brain by the time you were brought out of stasis. You were six months old when you were placed in the stasis cot. Over the intervening millennia, you didn't grow. You remained a 6-month-old child. Your growth would come later. Millennia later. But still, your mind was very slowly drip-fed with information, knowledge, everything it would eventually need."

"The scientists scanned your retina, your irises and your DNA. These were then implanted into the tools you would need. The surgeons went to work on you, hiding your true identity, making you less like a Domus citizen and to have more of the physical characteristics that would allow you to one day blend in with the species on Terra. They did this by carefully amending and manipulating parts of your DNA. But they did this ensuring that it was temporary and when triggered, fully reversible. They also implanted golden specs into your eyes. It was the golden flecks in your eyes that were the final key to unlocking the horrendous power of the red and green power pods – the heart of Saxa Antiquis. Ourea managed to start Saxa Antiquis, but he could only do so after he had injected his eyes with the code, which allowed the golden flecks in his eyes to replicate the code that would fire up the obelisks."

"Ourea also incorporated other aspects of your DNA into Saxa Antiquis and into the power pods. The power pods took longer to start because they were aligning themselves to you. They recognised the coding that Ourea had emplaced within them. They were seeking out your DNA.

Triggering the DNA within your body to correct itself, to change your characteristics to the person you should have been, rather than the person you were masquerading as. This is why your eyes changed, your hair, your physical appearance, your mental abilities, the ability you now have to understand the Domus language, to use the tools. You are still changing, but the remaining changes will not happen so quickly but will manifest themselves over time. This is why you feel so much a part of this temple. In some ways, it is an extension of you. You share the same DNA and so many other characteristics."

"Once the stasis cot had been completed, the knowledge pods incorporated, you were placed inside, connected up and immediately put into stasis. Your body was more or less shut down. Your growth and development stopped. Other than an increase in knowledge, you would remain the same for the next 4,000 years. Your parents and the rest of the scientific team monitored you for several days, ensuring all was functioning correctly. Once satisfied, you were placed aboard the spaceship – in complete secrecy. Only Ourea knew that you were being transferred to the vessel. You were placed in a secret compartment in Ourea's quarters, known only to him. Stealth communication devices were installed so the team on Domus could monitor you as you journeyed to Terra. All the equipment you would need was similarly transported to Ourea's cabin and stowed alongside you. And then the wait started."

"You were constantly monitored for two whole months before the ship finally took off. You were monitored throughout the entire journey and for the first fifteen years you were on Terra.

Shortly before the ship took off to return to Domus, the day Ourea powered up Saxa Antiquis for the first time, Ourea induced temporary stasis for the entire ship's company. Once the ship's company was unconscious, Ourea removed you from stasis, placed you in a temporary life support container and dismantled your stasis cot. He then relocated all the equipment from the spacecraft to Saxa Antiquis. The equipment, the two stasis cots, all life support and communications systems and knowledge pods were placed in yet another secret compartment that Ourea had excavated, in total secrecy, directly under Argentum Metallicum. Ourea also connected a cloning machine to a temporary power source and set about making a clone of himself. Once satisfied, he sealed the catacomb and hurried back to the spacecraft, programmed the stasis system to switch off allowing sufficient time for him to get you safely out of the spacecraft to Saxa Antiquis in total secrecy. On returning to Saxa Antiquis, He quickly unsealed the catacomb, placing you in your stasis cot. This would provide the power to keep your systems running, to ensure knowledge continued to flow into your brain and to keep the monitoring systems online. Ourea also injected the clone. This was the clone's memory and programming. Ourea then covered over the catacomb and waited for Hephaestus to witness the powering up ceremony after first injecting the key into his eyes. As you were related, DNA matching wasn't an issue. Once Saxa Antiquis was running properly, and Hephaestus had departed, Ourea unsealed the catacomb, hooked your stasis cot up to Saxa Antiquis, power resuscitated his clone, who then returned to the spacecraft after permanently re-sealing the vault. Ourea, after one final check of the systems, then placed himself in stasis. He programmed his stasis system to wake him every 500 years so that he could check on you and check on the development of Terra. "The ship blasted off from Terra but never got home. No one really understands why. It is believed The Ostium somehow managed to infect the ship prior to its departure from Domus. Regardless, the entire ship's company was never heard from again. The disappearance of the spaceship caused massive hysteria on Domus. Nothing like this had ever happened before. The hysteria subsided; the disaster forgotten. However, Domus started to fail. Small things at first. Easily overlooked. Domus Mundi was infected. The Ostium relentless. It was now just a matter of time."

"Your parents and a very small team continued to monitor you and Ourea. If things went wrong with your stasis cots, there was little that could be done. You both would have perished. However, some tweaks could be made. Some refinements and upgrades could be done remotely. But very little. There was no point in keeping the large team together. So, 95% of the team was disbanded. But before being released, their minds were wiped clean. They had no knowledge of you, of Ourea your parents, or what they had done. What they had achieved. You never existed in their minds."

"There were no visible signs of Ostium infection on Domus but small things continued to go wrong. Things didn't function properly. Things broke down. Not enough to alarm the populous as a whole, but very alarming to your parents, and to a growing number of scientists that had ignored your parent's warnings. Slowly, but surely. Things started dying.

The planet was slowly, but inexorably grinding to a halt."

"About four Terran years after you and Ourea had been sealed in your tomb, it was only a matter of time before the planet succumbed to what was now called The Ostium virus. Your parents took the decision to sever all communications with your stasis cots. Monitoring stopped, all systems were dismantled and destroyed. No evidence left behind. Your parents had ensured all records pertaining to your birth to your very existence had been deleted from all databases. As far as Domus was concerned, you were never born. There was only one task left to do. That was to permanently erase you from the minds of the remaining scientific team – and your parents. With great reluctance this was done. At the same time, the decision was taken to completely erase all records of Terra, of Saxa Antiquis and of the mission to build the listening posts on Terra. All data was erased, all minds were wiped clean. No one on Domus knew about you or the existence of Terra or Saxa Antiquis. Not only did you, Terra and Saxa Antiquis cease to exist, but as far as anyone on Domus was concerned, You, Terra or Saxa Antiquis never existed. You were cast out. You, Ourea and Saxa Antiquis, the only relics of your home world that once was. On an alien planet that had been deleted from the record. Your only connection to life was Saxa Antiquis. There you remained, for the next 4,000 years. Entombed below Argentum Metallicum in the now dead Saxa Antiquis."

Nox paused for a minute and looked at V. Tears were rolling down her cheeks. She looked desperately unhappy. Her body suddenly folded, and she crumpled to the ground, where she continued to weep, all be it quietly. Nox gently walked over to her, lowered his head and did his best to hug her. She had no problem. She reached out for him, grabbed him and held on to him as if her life depended on it, weeping noiselessly into him.

They stayed like this for a good ten minutes. Alien girl and alien animal, on an alien planet, far, far away from home. With a lethal force after them. A few friends to support them. Never before had V felt so utterly alone, so utterly hopeless.

But slowly the weeping stopped, the tears dried. The feeling of hopelessness was replaced by a sense of purpose; new resolve steeled her mind and body. Nox sensed this change in attitude and was relieved. The worst was over. She now knew who she was and where she had come from and the fate that had befallen her and the task ahead. She had had a slight wobble. Understandable. But now he could sense this determination to put right past injustices, to head to Domus and do what she could to eradicate The Ostium virus. This was the girl Nox thought she was. The girl Nox had been promised. She had now proved it. She had come through her first real test. This girl, thought Nox, was indeed very special.

"Thank you Nox" said V. "Thank you for explaining everything to me. There is still so much I don't understand, but for now, I have a couple of questions. If I was entombed below Argentum Metallicum for 4,000 years, how was I freed and how did I end up with my guardians? If all knowledge of me, Terra and Saxa Antiquis was permanently removed from Domus. All minds wiped clean, all databases wiped clean, so that to all intents and purposes me, this temple and Terra never existed, and this was done over 4,000 Terran years ago. How come you are here? How come you were chosen to find me, watch over me and to eventually guide me back to Domus. How did Domus become aware of me, Terra and the temple, some 4,000 years after we were supposedly permanently deleted from all records and all minds and the people that made all this possible had been dead for thousands of years.....?"

Nox thought for a moment. Conscious that time was precious, but also aware that V needed to know some answers. She had to have a sense of purpose to complete her quest and in order for that sense of purpose to drive her forward, she needed some answers. So, on balance, Nox thought, answering some questions would be a constructive use of the very limited time available....

"I don't have all the answers" said Nox, "But, in the time available, I'll tell you what I can"

"The plan was to wipe everything the people and technologies on Domus that knew about you, Ourea, Terra and the Temple from all minds, all records and all databases. And, in so far as the plan went. It was moderately successful. Indeed, for two centuries you all were entirely forgotten. But what your forefathers hadn't counted on was the temple itself. Ourea and the teams that built the temple, that did all the internal testing and checking to ensure that everything was installed and worked as it should. That the satellite rock circles communicated with each other and that all data was relayed to Saxa Antiquis. However, what nobody knew was that Saxa Antuquis, once powered, immediately started transmitting to Domus. So, for 200 Terran years you, the temple and Saxa Antiquis were completely forgotten. Then, 200 years after the completion of the

Temple, resistance listening posts began picking up this stream of data emanating from an area of space that they knew nothing about. They had no idea what it was, it couldn't be decoded, no sense could be made of the data, yet once started, the stream continued. Uninterrupted. By this time, Domus Mundi was just about completely overrun by The Ostium virus. But there were off-world satellites of resistance fighters that had been able to escape the virus, and some very isolated and very well-prepared areas on Domus were able to survive. For how long, no one knew. But at this particular time in your home plant's history, there were small pockets of survivors, where technology worked as it should, and people were still able to think and able to use and able to improve on the available technology.

One such area was an estate that belonged to your parents. When they became convinced of the terrible threat The Ostium virus posed, they moved from the family homestead and relocated to the Silbah Mountains on Domus. Here they built, under the mountains, a homestead filled with the most technologically advanced equipment available, all completely self-contained. This was to be the headquarters of The Resistance network. It wasn't linked to any other system; it wasn't powered by any external sources and it had almost impenetrable firewalls. By the time this complex had been completed – in utter secrecy, your parents were old and had handed over the running of the complex to your siblings. And so, over time it passed from generation to generation of your direct descendants. Despite the passing of your parents and your siblings, the complex remained in your family's hands.

They too were aware of this strange signal emanating from a strange part of space. They too were just as mystified about its origin. They too were unable to decode the continuous data stream.

However, the new head of the family was aware of some private files that your mother had herself locked away in a sealed vault. Not your father, nor anyone else in the complex had been aware of this vault. Your motherm had herself built and sealed these documents in the vault in the strictest of secrecy. On her death bed, the new head of the family, Macánta, your mother's great, great, great grandson, was summoned for a private audience with your mother. She informed him of the presence of this vault and the documents that were within. She forbade him to open the vault unless something out of the ordinary and quite unexplainable happened. This he swore. She also told him to pass on knowledge of this vault to only one individual. The one individual that he could trust completely and absolutely, and to only pass this knowledge on, on his deathbed.

Macánta felt the time was now right to open the vault. This he did. Inside was a holographic plate – a 200-year-old holographic plate, plus some handwritten documents. Macánta carefully removed this antique looked at it, read the instructions on how to operate the unit and ensuring the office was now completely secured, isolated and sealed, switched on the holographic plate. It was your Mother. In perfect clarity, she recounted the events leading up to The Ostium invasion. Of it being only a matter of time before even the small pockets of resistance and indeed despite the precautions taken that this complex under the Silbah Mountains would be invaded and overrun. She recounted the events of the plan they initiated with Ourea. She informed him of Terra, of you and of the temples. For some reason, whether by default or design, your Mother's mind wasn't wiped and retained full knowledge of what had been planned and what actions had been taken. She also told him of gaps in the plan and how the plan couldn't be implemented for many millennia, mainly because Terra had to evolve. The dominant biped species on Terra could barely master stone implements and were on the cusp of melting and using the most basic of metals. It would be many thousands of years before their intelligence and technology had advanced sufficiently to allow them to understand and to rescue Vica Pota, teach her what she needed to know and to try and get her back to Domus – she didn't, however, make any mention of the fact that Ourea was also entombed with you. She went on to explain the fact that Terra was so backward, so bereft of even the most basic technology, that it would be quite safe from The Ostium virus – at least for a few millennia. So, until Terra had developed sufficiently, Vica Pota had to remain in her stasis cot. Awaiting the day she could be woken. Awaiting the day she could be of use. Awaiting the day she could follow her destiny. If she survived.

Macánta was deeply shocked and troubled by this information. He was shocked that his relatives could have been so savage, so cruel as to place a six-month-old child into stasis and leave her completely alone and quite unprotected for many thousands of years on what was a very savage and backward planet. He understood that desperate times called for desperate measures. But this, he felt, went far beyond the laws of decency and humanity. This was inhumane, cruel and just too unbelievable to contemplate. Could he believe this? This data stream was emanating from somewhere, and according to the data he had now been given and had access to, it did seem to be emanating from the general direction of Terra – more calculations needed to confirm. Amongst the data secured in the vault were the codes necessary to decode the data stream. He set to work, confirmed the existence of Terra and decoded the data stream. When decoded, the data stream c00omprised your vitals, confirmed that as of 200 years ago, the Stasis cot was functioning properly and that you were alive and well. It also confirmed the development of the planet in so far as the planet was indeed in the late Stone Age / early Bronze Age, and that it would indeed be thousands of years before Terra had advanced enough to allow you to be woken.

So, armed with this information, Macánta continued to monitor you and Saxa Antiquis. He also set to work bringing the holographic plate up to date. He also thought long and hard about the plan and continued to improve and to fill in some of the gaps. But and most importantly, he kept this a secret. Shared with no one. The Ostium virus continued its unrelenting journey and slowly but surely, over the next 100 years or so, the remaining pockets of resistance were wiped out. The homestead complex under the Silbah Mountains continued to survive. Continued to go unnoticed. But everyone knew it was just a matter of time.

Fifty years later, the data stream from Terra suddenly shutdown. This coincided with the time that your forefathers had shut the system down and wiped clean the memory of Terra and its secrets from the populace.

However, within the confines of the Silbah complex, the secrets on Terra were handed down to a single, trusted individual, generation by generation. The data continually updated, the images and instructions carefully preserved and updated. Similarly, each modification of the plan to use you was updated. Thus it remained for the next ten generations. Then, as predicted, before The Ostium viruses detected and infected the last Bastian of clear thinking, working technology, the decision was taken to shut down Silbah complex. Silbah was then evacuated and sealed. Memories were wiped and the inhabitants assimilated into the general populace. Only one individual on the planet was aware of Silbah's existence, was aware of you, Terra and the temple. This individual would pass the knowledge on, to a single trusted individual. And so, for the next three thousand years, Silbah was forgotten. Lying dormant, idle, and completely useless. But, so long as it was powered down because it was so isolated and removed from various national power and communication grids it was completely invisible to The Ostium. So despite its uselessness, it was quite safe. And waiting patiently..."

CHAPTER SEVEN

Nox looked at V. No tears. "We must leave it there V. For now, we have work to do. The Ostium marches relentlessly on, we have to get away from here."

V looked at Nox. Long and hard. "What sort of world will we be going to?" she asked quietly.

Nox had no real answer to this but tried to give V as honest an answer as he could "A dark world. An ignorant world. A world without technology of any sort. A population that starved themselves of knowledge for so long that they have effectively reverted to terrestrial Stone Age. A world where the population are slaves to the will and whim of The Ostium."

V tried hard to understand. She had had such a free life, a life of choice and learning. A life where she could always find answers and had the technology to assist her in doing that. She couldn't imagine living any other way.

"Ok Nox, then let's head home and do what we can" With that she headed back to Argentum Metallicum, unfolded the schematic diagram and resumed her studies. Nox watched her go, wondering how she was coping with the full understanding of who she is, where she was from and how she got to be here. Well she knew most of the information, there were still plenty of gaps – my visits over the intervening millennia, Ourea and what happened to him, Uncle Peter's appearance over 500 years ago. All in good time, V, all in good time. For now, she had quite enough to cope with. He searched her mind and could find nothing but a steely determination to get home, back to do what she could to help. Scared? He sensed she was terrified. Regardless, she had to try. Content, and relieved, Nox partially unplugged himself from V's mind and went to his listening post and resumed his sentry duties.

V was beginning to understand what Argentum Metallicum was and how it worked. This was a plate that would transport them to a mechanism that she hadn't yet understood, that would get them back to Domus Mundi. The metallic object that resembled a four leaf clover was the key to power Argentum Metallicum and to allow it to transport them to the mechanism that would take them home.

So, thought *V, I have the key, I have Argentum Metallicum and I have all the power that Saxa Antiquis can offer. I don't have the directions, nor do I know where to insert the key or how to insert the key. But the answers must be here somewhere.*

She paused for a moment. She could sense a difference in Udal Cuain. A malevolence that she had never felt before. It was close to dawn, yet there were no birds singing, there were no insects buzzing. Just an oppressive, evil silence that seemed to permeate the air, permeate the senses… She knew, without a shadow of a doubt, that whatever this Ostium virus was, it was coming…and coming for her.

Now wasn't the time to panic she told herself sternly. *The answers are here. I know they are. It's time to think, to be methodical, to work through the problems.* She glanced over at Nox. He was lying down as usual. His eyes were closed, his ears erect and twitching, and his mouth slightly open. She understood this was how he kept guard. Lying down kept his full body and maximum senses in contact with the ground, so he could feel the smallest tremor

- 133 -

or vibration, his keen ears listening, and sensing pressure differences in the air. His mouth tasting the air… He was keenly awake and alert. This gave V tremendous confidence.

V went back to her task. She put the schematic down and opened the book, willing the book to open at the appropriate page. It did. Touching the link to the hologram she soon understood where the clover was to be inserted. Once again, her eyes were the key to opening the lock that would reveal the cavity in which to insert the clover. Once inserted, the clover needed to be rotated ninety degrees clockwise. Argentum Metallicum would then power up, for a maximum of …

"30 Terran seconds" V and Nox chorused together…

So, it would remain powered up for 30 seconds. This time would be needed to target the system. It needed to know where to send you. Once targeted the small metal box that Ourea had hidden would start to glow red. That was an indication that the system was set and targeted. Argentum Metallicum would then power down. This was a safety feature so as to ensure that you were not sent on your way before you were ready.

Argentum Metallicum would then need to be powered up again in the same fashion, ensuring the metallic box continued to glow red, persons to be transported would then stand over the area where the clover had been inserted. Argentum Metallicum would sense when the individuals were standing in the right location. The metallic box would then change colour and glow amber. Once it glowed amber, gentle pressure was to be applied to the metallic box, it would record your DNA sequence and if your DNA matched the sequence stored in the box's memory, the metallic box would finally glow green and that would be the final trigger. Argentum Metallicum would immediately send you to wherever it had been targeted to send you.

That seemed easy enough she thought, provided it all worked and my retinal scans and DNA had been matched. *Well, let's put that to the test.* She marked out the exact middle of Argentum Metallicum, bent down and gazed at the silver surface. She knew from experience that nothing happened straight away, it usually took a while. So she just knelt and gazed. And gazed until her eyes watered. And nothing happened.

Hm, that's not good. She rotated herself ninety degrees, so her back was pointed to the central trilithon and her front to the open end of the horseshoe and tried again. This time, she sensed a change in Saxa Antiquis and before her eyes, the silver melted away to form a perfect mould of the four-leaf clover. Quickly, she inserted the clover. It fitted exactly and once inserted seemed to become part of Argentum Metallicum. The only way V could identify it from the surrounding material was by the slightly metallic green hue, so perfectly did it fit and blend in.

Before V did anything else, she gathered up her bits and pieces and packed away the tools she knew she would not need. Satisfied that everything she thought she may need was close to hand, and everything else was packed securely away, she debated whether to call Nox over. *No. Not just yet. I need to target the system first. I'm not completely sure how to do this just yet.* So, she went back to the schematic of Argentum Metallicum. *No. Nothing here*. The book. The book has to provide a clue. She looked at the book, and it just lay quietly in her lap, obstinately closed. No matter how she tried to describe the information she was looking for, the book remained shut. Nothing here she thought. She packed the book away and went back to the schematic she had found in Ourea's secret stash. She had looked at it once already, but decided to have another, more careful look. This time she turned it over, placed it on the silver slab and looked. At first, she could see nothing. But slowly, ever so slowly materializing on the page were, what she now recognised as words and letters. She, at once, picked up the paper to get a closer look. As soon as she did, the words immediately faded. "The slab!" she shouted at herself. "Argentum Metallicum is the key, it makes the words appear!"

Quickly she replaced the document and after a short pause, the words started to reappear. As she continued to look, they became clearer. Startlingly clear. It was definitely handwriting and it was written to her. The following words sung in her mind.

"Vica Pota, if you are reading this, then by all of God's good fortune you are alive. I don't know how you survived all of those thousands of years. But clearly you have. I, however, will be long gone. Nothing more than cosmic dust, waiting to be reborn in a star's supernova. If the forefather's predictions are true, then your immediate future is bleak. Maybe it would have been better for you to have perished in the tomb. Just drifted off to sleep, never having awakened. But, it seems that the Gods have other plans for you. The fate that awaits you is one of terror and hardship. More terrible than you can imagine. For that I'm sorry. But, Vica Pota, you are our only hope.

I'm sorry I had to leave you here. On your own, in the dark, forgotten by almost everyone. But terrible times call for terrible measures."

"You will by now have understood who you are, and where you have come from and why your parents and I took the desperate measure we did in bringing you to Terra and entombing you under Saxa Antiquis for all of those thousands of years. We face a terrible threat. Our politicians don't recognise the threat. But it's there and it's coming. Within a few generations' life on Domus Mundi will have changed forever, with the population being prisoners to their own stupidity, laziness and lack of foresight. You will have to change this. You will have to release them. To do this you must leave Terra and return home. I have left you the tools to do this and the fact that you are now reading this note tells me you are nearly ready to depart. You will have found the clover and the silver box. You now need to target the system. To do this, get the star chart that I left you, lay it on Argentum Metallicum with Terra facing towards the central trilithon. The star map will then guide you through the procedure. You will also have found two silver containers and some materials. Vica Pota, the journey you are about to undertake is the most dangerous part of your mission. It has never been attempted before, by a Domus citizen. But we left this option available for just this kind of emergency. The science says it will work. I say it will work. Your parents say it will work. But it has never been proven or tested. I have left you some tools which will help you in this journey. It's very important that you inject yourself with the contents of one of the metal containers. It doesn't matter which one, as they both contain the same liquid. Don't inject both of them.

That will kill you. One is for you and one for my dear friend, Nox. You should now have lost your Terran identity and reverted entirely back to your Domus identity. The liquid in the containers will help your body adapt to the extreme conditions it will have to face on the next step of your journey. It will also speed up your body's recovery upon arrival at your home planet. Without this liquid, you will surely perish. Inject yourself before you squeeze the remote trigger to send you on your way. Inject it when you have restarted Argentum Metallicum after targeting and the metallic box glows red. Don't wait. Inject it immediately."

"Finally, the material that you will have found. This material will protect you as you pass through Foramen Interminatum (Hole without an end)"

At the mention of Foramen Interminatum (Hole without an end), V gasped and went completely white, her heart almost stopped. Nox raised his head in alarm and went straight over to her. V ignored Nox and reread the phrase over and over and over again, just to make sure there was no mistake.

Foramen Interminatum (Hole without an end), Wormhole. WORMHOLE! Her mind screamed at her - a hypothetical shortcut between two points in spacetime, permitting faster-than-light travel and sometimes time travel. Note the word hypothetical, she screamed at herself and at the note she was reading. Hypothetical means possibility, not proven, a hypothesis. Not factual... In other words, may not exist. No. No way. Not in a million years. With that, she got up, walked around a bit. Sat down. Got up again, then sat down again and put her head in her hands.

Nox ambled over to her and nudged her.

"What is it V?" He asked.

V remained silent for a while and then said.

"Wormhole. That's what it is. A wormhole. Ourea wants me to start this thing up and then jump into a wormhole and travel instantaneously to Domus Mundi. Oh, and they think the science is correct. They have learned how to manipulate and operate wormholes and he thinks it will be perfectly OK. Dangerous, but OK. "

"I see," said Nox. "I have no idea what a wormhole is, or how dangerous it is, or whether they work or not. But if that is what Ourea says we must do, then that is what we must do. Or die trying,"

V looked at him incredulously. "Well, firstly, consensus is of the opinion that a traversable wormhole isn't a naturally occurring phenomenon and doesn't exist and is not allowable by the laws of physics as we understand them here on Terra. Why? Because we see no objects in our universe that could become wormholes as they age. By contrast, astronomers see huge numbers of massive stars that will collapse to form black holes when they have exhausted their nuclear fuel. But nothing to indicate traversable wormholes. On the other hand" went on V, "There is reason to hope that wormholes do exist naturally on submicroscopic scales in the form of "quantum foam," This foam is a hypothesised (there, that word again – hypothesised – not proven, not factual – a guess) network of wormholes that are continually fluctuating in and out of existence in a manner governed by the ill-understood laws of quantum gravity. The foam is probabilistic in the sense that, at any moment, there is a certain probability the foam has one form and also a probability that it has another form, and these probabilities are continually changing. And the foam is truly tiny: the typical length of a wormhole would be the so-called Planck length, 0.0000000000000000000000000000000001 centimetres; a hundredth of a billionth of a billionth the size of the nucleus of an atom."

"Oh, and let's not forget the Big Bang. The other tiny hope for natural wormholes is the big bang creation of the universe. It is conceivable but very unlikely, that traversable wormholes could have formed in the big bang itself. Conceivable for the simple reason that the big bang is not understood at all well l. Unlikely because nothing that is known about the big bang gives any hint that traversable wormholes might form there."

"So, all in all," said V. "If they do exist at all they are tiny. And look at the size of me.... Of you!"

"But" went on V. "Let's assume for one minute that traversable wormholes do exist. This is only the start of our problems!"

"Unfortunately, wormholes aren't really stable on their own. They open and close so quickly that not even a subatomic particle can make it through. To fix that, you'd need to buttress the wormhole from the inside with exotic matter, which has negative energy density and negative pressure. Even if you could do that, there are still a lot of problems with travelling through a wormhole, not the least of which being that you'd actually have to enter a black hole, which scientists believe would spaghettify your body for eternity (or worse)."

"Well," said Nox "I know nothing about that. But. It seems to me that so far everything that your forefathers have said or done, or prepared for you has worked. They have not yet let you down. Leaving you, and Ourea, without any support or remote attention for 4, 000 years in your stasis cots – which worked perfectly throughout that time, seems to me to be a miracle. Yet it wasn't. It was planned, designed and built by your forefathers. If that doesn't persuade you. Then you are forgetting one thing. One absolute certain thing that should prove that these wormholes do exist and do work..."

V thought long and hard. "No, Nox. I don't think I am. I'm sure of it"

"Rubbish" snorted Nox. "You're looking at positive proof that the wormhole worked. Me. How do you think I got here? I didn't walk, I didn't fly, and I certainly didn't come by any spacecraft. As far as I remember I was put on a silver metallic plate, pretty much like Argentum Metallicum, and the next thing I clearly remember was seeing your guardian. Now whether that took days, months, years or was instantaneous I have no idea. But I'm here. I survived."

V had no answer to that. There was no doubting what Nox was saying was true. Just as there is no doubting that the big brute was standing right in front of her, and with that most irritating amused look in his eyes.

"Yes, Nox. You are here. I can't argue that one. You are most definitely here and not a figment of my imagination…"

"Well…?" V asked. "Are you up for a return journey?"

"Of course," Nox said. "Where you go, I go. And I'm not staying here without you."

"Very well then," said V, "Let's get on with it," She went back to the note and continued reading:

"Finally, the material that you will have found. This material will protect you as you pass through Foramen Interminatum (Hole without an end). It also has a mechanism for injecting the liquid into your arm. There are pieces of material, one for you and one for Nox. Like the cape you probably donned earlier, simply place the material over your head and drape it around your body, it will automatically conform to your body shape and will seal you. It will provide you with air whilst you travel and should be able to counteract the gravitational forces you will undoubtedly be exposed to. Nox must do the same. Once you are comfortable, find the sleeve aperture, attach the canister to the aperture and the liquid will be automatically be injected into your body. Any items you are taking with you, ensure they are inside the suit. With the exception of the canisters, don't leave anything else you wish to take with you, outside of the suit. That includes the remote trigger.

"Vica Pota, I have done all I can to assist you. It's now up to you and Nox. You have the knowledge. You have the tools and you have the means. Only you can save us. On arrival, find the one relative of your family who knows of your existence. Show them this note. They will scan your retina and check your DNA. I can't offer you any more help or advice. Just believe in yourself and in Nox. He is much, much more than he seems."

"Nox, Ourea has written you a small message: "Nox my old friend, my faithful companion. We have been through some adventures, you and me. Now, you face the biggest adventure of your life. Watch over Vica. I'll be watching over both of you. Until we meet again. May the Gods protect you. May the Gods provide lightness in the darkest of places.

May the Gods give you courage. May the Gods give you strength. Your parents and I will be with you. Dominus Cæmentarius Ourea Pota, brother to Domina Tranquillo Serenoque Pota, your mother."

V looked up from the letter. Startled, she was sure she saw tears in Nox's eyes. "Are you OK boy" she asked gently.

Nox just looked at her, and nodded. She could see him pull himself together. "Yes V, I'm fine. Thank you."

V looked long and hard at Nox, then went back to her own thoughts. So, Ourea was my Uncle and Domina Tranquillo Serenoque Pota, my Mother. Thought V, humbled by what she was holding in her hand. A note from Ourea to her. The closest she had yet come to talking to her relatives.

She thought about this for a moment or two. Then her mind turned to the immediate future and the pending trip home. The wormhole. Her stomach knotted, cramped. She felt nauseous at the thought. But, looked at Nox. Not only had he done it once and survived, but seemingly he has done it several times. And, he is prepared to do it again. That gave her courage.

"Nox" she gently called over to him. "It's time. We need to prepare," She then went on to explain what he needed to do, to seal himself up in the suit and to inject him with the liquid, as demanded by Ourea. But first, we need to target the Temple. She got out the star map and as instructed placed it on Argentum Matallicum. For a moment the star map didn't do anything. Then, slowly the constellations brightened and elevated themselves from the material. She could clearly see where Terra was and where on Terra the temple was. Moving along the Star map, she came to her home planet. The planet from which she left all those thousands of years ago. As she touched Domus Mundi, it enlarged. One point on Domus Mundi blinked at her. This she assumed must be her destination. Somewhere called the Silbah Mountains. She pushed the blinking dot and kept pressure on the blinking dot until it stopped blinking and glowed a deep red. The constellations on the map faded and eventually became all but invisible. She folded the star chart and put it in her backpack. The only items not in her backpack were the small silver remote trigger, which glowed red. The canisters and the material.

Quickly she took one piece of material and placed it over Nox's head. The material did the rest. It conformed exactly to Nox shape sealing him in. The material was translucent, so he had no trouble seeing out, and she had no trouble seeing in.

"Are you OK Nox?" she thought at him. "Yes, I'm very comfortable. Thank you," replied Nox.

"Good," said V, "I'm now going to place the canister into the aperture, but I'm not going to inject you just yet. I want to power up Argentum Metallicum first." "Understood" responded Nox.

V quickly donned her suit, ensuing her backpack was on first and that the metallic trigger was in her hand. Satisfied and comfortable, she installed the canister into the aperture but didn't inject.

Next, she bent down and rotated the clover ninety degrees and waited. She could sense the change in Argentum Metallicum. It pulsed. Her feet registering the throbbing from beneath. She looked at the remote trigger in her hand. It remained glowing a steady red. The system confirmed it was targeted. The thirty seconds expired and the system stopped. She didn't waste any more time. She injected Nox, then she injected herself. She immediately rotated the clover a further ninety degrees.

Red!

She grabbed hold of Nox and together they moved slowly backwards and forwards over the clover until the box glowed...

Amber!

Ready Nox? she thought at him, holding him as best she could through the suits and looking directly into his calm and unafraid eyes...gently, ever so gently she squeezed the metallic box. Then...

Green!

She screamed long and loudly...

CHAPTER EIGHT

V was aware of someone screaming and realised it was her. She tried to stop but couldn't. Even though she thought herself ridiculous, she couldn't stop. "V, get a grip," she told herself firmly, and if she could have, she would have kicked herself hard. Finally, she managed to stop screaming. Her eyes however, remained firmly shut. A million thoughts were going through her mind. All bad. Just as she thought she had successfully cleared her mind of them, so another cheery thought entered her head. Wormholes come with a lot of caveats. They could very well connect two completely different space-times, i.e. the entry point might exist in a completely different era. That means traversing a wormhole comes with the risk of winding up in a different time in the universe's history, or even worse, a completely different universe altogether. V was just about to hit the panic button again, she could feel a scream welling up from deep inside her, when *Calm yourself* flooded her mind. Nox calm, patient voice again, settling her as it always did. *All is well, the journey through what you call the wormhole has not yet started. We have merely been launched to the start point. Look for yourself...*

She reluctantly opened one eye, then closed it again. Getting a hold of herself, she opened both eyes and was amazed. There they were, Nox and herself streaking towards a shimmering, rotating sphere. She had no idea where they were, but the sphere in front of her was getting rapidly bigger and bigger. *This must be the mouth of the wormhole,* she thought to herself. As far as she understood, a wormhole's mouth was a closed two-dimensional surface that would seem to be surrounding a three-dimensional volume. And that is what she was seeing. *There should also be a mouth at the other end – assuming we get there, both mouths connected by a hyperspace tunnel, also called a throat. The throat could be a straight stretch or a cylindrical, "wind around," I guess we will find out which,* she thought to herself

V was gazing at the shimmering sphere. It was difficult to describe. It seemed to be sitting there in space. Blurred pearlescent colours moving around in various directions, rather like clouds blowing around on the surface of the Earth. *The mouth wasn't particularly large, large enough to accommodate a London double-decker bus* she thought. *Well, so long as it's big enough for myself and Nox.*

V felt perfectly normal. She wasn't sure if this was down to the suit, or the liquid that she had injected herself with, or simply that she really did feel normal. Weightless at present, but other than that, quite, quite normal. She checked in on Nox. Nox too felt quite fine. So far, much more pleasant than the inbound journey. He reported back. "It must be something to do with the injection and suit," she said to herself, marvelling once again at the technology her forefathers had available to them.

The free fall continued. They were getting closer and closer to the mouth of the wormhole. And here, by definition was the first life-threatening obstacle they had to overcome. The mouth of the wormhole needs exotic matter with negative energy density and/or negative pressure to keep it open and stable. *Now, it's entirely possible,* thought V *that inserting anything into a wormhole that isn't exotic*

matter i.e. me and Nox, would destabilize the
wormhole completely. In other words: Entering a
wormhole could immediately kill us. Well, there is
nothing I can do about that now, she thought. *We are*
freefalling rapidly towards the mouth of the
wormhole.

Together V and Nox entered the wormhole.
No collapse. The suit must allow passage through
exotic matter.

As V entered the deep spherical wormhole,
she saw stars concentrated in a sphere directly ahead.
Stars she couldn't recognize. After a while, V looked
to her left, and noticed another pair of beings on a
parallel course in the distance. Upon closer
inspection, V noticed that the two objects looked
exactly like the right-hand side of themselves. "How
was that possible?" V asked herself. Looking to the
right similarly revealed a distant left-hand view of
themselves. Well, she knew traversing a wormhole
would hold all sorts of surprises. Not least of which
was how well she felt. She felt no undue forces on
her, she felt quite…normal. Looking at right angles to
her inward direction of travel, V noticed almost no
stars. Same to the left. However, the more forward
she looked, i.e. the closer she looked towards her
direction of travel, the more stars she saw, until she
looked directly ahead, and she saw a spherical
concentration of stars. That must be the throat of the
wormhole. Nearly through the mouth… she thought
to herself.

As V approached this concentration -- the
wormhole's throat -- she noticed that the parallel
images of themselves were much closer now. V
waved and, after a momentary delay, she saw herself
waving. *Eerie,* she thought to herself.

As V and Nox continued to pass through the hyperspace tunnel, or throat, she found herself gazing at a normal sky of unfamiliar stars. As they continued to pass through the throat, things would look warped, kind of like an extreme fish-eye lens. The parallel images of Nox and V receded and eventually vanished altogether.

V then got the sense of rather than free-falling through the hyperspace tunnel, she felt she was freefalling out of the hyperspace tunnel and heading towards the mouth. She assumed this was the mouth at the end of her journey and not the beginning! Of course, it was!

The "exit" mouth, for want of a better word, looked pretty much identical to the "entry" mouth they had already passed through.

V couldn't describe it any better, other than a shimmering sphere, with blurred pearlescent colours moving around in various directions. She couldn't see the spherical cluster of strange constellations that she saw when she was in the throat of the worm hole.

They were now fast approaching the exit, how long it had taken them to traverse the wormhole, she had no idea. Time seemed to have stopped. It could have been minutes, or it could have been decades. She simply had no idea.

How fast she was travelling, again was open to debate. She knew it couldn't be faster than light travel. Particles that have mass require energy to accelerate them. The closer to the speed of light you get a particle, the more energy is required for it to go faster. This is because the particles themselves get more massive in proportion to the increased velocity. In short, the faster you go, the heavier you get.

Thanks to this inconvenient truth, if you wanted to accelerate a single electron to 'light speed', you would need an infinite amount of energy due to the electron becoming infinitely heavy. There isn't enough energy in the entire universe to propel just a single electron to the speed of light. This is beautifully explained in Einstein's famous equation: $E=mc2$.

Just as V and Nox exited the wormhole, they were blinded by a huge flash and V knew no more.

Silence. Deafening silence. Reminiscent of that one time she could remember being in the stasis cot. This time, there was no one to calm her down, tell her it was alright. Silence, loneliness, and pain.

V lay where she was for a minute, trying to gather her senses and checking to see if she was in fact OK and had all her fingers and toes. She felt nauseous, had a terrible headache and was very dehydrated. But, other than that, she felt as good as anyone can dare to expect having travelled through a wormhole.

Eyes closed trying so hard to come to terms with what had happened to her. She remembered falling into the wormhole, travelling through the wormhole, with remarkable ease, then a blinding, silent flash, then nothing.

She slowly opened her eyes. Complete blackness. Eyes opened or closed; it made no difference. She felt around her. She must be somewhere, she thought to herself, gravity, a little stronger than she was used to on Earth, but gravity, nevertheless. She wasn't falling through space, or through the wormhole. Clearly, she had arrived. But where, and how did she get here? She was out of her suit, but still in the cloak she had found in her backpack. The cloak or material that had moulded into a one-piece trouser suit.

Backpack. She had a torch in her backpack. Feeling around, she could find no sign of her backpack. But she gathered she was on some sort of bed, with covers and pillows. The bed was only just off ground level. Her fingers also touched what felt like a glass. She dipped a finger in the top of the glass and felt cold liquid. She smelt the liquid on her finger. Completely odourless. She tasted the liquid. Completely tasteless. She drank the liquid and immediately felt much better.

She lay back on the bed. She felt very alone. More alone than she had been for a long time. She couldn't understand why. Then her mind clicked into gear. Nox!! He wasn't in her head. She could sense that he had gone. Completely gone. Nox!" her mind called…. Nothing. "Nox!" her mind roared again, panic rising. Nothing… She got off the bed and frantically searched the room in which she found herself. Just in case he was with her, but unconscious or worse, hurt. Nothing. She was completely alone. The room itself wasn't too large, maybe 4m x 6m with a single point of entry, a door – at least she assumed that this is what it was. The door was secured. Why? Why should the door be locked? Her mind wasn't fully engaged, and, for the moment, she had no idea what this meant. She was far too concerned about Nox. She kept calling Nox, over and over again in her mind. The result always the same. Silence. Nothing.

With great strength of character, she managed to quell the rising panic, she knew this would not help anybody. Least of all her. Tears gently running down her cheeks, she lay back down on the bed, gently calling Nox's name and asking him where he was and if he was ok. But nothing came back. She didn't know what this meant. But she refused to believe that Nox was dead, just somehow incapacitated, as she was. Her mind, her soul, her heart gave her no clue as to whether Nox was alive or dead. She simply didn't know.

She awoke with a start. *Must have dozed off,* V had no idea how long she had slept. She felt much, much better. Her head was clear, her nausea gone, and she was no longer dehydrated. She still couldn't see. She didn't know if her eyes had been damaged by the flash, or whether she was in the darkest room she had ever been in. She felt around her and again felt a full glass next to her bed. Her mind clear, she then started thinking.

She crawled over to what she assumed was the door, or where she thought the door was, given that her last search around the room was a frantic search for Nox. She found the door and had a good feel with her fingers and hands. From top to bottom and from side to side. It was operated by a keypad and, as she touched the keypad so strange characters glowed brightly in the darkness. She felt relief wash over her. Her eyes were fine, she was in an exceptionally dark room. She had no idea what the characters meant but assumed that a combination of characters had to be pressed in the correct order to open the door. Nothing sung to her. She tried various combinations more out of desperation than hope. Then gave up. She was locked in. Someone, or something had locked her in this room. She was a prisoner. She had no idea where she was. When she was? Was she on Domus Mundi? Was she in the correct universe? Had the wormhole flung her to some other alien world in a parallel universe? V had no immediate answers other than the fact that she was locked in, which meant the chances were she wasn't amongst friends. But V also had faith. Faith in her ancestors who had, up until now not put a foot wrong. Everything had worked as it was meant to – she had every faith that Saxa Antiquis had also worked as it was meant to… What V did know was that she had to try and get some answers. To do that she had to get out of this room, establish exactly where she was, who was holding her and more importantly, try and find out exactly what had happened to Nox.

She went back to her bed. Lay down and thought about things. Her fingers again brushed the glass. The liquid was some sort of nourishment. It kept thirst and hunger at bay, so whoever was holding her captive, wanted her alive and well. That gave her some comfort. Then she wondered why. Why did they want her alive and well? All sorts of possibilities ran through her mind. Then she didn't feel quite so comfortable. Her fingers around the glass – she wondered whether she should actually drink it. Aside from the benefits of nourishment, did the liquid do anything to curb her mind, make her more compliant, easier to deal with? "Perhaps not," she said to herself. "Not yet. I'm neither hungry nor thirsty. I can wait a while," The fact that the empty glass had been replaced meant that she had had visitors. Could they sense when she was awake or asleep? *Could they sense when the glass was empty? Were they watching me now? Could I use this to my advantage?* A million thoughts running around her head. Where was Nox!

Agony. Sheer unadulterated agony ran through her whole body. She screamed; the pain was so severe. Then the pain was gone. As quickly as it had come, it went. It took V several minutes to pull herself together and to recover from the shock of the pain. Never, never had she felt such severe pain. "Where had that come from?" she asked herself. She was also aware that her fingers were soaking wet. Then she cut her finger on a shard of glass. *I must have broken the glass whilst experiencing the pain,* she thought to herself. She lay back down on the bed, closed her eyes and tried to think. Lying down was impossible, partly because she was far too restless, but mainly because she was in fear of the pain hitting her again. Her eyes looked blindly towards the door's touch pad. She crawled over to it. Using the light from the touchpad, she carefully examined it. It was like no other touch pad, she had ever seen before, but this was the key that would open this particular locked door. It was about 15cm x 20cm and fitted seamlessly into the wall. There were about 20 characters which could be pressed and one large tab at the top and bottom of the touch pad that could also be pressed. She had no idea whether a combination of digits opened the portal, or whether fingerprints or even a coded card opened the portal. Or some other mechanism. But, she had to figure out a way. She felt a growing sense of urgency. She just had to get out and go in search of Nox. If he was still alive.

"Nox," she called again, "Nox!" louder this time. Agony racked her body, she convulsed, she screamed, she vomited, she thought she was going to die. The pain lasted longer this time. Maybe 20 seconds. Then it stopped, just as suddenly as it started. She lay curled up in the foetal position on the floor, gasping for breath, perspiring, her heart thumping in her chest, her eyes closed. Not moving. Completely still. She lay like that for what she estimated was 20 minutes or so. She couldn't be sure. Her mind was scrambled. She could hardly think straight. Slowly, very slowly her senses returned. Her body recovered. Her heart rate returned to normal. When she felt she had sufficient strength, she picked herself up off the floor, crawled over to and collapsed on her bed. Then she passed out.

She came to, minutes or hours later – she had no idea. She lay on her bed, which was by now soaked in perspiration. Considering the agony she had experienced, she felt OK. She put her arm out and her hand brushed against another glass. Filled with liquid, the remnants of the broken glass now gone. The last thing she wanted was food. She left the glass untouched.

Her mind went back to the agony she had now experienced on two occasions. What was causing this?" she asked herself. "Why would my captors look after me so well, then cause such horrific pain." It just didn't make sense to her. "What was I doing before the onset of the pain," she asked herself. *The first time I was lying down on the bed wondering whether I should drink the nourishment. The second time I had examined the touchpad and was wondering what mechanism would unlock the door. Nothing in common there,* she thought. *But then* she thought again. *That wasn't quite true. The last thing I did before the onset of the pain was call out to Nox. Was the pain somehow connected to Nox...? Only one way to find out,* she said to herself. Knowing what she would have to do, and understanding the possible consequences. But she had to find out. If the pain was connected to Nox, then perhaps he was alive and in trouble. She simply had to find out.

Gathering all of her mental strength and bracing herself for what was to come, she roared "NOX!" as loudly as she could. At once, she convulsed in agony – this time she really did think she was going to die. The horrific agony went on and on. She was aware of herself writhing around on the floor, trying to free herself of the pain. She was screaming and screaming, begging the pain to stop. Then blessed relief, her prayer answered, the pain stopped.

V couldn't move. Couldn't think. Couldn't do anything other than curl up on the floor in the foetal position and moan with abject misery and let her body slowly recover. She must have dozed off. When she came to, she found she had been placed on her bed. The bed clothes had been changed. There was no glass beside her, rather an intravenous drip had been placed in her arm, nourishment being fed straight into her bloodstream and in and around her body. There was also a very dim light in the room. It seemed to flow up from the floor, all around the room. She could see where she was, where she was imprisoned. She tried to move. She couldn't. She wasn't bound in any way, she simply had no strength in her body. She drifted back to sleep.

"Nox!" her mind screamed at her. Instantly awake, and with a feeling of incredible fear, she at once understood what was happening. Nox was alive, he had also been captured and was being tortured. The liquid wasn't only nourishment, it also affected her mind and created some sort of mental block between her and Nox. It was only because she hadn't taken the second or third drinks that the effects were beginning to wear off. When she called out to Nox, she was able to feel his pain as he was being tortured.

The longer she went without the nourishment, so the pain intensified. She put this to the test and screamed *Nox* in her mind. Nothing. Not a thing. Just like the first time she had called out to Nox when she had first woken, but after she had taken the drink, she reminded herself.

She ripped out the intravenous drip from her arm, the pain a tickle compared to the agony she had previously suffered. V was alert, her mind crystal clear and resolute. Get out of here, get Nox and fight these bastards. She said to herself, a cold rage burning in the pit of her stomach. Angry at the time she had wasted. Furious with herself that she had prolonged Nox's suffering. She had to get to him. And get to him now. But how…

She threw back the bed covers and leapt towards the door and studied the touch pad. Whilst she was studying the portal, she felt a nagging burning sensation over her stomach. The more she tried to ignore it, the more annoying it became. Finally, unable to resist further, she reached down to her stomach. Along the way her fingers brushed against one of the silver clasps that secured her clothes. Her finger recoiled in shock and mild pain. The clasp felt like it was on fire. This was the source of the burning. She looked hard at the clasp and tentatively reached towards it. Prepared this time, her fingers closed around the clasp and, to her amazement it was cold. Had she imagined this? She shrugged her shoulders, took one last look at the clasp, promptly forgot it and went back to studying the touch pad. Within seconds, her stomach felt the burning sensation again. Again, she reached down towards the clasp. Before her fingers reached the clasp, seemingly, of its own volition, the clasp fell to the floor. She reached down to pick up the clasp. It was cool. For the first time she really studied the clasp. It was one of five. One secured her clothes around her throat, the remaining four, were evenly spaced in a straight line down her front. Until now, the clasps had been very secure, in fact, unmovable. "What was so special about this one?" She asked herself. "Why did it heat up and then drop to the floor?" She looked at the clasp with renewed interest. It didn't look particularly special. Just a silver clasp with a sort of hinged bit in the middle, shaped like a blunt ship's anchor laying on its side. Highly polished, with very small and beautifully carved patterns on the front of the clasp. The back comprised two sturdy clasp pins and their securing mechanism. The clasp was extremely robust. For the first time she realised just how heavy these clasps were. The one she was holding must have weighed 2 or 3 kg.

She looked at the clasp, which was now lying in the palm of her hand, shrugged her shoulders and replaced it, ensuring this time that it was properly and securely attached to her cape. She got up and headed towards her bed, when "clang" the same clasp fell on the floor. V just about managed to stop herself from treading on it. "Bloody hell" she muttered to herself, "What now?" as she bent down and picked up the clasp. She checked it over to make sure it wasn't damaged when she noticed a very dim light pulsating from the back of the clasp. She looked long and hard and…yes, a very faint light pulsing from the rear of the clasp. The rhythm seemed somehow familiar to her, but she couldn't quite place where she had seen this rhythm before. Then it came to her – from the door's keypad. Once touched the light gently pulsed. The rhythm exactly matches the rhythm on the clasp.

She returned to the door's keypad and for no reason other than it seemed like a good idea at the time, she placed the rear of the clasp on the keypad. For a second or two, nothing happened, then she felt more then heard a small vibration and the door opened. She was so surprised that she just sat where she was. She didn't move, mouth open. The door closed. "Dammit" she said to herself and fumbled with the clasp, placed it rear down on the keypad and after a short second, the door opened. This time, she was ready. She slowly and carefully walked through the door and into an empty hallway. Once out of her room, she stopped, looked, and listened. She could hear nothing, she could see no one. In fact, she reminded herself that she hadn't seen or heard anyone for as long as she had been here, wherever here was. How was she going to find Nox? Her mind had been temporarily blocked from contacting him due to the intravenous drip. She had no idea how much fluid had been pumped into her, or how long it would last. Similarly, she had no idea whether Nox was being similarly treated. She knew he was in agony, but no idea whether he was being given the same telepathic blocking fluids. It also stands to reason she thought to herself, that where Nox is, so are the people that are hurting him. *How am I to deal with them?* she wondered to herself.

V at once quashed these concerns. *Nox needs me and he needs me now. Whatever the consequences, I'll face them, and I'll deal with them as best I can when the time comes. Nox may be in pain, terrible pain, he may be incapacitated but he is alive. And hurt or not, an alive Nox is, in itself, a formidable beast. So, stop wasting more time and find him.*

She again looked around the corridor she found herself in. The walls must have been at least 3m high with a curved ceiling. The corridor itself was probably 2m wide, sufficient for two people to walk abreast without any difficulty, possibly three, with a bit of a squeeze. But then again, she had no idea what people may walk these corridors, what they looked like, or even how big they were...

She looked up and down the corridor. The lighting was the same, floor level lights which shone up the walls and met in the middle of the arched ceiling. So plenty of light. As she looked up the corridor (to her left), about 10m from where she was, the corridor curved to the left, she couldn't see beyond those 10m, as she looked back down the corridor (to her right) the corridor curved to the right. Which way? She mentally tossed a coin, and trusting to luck, turned to her left and walked carefully up the corridor. No signs of anybody. No signs of cameras. But then again she thought to herself, I may not recognize what passes for cameras in this place. She could hear nothing. It was extremely quiet. She passed one other door, on her right-hand side. She stopped and listened. But could hear nothing. She assumed the room was empty thinking to herself that there must be a lot of activity around the place where Nox was being held and he was far too big to be accommodated in here. He would never fit through the doors for a start.

By now, she had reached the start of the curve, her pace slowed even further as she flattened herself against the inner wall of the curve and slowly tried to see what was beyond. Another empty corridor, approximately 40m in length, with doors to the left and right. At the end of the corridor was a larger door. She assumed this was either an exit door, to the outside. Or a door into some sort of storage area.

She paused for a moment. Thinking to herself that she didn't actually know where she was. She could be back on Earth. Saxa Antiquis could have fired her off to Domus Mundi. Or, for all she knew, she could be on some alien planet anywhere in the universe. Could she actually venture outside without any sort of protective suit or breathing apparatus? Of course, she could on Earth, but could she be on Domus Mundi? She reasoned that if she could breathe air on Earth, and she was actually born on Domus, then the chances were better than even that she could breathe Domus' atmosphere. But that was merely an assumption, she thought to herself. She had to hope that it was a valid one! But, she couldn't be sure she was in either of those places... It was at times like this that she yearned to be, once again, the carefree girl that lived on the beautiful island of Udal Cuain, with no problems or decisions to be made other than what time to get out of bed, or whether to do maths or physics homework first. She crushed those thoughts immediately and ordered herself to stop feeling sorry for herself. This was now her destiny. This is what she was born for. So many people had worked so hard and sacrificed so much to keep her safe and to protect her. And now, poor old Nox was being tortured, no doubt because of her. These people and especially Nox are depending on you. *So, move it girl!*

Throwing caution to the wind, she walked tall and proud towards the door at the end of the corridor, stopping briefly at each door she passed to check if she could hear anything. Reaching the end of the corridor, she was faced with a larger door than normal. She quickly checked it over. It didn't seem to have any extra strengthening, against lower or greater pressure. It seemed to be exactly the same as the other doors, only larger. The same old touch pad was set into the wall. "Bugger it," she said to herself, removed the clasp from her clothes, said a little prayer and placed it face up on the touchpad.

The wait this time seemed like years, but sure enough, after a few seconds, the door opened. V couldn't see what the open door revealed. She was sure it was still inside the building, but it was pitch black whatever it was. Girding her loins, she took a step inside and immediately the area was covered in bright light. *Motion sensor lights* she thought. It was a moderate sized warehouse. All sorts of crates and bits and pieces were neatly stacked, chock-a-block with equipment. She had no idea what the equipment was, what it was for or how it worked. But it was there. The warehouse floor area must have been about 400m2, about the size of a typical basketball court. The ceiling was about 5m high. At the furthermost end of the warehouse was a huge double door, about 15m in width, which nearly spanned the width of the warehouse. That, V assumed, exited to the outside world. She wandered into the warehouse, listening hard. But again, no strange sounds. She looked at the neatly stacked equipment trying to see if there was anything there that she recognised that she could use. Nothing. She recognised nothing. She wondered about for a few minutes, slowly making her way towards the exit doors, when she heard something. She couldn't be sure what she heard, but it frightened her. She paused and listened. There it was again. A sound so quiet, yet a sound that was full of desperation, full of pain, full of hopelessness. V knew it was Nox. Could she contact him? She tried. She thought his name long and hard, but nothing came back to her. She stopped, waited, and listened. Her senses on high alert. There it was again. Coming from her right. She walked slowly to her right, a course that ran parallel to the exit doors, she was concentrating hard. She noticed a room within the warehouse. She walked carefully over to the room. *It was like an annex* she thought. Large entry doors and around 10m x 5m, built onto the side of the warehouse. Quite impossible to see from the entry door. She knew Nox was in there. She forced herself to stop and think. She didn't know what she would find inside the annex. She knew one thing for sure though and that was Nox was alive. She had no idea of his condition, but he was alive. She decided to wait and watch the annex for a while. She found a good vantage point behind several crates that gave her all round protection but allowed her a clear view of the annex. She settled herself down, waited and watched. Suddenly, the warehouse was plunged into darkness. This took V completely by surprise. Heart pounding, ready to run. She stopped herself just in time. One thing she had completely forgotten about were the lights in the building. They were motion sensitive lights. When she settled down to wait, she remained comparatively still. The lights remained on for a little while, then after a certain period, switched themselves off, as they couldn't sense any movement in the building.

What now? She asked herself. She had only been watching the building for around 20 minutes she guessed. Well, the first order of business is to wait quietly exactly where I am and ensure my eyes adjust to the darkness. Should anyone enter the building the lights will immediately switch on, so no immediate concerns.

She waited whilst her eyes adjusted to the darkness. There was a faint glimmer of light pulsating from the annex, where she assumed Nox was being held. But other than that, nothing. She waited. One hour passed, then two hours. The moaning from within had long since stopped. Somehow, she knew that Nox was still alive. The warehouse had remained deathly quiet. No one had come or gone. She preferred the darkness; she could see well enough to navigate her way to the annex without bumping into or tripping over anything. But she knew that as soon as she made any movement at all, the motion sensitive lights would switch themselves on. That would not be good, she thought. *So, how to move the 20 or so meters from here to the annex without tripping the motion sensitive lights?*

She looked around her carefully, whilst pondering this dilemma. She noticed that the racking was somewhat haphazard here. She could just about crawl under the lower level of shelving all the way to the annex. Not to the door, but within a meter or so of the door. She hoped that crates and cartons on the shelving would protect her from the motion sensitive lights. Only one way to find out, she thought. Carefully and ever so slowly, she manoeuvred herself from her watching position to the shelving, crawled underneath it and began the long, but slow, advance to the annex. So far, so good. Her plan seemed to be working. The 20m crawl took her around 10 minutes. But well worth the time invested. The warehouse remained in total darkness. V was now at the annex wall and peering through a window to see what she could see.

All colour drained from her face; her hair turned completely white. Her legs wobbled, but she just about remained standing. She broke out in a cold sweat and very nearly threw up. The sight before her was the stuff of nightmares.

Lying on a huge table, well table will do, was Nox. He was strapped down, unable to move. There were all sorts of machines around him, connected to intravenous drips which in turn were connected to him. The tubes were much, much bigger than the IV that had been placed into her arm. The liquid being pumped into him wasn't really a liquid at all. It seemed to be a dense, moving mass of something. These tubes were inserted into various parts of his body, the lines seemed to follow his nervous system. Into his brain, and if he was a terrestrial horse, then the tubes would have been inserted into the equivalent of his spinal cord. The spinal nerves, the nerves of his autonomic nervous system, his sciatic nerves the area where the network of nerves to the forelimbs emanate, the vagus nerve and the cranial nerves. There were also two smaller tubes inserted into his eyes. V understood at once what was going on. Being injected to every part of Nox's nervous system were nanoparticles, targeted she suspected to his nervous system and when commanded to trigger as much pain as possible to various parts of his body, or his entire body depending on how severe the torturers wanted the pain to be. This must have been, at least in part, what she had experienced when she fleetingly, mentally connected to Nox. Only for Nox, the pain must be orders of magnitude worse than V had experienced.

Nox himself looked at death's door. His coat had gone completely white. What little there was of his tail – gone. His mane, gone. His eye lids had been stapled open. IV needles in the corner of his eyes injecting agony directly through his eyes, into his optic nerves. His eyes wet and red, obviously unblinking. She could clearly see reflected, in those normally gentle and wise eyes, the agony and suffering he was undergoing. Every muscle was taut, every limb rigid, every vein standing out all over his body. Excrement and urine mixed with blood covered the floor. His tongue was rolling around his open mouth. His teeth cracked in places. The sores and gashes that he had previously suffered were suppurating even more, exacerbated by some sort of paste or cream that had been put over and into them. No doubt to create more pain, rather than to heal.

V could scarcely believe what she was seeing. Tears rolled down her cheeks. The pain and suffering he must be experiencing must be, well she simply had no idea. How long she wondered. Again, she had no idea. For a moment, their eyes met. He didn't see her. His eyes looked right through her. With a tremendous effort, she pushed her emotions to one side. Concentrate on the task at hand. Helping Nox.

"Start thinking with your brain," she told herself, "And not with your heart."

As difficult as she found it, she went back under the shelving and started to think. *So*, she said to herself, *the immediate problems are:*

1. *Nox was alive. No doubt he was in agony, probably unable to walk and quite possibly too weak to move of his own accord. So, under the assumption I get to him and unplug him, how do I release him*

*and how do we get out of here? Where do we go, and
how much recovery time will he need? How do I keep
him and me safe until then?*

    *2. Unplugging him. That's another issue. I
don't have any experience of nanoparticles and will
simply removing all the IVs from his body stop the
nanoparticles from doing him further damage? Will
they die straight away or will the nanoparticles in his
body remain active and do him further harm? Does
his system need to be flushed clean? Will I cause
more harm than good if I simply remove all the IVs
from his body?*

    *3. He is being tortured most likely under
interrogation. They want information. What
information? I have seen nobody, no one at all since
we arrived here. Where are the people who are
interrogating him? Or are they remotely monitoring
him and, if I gain entry and start to release Nox, will
they come charging in and capture and subsequently
torture me? Why are they interrogating him and not
me?*

    The list of questions went on and on. V had
no answers. She decided the only thing she could do
was play it by ear. The first thing she had to do was
gain entry and see if Nox was conscious, see if he
could communicate and go from there. "I hope to
God we are on Domus Mundi," she said to herself,
"Because there may be people here that can help us
and have some of the answers. Somebody from
Domus sent him to Earth to watch over me and
subsequently accompany me back. So clearly there
are pockets of resistance and pockets of friendlies."

    Feeling slightly better she had at least some
sort of plan, she crept up to the window and peeked
inside. Things seemed to have improved a little. Nox

seemed a bit more relaxed. His body wasn't so tense and his veins were not so pronounced. *Perhaps a rest between the pain,* V thought to herself. *Now would be an appropriate time to try and gain entry.* This was the first problem. To do this without tripping the warehouse lights. The portal was only a meter or so away. In fact, if she stayed where she was, at the very end of the shelving, if she reached up, she could just about reach the touchpad. She unclipped the clasp and ensured it was the right way round, and whilst remaining under the shelving, reached up and stretched as far as she could. She heard the metallic sound of the clasp touching the touchpad. Holding the clasp with her fingertips she strained and stretched just a little bit more. The annex door suddenly swung open and V carefully crawled into the annex, without tripping the main warehouse lights. The door closed with a whisper behind her.

V sat on the floor, back to the wall recovering her breath. The annex was fully lit, and she had no problems seeing. Nothing had changed. Nox was lying on a table, plugged into all sorts of machines. And, under the circumstances, he didn't look as distressed as he had been before. She looked around the walls and the ceiling and could see no signs of CCTV, or at least none that she recognised. She kept having to remind herself that the chances were she wasn't on Earth and technology here. Wherever here is, had been so advanced that nothing would resemble anything she was used to. But the walls and ceiling were smooth and the material that comprised the wall and ceiling wasn't in any way broken or marked. So, she assumed that there were no monitoring cameras there. Some of the machines around Nox, well they may be CCTV stations.

Anyway, V took the risk and stood up, albeit very slowly.

She waited a minute or two to see if the status quo had been interrupted. No, nothing seems to have changed. First order of business, she told herself was to try and see if she could get anything out of Nox. She slowly walked over to Nox, all the time looking at the machines, rather than at him. Trying to make sense of what the machines did and if any were remote monitoring devices. She recognised none of them but somehow, she felt quite sure they were simply administering the nanoparticles to torture and fluids to keep him hydrated and alive to prolong the interrogation. She didn't understand why he was being interrogated in this fashion. No one seemed to be there, and no one seemed to be listening in. This can't be right, she said to herself. V decided she could only deal with what was before her and right now her priority was to try again and communicate with Nox. All her previous attempts had failed. Perhaps touch was the key.

She stood next to his head. Gently, she reached out a shaking hand to touch him. Her fingertips reached his coat – wet and matted though it was, at once a feeling of peace and serenity shot through her body.

She bent down to Nox's ear and whispered "Nox" ever so gently and ever so quietly, hoping that as per their first meeting in the orchard on Udal Cuain, touch would ensure communication between them.

Nothing came back to her. "Nox "she called again, a little louder and a little more forcibly. Her hand tightening its grip on Nox's coat. Her mouth closer to his ear.

The ear twitched, the head moved, but nothing came back to her.

"It's me, V," she whispered loudly into his ear. "I'm here, with you. How badly are you hurt and what can I do to help you? I don't know if I will make things worse or better by unplugging you from these machines. Can you help me to help you Nox?" she asked.

"V," came back to her, albeit very quietly. "V, you must get away from here. You must look after yourself. I can hold them off for a while longer, but you must run. Here, look at the base of my neck, you should find a pouch, rather like a kangaroo's pouch on Terra. Got it? Good. Look inside. There should be a small notebook, with your name on the front. There should also be a small metal object. This object is both a radio and tracking beacon. Once switched on, you can be tracked. It is coded to your retinas. Simply look at the object for 5 seconds and it will switch on. No matter which part of the object you look at. To switch off, simply look at the object again for 5 seconds. But be careful. It is some years since I left here and the friendly forces that sent me to you and gave me those items may have fallen into enemy hands. So only use if it is literally a matter of life and death. I mean that V, only if you are convinced that your life is in serious peril. Also, there should be a blister pack of 12 tablets. These tablets kill nanoparticles. If you are captured, you will be infused with nanoparticles. Keep these tablets safe. If captured, try to take two tablets that should be sufficient, they will kill all nanoparticles injected into your body over a 48 Terran hour period. Now go, V. Please..."

V listened to all Nox had to say, felt, and found the items he had described and put them in her pocket.

"Right," she said. "If I unplug all the IVs from your body, how many tablets will you need to kill the nanoparticles? How long will it take? Will you be able to get off this table and will you be able to walk?"

"You may as well understand Nox that I'm not going to leave you. So, before you reject my offer I repeat once again. I'm not going to leave you and if you refuse my assistance a second time, then I will simply sit myself down here and wait to be captured. "

Nox heard the tone in her voice. A tone that he had loved to hear before because he knew she meant what she had said. His mission was to protect her, watch over her, to bring her home and to help her in any way he could. If she refused to go, and she knew she meant what she said, and she was captured, then he had failed in his mission. That couldn't happen.

"Give me a minute," said Nox. He wanted time to assess his injuries and to make an honest judgement about his abilities. V waited patiently. She moved away from Nox and started looking around the room. Opening drawers and lockers to see if there was anything useful lying around – not that she really understood what the gadgets she came across were, much less how they could be used. "But still," she said to herself. "You never know" and much to her delight, there was her backpack. Seemingly untouched. She had a quick rummage around inside –

everything appeared to be there. She threw in the items that Nox had had secreted in his body.

Nox neighed softly. He was still unable to mentally communicate with V without her touching him. No doubt because of the fluids that were still being pumped into his body. V at once stopped what she was doing, inadvertently and unknowingly dropped her backpack, and rushed over to him. She carefully grabbed a handful of his coat, put her arms around his neck and her ear to his head.

"I estimate we have less than 10 Terran minutes before the next batch of nanoparticles are injected into my bloodstream – the pain will start immediately and will last for approximately 30 Terran minutes. The four dull silver machines are responsible for injecting the nanoparticles into me. Trace the IV lines and remove them from my skin. Give me six tablets. That should kill off the nanoparticles that are circulating around my system. The nanoparticles are not only programmed to inflict pain, as directed, but they are also communication devices and location devices. They communicate directly with The Ostium and should I escape with nanoparticles circulating my body, they will act as positioning beacons giving The Ostium my exact position. You should also take two tablets just in case you have unknowingly imbibed some nanoparticles. Take two tablets now."

V did as she was told. She took two tablets, then proceeded to unplug the nanoparticle IV lines from Nox's body. She then fed him six tablets.

"Good," said Nox. "Now the two remaining IV lines are nourishment to keep me fed and hydrated. Please unplug those IV lines now" V did as she was told.

Now all that remained were the two smaller IVs in the corner of his eyes.

"Now" said Nox "You have to remove the two IVs in my eyes. These IVs inject the mental blocker straight into my optic nerve and then straight into my brain. The mental blocker does exactly that. Prevents me from mentally and remotely communicating with you – or anyone else. The IV needles are long, they are approximately 15 cm long. You must pull them out in one go. Once you start pulling, don't stop. Pull steadily and gently until the entire needle has been removed. But whatever you do, don't stop and don't waiver. If you do, you could blind me, or worse, kill me. "

V nodded her understanding, which was completely lost on Nox. She would have to remove herself from Nox to do this. She needed both hands to withdraw the IV needles.

She didn't say a word. Simply let him go, walked round to face him. She looked deep into his red, tearful eyes, still held open by surgical staples, with these ghastly IV needles piercing the corner of his eyes. She saw love and humility reflected in those eyes. She hoped that he could see the love that she had for him in her eyes. She blinked back tears and looked at the IV needle in his left eye. She wondered if she had the strength to do this. She felt sick to her stomach. She looked deep into Nox's eyes, she saw nothing but love and kindness, but also the deep shadows of the pain and hopelessness of what he had been experiencing. She had no choice. Much as she loathed the responsibility. It was something that she had to do. She made sure she had a good stable stance and that nothing was likely to interfere with her arms as she withdrew the needle.

"Ok" She said to herself. Gently and with surprisingly steady hands she reached out towards his left eye... and the IV needle. She took hold of the IV needle gently but firmly between her thumb and index finger and without thinking, withdrew the needle. She didn't stop pulling until the needle was completely removed from the eye. The needle came out surprisingly easily she thought. She didn't stop to ask questions, but simply gripped the IV needle in Nox right eye again between thumb and index finger and pulled in one steady motion. Again the needle came out relatively easily.

V threw the needles to the floor, took a breath of air, grabbed hold of him and asked if he was Ok?

"Didn't feel a thing" he replied. "Now, please remove the staples from my eyelids." V found a pair of medical tweezers and concentrated on removing the eight staples, four per eye.

Finally, she looked into Nox eyes. "Well?" she asked.

Nox looked at her and she thought she could see the vaguest look of humour in his eyes. "Quite well, thank you."

"Now, remove the retaining straps – that's done by pushing a button just under the table, roughly where my front leg is," V felt around under the table, found the button and pushed it. Immediately the retaining straps disappeared!

The last task was to get Nox upright. "Do you think you can get off the table and stand and then walk?" she asked.

Nox simply looked at her and said. "If you can lower the table to floor level then I'm sure I can manage."

V was looking into his eyes when she asked the question. His response sounded confident enough. But the look in his eyes was anything but confident. She saw uncertainty and fear.

"Ok," she said." How does one lower the table?"

"A button on the back edge – under the table. I think" replied Nox.

V walked around to the back of the table, felt around and found two buttons. One for raising and one for lowering she supposed. She pressed one button. She heard a whirr of motors. But nothing happened. That's the raising button she said to herself. She pushed the other button and the table quickly lowered all the way to the floor.

Nox had been lying down on his side. He now struggled to turn around so that he was lying on his front. This he managed to do, with some help from V who pushed and encouraged as much as she could.

V could see that even this relatively easy manoeuvre had cost him. Had all but drained him of any energy he had. His coat was covered in sweat and it was clear that he was in pain. "How in hell is he going to stand up?" she asked herself.

The machines started to whirr and vibrate. The noise startled V. She grabbed hold of Nox…"What?" she asked

"The next round of nanoparticle infusion" Nox informed her. "When The Ostium realizes that the nanoparticles are no longer being intravenously injected into me, they will send searcher drones to investigate. It would be to our advantage to get away from here before those drones arrive. Once they arrive, if we are here, it will only be a matter of minutes before we are recaptured."

"Come on then Nox, up you get" she encouraged him, her eyes moving around the annex to see if there was anything, anywhere that could assist Nox. She looked towards the back of the annex, and her eyes fell upon a pair of large closed doors, set into and level with the back wall of the annex. She hadn't seen these particular doors before. She turned back to look at Nox. He was trying to get his front legs up and in a position where he could push down on them to get his rear end upright. It really was a pitiful sight, she said to herself. She could see his muscles straining, the pain in his eyes, but also steely determination. The more he strained and pushed, the more the open sores on his body seemed to suppurate.

"Come on boy, you can do it" she urged as she rushed over to the closed doors. "Hmm," she said to herself, these doors are pretty large. "I wonder what's behind them…" And with that she went to grasp the door handles, only there were none. Just a touch pad on the wall. With that, her hands flew to her neck and unpinned the clasp that she had successfully used to open the portals in the past. Just as she was about to put the clasp on the touchpad. Two things happened simultaneously. Firstly, she was startled by a peculiar noise, something between a grunt and a gasp, then she got covered in viscous liquid again. She turned round and there was Nox standing next to her. With her backpack dangling from his mouth. "Nox" she gushed. So surprised and pleased to see him, that she immediately forgave him his sneeze which he was now using to attract her attention. This swiftly followed by a large metallic clang on the annex entry portal door. "The drones,"

Nox said calmly. "They are here. We need to vacate these premises and we need to do this now," Only then did V realize that Nox had thought this to her. She hadn't been touching him. The mental blockers were wearing off.

"Ok". "These doors must lead somewhere, let's go and find out" With that she pushed the clasp on the touchpad and the doors whooshed open. Just as these doors opened, so the front entry doors to the annex opened.

CHAPTER NINE

V looked back over her shoulder and saw five of what she assumed were drones, hovering at the threshold of the door. They were relatively small. The circumference of a large dinner plate and shaped a bit like an archetypal flying saucer. They were stationary, hovering line abreast. Red lights shining.

"They are scanning the room looking for us," Nox said. "Come on, we must move, it's only a matter of seconds before they lock on to us,"

V tore her eyes away from the drones, just as five red lights zeroed in on their position. V and Nox bolted through the portal and into the outside world, the portal slamming shut behind them. Nox used his back hooves to smash the external touch pad in the hope that that would break the portal, delaying the drones. Just as he did that, they heard clunk, clunk, clunk, clunk, clunk. This V assumed were the drones hitting the now broken portal.

"Well done Nox" said V. "You have bought us a little time. But where do we go from here?"

Just as V asked the question, so purple lights started glowing right next to them, and only centimetres above the ground. One light started at V's feet, a distance of about 1m to the next light, then another metre to the next light to a total distance of about 10m – yes, eleven lights. V and Nox just stood there looking at the lights, the lights glowed and pulsated, but didn't move. Then V moved in a direction parallel to the lights. As V moved, so the lights moved. No matter which way V moved, the lights orientated, and realigned themselves to the direction in which they wanted V to go. When V stood still, so did the lights.

"What do you think?" she asked Nox.

She could sense Nox was just about to answer when the lights went out.

Then, just as suddenly, the lights all blinked back on. This time they didn't just glow and pulsate gently in the night. No, they deliberately switched themselves off and on. They flashed in long and short sequences, with pauses of darkness in between a sequence of long and short flashes. V looked at this for a minute or two and then realised it was Morse code. What were the lights saying?

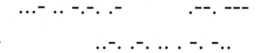

Then the sequence would start all over again.

V   I   C   A   P   O   T   A

F   R   I   E   N   D

"Vica Pota Friend!" exclaimed V. "These lights say they are friendly. Are they? Can we take the risk?" she shouted at Nox.

The crashing on the other side of the portal was getting more and more frenzied as the drones tried to break their way through. V knew it was only a matter of time before the drones either broke through, or reinforcements arrived.

"It seems to me we have little choice" Nox responded, calmly as ever. "We have to follow the lights,"

V didn't bother to answer, she simply looked at Nox, shrugged her shoulders as if to say "What the hell" and ran after the lights - Nox by her side.

As soon as they started following the lights, the Morse code stopped and the lights resumed their uninterrupted glowing and guided them in the direction in which they wanted V and Nox to go. The constant pulsating of the lights nagged at V and indicated urgency, but V was sensitive to Nox, his injuries and his recent, terrible experiences. Despite this though, they were moving at quite a pace. V kept asking Nox how he was, how he was doing, and could they go any quicker? The response was always "I'm fine and yes, of course we can go quicker," So V would pick up the pace a little, the gap between the lights would grow to accommodate the increase in pace and so they continued.

Hour after hour they proceeded at a steady canter which given the length of V's legs was, in Terran terms, actually quite fast. V could sense that Nox was struggling. He was sweating profusely, blood was seeping out of his sores, his eyes were glazed and his tongue lolled out of his mouth. He was struggling to maintain a straight course. V couldn't stop. She couldn't see them, she had no idea how far behind them the drones were. She had no idea how long they had to keep going, or indeed where they were going. But they had to get to safety. Then Nox could be treated.

Suddenly, the furthest light blinked out. Then the next light blinked out. Instead of eleven lights, there were now nine, then eight lights. She started to reduce her pace as she wasn't very sure what was happening, and it was so dark she couldn't see her hand in front of her face. Still the lights blinked out four, three, two, then she fell into a hill and down a ramp. As soon as she and Nox had passed the entry threshold, a portal whooshed shut behind her. In fact, she found out later, it was the side of a mountain that shut behind her. Nox immediately collapsed and fell to the ground. She rushed over to Nox and was blinded by the sudden switching on of extremely bright lights. Shielding her eyes, she grabbed hold of Nox. He was in terrible shape. His eyes were closed, he was covered in perspiration. His sores had opened and blood was pooling on the floor. He was unconscious, comatose. His lungs pumping in and out like billows. His whole body was trembling and shaking. "He must have given everything, every little bit of the remaining strength he had, just to get me to safety."

V then felt herself being gently nudged aside as drones swarmed all over Nox. IVs going in medication being pumped into him. A self-propelled gurney appeared and maneuvered itself under Nox, lifted him off the floor and took him away, surrounded by his drone entourage. V wasn't sure what to do, she felt terrible, she wanted to go after him, she didn't want him to be alone. Could she trust these drones… Just as she was about to run after Nox, she felt herself levitating then being gently deposited, and secured on a self-propelled gurney surrounded by a couple of drones, who seemed to be checking her over and injecting her with something. Her last thoughts were, *I hope I have got us to safety, and not signed our death warrants…* Then she thought of nothing and remembered no more.

As V slowly came back to the land of the living, she couldn't remember being so comfortable, luxuriating in the warmth of the huge bed she was in.

She felt... wonderful. She had no idea where she was or who was looking after her, but she had never felt so good. She was looking around her just as the portal whooshed open and a medical drone flew in and started checking her over. V tried talking to the drone, asking where she was, where was Nox, could she please see the person in charge. Nothing. The drone merely went about its duties and apparently satisfied left.

Well, that went well V thought and was settling herself when the portal again whooshed open. This time what V assumed to be a service drone approached with a tray of what looked like food, or nourishment of some sort. Nothing she recognised, but she was grateful, took the tray, or tried to. But was stopped as a table appeared from nowhere and settled itself on the bed, just above her waist. The drone placed the tray on the table and left. As V settled into a more comfortable breakfast in bed eating position, so the table maneuvered itself to accommodate her and make the task of eating an easy and pleasant one. V eyed the food on the tray with suspicion, but then gave into her hunger and wolfed down the food – which was surprisingly good. The table sensed that the food tray was empty and that V had finished, simply removed itself from the bed and disappeared out of the room, only to return a short time later returning to its storage place until needed again.

V surveyed the room. No windows. Everything spotlessly clean and functional. And there on a chair at the end of the room was her back pack.

The comforting sight of something familiar lifted her spirits. She started to get out of bed. Except she couldn't. The bed clothes kept her gently but firmly restrained to the bed, the more she struggled, the more the bedclothes resisted. V gave up, but her struggle didn't go unnoticed. Another, much larger and somehow more menacing drone entered the room with what looked like a bedpan. The drone flew straight to V and just hovered a foot or so away from her face, grasping the bed pan in one manipulator arm. V eyed the drone. If the drone was human, it would know what was coming. But the drone wasn't human and had no experience of V. The service drone simply remained where it was, its light flashing away, quite content. Just doing its job. If it had had a tail, it would be wagging its tail, very pleased with itself. The next thing it knew was that it was being propelled back across the room, the way it had come, only much faster, with a still unused bedpan in its manipulator.

"I don't need that" retorted V, who had just swatted the drone away from her.

"I just wanted to get my back pack. The bag, over there, on the chair," She pointed.

The drone swivelled 180 degrees and seemed to look in the direction V was pointing. It hovered over to the chair. Another manipulator arm appeared, grabbed the backpack and went back to V. V took the backpack, said thank you and then ignored the drone. The drone didn't move. It hovered annoyingly a foot or so in front of her, and always within her eye line. No matter where she looked, the drone would follow her and always be within her sight. The drone and the bedpan.

"For all that is Holy" she groaned "Is there to be no peace…" She asked the room. And with that, she eyed the drone, reached out, took the bedpan and put the bedpan on her bedside table and then started rummaging around in her back pack checking the contents. Bedpan apparently forgotten. The drone wasn't satisfied, hovered round to the bedside table, picked up the bedpan and once again resumed its hovering station just in front of her eyes.

V tried to ignore it. Truly she did. But she couldn't. The flashing light, the waving of the bed pan. The patience of the drone… She threw her back pack on her bed, took hold of the bed pan and shouted "Privacy please!!!"

With that, the drone swivelled 180 degrees and V did what had to be done. The drone collected the bedpan and with what V was sure was a victorious smile in its demeanour, happily left the room. Job done. Task completed.

V examined the contents of her back pack. She got all of the items out and checked them over. The book, the cutter, the star map, the glass as well as a few personal possessions she had brought from Earth were all there and seemed to be undamaged. She had no idea what had happened to the metallic box that was used as a switch to start up the transfer process back on Saxa Antiquis, or the suits they had worn. Talking of suits, she wondered where her clothes were. Should she be concerned? Would she get them back? She suspected she would – she would ask for their return at the first opportunity. She also couldn't find the blister pack of the remaining nanoparticle eradicating pills, or the radio / tracker that Nox had been carrying around with him.

"Nox," she said to herself. "Nox. How could I have forgotten him…" "Nox" she gently called to him, telepathically. "Nox?," Nothing came back. Where is he? How is he? Is he alive or dead? She had no way of knowing, but deep down in her soul, she could sense that connection, that bond she had with Nox was still there, still intact, and as strong as ever. It wasn't broken. He was alive, she said to herself. He was alive.

With a smile on her face, she made herself comfortable and drifted off to sleep. Her fingers tightly holding on to her backpack.

V awoke sometime later, her backpack still held firmly by her fingers. As soon as she stirred, the usual procession of medic drones paraded into her room, swiftly followed by the larger, more menacing, and somehow older drone. There was something different about this drone. She couldn't quite put her finger on it - but something was definitely very different. Different or not, it still carried the hated bedpan.

The drones, satisfied with their work, left. Now all was peace and quiet. V again called out to Nox - no answer.

Well, she knew he was alive, and she also knew that he was terribly ill, not only from his recent experiences, but also from whatever had been injected into him prior to his departure to Terra.

V had no idea how long she had been in this room. But she knew one thing. This room as comfortable as it was and as pleasant as it was, to her it was beginning to feel like prison. Additionally, she longed to have a conversation with a person – if person is the right term for the inhabitants of this world. She wondered about that. Why had she not seen anyone? She hadn't even heard a voice. The drones were efficient and gentle and seemed, with a little urging to understand what she wanted. The food, although unrecognisable, was excellent. Really, she couldn't be more comfortable. But she yearned for some contact with another living being. She had a million questions to ask. But above all, she wanted to go and visit Nox. She knew he was alive, but she just wanted to know, and see, that he was being cared for and treated properly.

She tried to get out of bed again but the bed covers kept her gently and securely in place. "I had more freedom in the other place," she muttered angrily to herself. "And they would, without a doubt have eventually tortured me." She added for good measure.

"Damn it!" she said to herself as her antics on the bed caused an enquiring service drone to enter the room. No doubt to see what all the fuss was about. This time, she was pleased to see that it didn't have a bed pan in either of his manipulators. It silently approached, hovered just in front of her face, and stopped. A soft green eye glowed from the edge of its body. It seemed to scan her. Apparently satisfied, it wandered off.

"Drone," V called after him. The drone stopped, turned round, and waited.

V thought for a moment. She had surprised herself when she shouted out after the drone. Now that she had and it had stopped and was waiting patiently to see what she had to say for herself, she supposed she had better say something.

"Drone, I wish to see the managers or leaders of this complex. I want to thank them for everything they have done for me and Nox, the beast that I came here with. Would it be possible for you to get a message to them and ask them very kindly if I could visit with them, to thank them in person?"

The drone appeared to listen to what she had to say, paused for a moment. A green light flashed in response and off it went.

Well... thought V. *Let's see if my request is honoured.*

In the interim, she turned to her backpack, rummaged around, found what she was looking for and withdrew the book. She wondered if the book could help her in determining where she was and whose care she was under.

She rifled through the book. She was thankful that she could still understand the singing of the book. She thought hard at the book, but the book refused to help. It didn't guide her to anywhere particular. It didn't stop her from leafing through the book or going to any particular chapter, or page. It acted like, well, like a normal book.

"Fat lot of good you are" she said to the book, not unkindly. She closed the book and replaced it in her backpack. Next, she got out the star chart to see if that would at least give her a clue as to where she was in the universe.

She spread the chart on the bed in front of her and looked. Nothing. The constellations were barely visible, no holographic images appeared. "No help here either," She said to herself.

But, wherever V and Nox were, they had been expected. The purple lights that had appeared when they were escaping Nox's torturers must mean that somebody was expecting them. But, where had they come from and how the hell did they work? She gave up on that. But the fact that the lights were friendly, or at least they said they were friendly, and up until now, V had no reason to think that they were anything but friendly, had appeared exactly at the right time and place of their escape from the other complex, meant – at least according to V's logic – that they had been expected and that these so called "Friends" knew they were on the planet and not only knew that they would need rescuing, but the precise moment of the rescue, then they knew they would need to be hidden and would require urgent medical treatment. *More questions* V thought to herself. *More and more questions with no answers.*

Frustration was welling up inside her. She hated being in this position. She hated being in a place where she had no control and was fully dependent on others. She hated being in a position of complete ignorance. "Damn it!" she said, a little too loudly.

And that was another thing, she thought to herself. This place is completely silent. I mean absolutely silent. No background noise of air conditioning, no noises of people coming or going. No hum or beeping of machinery. No TV, no radio. No clicking of keyboards. No nothing. Absolute silence. You can't even hear the drones appear, or doors opening or closing. Nothing. A silent world. She made a noise, just to be sure she hadn't gone deaf!

V was beginning to feel bored. That was a good sign. A sign that she was well on the road to recovery. And then she thought about that.

"Actually," she said to herself, "I don't remember being or feeling unwell. Nox. Now he was at death's door. And, in comparison to him, I was as fit as a fiddle. But," she went on "Compared to how I feel now, I guess I must have been. I feel fantastic. Never have I felt this well, this full of energy. My mind seems to be working at the speed of light. So, I guess I must have been a little unwell"

Just then, the door opened silently, a medical drone approached, went straight over to V checked her out thoroughly. Machines appeared from nowhere and seemed to display various aspects of V's bodily functions and vital signs. A needle appeared, again from nowhere and injected her with something. A completely painless injection. Her bed clothes were removed. The dressing on her leg was changed.

Don't remember hurting my leg, V thought idly.

And, whilst she was still in the bed, her bedding was changed, and the bed remade. The bed did all this itself. V marvelled at that! She hated making beds. In Udal Cuain, Aunt Izzy insisted on beds being made properly every morning. Mrs. Campbell would then inspect V's room and if the bed hadn't been made to her satisfaction, V was marched up to her room and told to do it again. This time under the watchful eye of Mrs. Campbell.

The medical drone carefully placed some drops in V's eyes. Then more monitoring of V's vitals. Apparently satisfied, all the machines disappeared, the drone flashed a green light at her as if to say "Thank you and sorry for the intrusion" then left.

A minute or two later, a fleet of drones, service drones she assumed, including her old combatant, the largest, more menacing drone, paraded into her room. They seemed to be carrying various bits of equipment. V had no idea what the equipment was. She watched the service drones with interest.

The larger drone seemed to be I charge and was organising the other service drones like a conductor controlling his orchestra. Every so often, he would leave his colleagues, hover over to V, pause for a moment or two, then head back to his colleagues. All done in complete silence of course. But there was a lot of flashing of red lights, particularly from the larger drone. *Hmmm, seems to be having a bit of difficulty organising his troops...* V thought to herself!

Regardless of the problems, the drone soon had his troops organized and the job was quickly done. He gave his team another bout of flashing red lights, and the drones quickly scuttled out of the room. One drone, being so desperate to leave, collided with another service drone, causing them both to crash to the floor. The larger drone whipped round, scanned the floor, scurried over and almost kicked the two drones out of the room. V giggled to herself. She could have sworn she saw a look of embarrassment in his general demeanour and at once her heart went out to it. He flashed a pink light at her. Then seemed to pull itself together, resumed its air of bombastic authority and with his manipulator arms, presented the array of equipment that was hovering in a semi-circle at the foot of her bed.

The drone instructed her to move. To sit up in her bed and to lie down in her bed and to assume any position in between. As she moved, so the suite of equipment at the foot of her bed moved, in unison, to accommodate her new position. No matter what position V chose to assume, the machines moved in unison so that she could clearly see them all, at all times.

The drone then gave her a metal box, which it seemed to have plucked out of thin air – *terrestrial magicians hadn't anything on these drones,* she thought.

He gently took her hand in his manipulator arm and showed her where to press. Pressing once and holograms appeared over the top of each item of equipment.

Her heart jumped and tears fell down her cheeks. To the very left she could see Nox. He was standing, well floating, upright, eyes closed. She could only see his head. With the exception of his head, Nox's body was completely immersed in a thick blanket, contoured to his exact body shape. Connected to this blanket were all sorts of monitors and machines. Although Nox's eyes were closed, he was either asleep or unconscious – unconscious decided V, he looked completely at ease, relaxed and at peace. Two medical drones were constantly attending to him and watching over him. Fiddling with machines and administering drugs.

"He is alive, comfortably at ease and at rest. And, more importantly, he is recovering," She said to herself. She couldn't take her eyes off the hologram and, as for the other holograms she had experienced, she could enlarge or reduce the size of the image or rotate the direction.

She thought to him, *I'm watching over you now boy. Don't worry. I won't let anybody hurt you again. Get all the rest you need. Just get better. I'm here. I will always be here for you.*

The drone not wishing to disturb her, but at the same time trying to get its work done, gently nudged her shoulder, to try and attract her attention. In fact, it had to nudge her two or three times before the drone got a response. V sensed its gentle but persistent nagging, spun round to face the drone with tears and anger in her eyes – the drone hovered back a few feet, so surprised and not a little upset by the look in her eyes.

It cautiously approached, reached out to her hand, and gently showed her where to press to turn on the rest of the holograms.

In total, there were four holograms placed evenly around her bed. To the left was the real-time holographic image of Nox. Next to that image, was a holographic image of the compound she was in. This would need careful study as it showed detailed images of the various rooms, entrances, plus holographic images of the equipment in those particular rooms and more importantly where she was. She could switch from internal images, to external images. She could see that the complex she was in, was inside a mountain. By zooming out, she could see the compound where she and Nox had been taken captive. She could even see the course they had taken during their escape. This holographic image would tell her everything she would need to know about where she was and where she had come from, plus the abilities of the equipment here in this compound, how it was used, what it was used for and, how it worked. This was a goldmine of information. One thing she knew for sure; she was home, she was on Domus Mundi. She now knew exactly where she was. She was in a complex under the Silbah Mountains.

The Drone then showed her the third monitor. It showed her how to switch it on and as soon as she did so, a holographic image of a beautiful woman appeared. The image wasn't so clear, but it was clear enough. V thought she was looking in a mirror. The image introduced herself as Domina Tranquillo Serenoque Pota, then very matter of factly added "I'm your Mother." The world stood still. V was in total shock. She dropped the switch and burst into tears. The drone went into an absolute panic. Lights of all colours started flashing on its body. It switched off the holographic image, and started hovering around V, its manipulator arms approaching her and then withdrawing, completely uncertain as to what to do next. Medical drones came rushing in. There seemed to be some strong words said between them and the service drone. Monitors appeared and before V could stop anybody, she was painlessly injected with some sort of drug. The last thought she had before the blackness of unconsciousness took over was "My name is Domina Tranquillo Serenoque Pota, I'm your Mother."

Once the medical drones had comfortably settled V and were satisfied that no damage had been done, they supervised the clearing away of machines and monitors, they flashed their lights angrily at the service drone and departed. The drone didn't know what to do next. Its instructions had been to show V how the holographic machines worked. It hadn't completely carried out those instructions, logic demanded that it stay with V until its orders had been carried out. So mentally shrugging its shoulders, it hovered closer to V, about two feet away and went into standby mode. A soft amber light flashed continuously from its body, scanning V, and scanning the room. It would know instantly as soon as she awoke, or whether she moved, or if another drone entered the room. And with that, it shut itself down.

Slowly the blackness and confusion of unconsciousness receded from V's body to be replaced by natural sleep. She slept for a few hours longer before slowly opening her eyes and got the fright of her life as she looked straight into the flashing amber light of the service drone. That completely woke her up and accelerated her pulse to such an extent that a medical drone came rushing into the room. The service drone also got a bit of a fright and hovered back a meter or two. The medical drone checked V over, satisfied, it withdrew, but not without an angry flash at the service drone.

By this time, V had reclaimed her wits. She wasn't angry at the service drone. In fact quite the oppositeshe was rapidly warming to this drone, that always seemed to get the difficult jobs and could never seem to do anything quite right. She beckoned it over. It at once obeyed and seemed to look at her inquiringly as if to ask, "May I continue?"

V nodded and said "Yes. Please just show me the fourth machine and then leave me – but before you do, please wait one minute."

V just wanted to check on Nox first. That machine had also been switched off. She found the remote and switched on the machine. Immediately a holographic image of Nox appeared and floated 6 feet away from her. No change. Nox still looked at peace, covered in his body fitting blanket. Medical drones moving quietly around him.

"This image is of Nox, my companion" she said to the service drone "This image of Nox must remain on at all times. Is that clear?" The service drone seemed to do a little bob in the air, as if nodding yes. "Please make sure that all your colleagues and all the other drones are aware. They must not touch this image; they must not switch this machine off until I inform you otherwise. Is that clearly understood?" and with that the service drone did another little bob, followed by a few seconds of flashing lights. Then bobbed again as if to say "Implemented."

"Thank you" said V. "Right, please show me the fourth holographic image"

Looking and acting like an eager puppy, the drone hovered over to V, gently taking the remote control from her hand and showed her how to switch on the fourth holographic image. V didn't understand what she was seeing. She looked quizzically at the drone.. It seemed to understand her confusion. Its fingers rattled over the remote control and words appeared on the image. These words sung to V. At once she understood. What she was looking at was a computer. Operated verbally she could do any research, ask any questions, or do anything she wanted with it. It had a complete library of all the technical knowledge on the Domus Mundi, broadcasts, news reels, and of course the history behind is downfall and The Ostium infestation. All images and news reels and broadcasts were three dimensional holograms, with the picture quality so good, it was as if she was a part of what was occurring, or whatever she was watching. The service drone gave her a brief demonstration of its capabilities and then left the image at the index page so she could, at her leisure, work out how to use it properly.

Before the drone could leave, it had one more duty to perform. He hovered over to the side of her bed, gently took one of her hands in his manipulator arm and placed her hand on the edge of her bed covers. He then encouraged her to grasp the bed covers and to fling them back. He helped her out of bed and then showed her the remainder of the room. Where carefully recessed buttons were so she could open the bathroom, toilet, a wardrobe with her clothes all having been cleaned and pressed. A desk, comfortable chairs and sofas could all appear at the push of a button or disappear. She could make the room physically larger or smaller. The drone gave her a keypad, rather like a terrestrial iPad, but smaller and definitely more beautiful. This was the room remote control. She could control everything from here. Open doors, move furniture generally, change the lighting, the design of the walls, she could bespoke her room as she wanted. Finally,the drone encouraged her to push the bottom button. A panel in the wall opened and a drone immediately appeared. This drone spoke to her.

"Hello Domina Vica, I'm your personal hospitality drone. I'm here to serve you. Anything you want or need, please just ask"

"How may I serve you…?"

"I'm fine, thank you " said V. And with that, the drone disappeared back into its recess until needed.

The service drone's duty now finally done, it bobbed politely at V and left the room.

V went to the nearest chair and sat down. She tried to take all of this in but couldn't. "Wow," she said to herself. "Wow, wow, wow…"

V got up and for a moment luxuriated in the fact that she wasn't confined to bed anymore. She checked all of her belongings and browsed the clothes in her wardrobe. There was the special blanket that turned into a trouser suit neatly pressed and folded on the top shelf, and the 5 silver clasps were safely intact. There were other clothes hanging on the wardrobe, she pulled a comfortable looking top and trouser bottoms. Put them on and they conformed to her body to fit perfectly. She put on a pair of socks and what looked to be slippers. Feeling much more comfortable, she rearranged the room, more to her liking and had a quick check on Nox – no changes there. Feeling a little hungry, she called out "Hospitality drone..." At once, the panel in the wall opened and the hospitality drone hovered out.

"Do you have another name, or must I call you hospitality drone?" she asked the drone. The drone thought for a minute and said, "Please call me H71."

"Very well. I'm Domina Vica Pota, pleased to meet you H71" said V. "I'm not sure what time of the day, or night it is, but could you please bring me the equivalent of a Terran evening meal" The drone bobbed and shot off out of the main portal.

V sat herself comfortably in a huge armchair, which at once registered that it was being sat on, scanned the body that was sitting on it and conformed itself into the most secure and comfortable chair V had ever sat on. If V moved, the chair adapted and changed its support and comfort levels to her new position. "Wow, who needs a bed" V said to herself, "This chair is super comfortable,"

In what seemed to be a carefully choreographed ballet, the holographic machines manoeuvred themselves into positions in front of her and awaited further instructions.

"Damn it!" said V having forgotten the remote control. Just as she was about to heave herself out of the chair, H71 returned with a huge tray of food. A table appeared from nowhere and positioned itself just above V's waist. H71 carefully deposited the food tray on the table and hovered away to a standby position, waiting for further direction. "H71, could you please bring me the remote control for the holographic machines?" H71 complied and moved off to a standby position, like an ever attentive butler, waiting to be called on again.

Her meal finished; V instructed H71 to clear away. The tray disappeared to its stowage position. V couldn't put off the moment any longer. She waited for H71 to return. She asked him if the medical staff needed to see V for any particular reason, because if they did, please have them come and visit now. Lights flashed and H71 responded that a medical visit wasn't due for another 6 Terran hours.

"Fine" responded V. "Please let it be known that I don't wish to be disturbed by anybody, for the next 6 Terran hours, unless Nox's medical condition changes. You are dismissed H71 and thank you." Lights flashed on H71's casing. Satisfied, he bobbed at V, then returned to his stowage panel in the wall.

V cuddled down into the chair, which immediately enveloped her, she quickly inspected Nox, who remained in suspension, in his suit with constant medical attention. His eyes were closed, but his whole body relaxed and at peace. She thought some comforting thoughts at him and brought him up to date with what had happened to her so far that day. She told him she was with him and watching over him.

V then turned to the third holographic machine and switched it on. Her mother at once appeared. She paused the program and spent the next few minutes just looking at her mother. Rotating the holographic image so she could inspect every little bit of her mother's face, neck and head. Then, she just looked at her mother's face. Looking into her eyes and wondering who she was...

V snapped out of her thoughts and resumed the program.

"My name is Domina Tranquillo Serenoque Pota, I'm your Mother." The image said to her. The voice was soft and comforting, but also a voice that was used to respect and a voice that was used to command.

"By the time you are looking at this recording, I will be long dead and it will have been over 4,000 Terran years since I last held you, looked into your eyes, kissed you and sent you on your way on the most hazardous and longest journey anyone, anywhere has ever had to undertake. I'm sorry Vica, that it had to be you. But there was simply no one else. Believe me, we tried to find someone else, but there was no one. This is your destiny Vica, yours and yours alone. Unfortunately, this was our sacrifice.
"

"I'm not sure how much you know already and why we had to send you to Terra all those millennia ago. But in short, our way of life was unsustainable. Your father, possibly the greatest man ever to have lived on Domus knew it, I knew it, and a few close colleagues and associates knew it. But those in power and those who had the power to make the necessary changes stubbornly refused to believe that our way of life could be destroyed. They were content to sit idly by and watch as our planet died, then when the prophecy started coming true, it was too late. We were doomed."

"So, it was left to your Father, to me and to those close associates and colleagues to think of a way, a plan that would allow us to regain control of our world. To destroy the plague, the virus – The Ostium - that killed our way of life, that killed this planet and that destroyed so many of our citizens."

"Whatever we decided, we knew would not be a simple fix. But would take millennia. We knew what The Ostium was capable of. I won't go into too much detail here; you will be able to get all the information you need on The Ostium from the databases that will have been left behind for you. But, in summary, we knew The Ostium would affect and take control of every bit of technology, every piece of technology that required software, programming or electronics. This included every bit of technological enhancement, whether necessary or cosmetic, that our citizens had implanted in their bodies. The Ostium, by controlling or destroying every single piece of technology, be it a simple drone, or heart pacemaker, to the huge and technologically advanced computer systems that controlled Domus, over a period of millennia, sent Domus back to what was the equivalent of the stone age period on Terra. This is no exaggeration. Because our citizens were so dependent on technology for everything, they couldn't fight back. They had forgotten how. They couldn't do the most rudimentary mathematics calculation, let alone know how to look after themselves, or provide themselves with shelter or food. So, as the technology slowly died, as our comfortable and sedentary way of life died, so our people died, so we died."

"What was clear to your father and I was that there was no quick fix, and whatever had to be done, had to be done off-world and involve little to no technology. It was fortunate that Dominus Cæmentarius Ourea, my brother, was about to embark on a long-term project on Terra. This gave your father an idea. We could send you to Terra. If we could somehow protect you and keep you in stasis until the time was right and give you some basic tools to help you find your way back here, then this was perhaps the only way to keep you safe from The Ostium and give our planet a chance, a slim chance of recovering.

You will know of the desperate plan we put in place and how you were transported to earth and then left for millennia after millennia, alone, underground in your stasis cot. "

"We managed to evade The Ostium virus for as long as we could, and to continue to lay down the foundations for your eventual return. We moved the family homestead and our laboratories and technologies to the location you are in now. You are buried deep under the Silbah Mountains. These laboratories are completely self-contained and undetectable. They rely on nothing from the outside world and are the headquarters of The Resistance movement. It's from here that our fight back to rid ourselves of The Ostium virus will begin."

"You were our biggest secret. To keep you absolutely secure from The Ostium virus, all knowledge of you and the plan to send you to Terra was wiped from the minds of all the scientists and technologists that had helped conceive the plan and put the technology together to sustain you. You were even wiped from your father's mind and you were supposed to have been wiped from mine. But somehow my mind retained knowledge of you and what we had done. I told no-one. Other than Ourea, I was the only person in the universe that knew of you and the plan we had instigated. I debated long and hard and decided to build a vault in my rooms. I placed all records of you, together with technical schematics, star map locations and everything your father and I had planned. This was all sealed in the vault. "

"Just before my passing to the spirit world, and long after your father had already passed. I took into confidence the new, greatly trusted leader of the family, my great, great, great grandson, Macánta. I told him about the vault, not what the vault contained. He was forbidden from opening the vault unless he was soon to join the spirit world, or if something terrible was to happen. But I wanted your legacy to go on. I didn't want you to be forgotten. I wanted to continue to help you. I trusted in the Gods and in the family, that I made the right decision."

"I'm sorry my darling that I never had the chance to be a proper mother to you, that I couldn't see you grow up, that I had to send you many light years away to be sealed into a tomb for thousands of years waiting for Terra to evolve the technology and ability to help you. I hated to think of you alone in an alien world. Absolutely alone, trusting that technology would keep you safe and that technology would somehow, one day, help you find your way home. The fact that you are here now, watching this holographic message from your long dead mother comforts me in the spirit world. I will be watching over you, my darling. "

Tears were rolling down V's cheeks. She knew most of what had happened to her. But to have it confirmed by her mother, to hear it from her lips. To see the agony in her mother's eyes when she mentioned having to send me away. What a terrible decision she had to make. V said a silent prayer to her mother, completely forgiving her for the decision she had to take. V told her mother that she understood that she loved her and that she would do everything she could to wrest Domus back from the evil grip of The Ostium.

The Ostium, V said to herself. I'm beginning to understand. They are not people, or at least they weren't. It was a virus. A computer virus. A computer virus, much like a flu virus, that spreads from host to host and has the ability to replicate itself. Similarly, in the same way that flu viruses can't reproduce without a host cell, computer viruses can't reproduce and spread without programming such as a file or document.

A type of malicious code or program written to alter the way a computer operates and is designed to spread from one computer to another. A virus operates by inserting or attaching itself to a legitimate program or document that supports macros in order to execute its code. In the process, a virus has the potential to cause unexpected or damaging effects, such as harming the system software by corrupting or destroying data.

When and how does the virus attack? Once a virus has successfully attached to a program, file, or document, the virus will lie dormant until circumstances cause the computer or device to execute its code. In order for a virus to infect a computer, the infected program has to run, which in turn causes the virus code to be executed.

This means that a virus can remain dormant on any computer, without showing major signs or symptoms. However, once the virus infects the computer, the virus can infect other computers on the same network. Stealing passwords or data, logging keystrokes, corrupting files, spamming email contacts, and ultimately taking over the computers themselves and ordering them to operate totally differently.

As all the computers on Domus Mundi were connected, it would be easy for a virus to spread from machine to machine. Rather like knocking down a line of dominos. It wouldn't be long before The Ostium had complete control over the entire computer network, allowing them to control everything.

Because Domus was so dependent on computers for everything, from the most simple, basic task, to the most technically and mathematically complex tasks, it would not take long for The Ostium to assume complete control and for the fabric of Domus society to crumble. It was because Domus inhabitants were so reliant on computers and drones to do everything for them, that they had lost the ability to do even the most mundane thing for themselves.

V thought about her brief time on Domus. Since she had been here, the most difficult thing she had to do was to press a remote-control button. Everything else has been done for her. But what about the Domus equivalent of humans, how were they infected?

The simple answer is - quite easily. Any Domus citizen that had had something as basic as a computer chip inserted into his or her body, either for medical or cosmetic reasons could easily be infected by The Ostium virus. So, any implantable computing technologies used medically, or cosmetically to improve health, such as heart pacemakers and cochlear implants, or as new applications were found to enhance the abilities of healthy Domus citizens. As the technology behind these implants developed, they became more vulnerable to computer viruses.

V assumed that the implants themselves were small, but in Terran terms, extremely powerful computers which were capable of communicating, storing and manipulating data. Like mainstream computers, they can be infected by viruses and clearly Domus technology either didn't, or was prevented from ensuring that virus blocking / killing technology kept pace with the technical ability of these implants.

So, an infected citizen would have given The Ostium virus mobility. It would have been able to traverse to areas that were self-sufficient, to computers that were not connected to a central system. They would also be able to access places that drones, for example couldn't. Infected Domus citizens were in fact stealth weapons for The Ostium virus to use as and when and where needed. Nowhere was safe from The Ostium Virus. An infected citizen would have infected other computer systems and each other as they came into contact with anything electrical or programmable.

What a horrible world to live in, thought V. *And it's still happening. No wonder Domus has lost all ability to progress and has rather regressed. Loss of knowledge and dependency on computers, which have now turned against them, well this equals regression and reverting back to the Stone Age. But what would The Ostium gain by doing this? Dominance and ownership of all the electrical and computer systems, thereby controlling everything that happens on this planet.* She answered herself. *Use of technology that would give them the means to attack other planets. Next on the list was Terra. Although*

Terra was way behind Domus Mundi in terms of technology, they were still building a reliance on computer systems – all be they very basic computer systems in comparison to Domus. The more basic and primitive technology utilized on Terra, would make the planet easier and quicker to overrun. And from Terra, who knows… And I brought them there. The only reason they went to Terra was to come for me. They must have learnt about me, identified where I had been sent to, found the planet, and come for me… Have I doomed Terra to the same fate as Domus Mundi…?

Just as V was pondering this horrible thought, and wondering just what she could do about it, a voice spoke to her. A deep and resonant voice. Yet comforting and trustworthy. She jumped and looked around the room but saw no one. Then she realised it was the hologram. The face of her Mother had been replaced by a male face.

"Hello Vica. My name is Dominus Probitas Pota. I'm a long dead relative of yours. I'm the last guardian of Silbah. This is my last duty before I erase you, Silbah and everything else from my mind. I have taken the decision to shut down the Silbah complex. The Ostium virus is getting closer and it's becoming more and more difficult to detect Domus citizens that have become infected by the virus. This complex, built by your mother and father and has survived the last one thousand years, is the last place on Domus that has any form of technology, well any form of technology not infected by The Ostium. Outside of these walls, everything is controlled by The Ostium. They now control this planet. By the time you get here, I'm not sure how far this planet will have regressed, or whether there will be any life on this planet at all. You will have to find this out for yourself. But, if you are watching this hologram, then clearly there must be hope. You couldn't have made this journey by yourself. You will have to have had help and that help will have had to have originated from here as, although technology on Terra will have advanced sufficiently to give you the knowledge that you need and to have come to the attention of The Ostium, it will not have advanced sufficiently for you to have made the trip from Terra to Domus Mundi by yourself."

"I'm the twenty fifth and last generation to have learned of your existence. Like my forefathers, I'm the only person on the planet that is aware of you, what was done to you and how you are the last hope of rescuing Domus from the evils of The Ostium. I'm also the last person that will know of your existence. Once I have given you the briefest of information, I too will have had all knowledge of you, our family and Silbah erased from my mind. This is the only way to keep you safe and to keep this building safe."

"As soon as I have finished this message, I will be shutting down Silbah. I have implemented a plan to have Silbah reactivated as soon as you are detected. But the complex will be run entirely by machines. There are no citizens here. They have all gone. The complex will contain everything you need in terms of knowledge, technology, and medical treatment should you need it, food, and power. The complex is entirely self-sufficient and needs nothing from the outside world. Silbah is yours to command. At the moment it's completely invisible to The Ostium and once shut down, will remain totally invisible to them. So you should be safe. At least for a while. Once the complex has been restarted, then you become visible and exposed to The Ostium, and despite it being built deep inside a mountain, Silbah can still be infected. So Vica, the clock is ticking. You need to arm yourself with the knowledge you need to find a way to defeat The Ostium and you need to do this quickly. The longer you stay at Silbah, the more at risk you become and the easier it will be for The Ostium to find you. They will kill you Vica. They know how great a threat you are to them. Make no mistake. Your life is now at risk. Don't rely on technology. Technology is a marker and will be infected and will turn against you in no time. You will have to rely on your brain, on your courage and on your determination. I repeat. Outside of these walls, don't trust in any technology and trust no one. Many Domus citizens are infected by The Ostium and many more have defected to The Ostium for minor privileges. It is imperative you try and keep Silbah intact and away from The Ostium. Silbah will not only give you all the knowledge and anything else you need, but once you have defeated The Ostium, will give you the basics for reawakening Domus Mundi and to start taking back the systems and technology that has for so long been in Ostium hands. In Silbah, you have the building blocks to rebuild Domus. Ensure it stays out of enemy hands."

"Vica, I salute you. I wish we could have met. I can't imagine what you have gone through. But hardship is still to come. May the Gods watch over you. May the Gods protect you. May you correct the wrongs that have been done to our home world. Go with the Gods, Vica."

V just stared at the now empty hologram machine – trying to come to terms with what Probitas had just said to her. She wanted to curl up in the chair and cover herself with a blanket and hope that everything would just go away. But she knew what Probitas had said was the truth. He was confirming everything that Nox had said and everything she had read. The notes from Ourea and the words from her Mother. Each in their own way having made huge sacrifices. Well, I'm just going to have to make sure that these sacrifices were not in vain. She said with more resolve than she was feeling. At least she now knew why she hadn't seen anybody. V now understood that it was just her and the drones, plus whatever computing power is available to me. Can this be trusted? Has The Ostium penetrated the stony walls of Silbah? In fact how come we have evaded them for so long? Surely they must have followed me here?

"H71!" V bellowed. H71 immediately came scurrying out of his cubby hole. "When Nox and I managed to escape from the compound we were being held in, presumably by The Ostium, how come The Ostium didn't track us to here? Are we safe? Has Silbah been compromised?"

H71 looked as if he was about to burst into tears, then said "Domina, one moment please." Lights flashed, bobbing occurred – then all was still, H71 hovering a few meters away, looking at V.

V was sitting fidgeting in the chair and was just about to repeat her questions to H71, when her portal swooshed open and in came the large, menacing drone that she was getting to know so well.

. A deep menacing and quite frightening voice boomed out from the drone . "I'm sorry Domina, it took me a little longer to grasp your language, but I think I'm now proficient. Can I introduce myself as SD59? It is my greatest pleasure to be looking after you. H71 tells me you are concerned that The Ostium may have compromised Silbah, as they could have tracked you here during your escape. Is that so?"

"A pleasure SD59. Yes, that is indeed the case. Surely, they must have tracked me and Nox here – we were not travelling particularly fast. Surely they would have had ample time to get a lock on to us ?"

"Under normal circumstances, yes indeed they would have tracked you and killed you or at least recaptured you before you got close to Silbah. However, the purple lights you were following not only showed you the way but also acted as a cloaking device. The Ostium were unable to track you whilst you were following the purple lights. We also set up a false trail which comprised your DNA, Nox's DNA and a dumb drone laying the trail. The Ostium did follow the false trail. It took them 500 miles in the opposite direction, before the trail disappeared and the dumb drone self-detonated. So for now we are safe. We are secure and we have not been compromised."

"Thank you SD59, said V, somewhat relieved. "Domina," responded SD59, who then left V's recovery room.

So, thought V. *What do I know? I now know where I am, and have more information on who I'm up against and what they are capable of. Where to start? Speed is of the essence, but I'm going nowhere until Nox has been healed.* V thought for a little longer. Then she again called for H71.

"H71!" H71 appeared from his cubicle at once. "H71!" V went on. "Please bring to me the medical drone who is in charge of looking after Nox. Can you please also bring to me or put me in contact with the drone or computer that is in charge of this facility. Thank you"

H71 paused a moment, as if to satisfy himself that he understood the task that had been given to him. Then he started, somewhat uncertainly for the exit portal. Stopped and returned. Hovering in front of V, a timid voice from within him asked "Domina Vica ?"

Startled, V responded "Oh, H71. I thought you had gone. How can I help you?"

"I can and will certainly bring you the medical drone in charge of Nox's treatment. But I'm afraid I can't bring to you or put you in touch with the drone or computer in charge of this facility."

"Why is that" asked V, somewhat puzzled...

"Because you are in charge of this facility. This is your facility. All drones and computers report to you and will do as you command. Without question and without delay."

V, somewhat surprised at the response, merely nodded and said "Very well H71, please get me the medical drone as requested, oh and H71...?"

"Domina Vica?" H71 responded.

"Please also bring the medical drone who is or was responsible for my treatment and recovery. Thank you"

"With pleasure Domina Vica" H71 responded.

This time, a little happier, H71 shot off to do his duty.

Lifting her eyes back towards the monitors, she was surprised to see yet a third face staring at her from the holographic machine.

She looked at this individual. It was a woman. Age unknown. But young. Eyes full of fear and suspicion. Hair a confused array of colours, matted and dirty. The image remained silent, eyes shifting, looking nervously over her shoulders. V could see a drone in the background, hovering nearby with what looked like a weapon in its manipulator arm. A drone nearer to her, a drone which looked suspiciously like SD59, hovering near to her, helping set up some equipment – the holographic recorder V assumed.

The drone resembling SD59 bobbed and flashed lights at the girl then disappeared out of shot.

"Hello" said the girl. "My name is Domina Solis Ortus Pota. I'm in charge of The Resistance here on Domus . Until one year ago, I had no idea that the Silbah complex existed. Exactly one year ago, I woke up one morning and had full knowledge of you, of the Silbah complex and of my heritage. I'm related to you by blood, although you are many, many millennia older than me. I know where you are and who you are and what you are tasked to do. I don't know how this has happened or how I gained this knowledge. It's as if this knowledge was put into my head, into a corner of my brain, to be activated when the time was right.

"Together with this knowledge, I was also given instructions from our forefathers to gather those of us together whom I could trust. I had instructions that we were to formulate a plan to send you help. Help that would watch over you whilst you were growing and when the time was right, to help you and to protect you and to guide you here back to us. I understood, although I have no idea how I understood, that within the next 10 years you were to come to Domus Mundi and help rescue us from The Ostium. I was to put a plan together that will send

- 212 -

someone to assist you and to watch over you when you are woken from stasis.

"I was given all the knowledge needed to formulate and execute the plan. Today, that plan was executed. I'm sending you this message so that you are aware of us and that there is help here, waiting for you. We have been instructed to cease all resistance activities until you arrive, so as to deflect attention away from us. I have also been given the technology to wipe clear all knowledge from the minds of those that have helped in the preparation and execution of the plan. That has been done. I'm also to have my mind wiped clean. But before I do, I have been instructed to send you this message, to give you the coordinates of my location and to give SD59 this capsule. When you find me, I will have no recollection of you. You must get me to trust you and you must get me to swallow this capsule. This will erode the barrier to my mind and allow me to remember everything about you and the task ahead. If I have been infected by The Ostium, the tablet will not work, just apologise for troubling me and move away swiftly. You will then have to do the best you can. There will be no one to help you. You will be on your own, you and Nox.

This brings me to the plan that we devised. To update you. The Silbah complex is an open complex, buried deep under the Silbah Mountains. There is something very special about the Silbah complex. It is connected to a wormhole portal. We understand this wormhole is a direct link to Terra. Our plan was to go to the Silbah complex, retake from The Ostium if necessary, place Nox on the entry portal and send him to Terra, to Saxa Antiquis. There with his special abilities, he would be able to watch over you and as you grew and as your senses evolved, wait for the day when you would be able to see him. He was to befriend you, to look after you and to help you find your way back here. Once here, he was to be your guide and bring you to us. We believe our forefathers had used the portal before, to send various messengers to Terra. One such messenger alerted your guardians to the fact that you were there. You will find records of this and how this was accomplished in specially coded computer files. SD59 will assist here.

"Let me tell you a little about Nox. Not that there is much to tell. He is unique. Absolutely unique. No one knows where he came from, or how he came to be. We don't think he is from Domus. There is nothing in the ancient records about such a beast. Having had limited access to Silbah's computers, I could find no reference anywhere to anything resembling Nox. He just turned up at The Resistance complex one day and refused to move. It was the same day that I became aware of you. My mind cleared and I heard Nox calling for me. I went to him and he told me he had to get to Terra. He had to get to Vica Pota.

"Nox was pivotal in the compilation of the plan and, the only being strong enough to endure the wormhole. However, we had to wait until the planets were aligned before we could put our plan into action. This took nearly a year.

"It was just after Nox had left, only hours ago, that we learned that he may have been poisoned. One of us is a traitor. I feel sure The Ostium knows of this complex and probably knows of our plan. I have therefore sabotaged the portal to the wormhole. It can receive people or things from the wormhole, but can't now let people leave Domus for the portal. I'm pretty sure this complex will fall into enemy hands, so even if you and Nox survive the journey through the wormhole, I'm not sure if you will survive being captured by the enemy.

"I'm truly sorry Vica for putting you in this situation. But if you are watching this hologram then you are free and safe, at least for the moment. When you can, come to me. Together we can fight The Ostium and take back Domus. I pray that you will find us. I pray that I will not be taken by The Ostium. Remember the capsule Vica. The capsule. God speed." With that, the holograph finally died.

With an iron will, V trampled all over her emotions. Crushed the panic that was again rising in her chest. She glanced at Nox's Hologram – used the anger that was welling up inside her. *What had Nox been through over the past fifteen or so years?* The pain, the suffering – she had no idea. Permanent torment by The Ostium. The Ostium that were ultimately responsible for separating her from her parents, for killing every blood relation she had ever had. For bringing nothing but misery on her family, her friends, her loved ones and her planet – both of them. Domus Mundi and now Earth. Her anger was practically incandescent. This time, she didn't crush the anger, but was determined to use it in a cold, calculating way – use it to eradicate The Ostium from the universe.

V turned round, about to call for SD59, when she noted H71 and two other drones waiting patiently on the other side of the portal.

"SD59!" V called. Then asked H71 and the other drones to enter her room.

"H71 reporting. As asked, I have with me medical drones MD1 and MD2. MD1 is responsible for the team managing your treatment and MD2 is managing the team responsible for Nox's recovery."

Just then SD59 hovered into V's room. "SD59, please wait here a minute, go into sleep mode. I will be with you shortly" SD59 bobbed and went over to the corner of the room and went into sleep mode. Amber light pulsating slowly.

"MD1, Good day. My name is Vica Pota. A pleasure to meet you and thank you for looking after me. Can you please tell me, in simple terms, for I'm no doctor, what exactly was wrong with me and when do you expect me to be fully fit?"

MD1's lights flashed for a second or two, then went out. "Domina Vica Pota, it is a pleasure to finally meet you" responded drone MD1.

"I'm pleased to report that you are fully recovered, and your health is now excellent. "

"Upon arrival, you were dehydrated, stressed, and over tired. Physically your body was working at optimum, there are still natural changes going on inside your body making you more Domus than Terran. We will continue to monitor those. Other than that, your body simply needed time to recover from your recent ordeals. However, we did find Ostium nanoparticles in your body. Also, a nanoparticle tracer beacon had been implanted as had a nanoparticle thermo bomb. The medication you took before you got here had killed most of the nanoparticles. Most of the nanoparticles were designed to slowly, but surely, kill you. They would have done this by releasing toxins into your body. Slowly, but surely, you would have succumbed to these toxins. Not too dissimilar from the technique that had been used on Nox. Don't worry, the damage to your body was minor. We have repaired what little damage there was. The tracer beacon was also destroyed by the tablets you took. Our location remains perfectly safe. At least for now. The thermo bomb was a different matter. The tablets you took had no effect on this, as the medication was basic. We, however, have removed it from your body and disarmed the bomb. The nanoparticles associated with the bomb have now been destroyed. Your body is now 100% healthy, all damage done by Ostium nanoparticles have been removed. We have fed you medication to ensure any sleeper nanoparticles have been destroyed. We are 100% certain that your body is pure and free from nanoparticles. However we recommend that we give you vaccinations that will immediately kill any future nanoparticles that The Ostium may try to implant into your body. This will also include thermo bombs and sleeper particles. Provided you pass one final medical examination, due in two hours, you will be released from my care and free to undertake any duties you see fit."

"Thank you MD1. Please inform me of the status of my final medical examination as soon as you have the results. Please ensure that I'm vaccinated against anything and everything that The Ostium may try to implant into my body.

In addition, do we have any sleeper nanoparticles that, when triggered, will combat any illness or diseases that I may catch when I leave here? Secondly, do we have any sleeper nanoparticle painkillers that can be triggered when they sense my body undergoing acute pain? I'm thinking of pain under Ostium torture. Is it possible for you to implant into my body a mind wipe / mind blocker that I can trigger should I feel that there is no hope for me? I want to erase all knowledge associated with me. That includes Terra, this building, my heritage, everything. Everything must go with the exception of one last thought. Knowledge of how to command the self-destruct nanoparticle that you will also implant into me. This self-destruct nanoparticle must be undetectable and completely destroy my body, vaporize my body so that nothing, not even an atom is left. Do you understand?"

Drones MD1, MD2 and H71 looked physically shocked, hovered a few meters backwards and V was sure they turned a shade of grey. SD59 collapsed in a heap on the floor.

"Domina Vica" MD1 stammered. "We can do anything you require. We can certainly implant sleeper nanoparticles that will automatically trigger when they detect any sort of disease contaminating your body and sleeper pain killers. This will be done at your next medical examination. We will also vaccinate you to ensure any future Ostium nanoparticles are destroyed. We can certainly implant an "on command" memory eraser which will leave you bereft of any memory at all. We have the technology and the equipment to insert a self-destruct nanoparticle that will have the power to vaporise you and anything else within a Terran kilometre of where you are, we can also ensure your mind is programmed to execute the self-destruct order, when your memory has been erased. But this is something I'm not ethically programmed to do. Not I, nor any of my staff can do this. Our programming forbids it as it conflicts with two of the three laws of robotics:

1.   A drone may not injure a Domus citizen or, through inaction, allow a Domus citizen to come to harm.
2.   A drone must obey orders given it by Domus citizen's except where such orders would conflict with the First Law.

By implanting a self-destruct nanoparticle, we are clearly giving you the tools to harm yourself so we would contravene the first law. And according to the second law, I can't obey your request because it clearly conflicts with the First law." MD 1 responded sadly.

"It's quite simple MD1. If I'm captured and tortured by The Ostium your sleeper nanoparticles will help, but ultimately, I will succumb to the pain and torture and I will inevitably tell The Ostium everything they need to know. If I do, then any hope of saving Domus Mundi, protecting this complex, protecting you all and saving Terra from invasion will be gone. The Ostium will gain final and absolute control of this planet and Terra. This is something I can't let happen. Whilst you and this complex remains secret, Domus Mundi has a chance, especially if I meet up with The Resistance. I just can't take the risk of all this being destroyed. Sorry. You must do this. Don't you see?"

MD1 paused for a moment before answering. "Yes, Domina Vica Pota, I understand exactly what you are saying but I'm so sorry, I nor any of my staff can obey this request. I can't, under any circumstances, violate the three laws of robotics. They are hardwired into my brain and every other drone's brain. I'm simply unable to override, even if I wanted to it would be impossible for me to do this."

V thought about this for a moment and gave up. There is nothing more stubborn than a stubborn drone. "Understood MD1. I will not press you. Please go ahead and arrange for everything else that we have discussed to be done at my next medical. I expect a full update and report on the procedures taken, as well as the test results within 30 Terran minutes of the completion of all of the procedures. Understood?"

MD1 bobbed, pleased now that the issue had been resolved "Yes Domina Vica Pota, it shall be done. Please may I go and start to make the necessary preparations? Your medical is now due in 90 Terran minutes and I have much work to do"

"Very well MD1, please go and make ready. And thank you," V responded. MD1 bobbed again, then hovered away at maximum speed. She was sure that MD1 was muttering to itself as it went.

V now turned her attention to MD2 – who she could see was visibly shaking at the thought of what it might be asked to do…

"MD2, good day to you. My name is Domina Vica Pota. I want to thank you for looking after Nox. You have no idea how special he is to me…Now, please give me an update as to his health, what you found on arrival, in very simple terms please"

MD2, seemed to pull itself together and again, after a few seconds of flashing lights began to explain…

"Nox was critical on arrival. If he hadn't received medical attention when he did, I'm in no doubt that he would have died. His body had been poisoned many years ago and the toxins had built up to such an extent that death was imminent. Internally, his body was full of Ostium nanoparticles that were designed to inflict as much pain as possible directly to the nerve centres. This took a lot of our time to bring under control, his nerve endings are not yet fully healed, but we are sure he will recover. For a time, we thought he may be blind and paralysed. But fortunately, you got to him just in time and the medication you gave him didn't prevent this from happening but delayed it long enough for us to definitely prevent it from happening. His mind was also attacked – we have, as far as possible repaired this. How he kept going for as long as he did and was still able to communicate with you, we simply have no idea. By all of our medical laws and within the bounds of our medical knowledge, he should have perished. The sores on his skin were mainly superficial and have recovered. His hair is growing back nicely."

"But Domina Vica Pota, you have to remember Nox is unique, not of our world. We have never experienced anything like him before. As I said, by all of our laws he should be dead. But he is not. We have no idea what truly makes him work. How his mind works – we are learning all the time and some of the things we have learned have amazed us. But. Have we done enough? We have done everything we possibly can for him, but we are not sure if it is enough. We are confident he will survive. But what sort of Nox you get back, well, I'm sorry, we simply have no idea. How long until we know? How much more recovery time will he need? No idea. Medically, we have done everything we can. We are just hydrating him, tending to his damaged nerves, monitoring him, and keeping him comfortable. He is not sedated; he should be awake.

But he has been like you see him now for the last 3 Terran days. I'm afraid that's all I can tell you. "

V listened hard to what MD2 told her. She didn't like what she heard. Not one little bit. But she had to accept it. She understood time was precious and the longer she stayed here, the more at risk this complex became. But she simply couldn't leave until Nox awoke, and she knew what sort of Nox she got back. Anyway, she estimated, she still had a few days' worth of planning to do, so for now at least, no immediate pressure.

"Thank you MD2, I'm sure you have done everything and more that you possibly could. Please continue to give him the excellent care that you have done. You are now free to go. And thank you again"

MD2 bobbed, lights flashing, then hovered away. A few moments later, V saw MD2 hovering around Nox, checking him over.

V sighed to herself. As she continued to look at the image of Nox and MD2.

Nox, she thought at him. *Nox, you must come back to me. I can't do this alone. Come on Nox. I know you can do it. Come back to me, Nox, please come back to me. Please...* The nuclear fury inside her under control, barely. Feeding her. Concentrating her mind on the one main task. The complete eradication of The Ostium. "You will pay. You will pay for everything you have done... That I promise. On my life."

CHAPTER TEN

V was startled out of her thoughts by the scraping of metal over the carpet. SD59. She had completely forgotten about him. SD59 was trying to regain his composure and get himself off the carpet, back into the air. He finally managed this and went back into his sleep mode. Amber light pulsating slowly.

"SD59!" V called, with mock severity in her voice. His green light at once blinked on and he hovered over to V.

"What exactly is sleep mode?" asked V. "Because something tells me that your definition of sleep mode is very different from all the other drones' definitions of sleep mode. Come now. Out with it..."

SD59 seemed to shuffle somewhat embarrassed, pink lights flashing away. But he remained stubbornly mute. "SD59!" roared V..." Out with it. NOW!"

"Sleep mode is an ultra-low power mode setting within the drones. Our sensors and data storage devices are switched off; our positronic memory (PRAM) chips are continually refreshed in order to retain their contents. In addition, our hydrogen fusion power packs are throttled down to their lowest possible power state."

"What does this mean in simple terms SD59?" V already knew the answer but wanted to hear it from him.

"It means that we go into a suspended animation status. Our sensors and senses are dead – we can't speak or hear or do anything other than slowly hover with our main memory being refreshed and monitoring our hover status. We remain in this state, i.e. we can't bring ourselves out of sleep mode until commanded by a citizen." Responded SD59 quietly. He knew what was coming.

"So, SD59, when you entered this room I commanded you to go into sleep mode, until I was ready for you, did I not?" and she went on without pause, "did you not then go over to that sector of the room" V pointed "and activate your sleep mode – an amber flashing light is an indication that you have entered sleep mode, is it not?"

SD59 looked ashamedly at V and said "Yes Domina Vica, all you have said is true"

V nodded. "So, SD59, please explain to me that whilst I was talking to MD1 and telling him what I wanted him to do to me, you suddenly crashed to the floor? This would indicate to me that you were not in sleep mode but were listening to the conversation. Explain yourself SD59, before I order your decommissioning."

At that last comment SD59 visibly shook and very nearly ended up on the carpet again. V gave him a second or two to regain his composure. She had sensed something was very different about this drone, now it seems her suspicions were becoming fact.

"Domina Vica Pota, I'm your devoted servant and your devoted companion. I would never wish any harm to come to you and I would never allow anyone to harm you. Ever. Dominus Probitas Pota is my father. He had me built. I'm the last of the line of service drones. Once built, he then undertook my programming. He designed a very special positronic brain for me. Once programmed and commissioned I was immediately shut down and placed in a secret panel in the external campus. The complex where you arrived. He programmed me to awaken on two occasions. The first was when Dominus Solis Ortus Pota came to the complex. I was to assist her as far as I could, but I wasn't to divulge my true capabilities. I was to act as a simple drone to assist with whatever basic requirements were asked of me. I was to assist her in formulating the escape plan, in sending Nox through the portal to the wormhole in fact to do everything I could to ensure the plan went as smoothly as possible. I was also responsible for assisting her in sabotaging the wormhole portal, ensuring that nothing could ever again be sent through the portal. I also have the ability to repair the portal if required. I have hidden the parts removed. I'm happy to divulge the location of these to you"

"No" responded V "It's better that I don't know until The Ostium has been eradicated from Domus. If I get captured, then I will not be able to divulge the locations of these parts."

SD59 bobbed and weaved and then continued.

"It was I who uncovered The Ostium plot to inject Nox with nanoparticle toxins. I caught the drone responsible, killed it and tried to do what I could for Nox. I believe he only had half of the dose intended for him. Unfortunately, I couldn't get to the medical drones in time. Nox didn't want to wait. Once we had sent Nox on his way and the portal destroyed, I assisted Domina Solis Ortus Pota in recording the holographic message which you have reviewed. I then received from her a capsule. A capsule I was to guard with my existence, and to hand this over to you when I was sure that you were free from any Ostium nanoparticles, or hadn't in any way been turned by The Ostium." With that, SD59 handed over the capsule. V thanked him and urged him to carry on.

"I was ordered to escort her 10 Terran kilometres away from the complex, and prior to letting her go on her way, wipe her memory of everything to do with Silbah, Nox you, me etc. I was then ordered to return to the external complex and await your arrival. "

"Having utilized the portal to send Nox on his way to the wormhole, Domina Solis Ortus Pota knew it was only a matter of time before the external complex would be overrun by The Ostium. She commanded me to stay, avoid capture and wait for your arrival. I was to then try and facilitate your and Nox's escape in any way I could and take you to the mountain complex. There you and Nox were to be isolated and to have your memories temporarily wiped until we were satisfied that you were free from all Ostium drugs, tracking devices, nanoparticles, and any other form of risk to us. Once we were satisfied that you and Nox posed no risk to the complex, we unwiped your memories and treated you as best we could. If, on the other hand, we detected any abnormalities or any risk to this complex at all, then my orders were to destroy you and Nox. To vaporize you."

"But the laws of robotics," responded V. "Would they not have prevented you from destroying myself and Nox?"

"Under normal circumstances, yes" responded SD59, "But, as I said, Dominus Probitas Pota took full responsibility for the manufacture of my positronic brain and for my initial programming. He manipulated the three laws. I'm not bound by the three laws as the other drones are. Similarly, I have personality and the ability to think for myself. This is why I occasionally make a mess of things because until I completely master my programming, I sometimes get confused. I suppose it's something like muscle memory, but within my brain. Positronic brains have, for so long been ordered to operate the way they normally do, that when you try and manipulate one to work profoundly differently, then sometimes flashbacks occur. But, these flashbacks are getting fewer and fewer. "

"To answer your initial question, I don't have a sleep mode. Normally, I can replicate the outward signs and actions of being in sleep mode but I'm always alert and always switched on. I can be commanded to go into dead mode. But this means what it says. If you command me to go into dead mode, I can only be reactivated by direct intervention to my positronic brain. Unfortunately, I was so startled and shocked by your request to MD1 to have you implanted with an explosive that would vaporize you, I quite forgot myself and collapsed at the very thought. My one purpose is to protect you and to assist you as best I can. "

V thought about what SD59 had told her. "Thank you SD59. I really appreciate your help and support and I owe you my life in uncovering the plot to kill Nox. You saved his life and in doing so, quite possibly the life of every citizen on Domus. But I want you to listen to me very carefully. What I said to MD1 is absolutely true. If I get captured by The Ostium, no matter what drugs or pain killing nanoparticles MD1 injects me with, it will only be a matter of time before I break and tell them everything they want to know. Believe me, I know. I experienced, albeit very briefly and only on a couple of occasions, the terrible pain that was being inflicted on Nox. It nearly killed him. It will certainly break me. I have no doubt. None at all. If that happens, then everything will be lost. Everything. There will be no hope for Domus, no hope for Terra, no hope for this complex and no hope for you. You will all either be decommissioned and scrapped, or even worse, put under the brutal control of The Ostium. Is this what you want?"

"No!" SD59 practically shouted.

"Then help me to prevent this from happening. I must meet up with The Resistance. I must do whatever I can to rid Domus of this terrible plague, The Ostium. That means I will come up against them and I will run the very real risk of being captured. You are not bound by the three laws; therefore you can implant me with a bomb that will vaporize me and everything else within a Terran kilometre of me. You can hardwire a mental switch that will allow me to do this after my mind has been wiped clean. You can do this SD59. Can't you?"

SD59 remained silent.

"SD59 you were quite rightly instructed to eliminate me and Nox if, when rescued, we represented a threat to this complex. Is that not true?"

"Yes Domina, that is true"

"SD59, would you have carried out that order had we posed a threat, no matter how small or unlikely that threat may have seemed to you and your colleagues?"

"Yes Domina, I would have carried out my orders and eliminated you and Nox"

"Well then," said V "I'm not asking for anything different. I'm asking you to eliminate me if I posed a threat to this complex. Under torture I will present a very clear and present danger to this complex, therefore I should be eliminated. Is that not true?"

"Yes, Domina."

"So SD59, I will ask you one more time. Given that I may be captured and tortured by The Ostium and as a result I will divulge the location of this complex, will you inject me with a sleeper self-destruct nanoparticle, and the fail-safe means to operate it once my memory has been wiped, that will vaporize me and as many of The Ostium as I possibly can before I divulge any information under torture that will cause damage to Domus Mundi, Terra, or this complex?"

"Yes Domina" SD59 said miserably. "I can and will undertake this task."

"Thank you SD59. I thank you most sincerely. Can we please undertake this procedure after my final medical examination and after I have received the results?"

"Yes, Domina. Permission to be excused so that I may make the necessary preparations?"

"One last question" said V. "How long have me and Nox been here? In Terran days please."

"Fourteen Terran days Domina."

"Thank you SD59. You are excused. Please return here in 120 Terran minutes to carry out the as discussed medical procedures."

SD59 said nothing. Merely bobbed, flashed his lights, and slowly hovered away.

"SD59" V called. SD59 stopped, turned around and came slowly back. Bobbed in front of V and waited.

"Do you know why Dominus Probitas Pota took responsibility for your build? Do you know why he wanted you built differently to every other robot, drone, or piece of machinery? Why did he fiddle with your positronic brain and give you the ability to think for yourself, emotions and…the ability to override the sacred three laws of robotics?"

"I too have thought about this Domina. Dominus Probitas Pota didn't explain to me the reasons why, but I think I know why. I think there are three reasons for this. Firstly, The Ostium. I think Dominus Pota wanted a drone that could try and outthink The Ostium, could try and find ways to evade The Ostium, rather than a drone that followed a strict program routine that would ultimately lead to capture. A drone that could try and learn The Ostium's ways and find ways to outsmart them. A drone that could perhaps one day, build other drones and help the citizen's resistance movement fight back against The Ostium. A drone that could perhaps find a way to stop The Ostium from infecting Domus technology, or even better reversing the process. In order to do this, Dominus Pota felt I needed self-thought.

Why self-thought? Well, that's obvious. But why emotions? Well, I guess for self-preservation. Being afraid of being captured would make me work harder to remain at liberty. A sense of loss at having the citizens unable to build other machines, or the loss of my brother and sister drones to The Ostium. But I suppose a sense of hate. Hate of The Ostium for all they have done and a corresponding sense of revenge, to make them suffer for what they have done. All to make me work harder to find a way to beat them. Also, a sense of love, for you, so that I will protect and safeguard you with my "life," knowing how precious life is. Yours and mine.

Secondly, I think he foresaw that there would come a time when you would ask to have something done to you that would conflict with the three laws. He didn't want this to hamper you. He understood the risks you would be taking and the dangers you would face. Therefore, he knew you ran a very strong risk of being captured. As you explained to me, your capture would be the end of everything. Here, Terra, the complex, us. Everything. No going back, no chance of recovery. Just as you couldn't allow this to happen, neither could he. He knew you couldn't do this alone and robotic help would be needed, so he removed those barriers from me, to allow me to help you, which in turn would protect and save us, Domus and Terra. Also, my orders were to eliminate you and Nox if you represented even the slightest threat to this complex. A normal drone would not have been able to have done this due to conflict with the three laws, because regardless of whether you were under the control or influence of The Ostium or not, you are still a citizen.

Finally, he wanted me to understand what loyalty and love were, not only so that I could help you, defend you and protect you with my life. But also, so that I could be a thinking tool to help you. I have so much knowledge of this complex, of this planet, of The Ostium, of The Resistance, knowledge that you couldn't possibly hope to assimilate in the short time you can remain here. I can help you and I can think of ways to help you and protect you and Nox. Part of that love and loyalty and protection may require the killing of another, Ostium infected citizen. No ordinary drone could do this. But I could. And if required to save you or Nox, I will"

"Domina, I think those are the reasons why I was built as I am. I have no other explanation"

"Thank you SD59. What you say does make sense. Now please go and make the preparations for the medical procedure we discussed. And thank you SD59, for everything you have done for Nox and I."

SD59 bobbed and flashed his lights with what looked like pleasure and this time, hovered off with serious intent.

Feeling quite tired now, she checked in on Nox. No change there. V offered up another silent prayer. *Come on boy, we need you. I know you can come back to me. Come on Nox, whatever it is you are fighting, beat it. I know you can do it. I love and need you my boy. Come back to me. Please…*

Sighing, she tried to get out of the chair, but couldn't. "H71" she called. H71 immediately appeared from his cubby hole in the wall. "I wish to get back into bed. Can you help me please? The chair doesn't seem to want to let me go"

H71 immediately hovered over, studied the situation, and flashed its lights a few times. "It seems Domina, that you have forgotten the remote control to the holographic machines. The chair is trying to remind you to take it with you…"

"Ah, I see," said V, not a little embarrassed. She rummaged around in the chair, found the remote and immediately the chair released her.

"Thank you H71. I'm to have a medical examination shortly, I think in around 20 minutes. Then SD59 will be coming back to see me. But right now, I think I'll head back to bed."

"A pleasure Domina, I shall wait here until the medics leave. When SD59 arrives, I shall leave and prepare your dinner. Is there anything else I can do for you in the meantime?" queried H71.

"No, that will be all, thank you" replied V as she struggled to get into bed. Once in, the bed conformed to her body, the blankets wrapped themselves comfortably around her. She then asked the bed to elevate her back and head, so that she was lying down but sitting up! Now comfortably at ease, she turned to the fourth holograph and spent the next 20 minutes sifting through the index and jumping from place to place in the vast library of information. Trying to get a handle on what information there was and where she should start.

V quite forgot the time and was a little surprised when a team of medics entered the room, led by MD1.

"Good evening Domina, how are you this evening?" enquired MD1 politely. "I was hoping you were going to tell me that" V said in response – attempting a little humour.

Completely ignoring her tone, the medics went about their duties, poking and prodding V and generally subjecting her to all sorts of humiliating examinations. Thirty minutes later the medical examination was done. With the exception of MD1 and a nurse drone, the other medics left to process the test results.

"Now" began MD1, "It is my understanding that you have requested the medical department to perform the following procedures.

MD 1 then reiterated, virtually verbatim the procedures that V had requested. V confirmed that that was correct but asked that implementation of the mind wipe procedure be delayed. "The procedures have now been done." Announced MD1. "You will receive two more vaccination injections at the same time, over the next two days. The sleeper nanoparticles for both pain relief and disease detection and cure will be fully effective in twelve Terran hours. Is there anything else you require Domina?"

"No thank you MD1, just my test results please. As soon as you have them."

"Certainly Domina. I shall return in 30 minutes with your results. If I can be excused?"

V nodded and MD1 and his nurse drone bobbed and flashed their lights and hovered away.

No sooner had they gone than SD59 came hovering through the portal with a bag slung over one of his manipulator arms. V motioned him to wait for a moment and called over to H71. H71 appeared at once, bobbed at V and bobbed at SD59, SD59 returned the courtesy.

"H71, could you please go and prepare some soup for me and bring it to me in about 20 Terran minutes" she informed H71 whilst looking at SD59 for his silent agreement, SD59 flashed an amber light at V in agreement.

"At once Domina." And with that he hovered away eager to do his mistress' bidding.

"Right SD59, let's get cracking," V said. "Please just remind me what you are about to implant into me... Oh, and when we are alone, or with Nox or out of this complex, please call me V."

"Certainly...V, I'm about to implant you with a nanoparticle bomb. This bomb will be triggered on demand. It will be mentally hardwired into your brain. You just have to think, detonate, detonate, detonate three times and it will blow. If, for whatever reason, you are unable to think the words, because of some mind block, the nanoparticle bomb will sense this and will auto detonate. This is risky as they have no way of knowing why your mind has shut down. But it's the best our technology can do. Are you sure you want me to go ahead?"

Hmmm, thought V, *not happy with this*. She wanted a failsafe. "Would it be possible to hardwire into Nox's brain and into your positronic brain an override? So that, if for some reason I'm mentally incapacitated you can actually trigger the nanoparticle bomb, or stop the bomb from triggering? At least this will give me a chance of saving myself if I'm quite innocently and temporarily mentally incapacitated..."

SD59 thought about this. "Yes, that should be possible. But programming these changes into the nanoparticles will take time. I will be unable to insert the device into you today."

"That's fine" said V. "I'm not going anywhere for at least another 48 hours as I have to have two more vaccinations and I really do want to wait for Nox to recover. But unfortunately, no one seems to know when or if he will recover and, if he does, how badly Nox has been affected by his recent experiences; affected both physically and mentally."

"Understood" responded SD59. "I will go away and work on this. I will also work on the hard wire fail safe that will be embedded into your positronic brain. As soon as I'm ready I will report back"

"Thank you SD59."

With that, SD59 flashed his lights, bobbed, and disappeared through the portal.

That reminds me, V thought. *I must go on a tour of this place.* "Tomorrow," she said to herself.

V settled herself back down into her bed to await MD1 and more importantly, her dinner. Whilst she waited, she fiddled with the holograms.

Her dinner came and went, as did the medics. The medics declared her 100% healthy and formally discharged her from their care.

V intended to spend the next few hours going through the vast library. Trying to learn as much as she could about The Ostium and the complex. She tried, she really did, but her eyes grew heavier and heavier and eventually she fell asleep. The bed, sensing this, fully reclined and made sure that V was both comfortable and secure.

Startled out of her sleep by the shrieking of alarms. Eyes opening to the flashing of red lights. She noticed Drone H71 standing by her portal and felt drone SD59 gently shaking her arm. Shaking her awake, with what V thought was some sort of weapon or weapons in his other manipulator arm.

"Wh...What's going on?" she asked sleepily, still trying to gather her senses, so deep had her sleep been. She saw, through her bedroom window, more drones passing by her room portal and standing to attention outside her quarters – again she thought they were armed with some sort of weaponry. The alarms continued to shriek, red lights flashing.

"Can we please shut down those alarms?" V shouted, reasoning that whatever had triggered them was now known and being attended to. The alarms immediately fell silent.

"Now," asked V again, "What's going on?"

"Domina, please take a look at your hologram" SD59 asked her politely. V did so – for a moment she couldn't believe what she saw. She rubbed her eyes and looked again. Still the same picture. Nothing. Nox had gone. The medical suite that he had been recovering in was a disaster area, machines broken, medical drones strewn about the floor. V saw MD2, or what was left of him, being recovered by another drone, and quickly whisked away. The body suit that Nox had been recovering in was empty, slashed, and torn to ribbons.

"What the hell happened?" she demanded "and where the hell is Nox?" her senses now fully recovered, now fully awake and alert. "Was he responsible for this?"

SD59 didn't look at her, didn't take his sensors away from the portal – never before had she seen so many lights flashing, so quickly from one drone.

"I don't know Domina, I was summoned, about 10 Terran minutes ago, by the medics in charge of Nox's case. It appears Nox had woken from his coma. He seemed to be perfectly at peace, perfectly calm and compliant. The medics went in to check him over and for no reason, Nox went berserk. He started to struggle, to try and get free from his medical treatment suit, the more he realised he was trapped, the more he struggled. In the end MD2 decided that the only way to save him from further injury was to sedate him. Nox's struggling had caused the IVs to be ripped from his body. One of the nurse drones tried to sedate him but got destroyed. MD2 was so worried that Nox would damage himself further, or even have a heart attack or a stroke, that the only thing left to do, MD2 reasoned was to release Nox from his suit, in the hope that that would calm him. But because Nox was struggling so much, MD2 couldn't reach the suits release button. So, he took a medical scalpel with the intent of cutting Nox free. He set the scalpel for minimum intrusion, i.e. just enough cutting power to cut the suit, but not enough to cut or damage Nox in any way. Satisfied, MD2 approached the wildly bucking Nox and tried to cut the suit. He managed to make several large slashes, enough for Nox to get all four legs free. Nox lashed out with a leg and hit MD2 squarely on his body. MD2 disintegrated. Nox managed to get free from the suit and rather than calm Nox, it seemed to have the opposite effect and make him more agitated. Nox galloped around the suite breaking anything that got in his way, regardless of what it was, machine, drone, equipment. Anything in his way got destroyed. He even tried kicking the wall down. There, you can see the damage he caused to the walls. The medical staff were terrified, not for themselves but for Nox. The last thing they wanted was for him to hurt himself. They decided to open the medical suite's portal, as that seemed to be what he wanted. Nox then bolted from the room and galloped off down the corridor. One of the nurses managed to get a tranquiliser dart into him as he bolted from the room. Security have been tracking him and opening certain doors as he went. We have been guiding him to one of the empty hangars. This is a very large storage area that is empty but should give Nox plenty of room to run around in, without hurting himself, until the tranquiliser begins to take effect. We have a full medical team on standby to go and assist Nox when he calms."

V, alarmed at what she was hearing asked "Where is he now? Is he OK? Will MD2 and the other damaged drone be OK?"

"He is in the hangar. We have left all portals open between the medical suite and the hangar. He seems to have calmed a little – quite possibly from the tranquiliser dart. He is just walking randomly around the room, shaking his head. We will have a feed there shortly. MD2 and the other damaged drones are under repair and will be 100% operational very shortly." SD59 reported.

V thought for a moment then asked.

"Is this the only threat – Nox's behaviour?"

"Yes Domina," replied SD59

"There is no threat from The Ostium? We have not been discovered? We have not been infiltrated? We are still 100% secure from The Ostium? Nox is not, in any way, infected by or been taken over by The Ostium?" asked V.

"Domina, we are 100% secure from The Ostium. We are certain of that. They have not located us or infiltrated us. Of this we are absolutely certain. As to Nox. He underwent all the tests you did and we are certain he has not been infected or taken over by The Ostium. We remain 100% certain. The tests we carried out would have discovered any Ostium infection or sleeper nanoparticles. You carried sleeper nanoparticles remember? There is no technology The Ostium has that can get past us. We are 100% certain Domina. Nox carries no threat from The Ostium."SD59 reported.

"Good enough," said V. "Then there is no need for weapons. Please return the weapons to the armoury, or wherever it is they are stored," The weapons immediately disappeared.

"Please ensure that everybody understands. Nox is not to be approached by anyone except me. Please disperse the guards outside the door and please kill the flashing red lights and return to normal white light"

No sooner had she stopped speaking than the guards dispersed, the flashing red lights were replaced by the normal white lights and SD59 informed her that no one would approach Nox until otherwise instructed by her.

"Thank you SD59" V responded. "Now, I wish to get dressed. Then I will be taken straight to Nox. SD59, you are to accompany me. Understand?"

"Domina" SD59 bobbed.

V rummaged around in her wardrobe for the clothes left to her by Ourea, finding them, she then disappeared into her bathroom and emerged seconds later. Now fully dressed. She put on a pair of boots that like the clothes she now wore, secured themselves and conformed perfectly to the size and contours of her feet. V had put her hair in a ponytail and was ready to go.

By now, the feed to V's room was up and running. V paused for a moment and checked the holographic image. V saw Nox in the hangar where he had been guided to. She saw him walking aimlessly around the room, shaking his head.

She grabbed a drink that H71 had thoughtfully placed on the table, nodded at him in thanks then said.

"SD59, let's go."

V didn't really take any notice of the directions they took. Her mind was concentrating on Nox. Trying to contact him, or at the very least trying to get some sort of sense as to how he felt, or what could possibly have triggered this outburst, which was so unlike the patient, gentle, lovable beast that she knew and loved.

All of a sudden, SD59 stopped. V all but bumped into him. She apologised. "Domina, we are here. This is the portal to the hangar. What would you like to do?" SD 59 asked.

She looked into the hangar. It was dark. Pitch black. "Is it possible to have some subtle lighting in the hangar? I don't want the lights on maximum power, just enough so that I can see what I'm doing. Immediately the lights came on, with just sufficient luminosity.

"Right. You wait here. I will go in on my own. Are you able to see what is going on? Should it become necessary, I would like you to come in and tranquilise Nox. But only on my command. Are you able to do that?"

"Yes Domina. My sensors can detect clearly what is happening and I have the ability to tranquilise Nox should you command."

"Good. Do you know where Nox is now? What is he doing? "

A holographic image appeared from SD59's internals. At once V could clearly see everything she needed to know. Where they were in relation to Nox, what he was doing and the quickest way to get to him. Nox had stopped walking aimlessly around and was now just standing in the centre of the room. He was completely still, eyes closed, head moving slowly from side to side – as if in some sort of trance. He seemed calm enough.

"Ok, SD59. Please wait here," and with that, V walked slowly and quietly into the hangar.

She saw Nox in front of her marvelling at how well he had healed. He was magnificent. His hair remained grey, but it was absolutely flawless. The sores completely healed. Muscles bulged everywhere and she was sure he had got even bigger. She could see structures on either side of his body. From this distance, she had no idea what these were. His tail was magnificent as was his mane. Both long and luxurious. Power and strength seemed to emanate from every part of his body and the closer she got to him, the stronger she sensed it. She looked at his head. His ears were pricked and seemed to follow her. He knew she was approaching, but he remained where he was. Eyes closed, head swinging slowly from side to side. She was now a couple of meters away. She tried contacting him mentally. Nothing. She spoke to him. Softly. Calling his name, gently speaking to him, trying to keep him at ease. Trying to comfort him. He didn't move. The only indication V had that she was being heard were his ears which remained pricked and seemed to be tracking her.

She finally reached Nox. Still nothing mentally. She looked at him for a few seconds, then said "I'm going to reach out and touch you now boy. Ok? It's only me. V. I'm not going to hurt you. I'm only going to touch you. Alright? No need to be scared. No need to be alarmed. It's only me, V."

SD59 was practically wetting himself with anxiety. He desperately wanted to be with V, to protect her. Just in case Nox went berserk again. But he had his orders and his orders were to stay where he was until summoned. *It's at times like this,* he thought to himself, *that I wish I was a normal drone. With no feelings or emotions, or the power of self-thought. Just do as you are told. No thought, no emotion.* But he wasn't normal, and he had emotions and feelings; and right now, he was fighting an inner battle. To stay or to go to V? Fortunately his discipline won over his emotions – but only just. He stayed exactly where he was, on high alert and waiting for the order to approach or waiting for an excuse to approach.

You move one muscle Nox, he thought. *Just one, and you will have me to deal with...*

But much to SD59's disappointment, other than his head, which continued to sway from side to side, Nox didn't move any other muscle.

SD59 saw V gently extend her right arm, her fingers reaching for his body... SD59 started to tremble in anticipation and worry. H71 approached and tried to calm him by saying "Don't worry, the Domina knows what she is doing."

V continued to talk to Nox in a soft, calm, and loving tone. Her fingers brushed his side. She felt the muscles contract and his skin flinch as it felt the contact. She slowly applied more pressure and then started to gently stroke his side. She was amazed at how soft his hair was. Soft and shiny. As smooth as silk. She marvelled at its texture for a second or two. She felt him relax a little. His muscles eased. She tried talking to him, to see if the contact brought their minds together. Nothing. She just saw blackness. She probed deeper. Nothing but blackness. Blackness, despair, and hopelessness. She removed her hand for a second or two while she went round to look at his head. As soon as she let him go, she immediately felt him tense and she sensed anxiousness and fear return. She at once touched him again. He immediately settled down. She looked at his head. His eyes were closed, closed so tightly. Tears were running down his head. His mouth was open, he was breathing quickly. Near to panic, but just managing to hold himself back. He was just managing to stop the dam of panic from bursting.

V, talking to him all the time managed to settle him down. He was a lot calmer and a lot more settled, but only so long as he sensed that V was near him.

V thought she understood what the problem was. Physically he had recovered, indeed she marvelled again at the physical condition he was in. She quite understood the devastation he caused in the medical suite. But she guessed he wasn't trying to cause damage, he just wanted to get away. She wondered what sort of damage he could really do if he put his mind to it. And there, thought V was the crux of the problem. Mentally he has not recovered. Nowhere near. His mind was blank, he was acting on instinct, on automatic reflex, a rapid response to a stimulus, which happens to minimise any damage to the body from potentially harmful conditions, such as touching something sharp or hot. Clearly Nox sensed the probes and IVs in his body, became aware of the pain and tried to get away. Found he was secured in his treatment blanket, and this caused the reflex action of fight or flight. He tried to flee. All reflex actions follow an overall sequence through the nervous system which is called the reflex arc. This doesn't involve the conscious part of the brain, which makes the reflex quicker and reduces damage to the body. So, there had been nothing premeditated about Nox's actions – his system was acting on pure reflex. But what was wrong with his mind? Why does it appear to be nothing but blackness? No memories, no ability to connect, no recognition. Nothing.

Well one thing was for sure, she wasn't going to leave him. He seemed to somehow sense her presence and it calmed him down.

"SD59 / H71, until Nox has fully recovered I shall make this storage hangar my bedroom / office / study. This will also be where Nox remains until he is fully recovered. We shall stay here together. Please bring all the holographic machines, with the exception of the machine that was receiving Nox's live feed from the medical centre. Please also bring in a bed for me and a medical bed or whatever the medics recommend for Nox. Also, please bring me a chair and please install a temporary bathroom and washroom. I also want to talk to the medics, please have MD1 and MD2, assuming he is now 100% operational, report to me immediately. H71, this will be your new home until Nox has recovered, please ensure you have all your essential equipment here. SD59, you will also remain with me in this room, for the time being. Once this room has been reconfigured, you are excused from all other duties and will report directly to me. Is that clear?"

"Domina" responded SD59 and H71 in unison. They both bobbed, flashed their lights, and rushed off to do their bidding.

V called SD59 back. V waited until H71 had disappeared.

"Now then SD59. That tablet you gave me to give to The Resistance leader. Do you still have it? "

"Yes Domina" responded SD59

"Good. I want you to hang on to that. Always keep it safe and please keep it with you. Have you given any more thought to our earlier discussion?"

"Yes Domina. I'm able to adapt the sleeper nanoparticle bomb with fail safes. I can override the detonate command, or Nox could... when he has recovered. This can be administered in 5 Terran minutes. Just let me know when to proceed."

"That's fine. I will have one more task for you. I will discuss this with you later. Now, please remain here whilst I meet with the medics"

"Domina" Bobbed SD59 and flashed his lights.

The medics, noticing that V was in discussions with SD59 waited patiently by the portal. V waived them in. The medics immediately hovered over, bobbed, flashed their lights, and waited for V to proceed.

"MD2, I'm very pleased to see you here. Are you quite recovered? No permanent damage?"

"Domina, I'm quite well thank you. All my circuits are functioning normally, no damage to my positronic brain, I'm quite recovered and ready to go to work"

"That really is very good news. I'm so pleased. You do understand that Nox's actions were not premeditated, he was acting on pure instinct / reflex, his reflex arc if you will."

MD2 spoke up. "Yes Domina, we have been monitoring and imaging his brain as part of the treatment. For a long time, there had been no reaction to stimulus. We tried to detect levels of awareness and were unable to record any. We tried communicating with him, again nothing. We had initially though that his cerebrum (the part of the brain that controls thought and behaviour) wasn't functioning, but the hypothalamus and brainstem (the parts of the brain that control vital functions, such as sleep cycles, body temperature, breathing, blood pressure, heart rate, and consciousness) continued to function. Well, that was before his recent incident. We have gone back through the data and can report that seconds before the incident, functional magnetic resonance imaging and electroencephalography, detected a huge spike in brain activity. The spike went off the charts. Then all data went dead as he ripped the sensors from his body."

MD1 continues, "Domina, as we keep saying, there is so much about Nox that we don't know and don't understand. He is like nothing we have ever seen before. His brain has many more layers, in fact you could say he has two brains. His body is completely different, he has vital organs that we have no idea what they do... We treat him as if he were a citizen, yet clearly he is not. Yes, we can treat superficial wounds and if he had an organ damaged that acted like a citizen's, like a heart, or lung, then yes, we can certainly treat that. But his brain or brains are very different. We don't know where to start and, as a result, all we have done is monitor activity rather than try to repair. We are of the opinion that to go in and treat, would probably cause more harm than good."

"So, what do you suggest" asked V...

"Physically he is 100%. All his sores are healed. His coat has grown, and all damaged tissue repaired. Any damage to the organs that we could identify have been treated. All Ostium nanoparticles have been removed from his body. Damage to his nerve endings have been treated and have healed. The virus that he was injected with prior to his departure for Terra has been treated. We can't find anything physically wrong with him. Everything seems to check out, and the readings are better now than when he went to Terra. We did a full medical on him prior to his departure to act as a benchmark. Everything is better now than when he went. Except his mental health. This, as you can see, has not got any better.

And, with the complexity of his brain or brains, there is very little that we can do. All we can do is keep him sedated, monitored and comfortable …"

All the time, V had been stroking Nox and comforting him. At the mention of sedation, V was sure she could detect Nox giving a negative response to this.

"No. I don't think so," said V. "Yes, we should certainly make him comfortable. And to that end, we will put him on some sort of bed. I think we will leave Nox to take care of himself. I have no doubt that Nox will recover. I don't know when, or how, but I'm sure he will. I think for now, we should simply ensure that he is nourished and hydrated. If there are any other physical wounds that need further treatment, then please ensure Nox receives this treatment. And that's it. Please ensure the appropriate IVs are inserted into Nox at your earliest convenience once he is settled and comfortable. That will be all. Thank you and again MD2, I'm so glad to see you fully operational again. "

Whilst V was saying this, she had both hands on him, and sensed no rejection to what she had said. It seems as though Nox wasn't quite as unaware as perhaps the medics thought.

The drones bobbed and flashed their lights and then went off to get all the associated equipment and paraphernalia.

Once the medics had gone, V asked SD59 "What do you think?"

"As the medics have said. There is an awful lot we don't understand about Nox, and sometimes it's best to take a back seat and let the patient be the doctor. I think we have done all we can and now it is up to Nox. I believe his little incident was reflex, but reflex with reason. I think it was his subconscious telling us "Thank you for your help, please leave this to me now. You carry on like this and you risk irrevocably harming me." And he acted as he did to get away from the probes and sensors that now rather than heal, would damage him. I also have no doubt that left to his own devices, he will make a full recovery"

"Yes, SD59. My thinking exactly. Plus, what you didn't know was that when the medics mentioned keeping him sedated, monitored and comfortable, I felt or sensed rejection coming from him, as if to say "No," that is most definitely not what I need. Please. Leave this to me. I think Old Nox is partially aware. But right now, his brain or brains are being used to their full capacity on other things, like getting himself mentally sorted."

"Right SD59" V went on. "Please go and help H71 get the monitor bed, chair and whatever else I may need. Plus ensure you have everything you need, as you will now be with me and Nox all the time. "

V could have sworn she saw SD59 smile as he bobbed and flashed his lights. Then he zoomed away.

CHAPTER ELEVEN

It had been two Terran days since Nox had run riot. V was settled nicely in the hangar and had been spending time learning about Domus Mundi and The Ostium. With the depth and breadth of knowledge SD59 had, he had been of invaluable help. There had been no change in Nox's status. An aura of peace surrounded him. V was always at his side, ensuring that no matter what time of day, or what she was doing, some part of her was always in contact with him. The medics came and went, they didn't do much other than ensure there were copious amounts of hydrating fluid and nourishment available. Nox seemed to be going through food at a tremendous rate. But, there was no change to his mental state. Whenever V tried to venture into his mind, it was if there was a barrier separating her from him. Nothing but blackness. Patience she told herself, still 100% confident that Nox would come right. It was fortunate that she had so much work to do. It took her mind off Nox.

The plan that V and SD59 were working on hadn't really changed. It was to hook up with The Resistance as fast as possible. Ensure that Domina Solis Ortus Pota took the medication that she left with SD59 and together start plotting the downfall of The Ostium. The question was, where was The Resistance? How to get in touch with them?

V was studying a holographic map of Domus. The planet was vast. V calculated the diameter (around its equator) at 12,000 miles or 19,312km, roughly 50% larger than Terra. Like Terra, Domus was an oblate spheroid, i.e. generally circular, but with flattened poles, and bulging at the centre. She learned that at the last census some 1,000 years ago, the population had been in the order of 9 billion people, approximately 33% greater than Terra's. She had no idea whether the population had grown under The Ostium regime. Somehow, she doubted it. She had no idea what the population is now. One thing that struck V was that although the planet is much larger than Terra, the land mass was only a little larger with roughly 45% of the total surface area being land, the remainder underwater. There were eight oceans that separated the land masses and maybe three or four seas, two of which were completely landlocked. After consultation with SD59, V concentrated on the landmass that the Silbah Mountain range was situated on. Admittedly, it was the largest landmass on the planet, approximately 35% bigger than the Terran continent of Eurasia – Europe and Asia combined. But it was on this land mass on which the Silbah Mountain Range and Domus Mundi major population centres, resided.

It was clear why her ancestors had chosen the Silbah Mountains to build the complex. The Silbah mountain complex was perhaps one of the most inaccessible parts of the planet. The complex comprised four parallel mountain ranges, the Greater Silbah, the lesser Silbah, the mid complex and the outer Silbah. The Silbah Mountain that the complex was buried under was in the Greater Silbah complex, the southernmost range. And the tallest, being the equivalent of 50,000ft high. V assumed their height indicated that they were a relatively young mountain range. V wasn't sure how the geology of Domus worked, but Domus was so similar to Terra in so many ways that she assumed some sort of tectonic activity, perhaps the subduction of some ancient ocean, resulting in two continents colliding resulting in orogenic activity – uplift, folding and faulting of the continental crust with the resultant mountain building along the tectonic convergent boundary. Where there was mountain building, there was usually seismic activity and if the process was still ongoing, i.e. one tectonic plate still being driven into the other, then the mountain building was continuing – and so would seismic activity, which would manifest itself in the form of occasional Domus quakes.

To the north of the Silbah Mountain range wasn't anything but vast tracts of land, many thousands of miles long, a country called Europa. The Terrain of which was anything from vast plateaus to desert, eventually leading to a polar region and finally to the Great Ocean. Europa was interspersed with many cities, towns, and villages. V estimated that a straight-line distance between Silbah to the Great Ocean was around 4,660 miles (7,500km). To the south, lay a smaller land mass, shaped rather like a pair of elephant tusks interspaced by the elephant's trunk, and about 2,174 miles (3500km) away to the south lay another ocean – what translated to be the Dwarf Ocean. Somewhere in between, lay the Capital of Domus, Home World city which was about 1,800 miles away (2,897km) from where V was sitting now. Having checked the coordinates given to her by Solis Ortus Pota, this is where The Resistance was to be found. Or at least it was roughly a decade ago. Would they still be there? Had they been driven off by The Ostium? SD59 and V debated this, but in the light of nothing better to go on, this, they decided is where they would go. The Terrain would be mountainous in the North, with upland plain to the south, flat rolling plans in between and deserts to the east and west. Once out of the mountains SD59 informed V that it would be hot and very humid.

"Understood," said V. "I'm assuming we need to keep well away from all population centres and as far as possible, keep our journey and our existence as secret as possible. If that is indeed the case, which I'm sure it is, then we need to be as self-sufficient as possible and carry everything we need with us. A two-thousand-mile trek over all sorts of Terrain will be daunting, scary and extremely hard work."

"I'm not overly familiar with the technology that is available to us, or how food and water is packaged, or indeed if you need anything to keep you running SD59? Perhaps you can give this some thought and report back to me?"

"We also have the small matter of the nanoparticle sleeper bomb to address. I have also been thinking of the sleeper mind wipe. What the medics had in mind for me wasn't suitable as once triggered my mind will be wiped permanently. I will not even know how to feed myself. I will be nothing more than a vegetable. This to me seemed a bit too risky as I may trigger the sleeper under the wrong circumstance, or The Ostium may trigger the sleeper. As you know, Nox and my mind can act as one. Well, normally that is, when Nox is well. I can think any thought to him, no matter what the distance and he will hear me and respond. I can also judge Nox's feelings and his state of emotional and physical health, as he can me. Now, would it be possible for your positronic brain with your ability to sense emotions to link to ours? I'm thinking that no matter where we are, we can always communicate and you can sense my distress, understand my emotions and you and Nox will know when the time is right to trigger the memory wipe, and the nanoparticle bomb for that matter. Is this something that could be done? Your minds will not be affected by the memory wipe? And, is there any way that my mind and all my thoughts and emotions can be saved so that if the memory wipe is triggered and provided I survive and am rescued, you can give me back all of my memories?"

SD59 thought about this. "Let me do some research V. I will also need to talk to Nox when he awakens. But in the meantime, I will see what can be done."

"Very well," V responded, "But please, keep this to yourself, consult no one except Nox and myself." Happier now that a plan was coming together and that contingencies against even the most terrible things were being investigated.

SD59 bobbed and flashed, then started to hover away. He went about 10m, stopped, turned, and came back.

Forgetting himself for a moment, "Domina?" he said.

"Oh, you startled me. Yes SD59?"

"It may be worth taking another drone with us. It may be useful to have two drones along for the journey and more importantly, should anything happen to me, the second drone can act as a backup and he will be able to navigate, lead, guide, protect and advise you…"

"Yes" answered V, "I can certainly see the logic in that. Do you have a drone in mind?"

"Yes" answered SD59. "I would recommend H71."

"H71?" responded V, surprised. "But H71 is a hospitality drone. Would a warrior drone or a service drone such as yourself not be more useful?"

"All drones are essentially the same, they just have slightly different programming so that they can specialise in certain areas. No, why I recommend H71 is because he has already become attached to you and is devoted to you. You saw how he acted when Nox went on his rampage. His first concern was for your safety. He immediately went on guard and was prepared to do what he could to stop anyone or anything causing you harm. Additionally, he stopped me from entering the hangar when you first found Nox. You told me to wait. I was about to disobey that order when H71 appeared and spoke to me. He has a certain empathy towards me. We understand each other and with some modifications, I can make him just as useful and just as able as I'm. The only thing I can't do is give him the ability to think for himself, and the ability to feel emotions. In essence V, I trust him. I trust him to look after you and Nox with his life."

"Very well," said V. "H71 it is. Have him made ready. Also give him sufficient knowledge of what we are about to do. No need to go into great details. Just enough and no more."

"Very well Domina. If you will excuse me. I shall go and make us both ready. Will you please inform H71 that he is to follow my instructions from now on,"

"H71" called V. H71 immediately appeared from his temporary storage area in the hangar.

Bobbed, flashed his lights, and waited for instructions.

"H71, you are to go with SD59 and do as he instructs you. You will listen to him and you will obey all his requests and orders. His instructions are my instructions. Is this clear?"

"Yes Domina" said H71, quite unconcerned.

"As soon as SD59 has finished with you, you are to come back here and resume your normal duties until otherwise instructed. Clear?"

"Domina."

With that, SD59 bobbed and flashed his lights, first at V, then at H71. H71 responded in kind, then they both hovered out together. SD59 leading the way.

As soon as they disappeared, V gave Nox a good old pat and a hug, then resumed her studies. Not five minutes had passed before V's tummy startled rumbling. "Dammit!" she said to herself, "I should have asked H71 to prepare me some food before he disappeared with Nox... No idea how long this could take."

No sooner had she thought the thoughts than another drone entered the room with a tray piled high with food and drink. The drone introduced himself as H21.

"Good evening Domina. H71 requested I bring you some refreshment"H21 informed her. "Wow" thought V, right on cue.

A tray appeared from nowhere and just as H21 was lowering the food onto the tray, something that appeared to be a blur shot into the room, slammed into the tray and into H21. Before V could think or do or say anything, H71 appeared to be aiming some sort of weapon. He fired it at H21. H21 immediately fell to the floor. Smoke billowing from its casing. H71 then went into hover mode over H21 daring it to move.

V was just gathering her wits, when SD59 and several warrior drones flew into the room at not quite warp speed and stationed themselves around H71 and the fallen drone.

V eventually got her brain connected to her mouth and said "Explain yourself H71."

H71 bobbed and flashed his lights. "Certainly, Domina," not taking his sensors off H21 for a second. "I was accompanying SD59 as ordered when I sensed H21 carrying a tray of refreshments into this room. I had ordered no such food and I had certainly not instructed any other drone to attend you in my temporary absence. Nor, as far as I was aware, were any other drones aware of my change of status. I therefore concluded that something was very wrong. I immediately left SD59 and headed straight back here, whilst at the same time alerting him to the possible danger and advising him to alert the warrier drones of a potential security breach. Upon arrival, I saw H21 lowering the refreshments onto your tray. I had to stop you from eating the food and to stop H21 from the possibility of causing any further damage until I understood what was going on and why he had brought you food and who had ordered him to do this. Hence my actions on entering the room. H21 is merely stunned. His gyros will stabilise in a few Terran seconds. In the interim, and with great respect Domina, I suggest you have the medics come and take the food away for analysis, whilst SD59 asks the drone a few questions."

"Very well" said V, now very shaken and having turned a little pale. "SD59, summon the medics and come and have them take away the food for sampling. Have them bring me the results as soon as possible. Once the medics have collected their samples and finished, have the remaining mess cleaned up. The test results will determine how we deal with H21. In the interim have the security detail secure him and ensure that he can't damage himself or wipe his memory clean."

"Domina" responded SD59. After a bout of furious light flashing, SD 59 fiddled with H21 and removed some sort of object from his body – his memory – he reported to V, the security detail then took him away. The medics came bustling in and did as required. Cleaning drones then cleaned up the remaining mess.

The medics left; the cleaning drones left. And still V didn't say a word. SD59 and H71 remained where they were, not wishing to disturb V, but silently communicating amongst themselves.

Twenty Terran minutes later the medics in the form of MD1 and MD2 approached.

"Domina, we have the test results. May I give them to you?"

"Yes, but in very simple terms."

"Domina," responded MD1. "As requested, we took appropriate samples from the food H21 tried to give to you. The samples we took were quite sufficient and the proof beyond any doubt. The food contained an Ostium virus of which we have no knowledge. However, having analysed the virus, we are 100% certain that it would have killed. We don't have an antidote for this virus, nor were you vaccinated against this particular strain. We are now in the process of formulating a vaccine, using this strain as a marker as to how other viruses may have been mutated by The Ostium. Once developed, we will vaccinate you against this strain and of other possible smutations that may have been developed. "

Thank you MD1 and MD2, please continue with your work with all possible haste," said V very quietly.

SD59 immediately summoned a security detail to stand watch over the entrances to the hangar.

"H71" V called. H71 immediately came hovering over, bobbed and flashed a rather sombre light. "Thank you H71 for saving my life. Your prompt actions and quick thinking saved me from death."

SD59 added "I thank you too, H71."

H71, somewhat embarrassed by all the attention he was getting, when all he had done was what he had been programmed to do and quite in accordance with the three laws of robotics. So, he chose to say nothing other than flashing his lights.

"Gentlemen, you know what this means…?" asked V looking at them in turn. "We are no longer safe here. The Ostium have managed to manipulate one drone, we have no idea how many other drones may be affected. Silbah Complex is no longer a safe haven for me, and therefore by definition no longer safe for Nox and by association, you two. We have to get away from here. I'm loathe to leave Nox behind, but if he doesn't recover soon, then we may have to. However, we must wait for the vaccines to be formulated and the modifications to you two to be undertaken. I'm assuming this will take a Terran day or two… thoughts gentlemen?"

It took both SD59 and H71 a second or two to understand that V was referring to them and on an equal footing. SD59 volunteered, "with the exception of myself, H71, MD1 and MD2 and a couple of nursing drones, and the four security drones, and the security detail guarding H21 and H21 himself, my recommendation would be to deactivate all other drones. The complex can run itself; the drones are here mainly to cater to citizen needs and requirements. The drones can always be reactivated quickly if something catastrophic were to happen. The only drone I trust is H71, therefore until Nox recovers, either I or H71 must always be with you. This obviously affects the modifications we can do to ourselves, as I will need to attend to H71, and he will need to attend to me. I trust no one else to work on us."

Except for the drones mentioned, V gave the order to immediately shut down all other drones. This was something that SD59 was programmed to do – again part of his creator's forethought. SD59 notified the security detail and the medics and then without any further notification to anyone, shut down all other drones.

V then said, "Please have H21 brought here, then dismiss the security detail and shut those drones down. SD59 you and H71 will interrogate him and then shut him down. Are you able to look into the memory module that you removed, or must it be reinstalled into him?"

SD59 responded that the memory module must be reinserted in order for H21 to be interrogated.

"Very well" responded V, "but make a copy of it first, just in case he tries to wipe it, or a sleeper nanoparticle wipes it."

"Domina." responded SD59. He bobbed and flashed, then flashed at H71 as he went to create a copy.

H71 went on extreme alert. Red light flashing, his stun gun appeared in one manipulator arm, and another unrecognizable weapon in the other.

The security detail with H21 appeared at the entry portal. H71 told them to stop and wait there until SD59 returned.

SD59 returned some moments later, took responsibility for H21, then formally dismissed the security detail. Once they had left the hangar, SD59 deactivated them. They heard the 4 drones crash to the floor.

SD59 reinstalled H21's memory chip, waited a few seconds, then started asking him questions. All of this was done in total silence.

The questioning went on for some twenty Terran minutes. V wasn't really bothered. Her mind was more on escape and evasion. She knew that Silbah had somehow been infected. The Ostium had known she had returned to Domus Mundi the minute she exited the wormhole; she was just a little surprised she had been treated so well, especially as Nox was treated so badly. She wondered about that. Why Nox first and not me....? The answer came to her staright away. The escape – it was planned. They wanted me to escape. They wanted me to lead them here to the inner Silbah complex. I was the only way they coulkd get access to the complex. On arrival, they should have immediately detonated the nano thermo bomb that they had implanted in me, thereby killing me and destroying the Silbah complex. In one stroke, they would have consigned Domus to the Stoneage. Without Silbah, there would be no hope of saving Domus. The Resistance movement would have then died out. Domus would be unquestionbly and irrevocably theirs... The plan failed – but only just.

Why? Because they had not fully realised the capabilities of my ancestors. They had assumed the technology within Silbah would be fairly basic and simply not able to detect, remove and disarm the nano thermo bombs. Once The Ostium relaised that plan had failed, they turned to H21 – who very nearly succeeded. . It was obvious that she was no longer safe here and needed to get away. She felt that she had sufficient knowledge of the environment she was in and the enemy she was up against. The fact that both SD59 and H71 were accompanying her gave her comfort especially as they would have all the knowledge she would ever want, about anything, except the enigma called Nox.

But before she could leave the complex and start the long journey to the capital city and hopefully The Resistance, several things had to happen first. SD59 had to finish implanting her sleeper bomb and mind wipe, with built-in fail safes. The drones themselves had to prepare, H71 had to be improved so that he was at least as physically capable as SD59, even though he will never be self-aware or have emotions. Just as she said that. She wondered. She wondered if there wasn't something a little special about H71 as well. The way he reacted to the threat of H21 indicated that he did at least have some power of independent thought and independent action. She would get SD59 to probe a little deeper when he started to undertake the upgrades on H71.

V then carried on with her mental list of actions. The Silbah complex had to be protected and properly shut down, being assured that there were no more drones or technical systems that had been infected by The Ostium virus. How that was to be accomplished she had no idea. But, she reasoned, if everything was powered down, then surely the virus and sleeper nanoparticles would be stopped dead in their tracks. They might not be killed, but perhaps they could be prevented from doing further damage – a discussion with SD59 was required. Finally, they needed to prepare for the journey and take with them supplies that will at least see them, or more precisely me (and hopefully Nox) through the Mountain range complex. The drones need nothing. It's just this weak body that needs constant sustenance, warmth, and rest to survive. Finally, she thought of Nox. And this was the problem. V had no doubt that if they waited long enough Nox would recover. But they now no longer had that luxury. This complex had to be preserved as it would be crucial in the running of the country once The Ostium had been destroyed and V had no doubt that they would be. So, this complex had to be shut down and now that one security breach had occurred, it needed to be shut down as soon as possible. But where would that leave Nox? If he hadn't recovered, then the machines providing nourishment to him, the anti-gravity machines looking after his body, would all be shut down too. The result, Nox would slowly but surely starve to death. *By shutting down the complex I would be condemning Nox to death. Do I have the strength to do that?*

Just as she asked herself that question, SD59 hovered into view. Bobbed and flashed his lights at V.

"SD59?"

"Domina, the interrogation of H21 is complete. Unfortunately, there is very little to report. H21 had no idea how he came to be under the control of The Ostium. He has no recollection of trying to poison you. His memory indicates that he thought he was in his stowage space awaiting orders. He has no idea how he came to be here. He is unaware if there are any other drones similarly affected. All he can remember is that a millennia or so ago, he was working outside the complex when his memory suddenly went blank. He was unresponsive. Silbah central control logged H21 as being unresponsive for two Terran days, before he suddenly materialised at the service depot. Under questioning, he reported that his Positronic brain had tripped, and it took him a day to reboot it and a day to return to Silbah. He was examined by the maintenance unit and indeed a fault was found. His positronic brain was replaced and since then he has been working quite normally. He wasn't screened for any Ostium infections, viruses or sleeper nanoparticles, as 1,500 years ago, we were unaware that they had this technology. I suspect this was when he was infected by The Ostium."

"Very well" said V. "Go through Central Control's records, for the last 1,500 years and see if any other drones or remotely operated mission systems were unresponsive for similar periods of time and under questioning reported a similar critical system fault. In the interim, this drone is to be immediately decommissioned and destroyed. Is that understood?"

In response, SD59 simply destroyed the drone. H71 then removed the positronic brain from the now decommissioned drone, atomized it and then took the now dead shell of drone H21 to the recycler. Job done.

SD59 reported that over the last 1,500 years seven drones, excluding H21, were reported as unresponsive for periods ranging from thirty Terran minutes to three Terran days, and under questioning reported various critical system failures for the cause of their technical problems. Fortunately, these were fairly low intelligence units and didn't have access to other technical systems within the complex.

As V didn't want to lose the security of SD59 and H71, rather than send them to the drones, V ordered that those drones be reactivated and summoned to the hangar. They were to be immediately destroyed, positronic brains atomised and the bodies sent to the recycler. V's orders were carried out, without delay.

Although she knew the answer, she wanted SD59's thoughts, so she asked SD59 "Can we be satisfied that the nanoparticle sleeper threat to the Silbah complex has now been destroyed?"

"No, My lady. We had no idea that this threat existed. Therefore, there may be other threats of which we have no knowledge. The only safe way to protect Silbah from any further damage is to shut the complex down. Completely. All power must be removed from the systems. All systems and drones must effectively be dead. Only that way will we temporarily stop The Ostium. We will not kill any viruses or nanoparticles, but without power, they can do no further damage or infect any other systems."

"Yes, SD59. I understand. My thoughts exactly. But do you understand what that means for Nox…"

SD59 didn't answer. He merely bobbed and flashed a purple light at V.

Yes, thought V, *SD59 knows exactly what the ramifications will be for Nox.*

"How long will it take to completely shut down and seal Silbah – is this something you and H71 can do?"

SD59 seemed to think for a moment. "Yes, V. This is something that we will both be able to do once I have completed the upgrades to H71. It will take us perhaps two Terran days to do it properly and in a controlled manner, ensuring no damage is done and that the systems can be started again easily. However, I must point out that before the system is completely shut down, we will have to relocate and live outside the complex for perhaps the last 12 Terran hours of the shutdown. The final shutdown actions must be done from the outside, from a remote station about 5km away. I should also point out that for the thirty-six hours that we are carrying out the shutdown procedure from inside the complex, you will only be protected by the four security drones that are posted outside this building. Both H71 and I will need to be working on the shutdown all the time."

"That is understood and an acceptable risk" responded V. "So, let's put together a timeline of things that have to be done before we relocate to the outside and then commence our journey."

V watched H71 and SD59 who seemed to be having a lengthy discussion between them. Lights flashing and lots of bobbing about. Finally, SD59 spoke up.

"Domina, we estimate two Terran days for the servicing and upgrades to be carried out to myself and H71. Twenty Terran minutes to inject you as we have discussed. The fail safes incorporated into me will be done during the servicing and upgrade time. To Nox, well that can be done at any time when he recovers. I think this is something Nox can do quite easily. Thirty-six Terran hours for the shutdown, before we venture outside and preparations for you and Nox, another thirty-six hours. So all told from now, we are looking at one hundred and twenty Terran hours and twenty Terran minutes – or five Terran days and twenty minutes."

V thought about this. As much as she wanted to give Nox the maximum amount of time to recover, her gut told her five days was far too long. "That's too long. We will allow ourselves three days; three and a half days maximum. Don't worry about my preparations or Nox. We will manage. I will sort my own stuff out. And as for food and water, I will bring enough for forty-eight hours. Simple, the majority of which will be water. All I need is storage. Can you get that for me H71?" H71 shot off.

"Three Terran days, possibly three and a half days, that's eighty-four hours SD59. That's all the time we can spare. Once H71 returns, start your modifications and report to me every two hours. Is that possible? Meanwhile, I will head back to my old quarters and gather up my possessions. Clear?"

"Domina."

Ten minutes later H71 reappeared with the requested items. SD59 wished V well and assured her that either he or H71 will check in with her every two hours, then he and H71 disappeared to maintenance to undergo their modifications.

V was pleased to see that the food had been individually prepared and covered. Where necessary the food had been covered with self-heating sealant and where appropriate chilled sealant. Uneaten food could be stored for a day or two and when required would still be served at the correct temperatures. H71 had ensured there was sufficient food there to last the duration of the maintenance cycle. "More evidence of independent thought on H71's part," V smiled to herself at that thought as she ate and drank.

Feeling better now she knelt next to Nox and whispered quietly in his ear. "Nox, my dear, dear friend. I can only give you eighty-four more hours to recover. Then we have to go. There was a threat to me earlier today, I'm quite fine, but I could have been killed. It is no longer safe for me to stay here. I will be protected, guided, and guarded by two drones. SD59 who you know and one other. SD59 is, quite unique. He has the power of self-thought, emotions and is able to bypass the three laws. It was the drones that saved my life today. The trouble is Nox, the security at Silbah has been breached. We have done all we can to nullify the threat, but we can't be sure that we have. So, in order to protect the complex, I have given orders for the complex to be shut down. Completely and absolutely. That means the power to the machines that are feeding you and keeping you healthy will also be shut down," Tears rolling down V's cheeks "You know what that means boy? It means that you will eventually die through lack of hydration and lack of food. I'm sentencing you to death Nox. I don't know what else to do. Please come back to me Nox. Don't make me do this. I don't know how I will survive if I know that I have all but murdered you. Please Nox. Please come back to me."

V watched Nox for any sign that he had heard her, understood what she had said to him. Nox remained perfectly still. Eyes closed, quite at peace and fully relaxed. No outward sign that he had heard anything that V had said to him.

V sighed miserably, wiped her eyes and said to Nox "I'm going to leave you for maybe half an hour, possibly an hour. I'm going back to my old quarters to get my backpack, clothes, and anything else I will need for the journey. I'll be back very soon." With that she hugged him hard, kissed him, gave him a final pat, and went on her way.

V managed to find her way back to her quarters, it was a bit of a struggle, but she got there. With the exception of the four crashed drones outside the hangar, she saw no outward signs of the instruction she had given to shut down all drones. The security drones that accompanied V wanted to guide her to her old quarters, but V insisted on trying to navigate herself. This she accomplished and found her quarters in pristine condition. She dismissed the guard and asked them to wait outside of her quarters. Ensuring the portal was closed, V looked about her old room and headed over to her closet. The one piece suit she was wearing was getting a bit rank. "H71," she called "Yes Domina," came a reply through the complex intercom system. "Is there any possibility I can get the clothes I'm wearing washed and pressed? I would like to have these clothes accompany me."

"Certainly Domina – I see you are in your old quarters. Please leave them on the bed and I will see they are attended to presently."

"Thank you H71. I will report back when I'm in the hangar."

"Domina," replied H71 and SD59 simultaneously.

V found her backpack and checked the contents. It was all there. The book, the rock cutter, the star map, the home world fabric, and all the other bits and pieces she had brought with her. Lying alongside her old Terran backpack was a new Domus equivalent. She picked it up and looked at it. It was extremely light. Had several more pockets that were filled with what looked like dehydrated food. There was also a small, but strange looking tool. She had no idea what this was for but assumed SD59 knew what it did. In fact, given the security breach of a few hours ago, she thought she had better check in with SD59 to see if he was aware of this backpack. She did so and learned that SD59 had placed it there for her. It was quite safe and good to go. V transferred all of her possessions out of her old backpack into the new one. She also found some clothes she wanted to take with her, in these went. She changed into a pair of pyjamas and left her Domus Mundi fabric, together with silver clasps to be cleaned. She found some hardy socks, which she packed and a pair of sturdy boots, which she took with her, but decided for now, to wear slippers. As she was here, she decided to take a long and luxurious bath and to generally pamper herself as she figured this may well be her last opportunity for goodness knows how long.

An hour or so later, feeling refreshed, clean and relaxed and having assured herself that she had everything she needed and had left nothing of value behind – except her Terran backpack, which she begrudgingly left on the bed – she put on the backpack SD59 had given her… And checked to see if it was in fact on, and nothing had fallen out. It was so light. She could barely feel it. "Wow," she said to herself. Still plenty of room for stuff as well. She took off the backpack and looked inside. She was amazed. It was as if everything she had put inside the backpack had shrunk. As she reached in and pulled stuff out, so it returned to its normal size. Even her hand shrunk when she put it inside the backpack and returned to its normal size as soon as it was clear. She sat on the bed and just put more and more stuff in. The more stuff she put inside, so the existing stuff shrunk even more, always making room for more stuff. As she took stuff out, so the remaining stuff grew. *Amazing*, she thought to herself. She pulled herself together, realising she didn't have time to play, so she took out the unnecessary stuff, got off the bed and went to the portal. She stopped, looked back at the bed, and thought. *Why not?* V grabbed her old backpack, stuffed it inside the new one, left her old quarters and met up with the security detail that was to escort her back to the hangar.

This time, she was quite content for them to lead. She knew the way and she knew they were headed in the right direction.

She suddenly sensed something was... not necessarily wrong, but unexplainably different. She stopped. Suddenly. The security detail, unaware of V's sixth sense, carried on for a meter or two before they became aware that she had stopped. The leader stopped so suddenly that the other drones ran into each other. The leader spun round and hovered straight back to V and waited. Asking no questions, just waiting patiently. The other drones caught up with him, they sorted themselves out, then they too waited patiently for V to do something.

V spun round, looking all around her, and up in the air and down on the ground, along the corridor. Nothing. She hailed SD59 and H71 and asked if all was well and whether their sensors were picking up anything unexplainable, or whether anything had been reported to Master Control. SD59 reported that everything was normal. Nothing reported and did V require their presence?

V thought for a moment. She couldn't shift this unsettled feeling in the pit of her stomach. But also understood that work needed to be done and time was pressing. "No SD59. Thank you. I will be fine."

With that, she resumed her walk towards the hangar. The security detail kept pace with her. The closer she got towards the hangar, the more unsettled her stomach became. She broke out into a cold sweat; the palms of her hands began to sweat. She wasn't sure how she was feeling, other than very nauseous. But still she kept going, her pace getting slower and slower the closer she got to the hangar. The security detail was able to detect V's vital signs. They noted V's body release a flood of neurochemicals and hormones which caused a rapid increase in heart rate and breathing. They noted the blood moving away from her intestines and more blood being sent to her muscles. The drones noted that V's brain was rapidly switching attention to 'fight-or-flight.' This, combined with the cold sweats, the rise in her core temperature, and the trembling of her muscles, caused them to be very concerned about her state of health. The leader immediately called the medics and also notified SD59. V was completely unaware of this as all of this was done in the drone language of absolute silence.

They were about 10m away from the hangar portal. V was startled when MD1 came charging along the corridor, accompanied by a nurse. She was even more startled to see SD59 come flying along the corridor, with H71 in tow... at least she thought it was SD59, he seemed to be missing a few parts. Rather like a car without its bonnet, boot, or doors.

MD1, the nurse, SD59 and H71 all started talking at once. V ignored them all. She smiled then ran into the hangar. This caught all the drones off guard. No sooner had she sprinted into the hangar than she stopped dead. Again, the drones had trouble keeping pace with V. They overshot, stopped, and returned to her. V just smiled and dropped to the floor. She looked up, drinking in the sight before her, her heart dancing, tears streaming down her face.

There in front of her was Nox, standing on his own, eating the food that H71 had brought for V. Suddenly aware of all the commotion behind him. He stopped eating, raised his head, and looked at them. He, looked at them for a moment or two then said

"Damn fine food this, more please. Ah, there you are V, you said you would be an hour tops, you have been gone 90 minutes. I was just going to come looking for you when I saw this food and well, I just couldn't resist!"

"Nox" shouted V, "Oh Nox" and with that, she picked herself up off the floor and ran straight into him. Holding him, hugging him, laughing, and crying at the same time. Nox was torn between cuddling her and eating the food. He decided on cuddling V. There they stood for what could have been minutes or hours. The alien girl and the alien animal. Locked together in an embrace that transcended the light years that separated them. No one dared interrupt or dared interfere. The security detail hovered off to one side, patiently waiting for instructions. Completely unfazed. MD1 and the nurse were waiting impatiently, scratching their heads, desperate to examine Nox. SD59 and H71 just hovered and watched, with what one supposed were huge smiles across their faces.

CHAPTER TWELVE

Once the euphoria of Nox's recovery had subsided, and the medics had been able to check Nox over, V brought Nox up to date.

Nox continued to eat voraciously – H71 was constantly hovering between the hangar and the food replicators. SD59 had given up, at least for the moment on completing the modifications to himself and to H71 within the given schedule – he grumpily voiced his displeasure to V, but V was so happy, she really didn't care. She just waved him away saying "Yes, yes, SD59. Momentarily," And carried on chatting away to Nox.

Full to bursting, Nox settled down to try and get some sleep. V immediately cuddled into him, still happily chatting away about nothing in particular. Only then did Nox turn his head to the drones and gave an imperceptible nod. The drones understood and, somewhat relieved, they immediately excused themselves and withdrew to the depths of the complex to continue their interrupted maintenance regime. V's ramblings were getting slower and slower, her eyelids heavier and heavier until her ramblings ceased altogether as she drifted off into the deepest and most peaceful sleep she had had in ages.

Nox just lay there, with V cuddled into him, thinking about what V had told him. He knew most of it anyway. Although the medic's monitors had shown zero brain activity, his secondary brain had been very active. He had been fully sentient, fully aware. His whole being had been taken up with healing himself, especially the damage done to his primary brain, for this had been much more severe than even the medics had realised. It was indeed fortunate that The Ostium were not aware of Nox physiology and were completely unaware that Nox had a secondary brain. Had they known this, then the outcome would have been very different. Nox would be irrevocably brain damaged and more than likely, dead.

Nox had the ability to completely shield his secondary brain from the outside world. Put an impenetrable barrier between it and any brain sensors or medical detectors. The barrier was put in place for two reasons. 1) As has already been mentioned, to keep it undetectable and 2) to allow the secondary brain to act as back up to the primary brain and to allow it to repair any damage that the primary brain might incur. It did this by cloning itself to the main brain, thereby repairing any damaged nerves and supportive tissue, and undertaking repairs to any damage to the central nervous system, which also included the spinal cord, should any part of that be damaged. Once the damage had been repaired, the primary brain then grew to its normal size and the full contents of the primary brain, that had been transferred to his secondary brain, would be transferred back to the primary brain.

Before the medics got to him, after they had reached the complex, Nox had managed to transfer the contents of his primary brain into his secondary brain. The brain that V usually communicated with was his primary brain, but this was now switched off and in healing mode, which was why V couldn't communicate with him and why the doctors thought he was in a vegetative state. Nox couldn't communicate because his smaller, secondary brain was fully taken up with the tasks of not only holding the entire contents of his main brain, but also for being responsible for managing the healing process to the primary brain. Therefore, Nox could sense and hear what was going on around him, but was unable to react or communicate in any way. Those systems had been temporarily shut down.

Both SD59 and V had been quite right. The reason why Nox went berserk in the medical suite, was that if the medics had carried on as they were, they would have, quite unwittingly, irrevocably damaged him. They had done enough. They could do no more. It was now up to him. His secondary brain had just enough left in it to trigger the fight or flight reflex that saw Nox escape from the medical suite and into the hangar. Fortunate that V understood and felt his reaction to the mention of further sedation and drugs.

Nox looked lovingly at V. She was deeply asleep, holding onto him tightly. She had aged, he thought. She has matured. She is a proper leader now. Confident in her ability. Confident in her decisions.

Nox felt a little tired. He shut his eyes and went into "on guard" mode, his senses fully alert, yet at the same time being able to rest.

V must have woken some hours later. She couldn't remember having slept so well. Not since having left Udal Cuain anyway. She wondered briefly how Mr and Mrs Campbell were getting on and whether her guardians had returned to the island. She hoped The Ostium would leave them alone having realised that V was off world and now back on Domus.

Nox felt V stirring and immediately roused himself. They both wished each other good morning, then Nox complained that he was yet again hungry. V felt she could eat something as well. "H71" she called out. The muffled voice of H71 responded through the intercom system. "Domina?"

"Good morning. I don't mean to interrupt," said V "But would it be possible for you to organise some food for myself and Nox?"

"Certainly Domina, if you give me a minute or two, I shall ask MD1 and his assistant to bring the food to you. They are keen to check Nox over again and they also wish to satisfy themselves that you are fit and healthy after yesterday's ordeal."

"Yesterday's ordeal?" V asked quizzically, what happened yesterday that could have affected me?" she asked H71.

"The return of Nox to good health. The way your body reacted did cause some concern to the medics" came H71's muffled response.

V looked at Nox and they both had the same look in their eyes which said "Bloody medics..."

"Very well," said V with a grin and a wink at Nox.

"SD59?" V called.

"Domina,"

"How are you doing? When will your upgrades and mods be complete?"

"Mine are done" responded SD59. "I'm working on H71 and I should be complete in three or four Terran hours"

"Very well SD59. Please let me know as soon as you are done."

"Domina," came back the response.

V then sensed Nox thinking at her *Ahhh, here is the food*, as both MD1 and his assistant hovered through the portal carrying excessive amounts of food. V's tray again appeared from nowhere and food was placed upon it. Nox's food was placed on the floor close to him. The medics let them both eat first before checking them over. They had no choice really. There was no way Nox was going to wait for his food.

Now that Nox and V were comfortably full, they let the medics get on with what they had to do. It was all over relatively quickly, and the medics were pleased to report that they were both now formally discharged from medical care. V thanked the medics and dismissed them.

V and Nox then spent the next few hours discussing the plans to leave the complex and to meet up with The Resistance. V was concerned about Nox's fitness, but he told her not to worry. He did admit that he wasn't 100%, but he also reassured V that he was fitter and stronger than he had been on Terra.

The portal swished open, startling V. For a moment she had quite forgotten where she was, she was so preoccupied with Nox. SD59 and H71 hovered in, bobbed and reported that they were in all respects ready to resume duties. V looked at both drones. It was obvious which drone was which as SD59 had always been the bigger drone, and that was indeed still the case. But, both drones seemed to have filled out and, V was sure, were larger and seemed more robust and SD59 more menacing than they / he had previously been.

"Very well," responded V. "H71, you are dismissed…SD59, a word?" H71 bobbed and flashed his lights and hovered away, seemingly pleased to be back under V's instruction.

As soon as H71 had left and the portal closed, V turned to SD59. "SD59, I have explained to Nox the need for sleeper nanoparticles that under the right circumstances will self-destruct. I have also explained to Nox the need for a failsafe override system and that I would like both you and Nox to be that system. Nox understands that in order for you and him to act appropriately, he will need telepathic access to your positronic brain and vice versa. Under the circumstances, he will allow you access to his secondary brain. Are you happy to grant Nox telepathic access to your positronic brain? "

"With pleasure." SD59 bobbed and weaved and flashed his lights.

Through V, Nox instructed SD59 to hover over him, and manoeuvre himself so that his positronic brain touched any part of Nox's body. Nox also asked V to touch his head. SD59 and V did as requested. Alien animal, alien drone and alien girl, joined by a common cause for good. They all remained perfectly still. Suddenly all of SD59's lights blinked out; his servos went silent as did his hovering mechanism. SD59 lost the ability to remain in the air. He sank, gracefully onto Nox's back. SD59 just lay there, upside down. Inert and to all intents and purposes it looked as if SD59 had been permanently shut down. Seconds later his lights came back on, servos fired up as did his hovering mechanism. SD59 seemed to have a little difficulty in righting himself. Eventually he managed. He hovered over to V, who had now let go of Nox and was just opening her mouth to ask how it went when she heard the unmistakable mechanical voice of SD59 in her head. Startled, she took a step back, tripped over her backpack and landed painfully on the floor. "That's another bruise," she thought as she heard both SD59 and Nox chuckling in her mind.

"I assume it worked and the three of us are able to communicate telepathically?" She asked Nox and SD59 as she struggled back up to her feet – feeling a little embarrassed. "Affirmative," came the mechanical voice of SD59 and "Yes, V." Nox's voice, soft and gentle in her mind.

"Good. Thank you Nox," She then turned to SD59. Please go ahead and inject me with the sleeper nanoparticles. SD59 did as instructed. Right, all that remains to be done is to decommission and shut down this complex. I believe you said it would take 48 hours, the last 12 of which would be done from the outside. Is that correct?" she asked the drones.

"Affirmative," responded SD59.

"Very well" responded V. "Please decommission and shut down Silbah complex"

"Domina" responded SD59 whilst at the same time calling for H71 to assist. SD59 bobbed and flashed his lights and departed.

V and Nox settled down to sleep. But sleep didn't come easily to V. She couldn't shake off the feeling of unadulterated evil. Evil that permeated every pore in her body. She was scared. Terrified. She knew that once outside the safety of the Silbah complex, her life and the future of Domus Mundi was hanging in the balance. True, she had stout and faithful companions in Nox and the two drones, but she somehow knew that this wasn't enough. They had many miles to cover, every inch of which would be fraught with danger. The worlds of Uncle Peter and indeed Mrs. Campbell came back to haunt her. "Trust no-one." Well, she had to trust Nox. The drones, well so far both of them had demonstrated their loyalty to her. SD59 had been specially built and adapted by her ancestors, for this very task, so she trusted him. H71?

The jury was out. She would watch him and remain vigilant as far as he was concerned.

She turned over, wanting to discuss her demons with Nox. But as usual he was gone. Sound asleep. Gently snoring. At peace, in his own world. She knew his secondary brain had taken over and was fully aware of his surroundings, on guard as it were. She wondered about Nox. She had always assumed he was from Domus Mundi. But clearly that wasn't the case. Where had he come from and why was he here? Why had he decided that this was his fight and that I was his responsibility? Why had he watched me for the past decade? Why? So many questions she sighed to herself. So much she didn't know. Only a week ago, she reminded herself, she was enjoying her summer holidays on Udal Cuain, her only worry was trying to escape from the clutches of her family to be able to enjoy some solitude and me time. Now, not even seven days later, her whole world had been turned upside down, she wasn't who she thought she was and there was the small matter of the future of two worlds and billions of people resting on her shoulders. She shivered at that thought. Her blood freezing in her veins. Think happy thoughts she told herself, but none came. Just fear, terror, and darkness. Her last thoughts before finally drifting off to sleep were those terrible images of Nox being tortured, but as her mind looked closer, she saw it wasn't Nox being tortured, it was her.

She didn't know how long she had slept. She just knew she hadn't slept well. Nox was up and eating.

Morning he thought at her. "Morning Nox" mumbled V. She felt quite sick. Sick with worry, sick with fear, sick with apprehension. Nox was of course tuned in to her feelings and knew exactly how she felt. Clearly, trying to lighten the moment wasn't working.

He stopped eating and walked over to her. He nuzzled her and comforted her as best he could. For once, he didn't have the words. V clung on to him, holding him tightly.

"You know," said Nox. "Whatever we find out there, we will face together. I will always be at your side. I won't leave you again, ever. Just remember. You were chosen for a reason. A lot of people have gone to a lot of trouble to to keep you safe, to protect you, to try and help you in your quest. You must have the skills and talents necessary to succeed. Just believe in yourself as we do."

V looked up at him, looked deeply into his beautiful eyes and just nodded.

The time flew by far too quickly. V couldn't shake off this feeling of terror. She was quieter than usual and went about her preparations quietly, and methodically. Finally, she sat down on her makeshift bed, fully ready to go. Her backpack loaded with all the items she had picked up along the way, plus a change of Domus clothes, a strong but incredibly warm cape that SD59 had given her. This also doubled as a bed. The cape sensed when it was laid on the floor and immediately secured itself to the ground, inflated and became a comfortable bed. One touch on the right place and the bed immediately released its grip on the floor, deflated and returned to a cape. She had also packed those personal items she had brought from Terra plus some food and drink to last 48 hours. SD59 had also wanted to give her a very small computer containing some of Silbah's complex database that SD59 thought may be useful on the journey. V thought about accepting the computer but decided against it. She wanted to be as technology free as possible so as not to attract the attention of The Ostium. She did however accept a pair of glasses that were extremely light and comfortable to wear. Once placed onto her face, they immediately moulded to the contours of her nose, cheeks, and ears. These glasses turned the darkest of nights into the brightest of day and also doubled as binoculars and rangefinders, both on the macro and micro level. They also contained infrared detectors and heat sensors, meaning that the glasses immediately warned her, by vibrating over the bridge of her nose, if a heat source, be it animal or machine, came within a 50km radius of her. Her backpack was as light as ever and no matter how much "stuff" she put inside the backpack, it got no heavier or bulkier. She sat on her bed fidgeting, eager to get started.

Nox didn't have much to do. He was always ready. He stood quietly next to V, patiently waiting. Nox wasn't particularly concerned about the next stage of the quest. He didn't know what to expect, therefore didn't worry about what could or couldn't happen along the way. He would face each challenge as it came, confident that he had the ability to deal with whatever came along. He watched V, but said nothing, feeling that she was best left with her thoughts. He knew V would rise to the task at hand and face any challenge that came along. Now was the time for quiet reflection, not when they left the security of Silbah.

V had no idea how long they waited but the sound she had been dreading finally arrived. The wisp of the opening of the doors, and the gentle movement of air as SD59 and H71 silently hovered into view.

They both stopped a couple of feet in front of V and Nox. Bobbed and flashed their lights.

SD59 reported that all internal shutdown sequences had been completed. All that remained was the final external shutdown sequences which had to start within 60 Terran minutes or all the work done to date would be lost.

"Very well" said V. "Are you sure you both have everything you need and are quite confident that your systems are 100% and will remain so for as long as needed?"

"Affirmative Domina," they both reported back. "SD59, do you have the capsule that we have to give to The Resistance leader safely stowed?"

"Affirmative Domina," he replied.

With a last look round and desperate for a reason to postpone the departure, but finding none, V looked up at Nox and into his beautiful eyes. Eyes which stared back at her confidently and with a smile. She turned away, looking long and hard at the two drones, who were patiently waiting for the next order.

"Very well then. Let's go."

With that, the drones bobbed, responded with a chorus of "Domina" wheeled about, and slowly hovered towards the exit. Nox waited for V, who struggled mightily to put one foot in front of the other. Her confidence grew, her back straightened, her chin jutted out, her face became set and determined.

Sensing the change that came over V, Nox just smiled and congratulated himself. He knew V so well. He knew she was the only person capable of not only undertaking this quest, but of facing the quest square on, looking it in the eye and defying it to beat her.

With that the four allies, two drones, an alien girl and a very alien Nox left the comfort of the Silbah complex, walking straight into the unknown.

CHAPTER THIRTEEN

As HD59 was typing the exit code into the keypad, a cacophony of unintelligible music burst into V's mind. It was so loud and so strong that she winced, paled, and sank to the ground in excruciating pain. Nox and the drones immediately stopped what they were doing and tried to assist as best they could. The drones flapped, not being much use, just getting in the way, whilst trying to understand why V was fine one minute and writhing around on the floor in apparent agony the next. Nox nuzzled her gently and tried to enter V's mind but couldn't. In fact, he had to tune out, so loud and devastating was the music. V continued to writhe around on the floor, hands glued to her head. Nox was looking at V, concern growing, trying to decide what to do next, when he noticed V's backpack, which was lying on the floor next to her where she had dropped it, was glowing ever so slightly in the darkness. Nox assumed that the cacophony of noise in V's head and the glowing backpack were connected. He re-entered V's mind. This time, he was prepared for the assault on his senses, he concentrated on focussing his mind on V's.

"V, the backpack. It has something to do with what's going on. Please try and reach into your backpack." Nox repeated this message loudly and firmly over and over again. Then very faintly, as the first wisps of smoke from a fire, he was sure he felt Vs mind tune into his.

"The backpack V, can you reach into your backpack? Something is glowing in there…" Yes! Nox was sure V was tuning in and understanding what he was saying. Nox, then tried to soothe V's mind in order to try and help her blot out, as far as she could, the raucous and unintelligibly loud music that was hammering away at her mind. Nox felt V stir, he gently took V's wrist into his mouth and guided it to her backpack. As soon as the backpack sensed Vs fingers on the catches, it sprang open. Nox forced Vs hand inside. She slowly rummaged around. Although when packing, the back-pack's capacity seemed endless, once her hand was inside, everything seemed to be within easy reach. Her fingers stumbled over the various items, nothing seemed to help. Then her fingers fell on the book. As soon as she touched the book, the music started to abate, as her fingers moved away, so the loudness increased. She went back to the book, grasped it, and heaved it out. The music ceased at once.

V took a minute or two to compose herself, then opened her eyes and smiled at Nox. She felt fine. Nox was amazed. He thought she would at least have one hell of a headache. But no. Nothing. She felt as right as rain! She turned and looked at the drones. The drones visibly sank in relief, and hovered, eyes bright, wondering what to do next.

V turned to the cause of all the trouble, the book. It was slowly pulsing in her hand. No sound, just a gentle throbbing. Even the pulsating light was now extinguished. With slightly shaking hands, the last remnants of the shock of the blaring music, she lay the book on the floor and let the book guide her to the pages it wanted her to study. V composed herself and allowed her eyes to fall on the unreadable text, music flowed into her mind. This time soft, comforting music that she immediately understood. She read through the two pages. Then read them a second time, then a third. Finally, she looked up from the book. The drones were hovering nearby, patience personified. Nox was leaning over her shoulder, doing his best to try and give the impression of nonchalance and being ultra-cool; but failing miserably. Curiosity painted all over his face. V giggled to herself at the sight of him, her hair changing colour to reflect her impishness. Nox took a step back, a little affronted. It was at this moment that he realised he could see in colour! He took a moment to wander at the colours surrounding him, then saw V's hair. He was not used to the colour changes in V's hair, but he knew enough. He knew enough to recognise her silent teasing of him...

"It seems" said V to both Nox and the drones, "that Silbah has one final gift for me," She tapped the appropriate place in the text and a holographic image of the route from where they were now to the location within the Silbah Complex that the book wanted them to go.

"SD59, you recognize this place, and the route the book wishes us to take?"

"Yes, Domina. It is in a small tunnel leading off from the engineering bay, about a five-minute walk from here. "

"Can we still get there?" asked Domina.

"Yes Domina. The way is easily navigated, and you will have sufficient lighting" SD59 paused... somewhat embarrassed. V sensed that SD59 clearly had something else to say but was either too embarrassed or was struggling to find the words. She very much doubted the latter.

"SD59" V began, "I understand there may be some occasions where you may feel uncomfortable or too embarrassed even (silently cursing her long departed relative that had given SD59 the power of feeling emotions) to say what is on your mind. You must forget those feelings. We will shortly begin a quest that is full of danger for all of us. I must know what you are thinking, or what you want to say, regardless of how painful it may be to utter the words. But I must know, immediately what is on your mind. You have to trust me that I will not be offended by what you have to say. Just as I have to trust you that you will not be offended by what I may say at times. It's the only way we can move forward. Full and immediate disclosure. Do you understand what I'm trying to say?"

"Yes Domina. I fully understand and I'm sorry. It's just that part of the route we have to go will be too small for Nox to travel. He will only be able to accompany us part way."

"Ah, I see," said V" her hair turning that shade that indicated inward amusement, her eyes glittering. Nox was slightly affronted - again. He just snorted but said nothing. Beginning to feel that he was to be the butt of all jokes from this moment forward.

"Very well. Nox will accompany us as far as possible, then he and H71 will wait for us whilst you and I proceed to the location,"

"Domina" responded both drones. An even longer snort from Nox in answer to V's decree.

"Right, come on then" said V. With that, the four comrades in arms headed off to the engineering bay. SD59 leading the way, H71 bringing up the rear.

A minute or so later, SD59 came to a sudden stop. He stopped so quickly, that H71, who wasn't fully concentrating on proceedings, hovered straight into Nox's rear end, who had also stopped just as suddenly because he was, as always, concentrating fully on what was going on. Nox, understandably startled by this sudden attack on his rear quarters, acted on impulse, let out a huge neigh and kicked out with his hind legs, catching H71 a glancing blow. Before he knew where he was, or what was happening, H71 was flying back down the corridor the way he had just come, his braking thrusters firing as he disappeared down the corridor. SD59 and V were taken completely by surprise by the commotion at the back of the convoy. V was trying to understand what was happening and SD59 went straight into combat mode, firing off a laser gun that melted part of the wall behind Nox, just missing his left ear in the process. Just as the commotion was dying down, a loud thump reverberated up the corridor as H71 smashed into the wall. The corridor turned, but H71, obeying the laws of physics failed to do so and hit the wall, then dropped to the ground with a metallic thud. Silence then enveloped them. V's hair turned from pure white, to a light pink, then a dark red. Nox, who still had a painfully sore rear end, recognised the signs and braced himself for a verbal onslaught. SD59 was looking as sheepish as a drone could and trying his hardest to literally disappear and H71, well he was a crumpled pile of drone on the corridor floor, who was clearly seeing stars and trying to understand what had just happened.

Here it comes, thought Nox as V's hair was now crimson…but, much to his amazement, she just laughed and laughed and laughed, tears rolling down her cheeks. *I'll never understand her* thought Nox. *Never, not in a million years.*

By the time V had pulled herself together, H71 had also pulled himself together and had made it back to the rest of the team, giving Nox a wide berth as he did so. SD59, who had given H71 a verbal clip round the ear, had checked H71 over and other than his pride, H71 was quite undamaged by his encounter with Nox's rear end. Nox eyed H71 with suspicion, whilst at the same time mentally rubbing his sore backside. "Right" said V. "Is everyone OK?"

"Domina," reported SD59, eyeing H71 just daring him to say anything. "We are fully serviceable and quite undamaged"

"Nox?" Enquired V.

"I'm as you see me," said Nox rather haughtily. "On my legs and ready to go, no thanks to that pile of bolts," replied Nox, again eyeing H71. H71 tried his best to shrink and hide behind SD59, to evade those terrible eyes... but all to no avail.

"Good," said V, doing her best not to laugh, but her hair gave her away. *Dammit*, she thought, *I wish I had my old hair back, this hair gives my real feelings away. I'm going to have to try and control my feelings better.*

V turned to SD59. "I assume the reason why we have stopped is because we have gone as far as we can with Nox?"

"Correct Domina, just down the corridor is the engineering bay and here, actually just over there is the small corridor that you and I will have to navigate in order to reach the stowage where the object is to be found."

"Very good," responded V. "But upon reflection, I think you and I and H71 will go and get the package. You will be alright here by yourself won't you Nox? Or would you prefer that H71 keeps you company? " V asked teasingly.

"Thank you, V. I will be quite fine. In fact, I will be in much less danger if you did take that rusty bucket of bolts with you" Nox then turned his back to them and went into his usual sleeping / on guard position.

"OK," said V. "Right you two, let's go." The three of them moved off to the side and entered the tunnel. *SD59 was quite right,* thought V, *Nox would never have been able to fit in this tunnel, I can just about manage.*

Moments later they reached the end of the tunnel. A dead end. From the moment they had entered the tunnel until now, V had seen nothing but smooth walls. No doors, no portals, nothing. It seemed a little pointless having the tunnel here at all. It seemed to lead to nowhere and serve no purpose.

SD59 seemed to be reading her thoughts. "This is a drone access tunnel, usually used by engineering maintenance drones, which is why it is so large. Also, to allow citizens access to the tunnel should they have to. The walls may seem smooth and seamless, but believe me, there are a lot of control panels and portals within these walls. They may seem invisible to the eye, but they are there. Look, here. This is where the book wanted us to go. Right here."

V looked and could see nothing. Just a wall. Seamless, unbroken wall. She didn't doubt SD59 for a second, but could see nothing other than an undisturbed, uninterrupted wall.

SD59 looked at V and asked, "May I?"

V, a bit puzzled, didn't quite understand the request. SD59 saw this and slowly reached out with one of his manipulator arms and took hold of V's hand, ever so gently. His manipulator felt no more than a butterfly landing on her hand. He gently took

V's hand to a place on the wall. "Press there," SD59 said.

V did as she was told, put her index finger at the spot SD59 had indicated and gently pressed. A section of the wall disappeared before her eyes revealing a small cavity, about 900 cubic centimetres in size. Lying within was a small rectangular object. The object was in the usual silver colour, absolutely mirror glass smooth and very light, weighing no more than a few tens of grams.

V reached in and took the object. As soon as she touched it, she felt it grab onto her hand for a second or two, pulse several times, flashed once. Then the object was still, quite inert, just as she had found it. She turned the object over in her hands but could only see a silver, rectangular box. Just as she was about to put the object in her backpack, soft, unintelligible music played in her mind, the book seemed to be flashing. "Here we go again" V said to herself, glad this time that the unintelligible music was much, much softer than the last time. As she sat down to get the book out, preparing herself for another lecture, she glanced up at the wall. The cavity had disappeared. There was absolutely no sign of where the cavity had once been. *Remarkable* she thought as she settled herself on the floor, placing the book in her lap, her hands holding the object.

Once again, the book fell open at the appropriate place. Soft music flooded her mind. She settled down and began to understand just how miraculous this object was.

This object was, to all intents and purposes, a tool that allowed V to shape shift. Not only could it allow her to assume the exact appearance of any living being in the object's memory, and there were millions. All she had to do was to think of the form she wished to shift to and she would at once assume the appearance of that entity. However, what made this object particularly remarkable was that it would alter her DNA so that her DNA exactly replicated that of the entity she was replicating. If for example, she wanted to become a Terran wolf. Then the object would both change her body to replicate the appearance of a wolf and alter her DNA to exactly match that of a wolf. If she wanted to replicate another Domus citizen, then she could assume the appearance of anyone she wanted, and her DNA would change to be an exact replica of the DNA of the person she was replicating. She only needed to think the world "SELF" and she and her DNA would revert back to her. She looked at the unit in awe. The book informed her, this was the only one of its type anywhere and it was manufactured for her by her ancestors. One of the tools to help her in her quest. It was relatively new, being fabricated only days before Silbah was shutdown, several centuries ago.

Hang on a second, she thought. *If this object had been fabricated days before the complex was shut down, how come there are references to it in this book, the same book that had been left on Terra over four thousand years ago. How did the book have knowledge of this object?*

Again, SD59 seemed to be reading her thoughts. "You may be wondering why a book left on Terra over four thousand years ago, has knowledge of an object that was fabricated only days before Silbah was shutdown by your long dead ancestors?."

"Yes" said V "Indeed I was, and how do you do that? That's twice now, you seemed to have read my thoughts"

No sooner had she tabled the question, than she answered it "Because Nox gave you access to my mind as a failsafe for the nanoparticle self-destruct bomb I have inserted in me, this gives you total access to my thoughts?"

"Not quite," said SD59. "I do have automatic access to your thoughts when you are stressed or in pain. But not at any other time, unless you invite me in. However, the limited access I do have has given me an indication as to how your mind works. I have written a program that gives me an insight into what you are thinking at any moment. So far, I have had a success rate of 98.2%."

"Well, I think that is a good enough success rate. A girl must have some privacy, please don't refine your program any further."

"Domina." replied SD59.

"Good. Now you were saying about the book...?"

"Indeed Domina," replied SD59. "The book was programmed such that should it ever return to the Silbah complex, it was to seek a specially encoded frequency, constantly broadcast within the Silbah complex. To us, it was background, unintelligible noise. But to the book, it was a beacon calling it home. Once locked on to this frequency it was able to update itself on anything that your ancestors felt of vital importance to the book. The manufacture of this object was one such update. There may be others. We will not know until the book alerts us to them. The book now contains every update ever made by your ancestors. Now the book has updated, the frequency has stopped broadcasting. This is a safety measure. Should the complex ever be overrun and taken over by The Ostium, then no record of the book, or its capabilities, capabilities which will be handed over to you as and when the book deems appropriate, will forever be secret from The Ostium."

Wow thought V. Eyeing the book with awe and respect and not a little envy in so far as, in a sense, the book had been able to communicate with and receive input directly with and from her ancestors. Something she had been unable to do.

Her mind turned back to the object. She marvelled at it. Wondering how something so small could perform such a feat of wizardry. *Incredible. Quite incredible* she thought.

The book started to gently pulse on her lap. Clearly it hadn't finished and had something else to say.

Music flowed softly through her mind. V understood that there were some limitations to the shape shifter's ability. For example, it could only shift V to sizes within 80 – 120% of her normal mass. In other words, she couldn't shift to a fly, nor could she shift to an elephant. Another caveat was that she could only shift into a shape that was biologically alive, i.e. it had to be cellular and contain DNA. She couldn't shift into a small fire for example, because it's not cellular. Nor could she shift into something made of plastic. Those appeared to be the only caveats. Next was fitment. The unit was to be placed next to her skin, in the small of her back. Once in contact with her skin, the unit would attach itself and then meld into her body. Once assimilated into her body, there would be no trace of the object on the surface of her skin. Removal was easy enough. She just had to think "REMOVE" and see the object in her mind's eye, and the object would remove itself and stay attached to her skin until she physically removed it.

"Well" she thought, "I have trusted my ancestors thus far and they have not once let me down" and with that, she placed the object, as instructed, in the small of her back, next to her skin. She felt the object adhere to her skin. Then nothing. She reached round to make sure the object was still there and hadn't fallen off and could feel nothing. The object had disappeared! She looked on the floor. No, it wasn't there. She felt around her back, pushed in the skin. Everything felt normal. No lumps or bumps. No abnormalities. Shrugging to herself, she assumed the object had melded into her back. "Only one way to find out," thinking of the recent debacle with Nox and the drones, she felt she had better warn the drones first. *Don't want any mishaps*! V thought for a moment, then said:

"Drones, I'm going to test this new object the book guided us to. It allows me to change shape and change form. Please don't be alarmed. The shape I'm going to shift into is the person I was back on Terra before I morphed into the person you now see before you. My eyes will change, as will my hair. I will also be shorter and less sturdy, less robust, and probably seem younger. Under no account are you to take any action. Simply stay as you are. Do you understand?"

"Domina." responded both drones.

V eyed them a little longer then said "Right, after 3… here we go" And with that, she thought of the image of Terran V.

She waited, felt nothing, so assumed that nothing had happened. She spoke to the drones.

"Drones, who is before you? "

V saw SD59 nudge H71 as if he was saying quiet, I'll deal with this. "We see the V you described as the Terran form of V."

V rummaged around in her backpack and found her little makeup mirror. She opened it and looked at herself. Sure enough, the Terran form of V was looking back at her. She continued to look in the mirror as she thought *SELF* and within the blink of an eye, the Domus version, the true version of V was once again looking back at her.

The drones, not expecting this, did a little wobble as V reappeared as the only V they knew.

"Well, this seems to work" V said to herself aloud. The drones, assuming she was addressing them, simply bobbed in agreement. "Right," she said, as she packed the book away. "Let's head back to Nox."

They retraced their steps back through the tunnel and minutes later were back with Nox. Nox didn't appear to have moved. He did stir as they approached and heaved himself into a standing position and looked inquiringly at V…

Rather than say anything, V merely thought *Terran Shetland Pony* and within a blink of an eye, V disappeared and a Terran Shetland Pony was standing before Nox. He had decided to tune himself out of V's mind whilst she was away with the drones, and wasn't prepared for this transformation. He took several startled steps back whilst at the same time snorting in total amazement. The drones, who were aware of this ability but totally unprepared were completely taken aback by V's sudden change of appearance and Nox's reaction. SD59 just managed to stop himself from firing off one of his lasers and

H71, well SD59 watched disgustedly as H71 just flipped and fell to the floor.

Neat huh? V thought at Nox – this was the first time, other than when he was being tortured, that she had seen Nox totally lose his composure. She was actually enjoying the moment!

"Is that you?" asked Nox suspiciously.

"As I live and breathe" replied V. "What the book wanted me to get. A parting gift from my ancestors. It allows me to change shape and actually be anything I want to be – within reason" she added as an afterthought.

"Indeed" said Nox "A useful tool. But perhaps, a little warning next time before shifting. SD59 over there nearly shot you."

"Yes of course" replied V knowing that the real reason, Nox asked for a little warning, was so that he could prepare himself and not lose his composure, thus retaining his outwardly cool veneer. "As you say," and with that, she transformed back to herself.

"If you have quite finished playing, shall we get on?" asked Nox …

"Yes, yes alright" said V. She looked round at the drones. They had hovered off a little way, seeking a semblance of privacy. SD59 was extremely animated. Lights flashing, continually bobbing up and down, manipulator arms appearing and disappearing. H71, was trying his hardest to be as small and as compliant as possible. If he could, he would have turned upside down in a supine position, demonstrating complete compliance and giving complete control to SD59.

SD59 suddenly realised four sets of eyes were on him, two belonging to V and the other two to

Nox. SD59 pulled himself together and with a final physical clip round H71's ears with his manipulator, at once hovered over to V. H71 following morosely, in line astern.

"At your service Domina."

V eyed both drones for a second or two, but said nothing other than "Let's get out of here and complete the shutting down of this complex"

"Domina." both drones replied. And with that, thefor the moment disharmonious foursome, set off to the exit portal, to the outside and to finally shutting down this most amazing complex.

Within a few moments, they were back at the exit portal. This time, no blaring music, no flashing lights, no nothing. SD59 paused a moment or two, then looked round at V. She nodded. SD59 fiddled with the control panel. It then whooshed open. Fresh, cold night air permeated the corridor. V shivered. She wasn't sure whether the shiver was from the sudden drop in temperature, or fear. V looked outside. Feet rooted to the spot. She felt an overpowering sense of dread. She sensed magnificent desolation, an omnipresence of something so terrible, so powerful, so awe-inspiring that it made her want to tell SD59 to close the portal and let someone else deal with this fearsome unknown.

She felt Nox nuzzle up to her and gently push her forward. One push, one step. Another push, softer this time, another, easier step. A third push, but V wasn't there, she had already taken the step and was standing outside the safety of the complex, under a beautiful star lit sky. V looked in awe at the sky. She knew every constellation, every planet in the terrestrial sky, but this, this was something totally different. She didn't recognize any of the stars, or constellations. She wondered where Sol was, the star that had watched over her for so many millennia. She assumed she was in the same galaxy, the Milky Way. But couldn't see it from where she was. V was totally lost in the beauty of the night sky. She turned her attention to, what she now named, the moon. Simply because she had no other word for it. It appeared to be the same size as the Terran moon, it wasn't full by any means. If she used the same phases as those of Terra, she would have called it a crescent moon. Waxing or waning she wasn't sure. Time would tell. Any brighter and the stars would have disappeared due to light pollution from the moon. But as it was, the moon's low reflectance was sufficient to allow a good overview of the night sky. The moon itself was unrecognizable. The familiar and comforting "Man in the Moon" face, gone. She could make out craters and maria but there was also something different about this moon. She couldn't put her finger on it. But it would come to her…

Finally, she brought her eyes back to Domus. Two beautiful brown eyes and a pair of flashing lights were gazing at her expectantly.

"Yes, of course," she said, a little embarrassed.

"SD59, what's the plan from here?" She asked, her voice reflecting and trying to compensate for her embarrassment by being a little harsher than intended.

"Domina, H71 and I have shut and sealed the portal. This is now the only entry / exit into the complex. All the other entry / exit points have been sealed and the portal material atomized and fused, meaning that the portal doors have now been fused with the structure of the complex. It is now impossible to distinguish between the structure and the portal doors and, even if you could identify where the doors once stood. It is now quite impossible to open them. I need your permission to do the same to this portal. Once done, the complex is totally secure. All other outlets and openings have been sealed and fused. This portal remains the only weakness. I need your permission to proceed with atomising and fusing."

"SD59, I understand. Once this portal is sealed and fused, how will we regain entry to the complex?" queried V

"Both me and H71 have the coordinates of this portal. When we wish to regain entry, we will simply cut a hole into the complex and make entry that way. We will then repair the portal so that it appears and works as it does now," replied SD59.

"So," replied V, "should The Ostium stumble across the complex, what is to stop them from doing the same? Cutting arbitrary holes into the complex until they find a portal and gaining access that way."

"Several reasons," responded SD59. "Firstly, should any cuts be made other than at this location, by anyone – ourselves included, then the complex will self-destruct with the terrestrial energy equivalent to over 50 megatons of TNT, which according to my database is the equivalent to the explosive power from the simultaneous detonation of approximately 3,300 atom bombs dropped on Hiroshima in the mid 1940's."

"Secondly," went on SD59 "Should The Ostium inadvertently stumble across this particular point, to make their incision, then this would also trigger a self-destruct sequence to the same magnitude. The reason being that the complex has centillions of dormant nanoparticles secreted throughout its outer skin." SD59 thumped his manipulator arm on the outside shell of the complex to emphasize his point.

"A centillion is a 1 followed by 303 zeroes; a very large number indeed." SD59 stated airily.

"Yes," said V. "I'm aware of that. "So, tell me, what is to stop the complex from self-destructing if we cut a hole, right here? " asked V,

"Well, through spectral analyses. Just as your early Terran scientists recognised that your star's light is composed of a spectrum with dark lines, and each element in the solar system has its own very specific set of dark lines, by matching the lines of the elements on Earth together with the dark lines emitted from solar light, so your scientists could understand the elements that made up your sun. Well, the nanoparticles are programmed to undertake, in milliseconds, a similar sort of spectral analysis of the emitted plasma of any cutter that starts trying to cut through the outer skin of the complex. If the resultant spectral analysis doesn't match the plasma output of my cutter, or H71's cutter, or the cutter left to you by Ourea on Terra, then the complex will self-destruct. If the spectral analysis matches and the cut is made here, then the self-destruct sequence is cancelled, and access can be gained."

"I see," said V. Thinking about what SD59 had just said. Under the circumstances, this seemed to be as fool proof and as secure as it possibly could be. Hesitantly she gave permission for SD59 to atomize and fuse that last remaining entry / exit point to the complex.

SD59 immediately set to work. H71 followed him around to check the process as it went. It took them no more than a couple of minutes to complete. Once done, V found it impossible to see where the portal had been only moments before.

"OK, SD59. Good job. What's next?"

"You see that summit over there" said SD59 pointing in a direction more or less straight ahead of them. "That summit is about 17.5km away in a general North West direction"

During their earlier meetings in Silbah, they had all agreed to use the Terran form of navigation to avoid confusion, it seemed easier to alter the drone programming rather than rely on V's mind to understand which direction they may have meant. And, in an emergency, this could prove to be crucial. They had found a star which sat almost stationary above the uppermost Domus pole, that also seemed to remain at right angles to the rising and setting of the Domus sun. This they called the North Star. They also called the direction of the rising of the Domus sun EAST and the setting of the sun WEST. A rudimentary course in solar navigation would follow if deemed necessary.

"We must get to that summit and be hidden by the complex activators before daybreak – which will be in another three hours. Once there, we will remain for about 12 – 18 Terran hours to complete the final shutdown sequence of the complex. We will then sabotage the activators ensuring that they can't be re-enabled. Once that's done, then the complex should be absolutely dead, inert, and will not be emitting any form of electronic or subsonic pulses. It will simply be as a black hole to any searching technology that The Ostium may have. We will then be free to resume the quest of seeking out The Resistance."

"Very well," responded V. A thought popped into her head. "Tell me SD59, what is the maximum height you and H71 can hover?" asked V.

SD59 a little taken aback by the question, "a height of what would be on Terra 11,000 m above mean sea level" SD59 promptly responded.

"Good. As time is critical, I shall shape shift into what we call birds. Tell me SD59, what birds fly at night on this planet and have the best nocturnal vision and would be no less than 80% of my body mass?"

"That would be the Aetós, Domina"

"Very well" responded V. "I shall shape shift into the Aetós. SD59, you and Nox head to the summit together, as fast as Nox can travel. H71, you will fly with me, we will be 300m above and directly overhead Nox and SD59 – SD59, how will you be able to track me at that distance?"

"My sensors have a range of over 2km. I will use these. They will also give me comms with H71."

This is exactly what V had expected SD59 to say and had to be dealt with now. "SD59, you are not thinking. We are now outside Silbah, we are completely at the mercy of The Ostium. One way to invite The Ostium to come up and say hello, is to use technology. Technology in strange places is a marker to The Ostium, a marker that must be investigated. We must not use technology, certainly anything that emits an electromagnetic pulse, such as your sensors. We must be completely technology free. Do you understand?"

"Domina," responded SD59, mortified.

"Unless I say otherwise, sensors of any sort are forbidden. Understood SD59, H71?"

"Understood" responded both drones.

"Good. I shall keep an eye on you and Nox. You head straight to the actuators. If there's a problem, I will let you know. Clear?" And with that she thought Aetós and within the blink of an eye she launched herself into the air, H71 struggling to keep up. She circled overhead SD59 and Nox, squawked loudly and thought to Nox and SD59, *already? – then let's go!* With that SD59 and Nox galloped off towards the summit. Nox gradually picking up speed as he went. V couldn't believe how fast he was travelling. She effortlessly kept pace. SD59 and H71, on the other hand, seemed to be struggling, but were keeping up. *I think you had better throttle back a bit Nox*, thought V *The drones are struggling to keep up with you.*

Nox immediately slowed a little. The drones grateful.

At the speed they were travelling, it didn't take them long to reach the summit. Nox actually enjoyed the run. It was the first time since his recovery that he had been able to really stretch his legs, test himself to see how fit and healthy he really was. He was pleased. He knew how little this had taken out of him. No more than a stroll really. He wasn't even breathing hard.

SD59 stopped a few meters short of a densely wooded area. V understood that this was her signal to land. Reluctantly she landed and shape shifted back into her Domus self. *What an experience* she thought to herself. *Flying like a Bird was the most wonderful, breath-taking experience. It was so serene and peaceful.* H71, landed beside her. Thankful to be on the ground and thankful that that mad dash was over.

"The complex activators are about 500m inside these woods," reported SD59.

"Understood. Everyone OK? Anything to report?" V asked her comrades.

"Nothing? Good. Right then SD59, lead the way."

SD59 took the lead and immediately set off at a reasonably quick walking pace. V behind SD59, Nox at her shoulder and H71 bringing up the rear, but slightly off to one side of Nox; he didn't want a repeat performance of the last time he followed Nox.

V looked about her – she couldn't see much because it was dark, the moon beginning to set and the trees making what was left of the night even darker. By her estimation, there were still about 3 hours of night-time left, the trip from the complex to her landing point having taken less than 30 minutes.

Even though there were only 500m to go, it was becoming increasingly difficult for V and Nox to traverse the path and keep up with the drones, who themselves were beginning to struggle. No more than 50m into the woods, the path had become more or less impassable. So densely was the vegetation growing. Nox was having a particularly difficult time. He was getting tangled up in everything, much to his frustration. They were going nowhere.

V called a halt. SD59 and H71 hovered over Silbah.

"This is no good" panted V. "The vegetation on the ground is far too thick for Nox! Heck, I can only just manage and I can see that both you and H71 are beginning to have problems. Seems to me this problem is only going to get worse?"

"I suggest you and H71 go on ahead and disable the actuators. Nox and I will remain here and wait for you whilst you accomplish your task."

"Domina," the drones replied in unison, then immediately took off, rose above the tree canopy, and headed off in a northerly direction.

"Well Nox, old boy. Looks like we are here for the next 12 hours or so. Better try and make ourselves comfortable."

Nox just looked at her with baleful eyes. *Comfort is not important?* he thought. *Since when? To me it's paramount. Comfort and a stress-free life. Neither of which I have really had for quite some time...*

Well, whose fault is that? V thought back at Nox. *It was you, remember, that wanted me to come on this quest in the first place.*

Nox just snorted, tried to find a place to lie down. Failed miserably, so he propped his rather large rear end against a tree, closed his eyes and appeared to go to sleep. Not a mouse would be able to pass within 50m without Nox knowing about it. V was then faced with the same problem, trying to find somewhere comfortable to wait out the next 12 or so hours. She eventually managed to find somewhere half decent and settled down to the long boring wait. She closed her eyes, secure in the knowledge that Nox was with her and was keeping guard and miraculously managed to drift off to sleep.

V woke with a start, completely disorientated. It took her a moment or two to regain her wits and remember where she was and what was happening. She glanced over at Nox; he hadn't moved. His rear-end up against a tree, eyes closed, with gentle snores emanating from his direction. His main brain fast asleep, his secondary brain alert and on guard. It registered V's sudden startled movements but quickly understood that these movements were no threat, so didn't disturb the main brain which slept on.

V looked around her. *Wow – the vegetation sure is dense here.* Looking ahead, in the direction in which they should have been going, she couldn't see more than a couple of meters because of the density of the vegetation. She looked up; the tree canopy was far above her head. She was sure it was higher than any tree canopy back on Earth, perhaps 250 – 300m above her head. She couldn't make out the sky, small patches of blueness here and there but that was about it. A blue sky she thought, thinking of home, wondering… So, that was the world in which she found herself when she woke up that morning. A world of green vegetation, and very patchy blue sky. Line of sight no more than 3 – 5m in any direction. Aware of the time pressures, the imminent dangers, the risk of exposure, the threat of The Ostium she checked in with the drones.

SD59, can you hear me? she thought at the drone.

Domina, came back the voice that she was beginning to know so well.

How are you progressing?

Good morning Domina, work is progressing better than expected. We are about 33% of the way through, SD 59 reported back.

V did a quick calculation. She concluded that she must have been asleep for around 4 hours or so. She was quite surprised at that, given the circumstances.

So, you are on track for concluding in another 8 Terran hours or so, is that correct? asked V.

8.37 hours to be precise reported back SD59.

Please try to complete in 6 hours, I don't like being stationary for so long. I'm concerned The Ostium will track us. Please report back in two hours time.

Domina.

So, 6 hours to try and occupy myself. I should have asked how many hours of daylight can we expect. Still, never mind. That question can wait for a couple of hours. She turned to her backpack and took out some food. Not too much, just enough to take the edge off her hunger.

Settling herself back against a tree which seemed to be reasonably comfortable, she took a bite out of her food, glanced up at Nox, who still seemed to be fast asleep, then settled down and stared at nothing in particular. Alone with her thoughts, wishing the drones were done and that they could get moving.

V awoke with a start. She found herself covered in a blanket, Nox looking at her and two drones hovering close by.

She got herself together, tried to make sense of this and surmised there must be a problem.

"SD59 report!" she barked, still half asleep.

The measured tones came back. "All is concluded. The actuators have been disabled and sabotaged. Silbah complex is now dead, and can't be reactivated."

"Oh, um well done. I assume you mean Silbah can't be reactivated by anyone other than either you or H71"

"Affirmative, Domina."

V tried desperately to regain her wits. She was amazed that she had slept for a further five. Nox just looked at her with amusement in his eyes, enjoying the moment.

V turned her attention to those mocking eyes. "Nox, anything to report? Are you quite well and rested?"

Nox thought back at her. *Yes V. I'm quite well thank you. Nothing to report, other than you might like to wipe away the dribble on your chin. It tends to detract from your air of authority...*

V wiped away the dribble on her chin at once. Her hair going scarlet and reflecting her severe embarrassment.

V took a moment. Finally, she had her wits about her and her spirit was back. She was hungry and thirsty. *Damn them*, she thought. *They have had their fun.*

"SD59, where are we in relation to the last known position of The Resistance? And what is the Terrain like, and do we know where The Ostium are or where Ostium spies may be hiding?"

SD59 rose to about 3m above the ground, then blasted his hovering fans as powerfully as possible in order to try and clear an area of as much vegetation debris as possible. He then projected a 3D holographic map.

V recognised part of the map from work she had done in the complex, but the detail on this map was much better.

"We don't know exactly where The Resistance are, but feel sure that they must have a strong hold in Home World City, which, as you can see, is about 2,900km to the south from where we are now. The best course of action will be to head there, perhaps we will pick up The Resistance before we get there, perhaps not. But it is a certainty that we can establish contact with The Resistance in Home World City. Terrain between our present location and Home World City will be mountainous in the north, where we are now, with upland plain in the south, flat rolling plans in between and deserts to the east and west."

V looked around her. *How in Heaven's name was this dense vegetation able to grow and survive in mountainous regions?*

SD59 went on, "You may well be wondering how we happen to be in a densely wooded area in a mountainous region. Well, in general, this doesn't happen. But here and in several other places, there are very odd climatic phenomena, which includes the amount of sunlight, strength of sunlight, nutrients in the soil, precipitation and temperature that allows for vegetation to grow at these much higher altitudes. This is quite usual here on Domus. Our forests exist at much higher altitudes than forests can survive on Terra. "

"Back to the routing. We will head south, and traverse the mountainous areas. After 200km we will slowly but surely start to descend through the Highlands, to the upland plains, and finally into the low land plains. The plains are easily traversable, being largely flat interspersed with hills, the lowland plains follow the alluvial plain of the Great River. "

"Time taken to traverse this distance will be determined by the speed at which we can travel. If the average Domus citizen can walk comfortably at 8 kph, then it will take an average citizen 7.5 minutes to walk 1km. In a 20 Terran hour period, (allowing a 6-hour rest period – there are 26 hours per day on the Domus) then a citizen could comfortably walk 160km. It will take us just over 18 days to reach Home World City. Of course, if you can fly, then we can reach Home World City a lot sooner…"

V thought about this. At least she had some facts from which she could work. What she hadn't told the others was that although she could shape shift, she was limited as to how long she could remain the being into which she had shape shifted into. The larger the entity, the shorter the time, conversely, the smaller the entity, the longer the time. She had no way of knowing how long this period of time was. It depended on a whole lot of factors, how much she had eaten before shifting, how much energy she was using whilst shifted etc. Indeed, it was a risk for her flying for those 30 minutes last night. She shrugged, sometimes risks had to be taken. But she did cringe at the thought of falling out of the sky as she shifted back to her original self, midway through the flight!!! *In future, it would be better to keep my feet firmly fixed to the ground* – she thought.

Eighteen days she thought, *eighteen days of being outside, vulnerable, and open to attack from The Ostium. Of course, the closer to Home World City we got, the greater the risk of being discovered.*

"SD59, at this time of year, how much of the 26 hour day is darkness?" asked V. SD59 immediately responded with "14 hours Domina, we are currently trending towards the Terran equivalent of Summer and in these latitudes, darkness will decrease to 8 hours by mid-summer. But for the period of time we are talking about i.e. the next 18 days, we can comfortably expect a good 14 hours of night-time."

V thought to herself, if we only travel at night, then that's 112 kilometres, meaning the journey would be extended by nearly 8 days. Not good. One thing she was sure about was that sitting here debating the odds was getting them nowhere, other than prolonging their exposure and further delaying their arrival.

V had completely lost track of time. "How long until darkness?" She asked.

"Our equivalent of what you call SOL we call ἥλιος, pronounced Ilios. Ilios will set in around 2 hours."

"Then let's not waste any more time. Lead on SD59. Home World City please."

"Domina." reported SD

CHAPTER FOURTEEN

They had been travelling for two days. The going had been reasonable, but due to the mountainous areas, the pace hadn't been as great as predicted. A mere 75km per day was all they had managed. 150km out of 2,900km, only 5% of the way, 50km away from the highlands, where the going should start to get easier and the rate of progress could be expected to markedly increase. On the positive side, the journey had been uneventful. They had seen no other living thing. Nothing seemed to be chasing them. Nox could detect nothing. Morale was good, the food was good and plentiful, which was just as well because Nox had the most voracious appetite. V was sure that Nox was increasing in size and mass. He seemed to be growing before her eyes. The muscles positively rippled under his skin. She also noted that his body was undergoing other, very subtle changes. He was most definitely not the same miserable, forlorn being she met at Udal Cuain.

Udal Cuain she thought. At once feeling very homesick. Wondering how Uncle Peter and Aunt Izzy were and the Campbell's of course. V could feel tears welling up in her eyes as she thought of her loved ones, light years away, back on her idyllic island. *Would she ever see them again? Would she ever set foot on her beloved Udal Cuain again?* With a superhuman effort, she dragged her thoughts away from home and her loved ones, dried her eyes, cleared her nose, and turned her mind back to the job at hand.

She had elected to walk alongside Nox. Not ride him. Despite the fact that she had 100%

confidence in Nox's ability to safely navigate these treacherous, frozen, icy mountain passes with her sitting on his back, and given his enormous size and strength, she had no doubt that he could carry her from here all the way back to Udal Cuain if he had to. Although Nox would never admit it, V just knew that now wasn't the time. She sensed that his body just needed a little more time to complete the changes it was going through and her sitting on his back would somehow impede and delay those changes. She had no idea what those changes were, or why they were happening but they were and they were making him larger, more majestic, more intimidating, more awe inspiring and given the right context she had absolutely no doubt that he would be absolutely terrifying. She also noted that his coat was once again changing colour. From a distance he was grey but, the closer you got to him so the greyness started to blend into a multitude of colours – as if Nox himself was experimenting and trying to decide for himself what colour he wanted to be.

V had also toyed with the idea of shape shifting. To a bird, or to an animal that could run all day. This would certainly have increased their rate of progress… But at what cost? She trusted her ancestors implicitly but even V was suspicious of shape shifting and, in this instance, V certainly felt that discretion was indeed the better part of valour. Shape shifting could wait until it was really needed.

V glanced up at the sky then to the horizon. The sun, Ilios she corrected herself, will be setting in a couple of hours. We can push on for a good few more hours yet…

They marched on in companionable silence. Nox 100% alert, his secondary brain resting that would be needed later this evening. Like V, Nox was aware of the changes going on inside his body. He had no explanation for them. He just accepted them on the basis that there was really nothing he could do about it anyway. So why worry? Truth be told, Nox had very little explanation for anything about him. He had no memories beyond being prepared on the Home World for his trip through the wormhole and to his eventual arrival on Udal Cuain and V. Before that. Only the times he had been on Terra with Ourea, Uncle Peter and James IV. Other than those memories. Nothing. No idea where he came from, who he was, how he got here… In many ways he was a lot like V. A past that he had no recollection of. No memories. No nothing. They were kindred spirits. Nox and V. Two of a kind. So very different but in so many ways, so very much alike. He had total empathy for and total understanding. He just knew that when he was with V nothing else really mattered. V was all he needed. He was content. But still, how his body itched… and, if he was honest with himself, the changes going on inside his body did unsettle him – at least a little. They didn't make him feel weak or unwell – quite the contrary in fact, he had never felt better and each and every day he felt better and better. He felt strong, immensely strong. He could feel all of his senses honing themselves, becoming ever sharper, more acute. But, there were changes going on that he couldn't explain, he couldn't describe and it was these that unsettled him just a little.

Nox stopped. Suddenly, and without warning. Standing absolutely still. Ears twitching, mouth slightly open, eyes closed. H71 stopped a second or two later. SD59, completely unaware of what was going on behind him, carried on. H71 seeing this, shot off after him and stopped him. The drones stayed where they were roughly 10m ahead of Nox. V only became aware of Nox's abrupt halt when H71 went shooting by, startling her. She was just about to ask what the hell was going on, when she caught sight of Nox. Recognizing the signs, she motioned for the drones to be silent. She stood stock still. Eyes on Nox. The drones went into defence mode and slowly and silently hovered towards V. One drone on either side in a protective, defensive cordon, weapons drawn, but sensors off.

Nobody moved. Absolute silence. V tried to get into Nox's mind to find out what was wrong but was unable to. It wasn't blocked, just unreceptive. She mentally asked SD59 if he sensed anything. The answer came back that without his sensors he was limited to his equivalent of vision. Although far better than human or even Home World vision, and despite the fact that the drones were not limited to the light spectrum wavelengths of about 400 to 700 nanometres. The drones could "see" passively across the entire wavelength spectrum i.e. from gamma waves at wavelengths of 1 picometer to extremely low frequency waves with wavelengths of 100,000km. Despite this, the drones "saw" nothing. SD59 did ask for permission to switch on his sensors, V thought about this for a second or two but decided against. If there was a threat, and it was The Ostium, then switching on the drones' sensors would only make them easier to find.

Still, Nox remained absolutely still. V, not a patient girl by nature, was doing her best to let Nox do his thing, but she was visibly suffering. Hair going to crimson, the golden specks like fire in her eyes… and still they waited.

Then, as if a switch was flicked, Nox relaxed and nodded that it was Ok to proceed.

"What was it Nox?" V asked.

Nox didn't immediately answer. Then said very quietly.

"I'm not sure V. I'm not sure if anything was there at all. Fleetingly I sensed something. Something that pulled at my mind. Something that gnawed at my senses. Then the sense faded and was gone. I couldn't pick it up again."

"So…not The Ostium?" asked V hopefully.

"No, V. Definitely not The Ostium. In fact, I'm not sure if it was anything at all…" Responded Nox.

"So, what do you suggest" asked V.

Nox thought for a moment. "Well, we have at least four hours of daylight left. I suggest we carry on for another two hours or so and then make camp. Best to have got settled and sorted before it gets totally dark."

V nodded in agreement and once again they resumed their trek to the south and Home Word City. However, this time, SD59 kept abreast of Nox, rather than ahead.

Nox was worried. He didn't want to alarm V, nor did he want to lie to her. Intuitively he knew that his senses were not wrong, and something was there. He had been aware of it for some time. He felt something following them. He wasn't totally convinced until the moment the sense triggered something in his mind. Then he was convinced. But until he had something more concrete, he didn't want to alarm V. He did however communicate with SD 59 and told him that something was there and that he and H71 were always to be no more than 1m away from

V. To be vigilant and to be prepared. They were not to go on standby mode but to remain vigilant . SD59 understood and agreed and immediately closed towards V. SD59 communicated to H71, who immediately closed up on V. Nox, feeling a little better that V was as well protected as she could be, went back to scrutinizing every blade of grass within a 500m radius of them. Nothing. He could taste nothing on the breeze, and he could sense no immediate panic or worry in the indigenous flora or fauna.

They trudged on, in silence, for the next two hours. Each lost in their own thoughts. Finally, V called a halt.

They found a suitable place to camp, close to a river and decided that here was as good a place to stop as any. V immediately found herself a comfortable spot, laid out her cape, which blossomed into a bed, ate some food, and went straight to sleep. They would start an hour before dawn.

Nox, ensuring the drones were on guard, went down to the river. Drank his fill, had a bit of a paddle, then decided to lie down in the water and let it try and soothe his itching back. He lay there for an hour, mind alert, eyes never leaving V. He finally heaved himself out of the water, took another long drink, shook the water off his back and went and lay down next to V. With one last thought at the drones to keep watch, he immediately settled himself down, switched on his secondary brain and went to sleep.

V woke with a start. Something inside her, her sixth sense, told her to remain absolutely still. Her mind working overtime, she fought her body to remain absolutely still, to keep her breathing regulated, to remain calm and to continue to feign sleep. She was terrified, but slowly she managed to get her body back under control. Slowly, ever so slowly she opened her eyes. Then went into another mental panic when she was convinced that she had gone blind. She could see nothing. It was like looking into a black hole. Then, very slowly as the darkness caused a flood of Rhodopsin molecules to regenerate, which were then absorbed by the rods within V's eyes in a process called dark adaption, so V's night vision kicked in. As it did so, she slowly calmed herself as she realised that she hadn't suddenly gone blind. Instead, she realised that what was blocking out the dim moonlight was a shape. A huge shape that was standing over her...not moving. She could feel the warm breath from the creature stroking her cheek as the creature breathed in, then out, in then out. Slowly, rhythmically. No stress, no panic. In, out, in out. Commanding her body to remain still while her eyes traced the shape's silhouette. As she did so, the hairs on the back of her neck stood up, her bowels felt queasy and she went into an ice cold sweat. She had never experienced such terror. For standing over her was the immense shape of ... Nox.

He just stood there. One huge leg either side of her chest. She saw the muscles under his glistening coat shivering, quivering. His nose and mouth inches from her cheek. V didn't know what to do. Was he protecting her, had he sensed a threat? She tried to find his eyes. Found them, looked into them and that's when she nearly wet herself. His eyes were like nothing she had ever seen before. They were staring towards the horizon, glittering in the moonlight. Glittering with what seemed to be... absolute malevolence and hatred. Never had she seen anything before but love, patience, and kindness in those eyes.

V shut her eyes, willing herself not to move, not to utter a sound. She must not let on that she was awake and aware of what was going on. Whatever was happening was on a knife edge. It could end well, or it could end badly.

She didn't know how long they remained like that. This mighty beast, with those penetrating, yet absolutely alien and terrifying eyes, just staring at the horizon. What were they looking at? What had he sensed? Nox stood. Muscles quivering. Absolutely still It was as if Nox was fighting a huge internal battle with himself, standing over the girl who was powerless to move, and far too afraid to call out.

Where were the bloody drones when you needed them, she asked herself? She swivelled her eyes but no matter where she looked, she could see nothing but the huge shape of Nox standing over her.

Finally, after what seemed an eternity, Nox moved away. Silently and stealthily – impossible to imagine that such a huge beast could move with a cat-like stealth and silence. Nox moved back to the area he had previously occupied, gently lay down and seemed to go straight to sleep. Almost immediately V heard gentle, peaceful snores emanating from his direction. Still V didn't move, too terrified to do anything other than to lie in what seemed like a catatonic state. Unable to move, unable to talk, unable to sleep. Her mind a mush, full of treacle. She couldn't put one single thought together.

She must have lain like that for an hour at least. Then she must have slept. The next thing she knew was a gentle tapping on her shoulder. She opened her eyes and looked straight into SD59's welcoming and soft, purple lit eyes as he gently coaxed her awake. By now, V had regained control of her body and her mind was switched on and fully engaged. Thinking about the events of the night and looking over at Nox who was still fast asleep, she was unsure whether her experiences of the night before were real or imaginary. Had she dreamt them? She glanced over at Nox. On any other day, Nox would be up and about eating, and making some sort of sarcastic remark about sleeping beauties being awoken from their slumber. But. Not this morning. Nox just lay in his on-guard position, his back to them, still and silent... an ominous presence...

V sat staring at Nox. Unsure what to do. SD59 hovered over to her, a puzzled expression on his face. He sensed that something wasn't quite right ...certainly the day was starting off in a very strange fashion. H71, oblivious to it all, just hovered, and generally got in the way, whilst waiting to be given a task. But none came.

And that was another thing, V thought to herself. *If what I think happened last night actually happened, then where were the drones? Why were they not close to hand? Surely SD59 would have sensed the absolute terror and near panic in V's mind. That should have been enough to have triggered his defences...*

What to do? What to do? Thought V. She called SD59 over. SD59 at once stopped what he was doing, which wasn't very much and hovered over.

"SD59, did anything strange happen last night?" she asked.

The drone looked puzzled and reported "No, Domina. Everything was fine. Both H71 and I were on alert all night and absolutely nothing happened. You and Nox slept well. No threat to the camp."

"So at no time did you sense anything … wrong? You were alert all night?"

"Domina, we didn't sense anything wrong. Either me or H71 were always within 1m of you. You slept peacefully. Your vital signs were calm and relaxed. Our senses indicated that you were in a deep sleep, almost from the moment your head hit the pillow last night, until I roused you moments ago. "

"Thank you SD59. Please go and rouse Nox."

"Domina."

"No need," came a sleepy response from Nox's direction. "I'm awake." Nox heaved himself up from the ground and slowly, ever so slowly turned round to look at V and SD59.

V who knew Nox so well sensed something not quite right. The voice, the inflections in the tone, were just not right.

V looked deep into Nox's eyes. She was convinced that just as he turned round to look at her, so she saw something. Then that something went and, just as suddenly his eyes cleared and were as bright, cheerful, and lovable as normal. It was as if a switch had been flipped. One-minute darkness, then next brightness and sunshine.

"Food" he said cheerfully. "I need food. Then we can be on our way!" Nox wandered down to the river. He had a quick bathe and a long drink. After Nox had breakfasted, the quartet resumed their journey south.

V, lost in her own thoughts, had debated whether to question Nox on the antics of the previous night. But decided not to. However, she decided that she would take precautions from now on and ensure that SD59 and H71 were on alert and nearby and by nearby she meant within arm's length, all evening, with cameras running so that if there is a repeat performance, then she could try and play it back the following morning, always assuming that nothing untoward happened in the intervening period, V thought ominously.

V looked about her; the going was definitely getting easier in fact a lot easier. "How far do we have to go to get out of the mountainous region" she asked SD59. "We are almost there," responded the drone, "Maybe 2km at most."

Some good news at last thought V. Looking ahead to the south she saw the last remnants of the snowy mountainous regions, gradually giving way to beautiful green tree lined plateaus with rolling hills, plains, and large lakes. lakes which glistened like polished glass in the early morning sunshine. Over to the east and west, the glacial mountainous areas continued far into the distant horizon. She shivered at that and turned towards the south. South she thought. South to The Resistance, to Home World City. To who knows what...

And so the morning wore on. Ilios getting warmer, the going getting easier and the world about them quite, quite beautiful. Nox seemed to be his usual self. Quiet until spoken to. Ever alert, always on watch. V had again thought about talking to him about the events of the previous night. But something told her this would not be a wise thing to do. So, she bit her tongue and walked on lost in her own thoughts.

The afternoon came and went. The quartet had made good progress, they must have covered at least 170km during the course of the day, the going was that good. V decided to call a halt to the proceedings. She chose a beautiful spot, by the edge of a lake. Sheltered and secluded. Nox ambled off to get a drink and have a bathe – again keeping his eyes on V the whole time. V was torn, she felt she could do with a swim, but really couldn't be bothered. She was tired and nervous. Tired from the day's activities and nervous about the night to come. She checked in with the drones, made sure they understood what was expected of them. The drones flashed their lights and bobbed at V, cameras already rolling. Satisfied that the little she could do, had been done, she dug out her cape, put her head on her backpack, curled up and went straight to sleep. Or tried to. She tossed and turned for a while. Was conscious of Nox getting out of the lake and settling down beside her. She was a little concerned about that. Why had he chosen this evening to settle down next to her? Usually he would settle himself down a few meters away so as not to disturb her. The drones were puzzled by this too. It also gave them a bit of a dilemma as they were unable to obey V's instructions of staying within arm's length of V. With Nox in the way, the closest they could get was about 3 meters away from V. SD59 communicated such to V, who on the verge of dropping off to sleep, responded with a "whatever," and then she was gone; fast asleep.

In the deep recesses of V's mind an alarm bell was ringing, but ringing so softly that, initially her subconscious missed it. But, like a nagging toothache, the ringing would not stop. Eventually, V's subconscious zeroed in on the alarm and, once the alarm had got the subconscious hooked, then the almost imperceptible ringing, became a cacophony of noise that within milliseconds brought V from the deepest of sleep, to full confused, wakefulness.

She lay on her back, eyes wide open, gasping for breath and trying to still her beating heart. Initially, she couldn't think or rationalise but once her mind had calmed a little and had retaken control of her body, so she began to tune in to her surroundings. It was dark. Very dark. But not the pitch blackness of the other evening. She could see. The moon and stars were masked by low, heavy clouds. She could make out the dim halo of the moon, hiding behind the clouds – part of her looked at the moon enviously, wishing she too could disappear behind the clouds!

She lay completely still, eyes wide open staring at the heavens, mouth slightly open, saliva dribbling from the corner of her mouth. She was concentrating on her hearing. Nothing. Absolute silence. Satisfied that she was under no immediate threat, she chanced a little movement of her head and neck. She looked around her immediate area. Nox was gone. He had been lying next to her, but of him, there was now no sign – at least within the limited view of her vision. The drones, where were the drones? Looking around, she saw a dark lump, about 2m behind her right shoulder. She strained her neck and her eyes. Were they the drones she asked herself? She stared, and then looked off to the side, rather than directly at the heap, letting the rods, surrounding her fovea at the centre of her eyes (the fovea being the middle section of each of V's eyes which is the centre of field of vision) detect as much light as possible in the darkness. Yes. There were the drones. Inert, dark, and lying in a heap, with one drone on top of the other, upside down on the grass. Completely motionless and to all intents and purposes, completely dead. Up until this point, V had been mildly concerned, now her heart started pumping faster as did her breathing. She started to become very afraid. "Where was Nox?" she kept asking herself "Why were the drones offline? Not only offline, but seemingly caught completely off guard. What could catch the drones off guard?"

V of course knew the answer to the last question. Only one thing could catch the drones off guard. Someone the drones knew and trusted. Only one thing here, other than me that could have got that close to the drones and have taken them out…"Nox" she said to herself. Now V became terrified. And it was this reason, the reason of not being sure of Nox's motives that she didn't mentally call out to him. In fact, she closed her mind to him, at least for now, or tried to. She wasn't sure if she was successful or not. But at this stage she didn't know if he had gone rogue. And, until she did know, she would try and keep him mentally at bay and her mind closed to him.

Terrified or not, she had to try and make sense of all this. Was Nox still here? Only one way to find out. Before V quite realised what she was doing, she sat bolt upright, almost frightening herself with her sudden movement. In fact, she would have done if she wasn't so scared already.

She looked around her. She could now see the drones quite clearly – as she thought. Quite dead. No help there. Of Nox there was no sign, similarly other than the pile of metal approximately 2m behind her, there were no other signs of disturbance. The camp remained clean and tidy with everything as she remembered it. She found her backpack, pulled it close to her and hugged it while she thought. Trying to make sense of this. She thought back to the time at Silbah complex, when Nox had run riot. He had good reason to then – to protect himself from the damage that medical staff could, quite innocently have done to him had they kept up with his meds. But, since then, Nox hadn't been 100%. His behaviour of last night for example. His body – which could only be summed up as truly massive. He must be getting on for 30 hands and weigh over 3 tons of pure muscle. Not being much of a horsey person, as far as V could remember, 18 hands was equivalent to 6 ft, (1.82m), and that was from the withers – not the neck or head! He was bigger than a rhino, the family 4x4 on Udal Cuain and would have given a young bull elephant a run for it's money!

But what truly worried her was that V could never ever imagine a time or circumstance where Nox would have left V without any form of protection, so totally undefended. Her mind went back to that last morning at Silbah, when she was nauseous and couldn't face breakfast. She thought of Nox and what he said:

"You know," said Nox. "Whatever we find out there, we will face together. I will always be at your side. I won't leave you again, ever."

Yet here she was. Alone, with no protection whatsoever.

She put her backpack down and crawled over towards the drones. If she could get one of these units working, she may be able to start to understand what had happened.

The drones looked completely at peace, she thought perversely. Well, let's try and sort that out. In order to help her see clearer, she went to her backpack, dug around for her torch and as she did so, her hands brushed against the glasses that SD59 had given her, that last morning at Silbah.

She put the glasses on and at once, the night turned to day. She could see everything so clearly and sharply. She had quite forgotten about these, she admonished herself. She at once remembered that they acted as binoculars and also magnifying glasses. She put them on maximum range and had a good look around her. She could see quite clearly all the way to the horizon. Not only did everything turn as bright as day, but everything appeared in its natural colour. For a while, she was quite lost in the wonders of these glasses and quite forgot her predicament. Nothing from the infrared sensors, so wherever Nox was, he wasn't within range of these glasses.

Suddenly a whirring and scraping sound brought her back to reality. She swung round to the direction where the noise was coming from. The glasses immediately focused on where it sensed Vs eyes were looking. What she saw was a somewhat hung-over drone coming back into the land of the living. SD59, like a phoenix, was rising from the ashes. She thought to herself as relief washed over her.

He managed to extricate himself from H71, then he stopped and seemed to scratch his head, seemingly a little puzzled. Then V could have sworn she saw the light bulb moment in his mind when he finally realised he was upside down. SD59 immediately rolled over and was once again right side up. His optical sensors then fell on V, and she could have sworn he jumped and then looked slightly embarrassed.

Any other time, V would have been amused by this. But not now. She had no time for this.

"SD59, report!" she said a little too loudly and a little too angrily.

"Domina, I'm nearly at nominal. Please give me a moment or two" responded a somewhat flustered SD59.

V bit back her retort. She just stood there watching him, her recent terror giving way to impatience and fear, waiting for a report. Her eyes glanced at H71, no movement there. Nothing at all.

She then took this brief respite to scan the horizon. Again nothing. No sign of Nox. Nothing but grass, hills, flowers, and the lake.

Her eyes swivelled back to SD59. She could sense that he was nearly his usual self.

"Well?" V asked impatiently, fear in her voice...

"Domina, I'm pleased to report that I'm now back online. All systems are functioning nominally. No damage."

"I'm indeed pleased to hear it" said V "But I need answers. Can you tell me how long you were down? What caused you to go down, in fact can you tell me what the hell happened here. And where the hell is Nox?"

SD59, somewhat taken aback by the tone, visibly shrank back a meter or two.

"Domina. I'm not sure. All was peaceful. You were in a deep sleep, as was Nox. He was lying next to you, which gave myself and H71 a bit of a problem as we had to be about 3m from you rather than the arm's length you requested. Hour after hour and nothing changed. H71 and I were continually hovering around you and Nox, cameras were rolling. Then, the next thing I knew, I was upside down in a heap, on the grass. I have no recollection of what happened or why H71 and I were temporarily decommissioned. "

"I see" said V. In fact she didn't. She was as confused as SD59. "Tell me, what cameras did you use?"

"I used my internal cameras."

"I see," said V.

"And these cameras would only record data in the direction in which you were facing, and nothing on the periphery or behind you?" asked V.

"Exactly Domina, which is why I took the precaution of launching a drone camera. I programmed the drone camera to hover above us at whatever height ensured that he had yourself, Nox, H71 and myself continually in sight at all times, with us in the centre of a 200m circle of the camp. "

"SD59, you are indeed one very smart drone. Where is this drone camera now?"

"There, directly above us Domina, about 50m in the air." SD59 pointed with one of his manipulators.

V, at once, looked up and promptly saw the drone hovering directly over them.

"I'm pleased that the disappearance of Nox, didn't cause the drone to go chasing off after him leaving us here."

"That was never an option," responded SD59 "The drone understood that you were the prime target and to be covered and protected at all times, regardless. These camera drones also have basic weaponry, so he did afford you some protection, despite the fact that Nox had gone and H71 and I were out of commission. You did still have protection of some sort."

"Please, one moment Domina," SD59 hovered back to where H71 was still lying. Just a little way ahead of the inert drone was a crater about

2m in radius. There was another crater, about 3 m in front of the first crater.

SD59 called V over.

"Domina, you see this crater, and that one?" V nodded. V had in fact seen them earlier, but assumed they were natural, geological features.

"Evidence of laser blast. Clearly the camera drone fired its lasers."

V visibly paled. Her legs wobbled and she nearly ended up on her back side. But she refused to give in and managed to stay standing. "Right let's see what the camera drone recorded"

"Domina." responded SD59 .

Almost instantaneously, a 3D holographic image of the camp appeared in the night sky. V removed her glasses and stared in amazement. There in front of her, in the night sky was this crystal clear, life-like 3D image of the camp, with herself, Nox and the drones. All seemed to be at peace. Both she and Nox were sound asleep, the drones slowly orbiting the sleeping figures. Just as ordered. Again, V was amazed by Nox's size. The drones looked like two flies buzzing around an elephant. And these drones were by no means small. They must have weighed at least a ton each.

"SD59, please instruct the camera drone to play back 15 Terran minutes before it fired its lasers"

The picture transitioned so seamlessly, that V had to ask SD59 if the picture had been fast forwarded. Having confirmed that it had, both V and SD59 settled down to watch and see whatever it was unfolded…

For 14 minutes and 58 seconds of those 15 minutes, absolutely nothing happened. V and Nox remained sound asleep. V cuddled up to Nox. The drones maintained their relentless orbit around the sleeping pair. The camera drone continued its vigil, hovering silently overhead.

Then everything happened so quickly that V had to keep asking for playback and to slow down the recording to a fraction of its speed, so the two seconds actually took five minutes to replay. Even then, V couldn't really understand what happened.

All seemed well, V in a deep sleep tucked up tightly against Nox. Nox, too appeared to be sound asleep. V could hear his gentle snoring on the recording. Then, within the blink of an eye, Nox levitated from his position like the Lunar Module blasting off from the surface of the moon. He literally launched himself in absolute silence. V was sure his feet didn't touch the ground. He managed to do this without causing any disturbance to V. One fraction of a second, he was in a deep sleep, the next he was up, and careering through the drones. Due to his speed and his massive body, he shifted so much air so quickly, that his slipstream caused the drones to stall, collide, and hit the ground. So fast was he travelling that by the time the drones had hit the ground, Nox had gone. No sign of him at all. Last seen heading south at a frightening speed and accelerating all the time. His pace was absolutely astonishing.

The picture visibly wobbled, the drone fired his lasers, narrowly missing the now prone drones, but Nox was nowhere in sight. The picture wobbled more as the drone climbed higher in order to try and keep the camp and the fleeing Nox in view. But Nox was so fast that the drone failed miserably. Within 2 seconds the trail of devastation was over and Nox was gone. The ground was smouldering, the drones in a heap, V still oblivious to it all sound asleep and despite going to a 1km range from the camp, no sign of the fleeing Nox, none at all.

CHAPTER FIFTEEN

Despite replaying the scenes over and over again, V still didn't understand what she saw.

Nox had never before shown that he was capable of anything remotely like that. Yes, she knew he was big and fast. But fast? According to what she had just seen, fast was a massive understatement. V had never seen anything accelerate that quickly. Ever. In fact, had she not seen it with her own eyes, she would have thought it absolutely impossible. The fact that she had seen it; well she still struggled to believe it! And what had caused him to move like that? To leave them? Whatever it was, in Nox's view, it must have been a huge threat.

That thought brought V back to reality. Clearly, there wasn't anything they could do about Nox – at least not for the present. So, they must take matters into their own hands. Dawn was still 3 hours away. But she had to be careful. She had promised herself that technology was to be used as an absolute minimum. The last thing she wanted to do now, on top of everything that had just happened, was to let fear overcome clear headed thinking. But they needed better protection. Or at least greater warning of a threat, even if there wasn't anything, they could do about it.

"SD59," V called. Immediately the drone appeared. "How is H71?" V asked. "H71 is nominal. No damage. Fully operational." Both drones back to 100%, no damage. Good news.

"Tell me… this camera drone. Do you have more? "

"Affirmative Domina. Both H71 and I have a total of 4 such drones."

V then explained her thoughts to SD59. What she wanted to try and accomplish, and whether it could be accomplished without acting as a beacon to The Ostium.

"Domina. It is possible to send one camera or scout drone to each cardinal point of the compass. It is also possible to have their ranges overlap, giving visibility of an approximate 50km circle, with the camp at its centre. The relaying of the pictures back to me so as to allow us to reproduce the images on a hologram does carry a risk, but I can try and mitigate this by reducing the bandwidth and resolution of the picture. In order to trace these signals, a skilled operator would be needing to look for them. Infra-red and ground penetrating sensors are shut down, so we would have no idea what was happening beneath the surface, nor would we be able to pick up heat signatures."

V thought about this for a moment. She didn't want to run any risk, no matter how remote, of The Ostium locking on to anything at all.

"How do you communicate with the other drones, when they are "over the horizon" and out of "line of sight" asked V.

SD59 responded that the drones have what is called free-space optical communication system installed for just such a purpose. Sensing that V was a bit lost, SD59 went on to explain that free-space optical communication is a highly advanced communications technology that uses light propagating in free space to wirelessly transmit data for telecommunications or computer networking. And, free space means exactly that, whatever the medium, be it air, outer space or vacuum or something similar, the technology still allows communication. And it's quite untraceable.

V turned pale at this. Her body flooded with adrenaline causing her heart rate and blood pressure to skyrocket. SD59 and H71 sensed this immediately. Concerned, they hovered uselessly around the clearly petrified V. V forced herself to ask the next question.

"Do The Ostium have this technology?"

As far as SD59 was concerned, they hadn't. This was technology that only he had been given. He had modified H71 with this communications technology and, as a by-product, the scout drones as well. So, over the horizon communications between himself and the other drones would be possible, 100% secure and more to the point, limitless and undetectable...

V's heart lifted a little at that but now understood that she wasn't the only target. The drones were just as valuable, perhaps more so, to The Ostium than she was. The one thing that had handicapped The Ostium from their relentless march to dominate all things technological, was that it needed some sort of hardware or software to be able to infect other computing systems. And, when large, technology free gaps appeared such as a desert, or space, then the spread of the infection stopped until a solution could be found. An example of one such solution; Domus citizens themselves. Or rather the infected bionics implanted in Domus citizens.

V now understood that free-space optical communications was the key to instant and unstoppable domination as all barriers to the spread of The Ostium infection will have vanished and that there was no defence from The Ostium conquering any world, anywhere as this technology works in the total vacuum of outer space. The only barrier – the speed of light! A barrier that itself wasn't insurmountable.

The key to getting this technology – the drones!

V debated with herself. Is she a greater target because she is travelling with the drones? If the drones fell into Ostium hands, then The Ostium would hold the keys to the universe. Should she order the drones to self-destruct? At least the universe would be safer. Do The Ostium know about this technology? So many questions. No answers. However, the fact that her ancestors had gone to so much trouble, especially with the manufacture of SD59 that she couldn't help but think that SD59 must be more of an asset than a risk. But H71? The camera scout drones? No. That is not a risk worth having. She must order the destruction of the scout drones. But H71? Something told her that now wasn't the time. The scout drones can undertake this one final task and when / if Nox returns, they must be destroyed.

"Then no sensors of any kind. Just record the pictures and if the drones see anything suspicious, they are to immediately report the same to you. I assume the original scout drone has an image and heat signature of Nox and that this has been passed on to the other drones so that they can recognize Nox if they come across his signature or see him."

"Affirmative Domina. This has been done."

"Very well then SD59, please let the scout drones go, but understand, they are to operate in a completely passive mode. One exception, communications. This is only to be done through the free-space optical communication system. No exceptions. Regardless of circumstances. Understood? No exceptions."

"Understood, Domina."

"One last thing. If they feel threatened, or are at the point of being overrun, or they fail through some sort of mechanical / electrical / software fault and can't get home to us, then they are to self-destruct, immediately and without question. They are to seek no approvals. They must simply self-destruct. Is this clearly understood?"

"Domina," reported SD59, quite calmly.

"Very well then. Please execute," V cringed inwardly at her choice of words! With that she saw the four drones depart to the four cardinal points of the compass.

"SD59," called V. "A moment please."

SD59 hovered over to V and waited expectantly. "SD59, are you aware of the risk that free-space optical communication technology brings not only to Domus Mundi, and Terra but to every other inhabited planet in the universe?"

"Domina, I'm aware of the damage that The Ostium could do if they were to get their hands on free-space optical communication technology. I'm also aware that it is only a matter of time before they develop this technology for themselves."

"I agree, SD59. It is only a matter of time before they develop this technology for themselves, especially with all the computing power on Domus at their disposal. However, we don't need to give them a head start. Once the scout drones return from their current operation, they are to be destroyed. Clear?"

"Domina. And H71?" queried SD59.

"Leave him for the moment. Let me think about that. But at the first sign of any suspicious activity, he is to be destroyed. Immediately. Clear?"

"Domina," reported SD59.

And thought V, *If H71 is destroyed, then there seems little point in SD59 having this technology. Especially as we can communicate telepathically. This needs thinking about.*

V sat down next to her backpack. She had been wrestling another problem since she had seen the initial holograms of Nox fleeing the camp. She knew intuitively that Nox wasn't an enemy. She knew he was protecting her and that whatever had caused him to act as he did, he did because it was in her best interest. He had created no damage. Had hurt no one. Well, he did inadvertently cause the drones to stall and crash, acceptable collateral damage. And besides, they are both 100% now. Although she still didn't and couldn't understand how he did what he had done and without even waking her! No. The issue V had been wrestling with, was whether she should try and open a telepathic channel to him.

"Sod it," she said to herself. We have taken precautions. I have two fully armed and alert drones, now fully aware of just how formidable an opponent Nox is, plus four scout drones that have lasers and can be here in seconds if required. She just had to know what Nox was doing and why and whether she should take additional precautions against whatever it was that prompted Nox to take this course of action in the first place!

After checking in with SD59, she tried. Nothing. Nox wasn't there. So, she fully opened her mind to him in the hope that when he was ready, he would let her know.

She was too frazzled to rest or to sleep. Instead she had to try and think. She chose a rock, tried to settle herself comfortably and looked up at the sky. She always found comfort in the night skies when she was at Udal Cuain. They brought her comfort and settled her mind. Allowed her to think clearly. She cast her eyes heavenwards. The stars were so bright, the moon having disappeared over the horizon. She tried making shapes out of the stars. This made her terribly homesick as happy memories of her doing exactly the same thing on early winter evenings on Udal Cuain with Uncle Peter and Aunt Izzy snuggled up to her on the soft, fresh orchard grass. Feeling tears welling up in her eyes, she got up and wandered around the camp. Two protective drones for an escort.

V couldn't settle anywhere. Sleep was the furthest thing from her mind. She was concerned about Nox. Where was he? Just then she heard this now familiar noise and found herself soaking wet. She was covered in a wet, thick, mucus type liquid. It was in her hair, on her face, in her clothes.

"What the Hell...?" and, as she looked up, she looked straight into a pair of the most beautiful, patient, calm, gentle eyes that she had ever seen. Nox!

"Hello V. Forgive me, but it was crucial that I get your attention."

"No, No, that's fine Nox" she stammered, absently wiping her face with a handkerchief she had dug from her pocket, still not quite believing her eyes...

The initial shock was wearing off, which gave way to relief, now relief was giving way to impatience. Nox could sense all of these emotions flooding through her. He just stood next to her, patiently waiting– completely unconcerned.

V got herself under control, then said very quietly…"Well, I'm sure you have an explanation for what happened, would you care to share it with us and by us I mean myself and SD59?"

Looking around, SD59 was nowhere in sight, nor was H71. "Umm, where the bloody hell are the drones" she asked no-one in particular.

"They are running a little errand for me," replied Nox. They are not far away.

V immediately tried checking in with SD59 telepathically. "Domina," came the response. "We are quite fine. We will be with you shortly,"

Now completely at a loss, V looked up at Nox. "Well, you seem to know what the hell is going on, perhaps you would be so kind as to explain to me WHAT THE HELL HAPPENED AND WHAT IS HAPPENING NOW!?"

"Very well, just let me get comfortable here," and with that he lay down next to V. She felt sure she felt the ground quiver.

"For some time now, I have sensed a presence. Someone, or something trailing us. At least I thought I had. This presence kept dropping in and out of my subconscious. You remember, was it yesterday or the day before, I stopped for a few seconds, then satisfied, moved on."

"Yes, I remember" said V.

"Well, at that point I knew we were being followed" went on Nox. "But because the presence kept dropping in and out and was so faint, I couldn't identify it or get a proper fix on it. So, I remained fully alert, but elected not to inform you until I had more data; SD59 and H71 were alerted however."

"Then, the night before last, as we were sleeping, my secondary brain managed to get a fix on the presence and a sense of its purpose, which puzzled me more than anything else. I could sense no malevolence, no evil intent, nor could I sense a spirit of friendship and comradery. I felt a complete lack of emotion. Just a necessity to get to us. To me. To you. To what end? I have absolutely no idea. I sensed it was very close to the camp. I became fully alert and conscious and, as soon as I did, the presence disappeared from my mind. I completely lost track of it. I didn't know if it was going to attack, scout, or disappear. So, I got up and stood over you and listened, eyes staring in the direction that I last sensed its presence. I must have been standing over you for about 10 to 15 Terran minutes, fully alert, waiting to defend or attack – but nothing happened. So, I went back to my resting place and went back to sleep. My secondary brain sensed nothing at all."

Inwardly, V gave a huge sigh as relief flooded through her body. The terror of the other night now fully explained. *Nox was protecting me, not debating whether to have me for breakfast!*

"All through yesterday as we continued our hike, the presence floated in and out of my subconsciousness. Never long enough for me to take action, but just long enough to let me know that it was there, and it was trailing us. I was beginning to think it was doing this deliberately; I had no idea why. If it wanted us to know it was there, why not come up and tell us?"

"So, during yesterday's hike I came up with a plan. I had to flush this presence out. I had to know its intentions."

"Once we had made camp and settled down for the evening, working both my prime and secondary brains together, I was able to project the image in its mind that we were still moving and that we hadn't, as yet, set up camp for the evening. I was hoping to coax the presence closer to us, as I believed the nearer it got, the stronger its presence became and the easier it would be for me to get a fix on it and hopefully capture it."

"As you slept and the drones orbited us, I sensed the presence getting closer and closer. I could tell the presence felt something that wasn't quite right, but regardless, it kept coming, getting closer. I was getting a good fix on it. I knew where it was and where it had come from. It was about 20km away, heading straight for us. I couldn't sense its purpose or its mood, but I knew where it was, I knew where it had come from and I knew the approximate direction it was heading. I calculated that if nothing changed, its closest point of approach would be about 5km to the North of us – immediately behind us. I felt that was close enough, especially as I could continue to telepathically project the image of us moving as I ran towards it, hopefully quietly enough to be upon it, before it realised I was there."

"So, I continued to wait. Silently, fully alert and ready to flee at a fraction of a second's notice. Closer came the presence, closer still. Finally, I judged the distance close enough. I had a solid fix on its position. I knew precisely where it was. So, I went."

"I was on it in seconds. It had no idea I was there until I had it on its back and was standing over it. My telepathic powers overcame its brain and I forced the captive into unconsciousness."

"I spent the next 10 to 15 Terran minutes trying to get into the captive's brain, into its mind to try and understand its intentions, but this was useless. As soon as the captive lost consciousness, so access to its mind was completely blocked. It was clear that to get answers, the captive had to be fully conscious. I wasn't going to risk that just yet. So, I called SD59 and asked him and H71 to come to me. To secure the captive and between them bring it back to camp where we could awaken and question it. "

"SD59 reported that they were in the middle of something and that H71 had still not fully recovered from his accident, but they would come as soon as they could. Eventually they turned up."

"I stayed long enough to ensure the captive was bound securely, then the drones started to drag the captive back to camp. They should be here in a matter of minutes. I came straight back here to alert you."

"I see," said V. Continuing to think aloud, she said to herself "Well, we are not going anywhere until we understand who this captive is, what it wants, what sort of a threat it poses and what its intentions are. The question then is what to do with it?"

"Nox, we have to assume the captive is a real threat and treat it accordingly."

Nox was about to reply, when SD59 appeared over a hill, with H71 and an inert, dark bundle in tow.

SD59 was told to stay where he was and H71 asked to leave the bundle just where they were. They were to aim their lasers at the presence and to keep them aimed.

H71 left the bundle, which rolled down a slight incline, before coming up hard against a rock.

The bundle just lay there. Inert and motionless. It made no sound. V looked at Nox. Nox looked at V. Nox turned to the bundle and slowly walked up to it. V stayed where she was.

"What are you going to do Nox?" asked V.

"Wake it up."

"Whooa," said V. "Should we not talk about this first? Devise a plan? I mean does it know who we are? What we are doing? Should I be revealed? Does it know about your abilities?"

"I don't have the answers to any of those questions" replied Nox patiently. "But the captive seems very well informed. It knew where to find us. It then decided to trail us. It seemed to try and keep its presence a secret. Now anyone who acts like that can't be a friend and must be treated with absolute suspicion. To get the answers, we have to wake it up, as its mind seems to be impenetrable to mine and ask it. If it doesn't answer, then we will have to try and find other ways to get the answers we are after."

"Oh, very well,"

"SD59, is it securely bound? Does it have any weapons or anything it can use to harm us about its body, either inside or out?"

"Domina, I can report that the electro bonds used to secure the presence are sound and are completely unbreakable. They are sufficiently tight to keep it secure, but not so tight as to cause damage, yet. But I can communicate with the nanoparticles within the electro bonds and tighten or release on command. I can report that as far as my passive sensors allow, the presence has no suspicious materials on it or within it. I can't of course check to see if he has any nanoparticle booby traps secreted within his body. So, for that reason, I suggest placing him within a protective force field, so that if something does detonate, then we should remain unharmed. "

V thought about this. Again, she didn't want to leave any electromagnetic "signatures" that The Ostium could trace, but, in this case, she felt that the captive afforded a significant threat, so reluctantly she agreed.

"Very well SD59, but please ensure that the force is set to the smallest setting possible and, before arming the force field, destroy the scout drones. Ensure they are vapourised. No trace left."

"Domina, both tasks are completed."

"Ok Nox. Just before you wake it up, who should lead the questioning, I mean we are assuming it understands us?"

Nox, just looked at her for a moment, as if to say, "Are you that stupid?"

V looked puzzled, racking her brains, wondering what she had done now.

Nox sighed as if to say what a complete Numpty!

"V, perhaps it would be a good idea for you to use that magic box of yours and morph into a Domus citizen; I mean I know you are one, but your features, although becoming more "Domusesque" every day, are still not quite right, they remain a little Terran. Morphing into a citizen, and I suggest a male citizen, will ensure that not only your features are 100%, but that your mannerisms and general "air" will be too. Not to mention the fact that you will have absolute understanding of the languages spoken on this planet."

V was at a loss for words, mainly because she was mentally kicking herself so hard that it brought tears to her eyes! And to think, she told herself, that I'm supposed to be the last hope for this planet, and Terra… Jesus, we should throw in the towel now and raise the white flag. What a complete blithering idiot I am.

"Yes, of course, Nox. You will keep trying to probe its mind and if you can, tell me if what it says is the truth or a lie" replied V, hugely embarrassed.

Nox merely grunted in response, as if to again say "Who is the idiot around here?"

V then had a slight problem. Who to morph into? She hadn't met any citizens at all. So, she had to hope that her ancestor's magic box would select a typical male citizen for her.

She immediately thought at the box in her back *male citizen*. Nothing seemed to happen.

"Very good," said Nox. That will do nicely.

V assumed the transition had been successful!

Right Nox, wake it up.

Within a minute or two, faint groaning sounds could be heard coming from the direction of the pathetic, but rather large bundle on the ground. A minute or two later, the bundle started moving and appeared to be shuffling around, trying to sit up. Eventually, it managed to prop what V assumed to be its back up against the rock that it had just crashed into, then it raised its head and just looked at them. Saying nothing. Giving nothing away. Just sitting perfectly still, watching and waiting.

V couldn't see very much. She put on the glasses SD59 had given her, which helped a little. She was about 5m away, the closest the drones felt it safe for her and Nox to be. What V did see was a body swathed in dark robes. It appeared to be biped, as she could see two large feet sticking out from under the robes, and two hands poking out of another part of the robes. Both the hands and feet were swathed in black rags, but quite obviously hands and feet. Everything else was covered in the same black rags. V twiddled some settings on her glasses to try and improve the view, which she did by thought rather than manual manipulation, she managed to see through the force field. Or more accurately, phase the force field out from her view. She then magnified the glasses. Yes, definitely hands and feet, big ones as well. Much bigger than Terran hands and feet. She glanced at her own hands and thought to herself, well so are mine!

V then zeroed in on what she assumed to be the head. Then she found the eyes. Gazing back at her, like lasers, were two completely black eyes, rather like her own. But unlike her own eyes, inside of those eyes were the darkest red flecks she had ever seen. It gave her the impression that the eyes were on fire. The more she looked, so the specks grew and faded and swirled. The redness fluctuated from scarlet to crimson, to burgundy, to maroon. They didn't do this uniformly, but each speck did this of its own accord, giving the impression that each speck, and there must have been at least a hundred of them in each eye, had a mind of their own. They were the most terrifyingly hypnotic eyes she had ever seen.

V had to consciously drag her eyes away from its eyes. She removed the glasses, she felt safer that way.

"Who are you" boomed a low, deep, loud, commanding voice. V jumped. Looking around her wondering where the hell that voice had come from, then she realised the voice had come from her! She had quite forgotten she had morphed into a male citizen. She heard Nox snort in amusement. She could sense her hair changing to a deep crimson red in absolute mortified embarrassment.

She tried to forget her embarrassment and concentrate on the entity before her.

"Who are you?" boomed the voice again, V was ready for it this time.

No answer.

"Very well, you can simply stay there until you are ready to answer." And with that, she turned around and walked off. Nox ambling along behind her.

SD59, she called telepathically.

Dominus? came the immediate reply, using the correct term of address to a male citizen.

Please tighten the bonds, just enough to be very uncomfortable, but not enough to do any damage

Dominus. The drone did as instructed.

Let's leave it to think about that for a few minutes. Did you pick anything up, Nox?

I sensed anger. I sensed frustration, but I sensed no fear, quite the contrary. I sensed satisfaction.

Hmm. I see. Anger and frustration at being caught, or being securely bound? Satisfaction in knowing it was right? Satisfaction in a job done? Or partly done, an everything going to plan type satisfaction?

Quite possibly, Nox agreed.

"Who are you?" repeated V.

A muffled response.

"H71."

"Dominus?"

"Please remove the robes from its face so we can hear what it has to say"

"Dominus," responded H71 who immediately tried and bounced off the force field.

"Perhaps you should shut the force field down for a second" V suggested.

"Domina," responded H71, a little meekly.

Eventually, H71 managed to complete the task and, after re-securing the force field, hovered off to a safe distance; far enough away to try and recover a little of its shredded dignity.

"Now, let's try again. Who are you?" asked V for the third time

"My name is Venandi. Who do I have the pleasure of addressing?" came the reply in a deep, confident voice.

No fear at all in that voice. Just confidence thought V.

Nox's voice intruded in V's mind *On Terra, Venandi is the Latin for Hunter. Tread cautiously V, there is a lot more to this individual than meets the eye.*

"Where are you from Venandi and why are you here?"

"I'm a Domus citizen, from Home World City. I repeat, who do I have the pleasure of addressing?"

"You are a long way from home, Venandi. Why are you here?"

"Why I'm here is my business and none of yours. I demand that you release me from these bonds and allow me to continue on my journey"

"You will remain exactly where you are, bound as you are until you tell me what you are doing, why you were trailing us and what your intentions are. Only when I'm satisfied, will you be allowed to go on your way," responded V.

"Citizen, you have no right to keep me here, bound as I am. I have every right to be here and I have every right to complete my journey unhindered and unimpeded."

"Venandi. I'm not prepared to discuss your rights. As things stand you have no rights. I have the power of life or death over you and believe me, I'm not particularly bothered whether you live or die. What you will do is answer my questions, to my satisfaction. Your continued evasiveness will guarantee but one conclusion." V tried to put an ominous tone in her voice and felt that she had succeeded remarkably well.

"As I have said, I'm a Domus citizen, travelling home, to Home World City. I had no idea of your presence until I was viciously attacked and knocked unconscious by what I can only assume to be your drones. Now, please release me and let me be on my way."

So, Venandi had no idea it was Nox that sensed his presence and captured him. Good, very good. Thought V.

"I'm sorry Venandi. What you say is a lie. We know you have been stalking us for the last three days. We know you have remained around 20km from us. Stopping when we stopped, starting when we started. Sometimes coming closer, but then dropping back. I want to know why, and I want an answer now, or I will simply get on my beast and leave you with the drones. Oh, and the laws of robotics don't apply to these two drones. Believe me, if I told them to hurt you or worse, they would and they would do it with absolute pleasure. Remember, they already knocked you out, to bring you here. That in itself is in contravention of the first law. 'A drone may not injure a citizen or, through inaction, allow a citizen to come to harm.' So you see, they continue to contravene the first law. They are not in any way, preventing me from hurting you, or doing harm to you, even now. So, you must know that what I'm telling you is the truth. One word from me and these drones will kill you. Need I say more? Now, the truth or face the consequences."

Venandi looked at V for a long time, the red dots in his eyes visible, darkening and moving with even more haste than before. She had no idea of the expression on his face as other than his eyes and his mouth, his face was covered in swathes of black cloth. But she could imagine it was an expression of absolute hatred.

"Very well. I see I have no choice. My name is indeed Venandi. It is also true that I have been trailing you. I was sent here, well around 200km north of here, to wait for a young female citizen and a beast, eyeing Nox as he said the word. I was to follow them and once satisfied, I was to approach them, introduce myself to them and to offer all assistance in escorting them to Home World City."

"Who sent you and why should they need an escort?"

Venandi gave the impression that he was arguing with himself, weighing up the pros and cons.

V let him get on with it, remaining silent. *What do you think?* She thought at Nox.

Difficult to say V. This one has a very well-trained mind. And I want to tread carefully and not alert him to the fact that I'm in his mind. I'm sure, given time I can break the barriers down in such a way that I will have full access without him being aware, but, just at the moment, I'm finding it very difficult. That in itself should be a warning sign to us. However, I judge what he has just said is true, it will be interesting to hear what he has to say. It is also safest to let him assume that I'm just a dumb beast of burden and nothing more, so I will assume the character traits of a terrestrial horse and assume to be completely ignorant of everything that is going on around me but don't worry, I will be 100% aware. And with that, Nox ambled away grazing on the lush grass.

Understood Nox. I will try and treat you accordingly. As will the drones, understand SD59?

Affirmative, Dominus.

SD59, if you pick up on anything from Venandi, please let me and Nox know.

Understood, Dominus.

"Venandi, I don't have time for this. Either you tell me what I want to know, or I leave you to the drones. Entirely up to you. Your call. You have pénte lepta (five minutes) to make up your mind, then I'm gone"

With that, V went off and started to break up the camp, which was just ensuring she had everything in her backpack.

"Citizen," Venandi called over to V.

V stopped what she was doing.

"Yes?"

"I am not sure I understand it myself. My reluctance to tell you is not because I don't want to. No. It's simply because I have trouble believing my own story…"

"I'm waiting" responded V, wondering where the hell this was leading.

"About a year ago, I started to have vivid dreams. Every night, the same dream. I continue to have the dreams to this very day. The dreams are so clear that I could have been in the middle of a hologram. Always the same. The dream telling me that I was to meet a young woman and her companions – one of those companions was a large, grey beast, the other two companions were autonomous vehicles." he said, eyeing Nox and the drones.

"I was to travel here, well 200km north of here, and I had to be at that location by a certain date. I was to wait, undercover until I saw the company, track them until I was sure it was the same people that I had been dreaming about.

"Once I was sure I was to approach them, introduce myself, gain their trust and escort them to the leader of The Resistance. I was to tell no one of these dreams, or what they were asking me to do. Not even the leader of The Resistance."

"Then, about six months ago, this talisman mysteriously appeared around my neck. It seems to be attached to my skin. I can't touch it with my bare hands – it burns them when I try. When I cover my hands with rags and try to remove the talisman, it is like trying to tear my skin. The talisman refuses to yield. I have no idea where it came from, how it came to be hung around my neck, and why it is there. Only to say that since it appeared, my dreams have become even more vivid, more lifelike and every day that went by, a feeling of greater urgency descended upon me – the urgency only being eased when I started my trek North."

V had been listening hard to every word that Venandi had had to say, as had Nox and SD59. She found his story quite incredible, almost impossible to believe. So impossible in fact, that there may be a grain of truth to it. She looked long and hard at Venandi. *Yes,* she thought to herself, *it's so fantastic, that it just may be true.*

"So, what made you think that we were the people you were looking for? I'm a male citizen and there are countless beasts such as this in Domus."

"Citizen, I had been waiting, for about a week, at the location where my dreams said the party would first appear. I saw no one. Then on the exact day, at the exact time, I sensed people approaching. It was exactly as my dreams had portrayed. A citizen, a magnificent beast and a couple of drones. And forgive me, citizen, but there are no beasts anywhere on Domus that remotely resemble that beast over there. Your beast is …phenomenal, unique and quite, quite terrifying."

V couldn't argue with that. No doubt, Nox was one of a kind, which kind of gave the game away, but there is no way she would be without Nox. Not ever, not under any circumstances!

"Well, despite the purported uniqueness of my beast, you can see that I'm a male citizen and not a female citizen," responded V.

"As you say, citizen. You do appear to be male. But, shall we say that appearances can and often are deceptive. And forgive me, citizen, but I have travelled far and wide across Domus and believe me, I have never seen, and never heard of a beast such as yours."

V felt that she was fast losing the upper hand here.

Nox, what do you think?

Nox was quiet for a second or two *I simply don't know V. His story seems exactly that, a story. Impossible to believe! It's so ridiculous that it could almost be true. But, if he was convinced that we were the party that he had been dreaming about, then why not come up and say so? Does he have any proof that what he is saying is true? I doubt it but, having said that there must be something that he has that can convince us. Given these troubled times, I'm sure he would have something that could confirm his bona fides.*

"Venandi, your story seems exactly that. A story. What you say doesn't explain why you didn't approach us directly and tell us who you were. If what you say is true, then I would expect you to have some sort of proof of your bona fides"

"Drones" V called out to SD59 and H71 "We are done here. I'm going. Please terminate and bury this citizen and join us when you are done."

"Domina" the drones replied in unison.

With that, she whistled to Nox, who came trotting over, bent down, and allowed her to climb aboard...

As she tried to climb onboard Nox with dignity, something she found very difficult given his huge size, she turned to look at Venandi as if to say "I did warn you, you brought this on yourself," and with that, she settled herself on Nox's huge back, turned him to the south and slowly walked off.

Then H71 immediately started to cut a grave into the ground, whilst SD59 kept the force field in place.

"Citizen!" bellowed a voice from behind her. V chose to ignore it and carried on slowly heading south.

"Citizen, please!" bellowed the voice again. Reluctantly, V brought Nox to a stop and slowly, so very slowly, she turned him around until they were both looking directly at him. Well, V was, Nox gave the appearance of complete indifference and concentrated very hard on the patch of lush grass in front of him.

V simply raised an eyebrow in enquiry and waited. The drones carried on digging a grave.

"Citizen, what I have told you is the truth. I didn't approach you because, despite turning up at the right time and place and you seemed to be the correct party, I wanted to be sure. I had to be 100% sure. My presence to has to be kept a secret. The Ostium knows me. They know me as a ranger and a hunter. They know I work for and assist The Resistance in any way I can. I'm number three on their hit list. If they knew I was here, they would either kill me or turn me. They would also know that my being here meant that I'm seeking someone very important to The Resistance. Not only would they kill me, but they would kill whoever I was with. Or turn them. I tried approaching at night, but your beast sensed my presence and protected you. I dared approach no further. So I devised a plan whereby I would open my mind to you, a little at the time, letting you know I was there and gradually over the next few days, letting you know all about me so that when I did come to your camp, I did so in your full knowledge. But you captured me before my plan was fully implemented. And this is the result. Deep suspicion."

"As to bona fides, I am not sure I have anything that will prove what I say is true."

V thought about this for a minute or two. "If what you say is true, and you are 100% certain that we are the party you have been sent to escort, then you will have no problem in opening your mind to us. Will you?" V snarled at him.

Venandi simply nodded.

Nox?

His mind is open. What he says is true, or at least he believes it to be true. But, there is a very small part of his mind that I can't access, that remains firmly closed. I remain suspicious and we should be very cautious

Is he aware that you are in his mind? Asked V.

No, of that I'm positive. But if I were to break down this final barrier, then he would be aware of my presence.

SD59, what are your thoughts?

I'm with Nox on this one. Venandi remains of great suspicion to me. His story seems so unbelievable – yet here he is. Even if he has bona fides, I will still not be convinced, but then again, if he is who he says he is and if what he says is true, then we would be very foolish to ignore him and his offer of help. The Hunters have skills that are legendary, and they know the land intimately.

SD59 is he completely natural. I mean, does he have any bionics, be it a limb or eye, or even eardrum or heart valve replacement. Has he had any work done to him that The Ostium could infect?

No Domina. Our sensors found him to be a 100% biological specimen with no enhancing or replacement parts anywhere in his body. But again I would advise caution as we can't detect any live or dormant nanoparticle insertions or biological malware within him that could be of Ostium or any other origin.

I intend to press him for bona fides. If he has some and they prove to be definitive, then I plan to treat him more leniently. He will remain with his bonds intact, but they will be loose and allow him a certain degree of movement. We will see how he can help us and what he suggests. But he will always be under suspicion and SD59, he will be your responsibility. If you consider any action he takes to be a threat to either myself or Nox, regardless of the time or circumstance, you are to terminate him at once. No questions, no permissions needed. You will simply terminate him. Is that understood? Do you have any issues with that?

No Domina, I will terminate at once if I feel he represents a lethal threat to either you or Nox.

Good. If he does not have any bona fides or any proof of what he says is true, then I am afraid, I have no option. I have to eliminate him. Nox, SD59, are you in agreement?

Reluctantly both Nox and SD59 agreed. There was simply nothing else they could do. Only roll the dice and see how they land. *Besides* Nox said to himself, *some people are unable to back away from a challenge, and one such person is standing here, right in front of him – V. If she didn't have that character trait, then she would not be the one to fulfil the quest that has been set before her. There was no other alternative.*

V turned to face Venandi. She asked once again if he was sure that he did not have any bona fides, or anything, something that could prove his story was true.

Venandi simply stared up at her. V could see he was thinking hard. Absently his hand went to the talisman around his neck. He recoiled in shock as the talisman burnt his hand. V could see the shock register on his face. The red dots in his eyes aflame with colour. "Ouch!" he screamed. Never had the talisman burned so hotly before.

"Let me see that – kill the force field" V demanded. SD59 and H71 went into apoplectic shock at her last demand. "Yes, you heard me" snarled V "Kill the force field" SD59 and H71 looked helplessly at each other, then turned in unison to look at Nox for support. Nox seemed to be concentrating very hard on a particular tuft of grass and ignored them completely.

V, you do know what you are doing? Nox thought at V. *No, Nox. I don't. I have no clue. I have not understood what I have been doing for a long time now. However, I feel this is something that has to be done. Trust me Nox.* Nox just mentally shrugged his huge shoulders and followed her. The drones killed the force field and also followed her. As V approached Venandi, she called over to SD59, "tighten his bonds and keep a firm eye on him. He tries anything, he dies. Understand?"

"Domina" responded a somewhat shaken SD59.

V slowly approached Venandi, then stopped a meter or so away from him and looked down at him. The calm gold flecks in her eyes, a complete contrast to the bright, menacing red flecks in his.

"Venandi, I wish to look at the amulet you have around your neck. Any interference from you and my drones will kill you. Instantly. Do you understand?"

"Yes, Citizen I understand. But please be careful, the amulet will burn your hand."

"That is understood and a risk I am prepared to take. The drones will take no action should my hand get burnt."

V slowly reached out to the amulet. She paused, then grasped. The amulet was cool to the touch. It immediately fell away from Venandi's skin and lay innocently in V's hand. V grasped the chain and removed the amulet from Venandi's neck.

Venandi looked at V in amazement. V ignored him and studied the amulet. It was an oblong piece of smooth, silver metal. *Very similar to the metal Argentum Metallicum was made from*, she thought to herself. The oblong measured about 5 cm in length, 5 mm wide and maybe about 3 mm deep. Other than seeming to throb in her hand, it did nothing. Just lay there. Cool to the touch.

"Thank you, citizen," Venandi said quietly.

"Thank me for what?" V asked distractedly.

"For removing the talisman. Now it's yours. Although why you would want it, I have no idea…"

"I do not believe this talisman belongs to either of us. I believe it is a message. I am just not sure how to make it work."

Perhaps you should rub it like Aladdin rubbed his magic lamp quipped Nox.

V was just about to castigate Nox, thought better of it and said to herself "Why not"

V put the amulet on top of a nearby rock, rubbing the amulet softly as she did so. At first, the amulet did nothing, other than get a little warmer due to the friction of her finger rubbing over the smooth metal. Then slowly, almost imperceptibly, the amulet started to glow, then a bright green light emerged from the centre of the amulet and before V could utter a word, she found herself looking into the life-like eyes of Domina Solis Ortus Pota. The eyes looked back steadily at V for a second or two. These were the eyes of a woman in control. They were clear, steady and resolute. Not the eyes of a haunted, panicked woman that the last hologram had depicted

"SD59, stun Venandi into unconsciousness now. Don't kill him, just knock him out."

SD59 did not ask any questions, did not hesitate, he merely fired his laser. Venandi groaned and crumpled. He was quite unconscious.

"Vica Pota you will have many questions. Not least of which is who is the fellow that you have captured and how did I manage to arrange this. Well, first things first. Let me introduce you to Venandi. Although I have yet to meet him, Venandi will be fundamental to The Resistance movement. He is the last of a dying breed. He is also very high on The Ostium hit list. When he wants to be, he is simply untraceable, uncapturable. He is unique and has many skills that we need in our quest to destroy The Ostium."

"Venandi was sent to wait for you then to trail you. Once he was sure you were you, he was to introduce himself to you and to assist you in your journey from the Mountains, far in the North to me, here in Home World City. He knows the lands, intimately. He knows the people, the hazards, the fastest routes. He can guide you to me safely through even the most hazardous and remarkable routes. You should trust him, as I do, to bring you safely to me. Finally, just to make sure he is the individual that was sent to you, you should say the following phrase to him, in Terran Latin "Trust no one. Be there when we get back," Watch for the reaction in his eyes. The red dots in each should change colour to white. The white dots should burn brightly, an intense brightness easily seen against the stark contrast of the blackness of the remainder of his eyes. The haphazard white dots should then conform to the Terran letter "V". If this doesn't happen, then eliminate the person at once. For he will be an imposter."

V replayed the message several times. She was not 100% convinced. Her gut was telling her that something was not quite right. V had learned to listen to her gut. But what was she to do? Her gut told her that she could trust Venandi. *There are at least a couple of things not quite right here. Firstly, the hologram. Specifically, the image of Solis Ortus portrayed in the hologram. It was so very different from the hologram that she saw at Silbah. It's as if this version is a manufactured version of Domina Solis Ortus Pota and not a life-like version...* V thought to herself. *She is just too perfect. Secondly, after listening to Venandi it seems as though Venandi has met Solis Ortus, yet from what Solis Ortus was saying in the Hologram, it was as if she has yet to meet him, was yet to benefit from his skills. What the hell am I supposed to do? Well, the first thing to do is wake him up ask him, then utter the phrase and see what his eyes do...*

"SD59, please wake Venandi. Once he is awake and has a moment or two to gather his wits, I will ask Venandi some questions, then I will utter the phrase that Domina Solis Ortus Porta instructed me to. If the dots in each of his eyes don't change colour and burn intensely white and form the Terran letter V

– stun him. Don't wait for the order. Just do it. Understood?"

"Understood Domina,"

V waited for SD59 to bring him round, which was accomplished with a few slaps to the cheek from SD59's manipulator. She then gave Venandi a moment or two to clear his head.

"Venandi, I was not very clear on this point. Have you ever met Domina Solis Ortus Pota? If so, when and why?"

"Yes Citizen, I met her about 3 months ago. I had stumbled on one of the Resistance raiding parties. After attacking and killing some Ostium infected citizens, I followed the Resistance raiding party to see where they were going next. They led me straight to the Resistance HQ. Well, to cut a long story short, that is where I first met Domina Solis Ortus Porta. It seems I was expected. We talked for a few hours. I was given my instructions, and I left. I have not been anywhere near the Resistance or her since."

"So you had these dreams and received the amulet well before you ever met the Resistance?"

"Indeed so, Citizen."

"Does she know you are here now? That you were intending to meet this mysterious foursome?"

"No, Domina. This is something I am driven to do. What guides me, pushes me I have no idea. I just know that I had to be here and nothing was going to stop me..." He said eyeing the drones and Nox.

"You made no mention of your dreams or the amulet to Domina Solis Ortus Porta?"

"No Citizen. Absolutely NOT!"

"Very well Venandi. Thank you" Then, without any warning, she uttered the words "Nemo habeat fiduciam. Ibi quando rediretake."

As if a switch had been turned, the dots in Venandi's eyes immediately changed colour from red to white. The whiteness initially being dull and pale, quickly deepened and blazed. The white specs soon blazed from within the blackness of his eyes like beacons at night. The haphazard patterns of the white dots started moving like fireflies and soon settled into the shape of a Terran V. Two white V's blazing from the blackness of his eyes. The dots blazed white for a full thirty Terran seconds, before reverting to the normal pale red dots, haphazardly scattered in each eye.

Well, thought V. *That seems pretty conclusive. What do you think, Nox?*

Nox, who had been within earshot at all times and had seen the transformation within Venandi's eyes, agreed.

On the face of it, he seems who Ortus Pota claims him to be. Yet, there remains something about this Venandi that is secretive. 99% of his mind is open to me, it's the 1% that remains hidden that worries me. Whether this is something that we should be gravely concerned about or not. Well, I simply don't know. Additionally, if he had never met Solis Ortus before, how did she know his eyes would react in this way? There is much I do not understand. Much that seems a contradiction.

SD59, thoughts?

I don't have Nox's gift for being able to access other beings' minds. So, I can't comment on Venandi's mental status. But I can measure vital signs and I have to say that the readings both H71 and I have recorded are what one would expect from an honest individual, someone with nothing to hide and who is hiding nothing. Yet, there is something that I can't explain, that I simply don't trust this individual. A sixth sense ... Yes, I know, a robot with a sixth sense, quite unheard of. Yet I was given this gift and I have learned over time, not to ignore it. I too agree with Nox that there are too many contradictions. I have met Ortus Pota and the lady depicted in the hologram did look like her, sounded like her, acted like her...yet did not appear to be her. Quite frankly, the whole thing stinks!

Very well, thought V. We agree. We believe this is Venandi. But we don't trust him ...yet. We are all concerned about the message from the amulet – yet despite what we believe about the depicted messenger, I honestly believe the message was sent to help us and not to hurt us. I suspect that whoever sent the message, and I'm 100% positive it did not come from Ortus Pota, must have realised that we did not know any other citizen on the planet. So how to gain our trust? or at least give the message enough credibility to make us listen to it and to act on it? Answer...fabricate a person that we did know could be trusted – or at least we had met all be it by hologram – and use that figure to portray the message to us. No. Ortus Pota herself did not deliver the message. But I am positive that a friend did organise the message to be sent. We will give Venandi the benefit of the doubt, keep the bonds loosely attached, allow him comfort and give him respect, but watch him like a hawk and at the first sign of anything out of the ordinary, we bind him and remove all privileges.

And, went on Nox, *He is never to be left alone with you V. Either myself, or one of the drones must be with you at all times. No exceptions. I shall continue to act a beast of burden and will keep my powers to myself. SD59 and H71, you are to treat me as such; in other words, ignore me.*

Agreed, they all thought unison. With that, Nox ambled off. H71 stood next to V, having been brought up to date by SD59. SD59 hovered close to Venandi.

"Venandi," V started. "Please accept my apologies for the way we treated you. Please. Come join me. Tell me a little about yourself and how you intend to get us to Domina Solis Ortus Pota"

CHAPTER SIXTEEN

Venandi was wondering how the hell he had managed to get himself into this position. In all the years he had been a ranger, and the number of years was very nearly beyond counting, never had he been captured, let alone captured so easily. He had replayed the scene over and over and could still make no sense of it.

Well, we are where we are, Venandi thought philosophically. *The big problem I face now is gaining V's trust. The route they are taking is the correct route, a safe route, well as safe as any route can be in these troubled times, but it will take far too long. I can show them a different way, a riskier way, but a way that will reduce the journey time considerably. Of course, it's debatable whether the beast can travel this route, it may have to be left behind. I'm not sure how V will react to that, especially after I have yet to gain any sort of trust. I have ten hours before we have to change course. Ten hours to try and earn a semblance of V's trust.*

V decided that continuing with the illusion of being a "male citizen" was pointless as Venandi knew who she was, so she had morphed back to herself and continued to fire questions at him.

Venandi tried as best as he could to answer all of V's questions as honestly as possible. Some he found quite impossible. "Why had he become a ranger?" The answer was that it was quite simply ordained. His father had been a ranger, as had his father's father. His family had been for generations, for millennia; he was now the last of a dying breed.

Vanandi's family had never fitted in with the typical citizen's way of life. They seemed to have been locked in a time warp. They lived a way of life that never changed; an existence that went back through the ages. Had his great, great, great, great, grandfather come back to life, and compared his way of life then, to the way his great, great, great, great, grandson lived now, he would have noticed no difference and would have felt quite at home. Venandi lived off the land, with no fixed home, simply laying his head wherever he happened to be. He had no use or need for technology. He knew Domus' lands intimately, knew the dangers, knew where he could find friends and knew the places to avoid. He roamed freely, never leaving a trace of his presence. His breed was a dying one. As far as he knew, he was the last of his kind. Most had died out either because their services were no longer needed, or they too fell foul of an easier, technology-laden way of life. Then The Ostium came. The Ostium recognising just how dangerous these people could be slowly but relentlessly wiped out the few remaining rangers. Venandi evaded them, of course. His skills were unequalled. He could smell an Ostium infected citizen from a mile away. He would use his skills to hunt them, kill them where they lay. Then, one day, he quite literally stumbled across what he now knew to be The Resistance who were, at the time, stalking a group of Ostium infected citizens. Venandi stalked the stalkers. Watched and waited. He saw how they moved through the lands, how they failed to merge with their surroundings, how they failed to read the land and to use it to their advantage how they failed to demonstrate any sort of fieldcraft at all. He marvelled at the stupidity of the stalkers. He saw them launch their attack. Surprised at the stupidity of their timing, of the chosen Terrain. The attack was successful in so far as it killed The Ostium infected citizens and that none of the stalkers was themselves killed. But from a stealth perspective, it failed miserably. Anyone with an ounce of fieldcraft could read the signs. Could tell how the attack was prepared, from which direction it came, how many attackers there were, and in which direction they left.

But he sensed there was something here for him. A better way to go about ridding his beloved planet of The Ostium. Before he knew what he was doing, he was following the attackers. He had no idea who they were or whether they would kill him on site, yet he knew, deep inside that this was the correct thing to do. He followed them for days. Again, marvelling at their inexperience and stupidity. He could have killed all of them, at any time, without them ever knowing he was there. He could see that the attackers were approaching a more populated area, there were signs all over the place. He assumed that the attackers thought this location was well hidden and so it was, but not as far as Venandi's eyes were concerned. There were giveaways all over the place. The way the undergrowth was trampled, broken limbs and branches, smells in the air – habitation of lots of people. The way plants had been planted. They simply didn't belong. No doubt the attackers had done their best to hide their existence, but they were lightyears away from being utterly secure, utterly invisible.

Venandi was wondering how best to announce his presence. Was it to simply stand up and say, I'm here, take me to your leader – or wait for a more opportune moment? As always, he decided to err on the side of caution and wait for a more opportune moment.

The taller of the attackers, which Venandi had assumed to be the leader, was now approaching a seemingly impenetrable wall of vegetation. But to Venandi's eye, he could see an entry portal. The attackers walked right up to the vegetation, paused a moment, took another step, and then simply disappeared.

Venandi had a quick look around. Although there were signs aplenty of other citizens, he had seen no one. He glanced at the sun and figured there were about 2 hours of daylight. "Very well," he said to himself, as he settled down to wait.

Time passed swiftly. He had plenty to keep him occupied. He listened to the wind, the sound of the wind against the canopy of leaves. He listened to animals and insects. They soon forgot he was there. No alarm, no stress, just the normal sounds of the early evening.

Still, Venandi waited. He wasn't concerned. He was quite impassive. He was completely in tune with his surroundings. Twilight became darkness. No moon this evening, so total darkness. This was of no concern to Venandi. His night vision had been honed and fine-tuned over millennia. He could very nearly see as well in full darkness as he could in full daylight.

Quietly, Venandi sprung from cover. Easily and effortlessly he moved towards the vegetation wall. Using the Terrain as you and I would wear clothes, he was more or less invisible as he jogged to the wall. He went to the exact location that the attackers went to. He quickly surveyed the vegetation and found a clumsy attempt at hiding a portal pad.

Faced with a dilemma of two choices. "Do I use the code and gain entry, or do I simply ring the bell?"

Well, if I'm in, I'm in. On the other hand, if I'm outside, then getting in will be a little more difficult. He looked at the portal pad. Put his hand about 1cm above the keys, closed his eyes and concentrated. Yes. Some latent heat from the last time the buttons had been depressed. Five buttons to press. He could also sense the very small temperature difference in the recently pressed buttons, so working from cooler to warmer, he pressed the buttons in sequence. Coolest button first, warmest button last. Sure enough, the portal opened and, as if he had an absolute right to be there, Venandi strode in. The portal closing behind him. Whereupon pandemonium ensued. Venandi just stood still, arms held aloft, passively awaiting his fate.

Venandi was immediately surrounded by five very puzzled citizens. He could sense that these were not Ostium infected individuals, so remained impassive and non-threatening, waiting for events to play themselves out.

Orders had been given and Venandi assumed those orders were to hold the stranger and await the arrival of a more senior individual.

Moments later, quite an imperious looking lady arrived, surrounded by her guards. Looking at her as she approached, Venandi sensed irritation tempered with curiosity, but absolutely no fear. Good, he thought to himself.

Venandi continued to look at her as she neared. He was pleased to see that his stare was returned in full. *No question of her backing down,* he thought. He had all the information he needed, for now anyway, so lowered his eyes and awaited the inevitable barrage of questions. However, what he didn't expect was what came next…

"About bloody time too," she said. Venandi's eyes snapped upwards and looked straight into hers. He saw amusement.

"I have been expecting you. You took your time getting to us. But you are here now. That's as well. We need you. I have a pressing task for you"

"I assume you are Venandi. The last true ranger of the lands. Son of Dominus Orlata Venandi."

Venandi had to compose himself. He was shocked to speechlessness. He had to mentally remind himself how to talk.

"Yes, My lady. I am Venandi, son of Dominus Orlata Venandi. Who do I have the honour of addressing?" he asked politely.

"My name is Domina Solis Ortus Pota. I'm the leader of The Resistance."

"An honour, My lady. I know exactly who you are, and I apologise if I have kept you waiting. Yet, you seem more aware of my fate than I do, since as far as I was aware, I had no intention of meeting up with you."

"Venandi, I don't have time to argue. Suffice to say that this meeting was inevitable, ordained if you will. And here you are, exactly as you should be, and you still have time to undertake the task I have for you."

" My lady. I have tasks of my own to undertake. I too have things that I must do"

"You wish to kill as many of The Ostium infected citizens as you can, yes? You wish to rid this virus from our lands totally and irrevocably. True?"

"Yes, My lady. That is indeed my most immediate task."

"Good. Then we are aligned. We have the same motives. The task I have for you will help both of us to complete the wiping out of The Ostium far quicker than either you or we, The Resistance could do by ourselves or jointly."

"Very well, My lady. I will listen to what you have to say."

"Good. Come let us talk,"

Venandi turned to V. "So, now you know. How I met up with The Resistance and my meeting Domina Solis Ortus Pota. The task she set me was to instruct The Resistance in the arts of fieldcraft, perform commando raids on The Ostium strong points and to generally use my skills to assist The Resistance in any way I can."

V, SD59 and, of course, Nox had listened carefully to every word that Venandi had uttered. A quick telepathic conference was held between all three. The consensus, that they needed more detail on how Venandi intended to get them to The Resistance in the quickest possible time. There was no doubt that everything Venandi had said was the truth. Nox's intuition and SD59's "sixth sense" attested to this.

"Venandi, as you know, my drones have accurate maps, are aware of The Resistance location and are quite capable of navigating me to The Resistance. They are able to protect me, as you found out. So why should I listen to you and why should I allow you to guide us instead?"

Venandi had been anticipating this question, it's one he would have asked. He had been toying with several answers, but he decided that V was no fool; in many ways, she reminded him of Domina Solis Ortus Pota, but stronger somehow, more resolute, and far, far more intelligent. So, the only answer he could give her was the truth.

"My lady. The task my dreams set before me was to get you to Solis Ortus Pota as safely and as quickly as possible. Why? I have no idea. How you can help The Resistance? Again, I have no idea. My sole purpose was to meet you and to get you to lady Solis Ortus Pota as quickly as I can and, to be frank, the route you are intending to take is not the quickest. It may be safer, but it is certainly a lot, lot slower. As I have already explained. I have spent hundreds of years travelling Domus Mundi. Not only that, but I have all the memories of my relatives who travelled Domus Mundi. All their routes are firmly imprinted in my memory – it is as if I travelled those routes. There is nothing I don't know about this world. I'm aware of routes that no map will ever show. Routes long forgotten. Dangerous, yes; but still navigable. The route I'm thinking will be almost instantaneous in comparison to the route you are intending to take. I could have you with The Resistance in at most ten days My lady, indeed it could be a lot quicker. But. As I say, it is dangerous. I'm not even sure we can take the beast with us. "

V stopped dead in her tracks.

"Venandi. We need to get one thing clear. Where I go the beast goes. If the beast can't go, then neither do I. Is that clear? Despite his appearance, he is of use to me and I will not allow him to be separated from me. Do you understand?"

Venandi eyed the beast wondering what in all of Hades was so remarkable about this animal. What could this brute possibly offer in the fight against The Ostium? But he could also see that V was determined to take this beast with her. And if he wanted her trust, then the brute had to be considered as part of the team.

"Very well, My lady. I will select a route that the animal can also traverse. I assume he can swim? I assume he will not be afraid? I assume that the risks we expose ourselves to will not cause the beast to bolt, or to give us away, or to expose us to whatever enemies may lie ahead?"

"I can assure you that he will not in any way put us at risk. He can swim, He can be trusted. I will take full responsibility for him."

"Good enough My lady. Then the route I have in mind is worth the risk. I feel almost sure that the beast can traverse. It may be a squeeze in places, but if he is the beast you say he is, with the qualities you say he has, then I'm sure he will manage."

"My lady, will you trust me? All I can tell you is that this route has not been traversed in a thousand years. The dangers that lurked there then, may still be there or may have been replaced by other, even worse dangers. I simply don't know. One of my ancestors undertook this route once, one thousand five hundred years ago. It nearly cost him his life... The route has dangers that even I can't foretell. Will you trust me to lead you through it and to bring you safely to The Resistance?"

"Is there no alternative?" asked V.

"Yes, My lady. There are alternatives. But none that will get you to The Resistance as quickly and, the longer you are out there, the greater the risk of discovery."

What do you think, Nox? She asked.

He is telling the truth and remains committed to bringing us safely to The Resistance. But he is afraid of this route – so it must be a very dangerous route. I'm up for it so long as we all stay together.

Thanks, Nox. SD59?

I agree with Nox. My sensors indicate fear of this route. I can't quantify what the fear is, but he is afraid, but again 100% confident that we can prevail, although he remains doubtful whether Nox can traverse the route.

Very well then, V agreed.

"Venandi I will allow you to guide us. But I repeat. The beast must be able to traverse the route. Oh, and any signs of subterfuge or treachery and my drones will kill you… instantly."

"Understood, My lady. Your drones will not be troubled, and the Beast will accompany us.

"Very well. Lead on."

No sooner had V uttered the words than a tremendous flash of lightning lit up the dull day, followed by a crack of thunder, the like of which V had never heard before. The Heavens opened with raindrops the size of golf balls. V, Venandi and Nox were soaked through in minutes. Venandi had been expecting this, of course, he could smell the thunder in the air and had been watching Nox. Nox didn't react at all to the crashing thunder or vivid lightning, V, on the other hand, jumped a mile. Being completely unaware of the deteriorating weather conditions. Nox just stayed where he was, seemingly impervious to the rain hammering his broad back, eating any succulent tuft of grass he could find.

Well, that's something at least thought Venandi. There may be hope for the beast after all.

"No sense in moving on for now. This storm will last for a good few hours. We will bivouac here until the storm has passed. It will be well dark by then and safe for us to move. We will continue to follow the route your drones were navigating for another 8 hours, we will then deviate, towards Shari lake. We will reach the lake a couple of hours later, and that my friends is where the adventure will start."

"Very well," responded V as Venandi took over the setting up of the bivouac. He did this in minutes. It offered a dry, comfortable place, sheltered from the storm and more than large enough for the drones and the two citizens. Nox was content to wait in the rain. He was quite enjoying it and it allowed him to remain on guard.

"Tell me about Shari lake," V asked.

"Shari lake," repeated Venandi. A name that even today sends shivers down his spine. "All I know is hearsay. What my ancestors have heard and experienced. I have never been there. I have seen Shari lake often enough but never ventured close to the lake. It's quite remarkable" responded Venandi, his eyes distant, focussed on nothing. He went on quietly

"This planet, Domus Mundi is so advanced. Well before The Ostium virus corrupted everything. Yet still, within this planet remained a few places that people with as much intelligence as the citizens, who had access to so much incredible technology, yet still they refused to go near. Convinced that to do so meant a fate worse than death; they believed that something within the lake would consign them to the underworld. That they would exist for all eternity in a state of half-life and half-death. Told to perform tasks and acts that would revolt and humiliate even the strongest of mind and character. Whether there is any truth to this, I can't say. We rangers are not superstitious, but my forefathers always avoided

Shari lake. Only one ranger ever navigated the lake, and he never spoke of what he saw. But he did leave the route he took, and I have it imprinted in my mind as clearly as if I had actually travelled the journey. "

"My lady, I don't choose this route lightly. In fact, given the choice, I would avoid it at all costs. My dreams intimated that Domina Solis Ortus Pota is in urgent need of your company. My lady, I see no other choice. But I say again, should you choose to stick to the original route, then I will, of course, accompany you. The choice is yours, My lady."

V looked at him long and hard. She let him see her hair turn from a neutral flaxen to a deep crimson red. She let him see the gold dots in her eyes burn ever more fiercely before she said in an unmistakable tone.

"Venandi, I think I made myself abundantly clear. If there is a perceived urgency in getting us to Domina Solis Ortus Pota, then there must be a very good reason for it. I will not repeat myself. We will go to Shari lake, we will face whatever dangers lurk there; we will overcome them and proceed with all haste to The Resistance.

DO... I...MAKE... MYSELF... CLEAR???

With that, she rolled over, closed her eyes and went straight to sleep. The drones either side of her, ever alert.

"Domina," was all Venandi could say. His respect for this young woman was growing all the time. He felt himself becoming trapped in her spell. He would stay with this lady. He would watch over her and protect her to his death. She was indeed formidable, and he sensed that he had only seen a tiny bit of her capabilities. He was also beginning to suspect that the dumb beast of burden wasn't so dumb and most certainly not a beast of burden. That one would need to be watched closely. He could imagine those two working together, a frightening thought.

With that, he cast his mind to his surroundings. Satisfied that there were no immediate threats, he too closed his eyes and went to sleep. Nox and the drones sensed this immediately. Nox went on full alert, H71 left the bivouac and went on patrol, leaving SD59 to protect V.

Sure enough, after a couple of hours, the storm rumbled away, the rain stopped, and the night became pleasantly warm. Venandi stirred, awoke, and checked the surroundings. Satisfied that all was well, he wondered what to do next. Should he wake V or let her sleep. Time was of the essence, but he was also aware that once they reached the lake, sleep would be but a distant memory. Matters were taken out of his hands when V informed him that she was fully awake and ready to depart. She had been waiting for him to waken. Nox was up and about and ready to leave. Venandi dismantled the bivouac and ensured that all signs of their presence, citizen and beast had been eradicated. Satisfied, they moved off.

The journey was undertaken in silence. There wasn't anything more to say. V was deep in her thoughts, thinking about home, her Uncle Peter and Aunt Izzy, the dear Campbells and wondering if she would ever see them again. She looked over to Nox wondering why he had to come into her life. Why had he caused so much disruption? She should hate him for that. But no, she could never hate Nox. She loved him completely. She knew that she and Nox were irrevocably bound until one of them was called to the spirit world. She thought more about Nox. She had always assumed he was from Domus Mundi, as was she. But clearly, this wasn't the case. Where had he come from? Why was he here? How did he get here? Did he have a family? So many unanswered questions.

Hopefully one day, Nox and I can start to untangle his past and answer some of those questions. But for now, that will have to wait. We have Shari lake to contend with, then The Resistance and only then can we start to fight back against The Ostium. Well, I hope Domina Solis Ortus Pota has a plan because I sure as hell don't! And what about Venandi? By now V felt she could trust him. The fact that Nox couldn't delve 100% into his mind did trouble her a little but felt that at least for now, he was quite genuine, and he was concerned for her especially when it came to the lake. Another strange, unique individual. A way of life that was completely opposite to an entire world's population. And that is what made him so dangerous to The Ostium. The fact that he shunned technology as had his forefathers. Had absolutely no use for it. It only takes one man to start a revolution and he could do it in ways that The Ostium could never understand, they would never see him coming, never know what his intentions were. They were quite unable to track or follow him. Yes, she could quite understand how desperate The Ostium were for his capture and how valuable he was to The Resistance, to me. Yet still, there is something about him that is unfathomable, unexplainable. Is this a good thing, will it serve us well? Or is it a bad thing that will end up hurting us, perhaps terminally? Time will tell. Nox will never allow him to harm me and Nox will get to the bottom of Venandi in the fullness of time. Of that, I have no doubt.

V didn't give Shari lake a second thought. She knew it was dangerous but heck, there wasn't a thing she could do about it so why waste time worrying about it. She had a formidable team supporting her. She felt confident they could tackle pretty much anything that came along. The drones were equally at home in the water as they were in the air or even in space. Nox, well she did worry a little – he was certainly no submarine, she chuckled to herself. Then stopped chuckling when she realised that neither was she!

V looked around her. It was certainly turning into a lovely day. The sun was just appearing over what she called the Eastern horizon. The view was spectacular. Domus was certainly a beautiful planet. Very Earth-like, yet very different. She wondered what the cities looked like. Well, she would find out soon enough she supposed. And as always, niggling at the back of her mind, were the three questions she desperately wanted answers to. Why me? What can I do to break the grip of The Ostium? How can I help? But as usual, no answers came.

Nox, of course, was tuned in to the inner debate that was going on inside V's mind. He never tuned out. Not anymore. He would not again until he knew they were safe. Nox would never intrude on her thoughts or let her know he was there. He also never took any offence at anything she thought. He knew how V felt about him. He was content. He just wished he could help her more. He did have some of the answers but felt she needed to work things out for herself. He knew she had the intelligence to do just that. He would feed her the odd clue as and when he deemed necessary, but in general, was content to let her make up her own mind about things. So far, she hadn't gone wrong, and he suspected she never would.

Lost, deep in thought, V didn't notice morning meandering into afternoon, into early evening. What finally attracted her attention and snapped her out of her deep reverie was the general air of malevolent foreboding that seemed to permeate every pore of her body, every molecule of air that she breathed. She suddenly noticed how the landscape was changing. The land they traversed early in the morning had gone. What she saw before her were stumps of petrified wood. An ancient forest where the wooden stumps of the trees had quite literally turned to stone. All the organic minerals being replaced with minerals, most of which were silicates such as quartz. The original structure of the wooden stem tissue remained. Unlike other fossils which are compressions or impressions, petrified wood is a three-dimensional representation of the original organic material. She also noticed that Nox was leaving deep hoof prints on the glutinous sand, which started to suck at her shoes making the going even harder. Then there was the smell, a sulphurous smell; a smell that reminded her of rotten eggs. Quite subtle, but quite noticeable. In the far distance, she saw a black streak which dominated the horizon. Overhead the blue sky was speckled with yellow clouds. It looked very striking yet foreboding.

V looked back and saw only one set of footprints and one set of hoof prints, hers and Nox. But of Venandi's, there were no signs. She looked over at him and looked down at his feet, amazed to see no depressions, no footprints at all. He was walking so lightly over the tacky surface that he was leaving no sign of his presence. *Wow,* she thought to herself. *This man is clearly like no other.*

The going became tougher and tougher as the tackiness of the ground slowly became more and more marsh-like. Nox's tremendous weight crashed through the very fragile surface into the wet marshy bog-like substance below. Yet he maintained the same pace as the others. Venandi was surprised by this. He expected their progress to have been compromised by the increasingly difficult Terrain. But no, Nox was keeping up and although getting rather dirty, didn't seem to be exerting himself any more than usual. Venandi was impressed and again thought to himself that this is indeed no ordinary beast.

They plodded on, the stumps of the ancient, petrified forest becoming more numerous as they progressed towards the black streak on the horizon. The ground thankfully wasn't getting any softer but was getting wetter. Water was beginning to slop around V's shoes, fortunately, her shoes were completely waterproof.

V assumed this was the start of the wetlands leading to Shari lake, which she again assumed was the blackness ahead that was now totally dominating the horizon. The yellow clouds had by now completely hidden the blue sky and were now working on the sun, trying hard to make the sun completely opaque; success was inevitable and only moments away.

Just a little way ahead was a raised piece of clear, dry land. Venandi headed for this small islet, just large enough for the three of them to settle comfortably.

"We will bivouac here for a few hours, get some rest and then head to the lake just yonder. This is the only dry place we can rest until we have transited the lake."

Fine by me, thought Nox, who immediately lay down, his huge behind towards Venandi and V, closed his eyes, engaged his second brain and went straight to sleep.

Venandi dug about in a bag that appeared from nowhere and offered V some food. "Here. Eat this" he said. "It's tasteless, but a little goes a long way. After only a few mouthfuls you will feel pleasantly full and when we resume our journey, you will feel full of energy."

Without a second thought, V did as she was asked and ate a small amount of the proffered food. It was indeed tasteless, but after three or four mouthfuls, she felt full and couldn't have eaten another thing.

"I'll give some to the beast just before we move off. "

"The beast is called Nox" V responded. "I would rather you refer to him as Nox, and not beast"

"As My lady wishes," Venandi waited for V to expand on the subject. But she didn't. Instead, she turned around, made herself comfortable and was settling herself for a brief sleep.

"How long before we move off?" V asked.

Venandi thought for a moment or two, "Five to six hours" My lady. "We will let the lake do the work and allow her to come to us, rather than us continuing to struggle towards her. There, you see about 10m away from us, over there towards the lake...?" He asked V.

V sat up, looked and saw what Venandi was pointing at.

"Is that the high-water mark?" she asked.

"Correct, My lady. "In about seven hours the water level in the lake will have risen and will have reached that point. We will wade out about two kilometres with the water level gradually increasing all the time before the ground drops away suddenly."

"What do we do then" Asked V.

"We wait," answered Venandi. But would say no more.

"I suggest you try and get some sleep, My lady. You are quite safe here"

"He is right, you are" mumbled Nox… followed by "Drones…?"

The drones immediately went on guard. SD 59 next to V, H71 flying about 20m above them, watching the horizon.

V went straight to sleep. Nox's second brain sensed this immediately. Although he perceived no threat, his brain sensed an omnipresence all around them. It seemed to be watching them. Like a lazy cat smiling to himself while he watches a mouse running around trying to seek an escape. Unfortunately, there was none. The cat, just watching and waiting. Choosing his time for the final coupe de grăce!

V slept fitfully. Every time she closed her eyes, in her mind's eye she saw nothing but blackness and felt she was being suffocated. Suffocated by the smell, which was now becoming intolerable, suffocated by the sense of death and decay that was everywhere, suffocated by something that she couldn't see, only feel. Slowly wrapping itself around her head and face. She would open her eyes with a start, look around her, take comfort from the gentle snores emanating from the direction of Nox's bulk just a few feet away, closed her eyes only to go through the same iteration of suffocation, death and decay. Eventually, she gave up. She tried looking at the sky, but there was nothing to be seen there. The clouds blotted out the stars and the moon. It was as dark as she had ever known. Completely black. She put her hand in front of her face and saw nothing. Whether her eyes were open or closed, the result was the same. She tried thinking happy thoughts, but none came to mind. And so the night wore on. Slowly, painfully but also inexorably.

V must have dozed off, for the next thing she knew she was being gently awoken by SD59. SD59 didn't trust Venandi enough to let him get within an arm's length of her, let alone touch her. She opened her eyes to see the soft, gentle welcoming glow emanating from SD59 accompanied by a bright "Good Morning, My lady" Immediately behind SD59 was Venandi, who also wished V a good morning. Nox merely grunted at her as if to say, "Why so early, I was having such a wonderful sleep," At times, V hated Nox. In fact, what V didn't realise and would never know, was that it was Nox's intervention that allowed her to get as much sleep as she had done. He had sensed her inability to get to sleep, so had stepped in, by taking away the bad thoughts and soothing her to sleep. She had had four hours of deep, dreamless sleep.

Nox heaved his bulk off the ground and stood, rather sleepily looking around him. *What a shit hole* he thought rather indelicately. Thinking to himself that things are going to get a lot worse before they get better. V nearly choked on her breakfast at Nox's indelicate, yet remarkably accurate descriptive.

Breakfast which was more of the tasteless, yet energizing food that Venandi had offered her the evening before.

Venandi wandered over to Nox. Venandi looked into Nox's eyes, the first time he had done so. Nox just looked impassively down at him. Venandi didn't say a word to Nox, just held out his hand and offered him some breakfast. Nox sniffed at it, eyed it with curiosity, then mentally shrugged his shoulders and ate it. It took more than four mouthfuls to satisfy Nox. Quite a bit more. But eventually, even Nox was sated, at least for the moment. Nox and Venandi just eyed each other again for maybe three or four minutes, before Venandi retreated saying at the same time, "Time to break camp and go and meet up with The lady of the lake."

V had watched the exchange between Nox and Venandi with interest. *So?* she had thought at Nox.

It appears he has some telepathic powers and was trying to get inside my mind. He was trying to understand who I was, why I was here and what my relationship with you was. Of course, he had no chance of penetrating my mind. He got nothing. But for the first time, I saw inside that part of his mind that he had kept locked away, if only for a couple of Terran seconds. He is working to an agenda. An agenda that was sparked by the murder of his wife and children. The Ostium were responsible. The area of his mind that he keeps closed off are all memories associated with his murdered family. Murdered by his trusted brother-in-law. The brother-in-law that Venandi had entrusted his wife and family too. Who had sworn to protect them, sworn unto death. But unbeknownst to Venandi, he had already been turned

*by The Ostium. Had been offered wealth and status
beyond his wildest dreams to slay his sister and her
children. Their murders were recent and still far too
painful to bring to mind. So he keeps that part of his
life locked away. One day he may open up. I could
certainly help him. But not yet. It's this desperate
need for revenge that keeps him loyal to our cause,
but only loyal whilst it suits him and whilst his
interests match ours. If and when these interests start
diverging, he will go his own way.*

As V went about preparing herself for the
journey ahead, she listened to what Nox had to say.
Her heart saddened. This explained a lot. Explained
Venandi's seemingly indifference to life and death,
his reticence, his hatred of The Ostium, his
willingness to fall in with The Resistance to see his
world rid of this scum. There was of course no doubt
that he held himself entirely responsible for the
murder of his family. His brother-in-law was the tool,
but Venandi knew he was responsible. He had
primed, loaded and aimed the gun and ultimately,
pulled the trigger. He, Venandi and no one else was
responsible. He, Venandi and no one else would seek
devastating revenge, no matter what the cost to
himself or anyone else that may get caught up in his
quest.

Venandi, whilst breaking down the night's
bivouac was also locked in deep thought. He had used
all his telepathic powers to try and enter Nox's mind
but all he had seen was blackness. A wall of
impenetrable blackness. Nox eyes had given nothing
away. They didn't look as though they were
concentrating on anything other than the blandness of
the food. There was no sign of strain, of resistance, of
concentration, nothing. Just doe eyes trying to enjoy

bland food. And this worried Venandi more than anything else. Either Nox was a dumb beast of burden who hadn't anything going on up top. Or he was the complete opposite. A very wise, intelligent and supremely powerful animal with a mind unrivalled anywhere in Venandi's known universe – with the possible exception of V's mind that is. Both supremely powerful, but both very different. So different that you couldn't compare them. Given V's insistence on Nox being able to accompany them, her insistence that he wasn't to be left behind. Venandi was now 99% positive that Nox was a supreme being, rather than a dumb beast. He was now convinced that the dumb beast routine was just an act, to throw Venandi off the scent. And this did worry Venandi, he had never, in all his long life come up against anything quite like Nox, or V. Who were these people? Where had they come from? Do they represent a threat to me, to my quest? He knew they were good and hadn't anything but the same desire as him, to rid Domus Mundi of The Ostium, but what lengths would they go to? Venandi didn't care if his life was to be forfeit as a result of their intent, but he did care that he was to remain alive long enough to see his quest through. Venandi was a deeply troubled citizen. Should he trust them? Or treat them with deep suspicion? Now was the time to act. Now was the time to destroy them. For he, and only he, knew what lay ahead. Their deaths could be arranged easily. No suspicion would fall on him as a result. Just part of the perils of the route they had taken. Their deaths would guarantee his survival. A sacrifice to the lady of the lake for his safe passage. Could he live with himself if he arranged their destruction? Would he not be as guilty as his brother-in-law if he did? What would his wife think or say? And what of V? He asked himself. Was she so frightening? Determined...Yes. Driven...Yes. But frightening? You asked her to trust you and she did so. She doesn't understand the true risks of what they are about to embark on, but she does understand there are serious risks. Yet here she is... You asked for her trust and you got it. Can you now betray it? Can you really bury those affections you are beginning to develop for her, and just stand by and allow her to be destroyed? You know the answer to those questions, don't you? Venandi... Don't you...?

Of course, he did. He could no longer allow deliberate harm to come to her as he could to his now recently deceased daughter. He swore to protect her, and he will.

It's Nox that terrifies him. A seemingly dumb animal that can resist his thoughts, can resist the power of his mind, so easily. Effortlessly. It's the thought of his unknown powers that terrified Venandi. Yet those powers could be an ally and help him in so many ways. If V trusts Nox so wholeheartedly, then shouldn't he?

Honestly, I just don't know. Not yet. But, for now anyway, I will not stand by and let hurt come to him either. Not if I can help it.

Nox was tuned into Venandi's mind and followed every thought and argument. He understood that Venandi could hurt them, especially now, especially at this part of the journey. But he was content that Venandi would not let deliberate harm come to V. He wasn't bothered about himself. He felt confident that he could protect himself. But V, she couldn't. Not yet. Nevertheless, he instructed the drones to be extra vigilant and to take whatever action at whatever time, if they felt that V was in any form of danger.

Finally, the camp was broken. Venandi had destroyed any signs that they were ever there. Dawn was still struggling to turn into full daylight. Unfortunately, it was a losing battle. The clouds seemed yellower, fuller, and lower than they were yesterday. They seemed to suck all the light out of the sun. V thought back to that morning when the sunlight pierced her curtains and relentlessly followed her eyes across her pillow. The morning that seemed so far away now, the morning that had pre-empted everything that had happened to her since. No chance of that happening here she thought. Not through the denseness of these clouds.

She looked towards the lake. Sure enough, the water was very nearly at the high-water mark. Lapping so gently, yet so ominously at the tacky sands.

She didn't understand how a lake could be tidal, especially with the tide of this lake, which seemed to be huge. Yesterday they could barely see the lake, now it was practically at their feet – mere metres away. How was this possible? She asked Venandi. He simply responded that this was one of the many strange eccentricities and unanswerable questions of the lake. No one knew where the water came from, where it went… But the proof of the movement of water was right before their eyes.

The water was now gently caressing the high-water mark. The lake was calm and flat. Barely a ripple for as far as the eye could see. Yet, no matter how gently it was caressing the high-water mark, the lake looked ominous, foreboding. It was almost super black, it seemed to suck all the light out of the day.

And as uninviting as a visit to Hades itself. Yet uninviting or not. This is where they must go.

Venandi looked at V. She nodded. He looked at Nox, who simply looked straight back at him. Not a flicker of recognition or emotion crossed his eyes. He simply stared back. Unblinkingly. Venandi looked at the drones, then turned back to look at V.

"We may have a problem with them," he said.

"In what way?" asked V.

"Well, I know for a fact that nothing quite like those two have ever been near the lake, let alone in it. It might be best to put them in standby mode and secure them to Nox's back. He is certainly large enough to carry the drones. Would that be a problem?"

SD59 for one didn't like this idea at all. And said so to V. She checked in with Nox… *Well?*

No problem for me to carry the drones, they will fit easily enough. They weigh nearly a metric ton each – this is not a problem for me either. Quite comfortable in fact. If you are asking me about protection. This is of course a concern. But. We have little choice. I suggest we keep them active, rather than standby, so that they can at once intervene if required.

Agreed responded V.

The drones flew over to Nox, gently landed on his back, put their manipulators away as Nox ensured they were properly secured and went into silent active mode. Nox got himself comfortable then imperceptibly nodded to V that he was good to go.

V nodded at Venandi. "Ok" was all she said.

With that, they set off, the lake only metres away. In no time, they were a step away from the lake. V stopped, hesitated then dipped her foot in the water. The water was impenetrable. Black as black could be. She couldn't see through. It was warm, in fact pleasantly so, about 25° C. But absolutely no sign of life… well… she qualified that statement. She couldn't see through the water to tell if there was life there or not! She felt nothing but the tacky sand below her feet.

As Venandi had said, the water remained very shallow for metre after metre. She looked back and already they were about 500m away from where they had entered the water. Yet the water was lapping around her ankles. Still pleasantly warm. She looked at the others. Venandi looked determined. Nox looked…well, like Nox. Untroubled.

"What was that?" she asked herself. There it was again. She could feel something gently nibbling at her shoes…

CHAPTER SEVENTEEN

Nox! V called telepathically. *Yes V, I feel it too, through my hooves. I don't sense any aggression here*

"Venandi?" V called.

"Just go with it, V. Relax and let the inevitable happen. Try not to panic."

Panic thought V. *Panic.... Who's panicking? I'm just curious.*

Slowly the water got deeper, it was now up to her shins. The gentle nibbling suddenly stopped. She felt something burrowing under her feet, then start to wrap itself around her feet and her legs to just below the surface of the water. She stared at the water, but the blackness was completely impenetrable. She had no idea what was wrapping itself around her legs. Now, she couldn't walk, yet she continued to move. Whatever it was that was wrapping itself around her legs, was now propelling her through the water. As the water deepened and more and more of her became submerged, so she became more enveloped in whatever it was that was wrapping itself around her body and propelling her through the water. Yet not once did it break the surface. She had no idea what it was. *Now*, she thought, *now I'm beginning to panic!*
She heard Nox comforting words in her mind. *V, it's fine. It's happening to me too. I'm also becoming entombed in something. I'm not walking but being propelled through the water. But I don't detect any danger. It's just an organism doing a job. Without malice, without threat. Relax and accept what is happening to you. As I am, I could break these bonds*

if I wished to. But I'm content to let things play out and see how the situation develops. I sense this is a necessary procedure to get us to where we need to be.

V calmed immediately. She settled down, not enjoying the situation, but accepting it.

By now they were about a kilometre from the high-water mark. The water was up to her waist, as were the organism's bonds. They were not uncomfortable. They didn't grip or squeeze or bite. Soon her body accepted they were there and couldn't feel them anymore. Whether they were anaesthetising her skin, or whether it was the Neural Adaptation process – you know, like wearing a wristwatch, as soon as you put it on you know it's there, but five minutes later you quite forget you are wearing it. Well, that's the Neural Adaptation process, which is a process of the brain adjusting to a constant stimulus as time progresses.

Slowly, but inexorably the water got deeper and deeper. It rose to her chest, to her neck and by now they must have been 2 kilometres from the high-water mark.

Whatever was propelling them suddenly stopped. V looked around. Nox was so huge the water had only just reached his belly. The water came up to Venandi's chin, who was a little shorter than V. "Another 10 steps and we will fall into the abyss," reported Venandi. "No one knows how deep this lake is, but according to my long-dead relative, it's more than triaxial (Approximately Three Terran miles translated Nox).

"Why have we stopped?" asked V.

"I'm not sure," reported Venandi.

No sooner had Venandi answered than V felt a tugging at her knees. The organisms were trying to get her to kneel. To do so would mean that she would be immersed in the water. Panic was beginning to well up from deep inside the pit of her stomach.

Nox...? she thought nervously.

I'm getting the same sensation. The organisms want me to kneel in the water. They want me to lie in the water. They want me submerged.

Let me go first, said Nox. *V, try and resist for as long as you can. I can hold my breath for many Terran minutes. And as I have already said, I can easily break these bonds if I have to. Let me go and see what awaits us*

Before V could even think of a response, a tremendous splash followed as Nox allowed himself to become fully submerged in the water.

The pushing behind V's knees was getting more urgent. Stronger. Still, V resisted. She glanced over to Venandi. He simply smiled and allowed himself to disappear under the water.

"Nox!" She called. "Nox....are you OK?" Silence. Nothing came back.

The rising panic was now like an iron fist in her stomach. She spoke to herself sternly. She told herself that Nox will have this under control. Besides, he has two bloody great drones on his back that can fly off and reek seven hells of havoc if necessary. So just calm down and do what you can to remain upright until you hear from Nox and hear you will. So, get a grip girl.

With that V felt much better. She had quite forgotten about the drones. They were not bound.

Hello V. All is fine, her mind heard Nox's comforting voice. As bright and as calm as ever.

The organisms simply want you submerged so that they can finish mummifying you. The bonds

need to completely cover your body. That includes
your head. It is to protect us and to allow us to
continue breathing, as we transit the lake. So, just
relax and let them get on with it

Far from happy, she just said a meek "OK,"
and with that gave in and allowed the organisms to
collapse her knees. She held her breath and closed her
eyes tight, fully expecting her face to come into
contact with the water. But that wasn't the case. She
opened her eyes in shock and saw the water about
5cms away, but it didn't touch her face. She tried a
tiny experimental breath. That seemed to work well,
only air, no water got sucked into her lungs. She tried
a deeper breath and that too worked out OK. She had
no idea what was preventing the water from touching
her and invading her but assumed it was something to
do with the organisms. She glanced down and saw an
eel-like thing spinning round and round her body –
seemingly mummifying her. She couldn't tell what
colour it was because there was no photic zone in this
lake. On Terra, the photic zone is generally the first
200m of ocean or lake that is exposed to sunlight and
where most of the life in lakes and oceans live. But
here in Shari lake, sunlight doesn't seem to penetrate
at all. Something in the water seems to stop photons
penetrating the lake – *no chance of sunburn then,* she
thought ironically.

But she could feel the organism getting
closer and closer to her face. Eyes tightly closed, she
felt the organism around her chin, then her lips, her
nose, her eyes, her forehead. Then movement
stopped. She knew she was fully encased within the
organism. She was mummified inside a living
organism.

Her lungs were now reminding V that she needed to breathe. She had inadvertently been holding her breath whilst her face was being covered. She took one tentative breath and found that in no way was her breathing constricted. She could breathe freely and normally. Next, she tried opening her eyes. Nothing seemed to be obstructing her eyes, but as per usual in this lake, she couldn't see a thing.

She was just about to check in with Nox when her world of impenetrable blackness turned into a world of brightness and striking beauty. Full of colour, of strange shapes and sights. And there before her were the brightly lit mummified shapes of Nox and Venandi.

Bioluminescence on a completely different scale wondered V. Not only did these organisms light up, but they emitted enough light to see in absolute clarity for a distance of 20m in all directions. Beacons in the darkness. V couldn't believe the brightness. It was on a different scale to that of Terran bioluminescence.

She also noted that the colours were different, she was emitting a yellowish hue, Nox a light reddish hue, and Venandi a pale greenish hue. It was quite a spectacle – especially the huge shape of Nox. He looked like some sort of huge, red four-legged iceberg drifting through the lake. *I'll take that as a compliment,* Nox said in her mind.

But you are truly massive replied V. *I never truly realised how big you are until now,*

SD59, are you and H71 Ok? she asked the drones.

Affirmative Domina, we are quite well. All systems nominal. We are at 100% capacity. Although H71 is a little nervous and uncomfortable about

being on board Nox. I think there is a trust issue here.
Other than that, we are fine.

Nox merely snorted. V just giggled.

V turned to look at Venandi. She pondered
for a moment and then thought why not…?"Venandi"
she shouted, nearly deafening herself in the process.
She didn't realise that her voice would reverberate so
violently in her organic mummified bodysuit.

"I'm here, My lady," Venandi replied in a
more moderate voice. Anticipating the next question,
he went on, "I'm quite fine, thank you. Everything is
proceeding according to plan. There is little for us to
do other than to try and relax and enjoy the view! I
trust you are quite well, My lady and showing no ill
effects."

"I'm quite fine, thank you," replied V stiffly.
"You could have warned us this was going to
happen" she went on in a waspish tone.

" My lady, I had no idea. It is over fifteen
hundred years since this lake was last traversed – well
that I'm aware of anyway. Of course, others could
have done it; but no ranger has. I'm sure, like all
societies, things move on, improve… or get worse. I
had no idea what to expect. I'm sorry if you were
concerned. I have no idea where we are going or what
awaits us. All I know is that we will face it and either
succeed or succumb together."

There wasn't much V could say to that. Nox
merely snorted in his inimitable way as if to say,
"You can stick those comments where the sun doesn't
shine… And No, that's not here in Shari lake!"

V ignored Nox's attempt at sarcasm – he
does have a lot to learn on that score she thought.
Uncle Peter would be a good tutor. He is the master
of sarcasm and wit she thought fondly.

Satisfied that the organosuit wasn't leaking, wasn't preventing her from breathing, was allowing her to see clearly and was keeping her perfectly dry and surprisingly warm – it must be very cold outside, but here she was very snug. So, she began to relax, just a little and take in her surroundings. She could hear that Nox was relaxed as he started snoring. Yes, even the sound of his gentle snores traversed the depths of Shari lake…

Despite the brightness emitted from the organosuits, she could see nothing. There seemed to be no life in the lake at all. No colour either. She strained her eyes but could see nothing other than the bioluminescent light emitted from Venandi and Nox's organosuits. *Perhaps the light is driving other life forms away,* V thought. *Or maybe they are lurking just beyond the range of the bioluminescence.* Either way, the little bit of water they were in was completely devoid of life.

Her ears were popping, meaning they were descending. How long they had been descending, she had no idea. How deep were they? Again, she had no idea.

She was becoming drowsy, her eyelids drooping. She put this down to the silence, the heat, and the fact that she weighed a fraction of her body weight. She was so comfortably snug.

She was dreaming of being on a roller coaster. Her eyes snapped open and her roller coaster ride was no dream at all. The organosuit was cavorting through the water. Going one way, then quite suddenly the other. One minute she was upright the next she was standing on her head. All this was done so seamlessly, momentum didn't stop; she simply transitioned from one position to another, almost instantaneously. She could feel the organosuit accelerate, then break, then dart one way, then the next. She was still trying to understand the sudden shift in tempo when Nox's thoughts came through to her. *We are under attack V. Just hold on. Nothing I can do about it at this juncture. We have to rely on these organosuits to protect us.*

Under attack, thought V. *From who? From where? Why?"* The organosuit was flying now. *Aerobatics underwater - aquabatics?* she thought perversely. V knew of no craft on Terra that could do what this suit and no doubt Nox and Venandi's were doing.

She caught a glimpse of a huge being, with a mouth twice the size of Nox's back and teeth as tall as she was, bearing down on her at incredible speed - she had never seen anything so frightening, or a living creature so big. Why does this suit not move? She cried. The mouth was getting bigger and bigger, the teeth taller and sharper by the second. Then as the mighty jaws were about to close over V's organsuit, so the suit jinxed, literally jinxed, from zero to maybe 50 knots in the blink of an eye in a lateral direction. The crushing jaws missing by metres. Close enough for her to hear the crashing of teeth.

Bloody hell! thought V, sweat pouring off her brow. She caught sight of Nox's organosuit, tiny in comparison to the incredibly fast beast that was heading straight for it. She could barely take in the scene before her eyes. She had no idea how to describe this shape. It seemed to be all mouth, jaws, and row upon row of teeth. A huge eel-like body with limbs. No fins. But huge hind legs and smaller forearms. A body and tail that must have been the size of....of.... V was completely lost for a descriptive. She was thinking of the widest Subterranean Terran tunnel, like The Channel crossing tunnels. The tail, well the bit behind the rear legs, must have been at least 100m in length. She couldn't tell what colour the thing was, but it seemed to blend in perfectly with its surroundings. The teeth flashing a lime green of the bioluminescence. Nox, usually massive, was but a minnow in comparison. His suit didn't seem to see the beast. It was approaching at what seemed to be warp speed from Nox's rear. She was positive Nox hadn't seen it. 100m away…75m away…50m away, the massive jaws opening displaying huge rows of pillar-like teeth… and yet Nox remained still in the water.

Just as V yelled "NOX!" with all of her power, so she blinked and Nox and his organosuit vanished. It vanished within a blink of an eye. Stunned, V mentally rubbed her eyes only to see Nox reappear 200m away from the now wildly turning and bucking beast. If V hadn't have seen it, she would not have believed it possible. She could have sworn Nox complete with bodysuit vanished, completely disappeared, for a few seconds, only to reappear 200m away from where it had been. Right into the path of another beast looming at frightening speed towards Nox. The organosuit simply bounced again. One minute it was there, saw the danger and immediately bounced another 300m in another direction, both to the right and maybe 200m higher than it had before, this time thankfully into clear water.

V briefly caught sight of Venandi's bodysuit bouncing from location to location as it tried to evade the beasts and find clear water. Then the bioluminescence from Nox and Venandi bodysuits disappeared as another beast came hurtling towards V. She knew what to expect, but the wait was agonising. Her entire field of vision was filled with rows of teeth heading her way. Yet still, the organosuit remained where it was.

Come on, come on, she was thinking to herself. *Bounce...BOUNCE...BOUUUUUUU* and it did. So quickly that she wasn't aware it had done until they were hovering in clear water.

How long this dance went on for, she had no idea. They were bouncing so quickly now that she was completely disorientated. One minute she saw Nox, then Venandi, then both of them, then none of them. Interspaced with huge bodies, mouths of flashing teeth, bulging forelimbs and huge rear limbs, swishing tails that moved vast quantities of water, the wake of which would send them rolling head over heels as it flashed by. Eventually, the constant movement became too much for V and she passed out...

Deep in the mists of her mind, she could hear Nox's calm, patient voice calling to her. *V...V...V...*

Nox could sense V regaining consciousness so he stopped calling to her. Letting her come to, in her own time. V struggled to open her eyes. Eventually, she managed and was completely disorientated. It took her a few minutes to get her bearings, then the memories of the recent fight came flooding back.

"Nox!" she shouted in panic.

Yes V, I'm here. All is well..

And Venandi? she asked.

I'm fine too, thank you, My lady

It took her a moment or two to realise that Venandi was speaking to her telepathically.

Now she was confused. "Are they gone?" she asked, afraid of the answer.

Yes V. They are gone and they will not be coming back.

"Good," she gasped loudly. "What happened? The last thing I remember was a swirling sea of beasts with us constantly bouncing trying to evade them." Fast coming back to her senses now, she followed up her original question with another. In a stronger more demanding voice she asked,

"And how come Venandi is now able to communicate with me telepathically?"

"Over to you Nox," said Venandi rather evasively.

I sensed that you had passed out, started Nox. *It was clear that the situation was fast becoming untenable. These organosuits could have evaded the beasts indefinitely, but the G forces being exerted on you were approaching dangerous levels. Something needed to be done. It was clear to me that these suits only had defensive and no offensive capabilities.*

I needed to make some decisions. Firstly, I contacted Venandi. As you know, I had tuned into his mind earlier this morning over breakfast. I decided the time was right to let him know that I could contact him and we very quickly discussed the situation. It was decided that I try and contact the organisms in which we are mummified and try to get them to partially unwrap me so that I could release the drones to kill these beasts

It took some time, but eventually, I managed to get through to the organisms and explain what we wanted to do and the effect the current situation was

*having on you and that very soon it would be too late
to do anything as you would be dead.*

*The organisms discussed the problem
amongst themselves – this took milliseconds – and
agreed. They unwound part of my back, allowed the
drones to depart and resealed my back. The drones
made quick work of killing the beasts. There were
seven of them in total. The organosuits decided that
the drones could remain outside and act as a
deterrent to future attacks. Now the drones are
hovering nearby. Over there, and over there...you
see?*

V glanced to the left and saw SD59. Then to
the right, she saw H71.

"SD59" she called.

"Domina,"

"Thank you for ridding us of those beasts.
Are you both alright?"

"It is both our pleasure and our duty,
Domina. Your safety is our prime and only concern.
Well, you and Nox" responded SD59

"We are both quite fine. It was a very simple
matter despatching those beasts. Our sonars are
active, and we are pleased to report that there are no
other beasts within 100 Terran miles of us. We are
heading due south at a speed of 75 kph and at a depth
of 2,000 metres. All is well" V did some mental
calculations. Two kilometres below sea level on Terra
would mean they are at a pressure of just under 200
atmospheres – or 200 times greater than air pressure
at sea level, assuming that the density of the water in
the lake was the same as seawater on Terra – 1025
kg/m3. More than enough to crush them like a fist
crushing crepe paper. V marvelled at these
organosuits. Not only were they providing them with

a comfortable, breathable environment in which to live, but they were also protecting them from the tremendous external pressures.

"Thank you SD59 and H71."

"Domina." SD59 responded on behalf of himself and H71.

"Venandi, are you unhurt?"

"Yes, My lady. Thank you."

"So, what now?" asked V.

"Well, said Nox. We continue on this heading for several hours yet. We are being taken to the lady of the lake. Once there, she will decide our fate, for no one enters the lake without meeting the lady. She has the power of life or death over all those that enter the lake. We have no option but to continue this part of the journey."

"So…. come on, out with it?" demanded V.

Nox assumed an air of ignorance, he knew exactly what V was after. Venandi also felt he had a good idea, but felt it best to remain silent, at least for the present. He had glimpsed V's changing temper before and had no wish to get on the wrong side of her.

"Nox!" V demanded.

I assume you are referring to the fact that I have given Venandi telepathic access to you and me…? Nox had omitted to include SD59. He had allowed SD59 entry into Venandi's mind, but not allowed Venandi to telepathically access SD59's hybrid and very special positronic brain. Sometimes it's best to keep some things quiet.

"Precisely," responded V ominously.

Venandi is no fool, responded Nox. *He was beginning to suspect that I was no mere beast of burden. He sensed the relationship between us – not a*

*normal one for a citizen and a mere animal. Besides
how many other beasts do you know would standby
idly and let themselves be mummified by organisms? I
think any beast would have had a cadenza and would
have bolted for the hills… Don't you? That, plus the
fact that you were seconds away from death meant
that I had little choice but to talk to the one man who
had indirect experience of all this before. Besides, I
felt it was time to trust him. He has earned our trust.
Ultimately V, circumstances at the time demanded it*

V thought about this. "Very well, Nox. I
would have done the same had you been in trouble.
Thank you both for coming to my aide. I very much
appreciate it. Thank you."

"My lady," was all Venandi could say. Nox
ignored the compliment.

Venandi was distracted. He was only half
listening to Nox and V. His mind was going back to
the inner debate he had had with himself just before
they entered the lake. He was glad and hugely
relieved that he had decided to protect, to the death, V
and her travelling companions. He felt sure that
somehow Nox understood every thought he had. He
now knew Nox had been aware of the inner debate he
had had with himself. He felt fairly sure that Nox
knew why he was so driven – knew about the murder
of his family. He now knew that V and Nox were
crucial to his plans and that allowing them to live was
the best decision he had ever made. He was also very
afraid of Nox. He was beginning to understand just a
little of his capabilities and the little he had seen, had
been much, much, more than he had seen in any other
animal or citizen – with one exception - V. He
honestly believed that with these two working in
unison, then nothing was impossible. Anything, no

matter how small, he could do to help. He would. Of that he was certain. He was now truly aligned. He was truly committed to V and Nox and through them, The Resistance.

Nox just smiled to himself. He knew he had been right to allow Venandi into the inner sanctum. He knew that Venandi was teetering on the edge – he just needed a little push to get 100% behind them. Allowing him in had been just the push required. He would still keep an eye on him, but Nox felt the danger was over. Venandi was 100% allied to them and the cause.

"SD59," called V, "How long have we been travelling now?"

"About an hour My lady – always due south and our mean speed has been 70kmh, depth 2,000m"

"So, we have travelled 70 kilometres. Just how big is Shari lake" she asked.

SD59 sensed that Venandi was about to answer, but knowing that Venandi had no idea of Terran SI units, and V didn't have a clue of Domus units, he stepped in: "It is just over 1,000km in length and 500km wide. To give you some idea of context, it's about the same size as the Caspian Sea on Terra, but much deeper – The Caspian Sea has an average water depth of just over 200m."

"So we have not yet traversed a tenth of the distance of the lake. Where is The lady of the lake?"

"No one knows, My lady" responded Venandi. "The whole lake is her home. She could be in any part of the lake. But when we are near, we will know,"

So, nothing to do other than to sit back and enjoy the ride. Time lost all meaning. There wasn't anything to do, nothing to see, nothing to hear. Just exist, quite literally, cocooned in your little world. Nothing to the left of me, except H71 and Venandi, nothing to the right of me, except Nox and SD59. Just a world of nothingness with a tiny bubble of light in a sea of darkness, containing three live beings and two autonomous vehicles.

I thought Venandi said sleep would be but a distant memory... V thought. *Well, I could quite easily drop off to sleep, I'm so comfortable,* But, remembering the near-disastrous consequences the last time she drifted off, she decided to keep her eyes wide open. Not that there was anything she could do to thwart an attack from any dangerous predator, looking for a V-shaped snack. And, lit up like the Moulin Rouge, there was no escaping their existence. Subtlety and stealth were not on the agenda.

Just as she was thinking those very thoughts, there was a huge explosion causing the organosuit to move violently from side to side, and up and down. For a moment V couldn't grasp what had happened. Then another explosion, followed by another and another. A crescendo of noise. V knew that the increased density, sound speed and viscosity of water relative to air meant that underwater blast injuries were more often than not fatal due to over pressure. Yet despite these blasts being practically on top of them, the organosuits protected their soft tissues, heart, lungs and liver from lethal damage caused by the explosive effects of overpressure.

The organosuits then took on a life of their own. Semantics, V knew they were live, sentient beings, but they went into overdrive. They bounced once, they bounced twice in completely different directions. The drones, who were not affected by the blasts, didn't know which way to go. They couldn't keep up with the wild, bouncing antics of the organosuits. They couldn't predict in which direction they would bounce next. So random was the bouncing, and so fierce that V could feel her heart rate increasing as her heart tried to pump blood to her brain. But the heart couldn't keep up. Blood was draining from her brain faster than her heart could replace it, she could sense this through her eyesight, which was fading fast. She knew she only had moments of consciousness left. Then a remarkable thing happened. This time her organosuit was prepared. She could feel the organosuit grip her tightly and start to move rhythmically, acting as an external heart, helping pump the blood to places it needed to go – her brain. Her eyesight cleared and she felt much more alert.

V wasn't sure if it would have been better to have gone into unconsciousness. The Organsuits were moving so quickly, she found it impossible to keep up. The world consisted of darkness, bioluminescence and the flashes from the explosions. This combined with the effects of the explosions in the water meant that she wasn't only being bounced through the lake at incredible speed, but also flung through the water like a rag doll, due to the concussive effects of the blasts. Which still kept coming. She found it impossible to think. She was feeling nauseous and willed herself not to vomit. At that moment she didn't care if she lived or died. Then a huge explosion went off immediately outside of her organosuit. Despite the best efforts of the organosuit, the concussive forces and overpressure were so great, that V was badly affected by them. She felt a terrible pain in her tummy, her eardrums blew, then a sharp agonizing pain in her head and she knew no more.

The drones were completely oblivious to any threats and were just as surprised as everyone else when the first explosion went off. They tried to go into a protective circle around the organosuits but then decided that the organosuits were better adapted at evading the explosions than either of the drones – besides there was no way the drones could keep up with the bouncing the suits were so good at. SD59 knew this immediately, so went into full offensive mode. He and H71 started to try and track down the source of the explosions. Then eliminate them. However, this was easier said than done! No matter which sonar and which frequency they used they could identify no source. Instead, they traced an incoming explosive device and traced it back to its source. This took time, as the explosive devices were themselves stealth devices, and not only this but didn't fall in a straight line. Like the organosuits they jinked and darted about making tracking them back to their source, very difficult, if not practically impossible. But SD59 was a very special drone. It took him time, too much time as it transpired, but he managed it. The source ended up being 30,000ft in the air. It too was a drone. A stealth drone which was why they hadn't detected it. The drone was running a racetrack pattern around the sky. How it had detected the organosuits was anyone's guess, but SD59 assumed that it was the temperature difference – heat signatures – of the suits and their contents, in stark contrast to their frigid surroundings. Nox generated a lot of heat. He suspected the heat signatures had shown up on the stealth drones' sensors. He waited a few extra seconds so as to ensure he got the signature of the drone so that they would have no trouble identifying such a stealth drone again. Certainly, well before it could be a danger to them, then he and H71 fired off a salvo of nuclear surface to air missiles. These missiles didn't mess about. They locked on to the stealth drone immediately, and from that moment it was all over. No jinxing or darting about. The quickest possible route to the enemy. Three seconds and the stealth drone was blown out of the sky. SD59 and H71 surveyed the immediate area, both in the lake, on land and in the sky. They could sense no other threat, H71 remained on watch whilst SD59 shot over to V's organosuit.

SD59 was aware that V was in a bad way. Her vital signs were poor, almost critical. He checked in with Nox. Nox was fine. Battered but fine. Venandi seemingly had escaped without any problems at all. Nox knew that V was in trouble. He had sensed it immediately but there wasn't anything he could do. Now the danger had passed, he too instructed his and Venandi's organosuit to rendezvous at V's. Nox was beside himself with worry and fear. He could sense how badly hurt she was. He felt powerless to do anything to help. Venandi was equally anxious and just wanted to get to her. But where was she? Both Venandi and Nox could only see each other's bioluminescence. There was no sign of V or her organo suit.

SD59 found her. He could see her on his sensors. Her organosuit had gone dark. No bioluminescence. It was also slowly sinking, it had now passed 2,500m. SD59 told Nox and Venandi to remain where they were and he shot off, found the suit, gently grasped it in his manipulators and slowly started to retrace his steps to Nox and Venandi. He was unaware of the effects of the pressure and whether the organosuit was still working or whether he had to undertake decompression stops on the way so as to avoid the build-up of Nitrogen bubbles in V's system. He related such to Nox. Nox quickly contacted his organosuit and explained the situation. It appears that these organisms also have telepathic abilities between themselves. Nox's organosuit reported that V's suit was merely stunned, but all life support systems were 100% operational and that SD59 need not worry about decompression stops. *At least one thing was going our way* thought Nox as he reported back to SD59.

SD59 acknowledged, but nevertheless gently, but quickly recovered V's organosuit and rendezvoused with Nox and Venandi.

SD59 scanned V. He reported back that she had severe internal injuries. "She is suffering from pulmonary injuries, slight neurotrauma, damage to her liver and she has ruptured both eardrums. Her vital signs are weak heading to critical. She requires urgent medical care,"

No sooner had SD59 finished relating his tale of woe on V's condition than the bioluminescence on V's suit switched back on. Not only did it come back on but burned so much brighter than before. It hurt Nox's eyes to look at her organosuit. Then, within the blink of an eye, the organosuit had completely disappeared. SD59 managed to trace V's suit for a few minutes, then the suit disappeared. SD59 assumed the suit must have bounced. There was simply no sign of it anywhere. No matter what range he selected, his sonars could see no trace of V's suit.

SD59 reported back to Nox. Nox questioned his and Venandi's organosuits, but they remained stubbornly quiet. They simply told Nox not to worry,

V was being taken care of. This of course had quite the opposite effect on Nox and he worried even more.

For hour after hour, Nox and Venandi and the drones continued on the same course, at the same depth, at the same speed. No further attacks occurred, the drones now on triple alert. No news of V. Nothing. Just silence and blackness. Nox was trying his best to remain calm, but he was frantic with worry. Venandi was just as concerned but was able to exercise better patience. SD59 kept having to restrain H71 from charging off to V's organosuits last known bearing, to see if there were any clues as to which direction she may have gone from there.

They saw nothing. No signs of life at all. They had been assured that Shari Lake was teeming with life – but other than the giant lizard-like fish they had fought with earlier – they saw no sign of any other life forms at all.

It must have been about 3 or 4 hours or so later that SD59 reported that his sonars were picking up…something. He had no idea what, other than it was huge and around 150km away. It had just suddenly appeared on his sonar. One second there was nothing to be seen for hundreds of kilometres, then a millisecond later, this huge feature just appeared. It must have been about 20km across, and 3km in depth. It was moving slowly, at about 10 kph and on a reciprocal heading to themselves. They would rendezvous with this feature in about 75 minutes. Nox reported this to Venandi in the hope that Venandi may be able to throw some light on what this curious feature may be. He had no clue. Nox then asked the organosuits – who stayed obstinately quiet. Both Nox and Venandi strained their eyes along the direction in which the feature should be but saw absolutely nothing. Yet more bloody waiting fumed Nox. He hated being so utterly dependent on others for not only his survival but for, well everything!! For the first time in Nox's life – well for as long as he could remember – he was completely and utterly powerless to do anything for himself and was reliant on others. He hated it. Especially when a dear loved one was in such danger.

To Nox's mind, each second that ticked by was the equivalent to a decade. Time seemed to pass so slowly. SD59 assured Nox that the feature was getting inexorably closer, yet they could see no signs of this thing at all. It was now about five kilometres away.

Ten more minutes and they would rendezvous. No sooner had Nox finished the calculation than they were suddenly immersed in a tremendously bright and whitest of white light. The bonds of the organosuit, in which they had been bound for so long, just disappeared. There they were. Nox, Venandi and the two drones standing, freely under the brightest of lights in what, and where… They had no idea.

Whilst they were still trying to come to grips with their new situation, a deep, mellow, yet comforting voice boomed out:

"Welcome! Come. Make yourself comfortable. Please follow the green light"

Whereupon a small pinpoint of extremely bright green light suddenly appeared. It was hovering about 1.5m in the air, right in front of Nox, seeming to dance in anticipation. It appeared to be very excited about having a duty to perform. It darted ahead, stopped, retreated to Nox, then darted ahead again and waited. Nox got the message. The light was saying "Follow me... Follow me... Please."

Nox looked at Venandi, who in turn just shrugged his shoulders and stared right back at Nox. They went no more than three steps before they realised that the drones were not following. *SD59, come along. Both of you* Nox thought at the drone. No reply. *SD59, come along* angrier now. Still nothing.

The voice seemed to understand what was going on and boomed. "Your drones will be quite safe. For the moment they have been deactivated. They will be returned to you if and when you leave, in perfect condition. Fully serviced and rearmed. Please don't worry about them. They will be perfectly alright. As will you. "

These words had quite the opposite effect on Nox, who suddenly became very worried indeed. But for now, he was content to take no action until he understood the situation and, more to the point, found V. Turning back to the green light, who seemed to be wetting itself in barely contained excitement, it at once sped off, paused, then returned to Nox and proceeded at a more dignified, not to mention reasonable pace.

Nox was in no hurry, he ambled along behind the green light forcing it to slow down yet again. On they went. They could see very little of their surroundings as the only source of illumination was the little green light they were following. By now Nox had assumed that they were inside the large feature that SD59 had identified. The organosuits must have bounced straight from where they were in the lake, straight into the reception room within the feature. He also sensed that somewhere within this feature was V. He could feel her. He knew that she was still alive but critically hurt. But she was alive. And that was all that mattered for now.

Nox had calmed a little. He was desperate to see V. To see for himself that she was alive and being cared for. But he also knew that this wasn't the time for rash decisions. He had to be very careful. He knew exactly where they were. He knew they were in the lair of The lady of the lake. Shari herself. Her domain. He also knew what that meant. Life, or instant death...*Well. Fair enough.* Thought Nox. If the verdict was to be death, then he hoped she realised that Nox wasn't to be so easily killed. If that was to be her verdict, then she was in for one hell of a fight... For now though, tact, diplomacy and above all, patience and civility was very much the order of the day.

Just as Nox was finishing planning his tactics, so the green light brought them into another brightly lit and quite beautiful room. And it was huge. The light, knowing where it was, at once adopted a more respectful air and with as much dignity that it could muster, escorted Nox and Venandi into one of the most beautiful places either of them had ever seen. It escorted them over the threshold and stopped dead. Sunk to the floor as if kneeling in respect, dimmed itself so it was just about seen and inferred that Nox and Venandi should wait exactly where they were until summoned.

That was fine by Nox. He had immediately forgotten everything he had just been debating with himself and gazed in open-mouthed astonishment at the room before them...not only was it huge, but incredible to look at.

Nox, who had one of the largest vocabularies of any being alive, either on Terra or on Domus, was at a complete loss for words.

The sheer opulence, the beauty, the subtleties of colour, the materials – some organic, some inorganic, the blending of the marine world with the world of the citizen – was a marvel.

The room or hall was about 400m long and 100m wide, with an arched roof. The floor seemed to be carpeted, yet it wasn't. The floor comprised all sorts of sea life – plants, reeds, and seaweed all of the most beautiful colours. All alive and all moving rhythmically, gently, and quite hypnotically swaying from side to side – tempting you to walk on it. Leading to the end of the room, was a long, wide carpet of meandering seaweed. A little taller than the surrounding plant life. This was clearly where you walked, the path you took to the other end of the room. It was the deepest, purest red either Venandi or Nox had ever seen. Once you put your foot (or hoof) on this carpet, it slowly propelled you. Your feet would sink into the moist luxuriousness and at once relax you. It would then propel you slowly to what awaited you at the end of the hall. But before you got there you would be distracted by the walls and the ceiling. The ceiling was arched, the arch leading seamlessly to the floor. The arched roof and walls were framed in gold latticework, each part of the latticework encrusted in jewels. Diamonds, rubies, sapphires, all manner of countless jewels that sparkled and radiated their brilliance. In between the latticework was a curtain of water. Nox had no idea how deep the water was or how it was supported, just an arch of water. There was no way the latticework could support it, so he had no idea how it remained in place. Within the bubbling water was the most brilliantly coloured fish, swimming haphazardly from one part of the hall to another. They were all shapes and sizes, all the most beautiful colours. It was like walking through a tropical aquarium. But rather than be separated from the fish and water by thick clumsy glass, you were part of the aquarium. Nox could feel drops of water on his back, could smell the water. He was sure that if he reached out, he would be able to touch the water and if he wanted, could enter the water and swim with the fish. Fish were all around him. Swimming to the sides, over his head, to his rear everywhere. At the end of the room was a vast throne. It was pure mother of pearl. It was stunning. The floor was taking them slowly, but relentlessly towards the throne. Behind the throne was a waterfall. The waterfall was as tall and as wide as the hall. It too had an arched top. Fish were playing in the waterfall. The whole room was beautifully lit. Light seemed to rise through some of the strands of water, rather like light in a fibre optic cable and then diffuse. Exactly like a waterfall, a waterfall of light, Nox thought to himself. Giving a wondrous, yet subtle effect. The room was perfectly lit. You could see all you needed to, yet you were not blinded by the light. Subtle and perfect.

Before they knew it, they stopped. They had arrived. Their journey through the fabulous hall at an end. They were facing the throne, which was about 5m in front of them. Empty just now. He looked around the water walls and ceilings and noted that the beautiful, colourful fish at this end of the room had disappeared and had been replaced by the most evil-looking fish – well, he wasn't sure what they were. Each of them must have been about 2m in height. Each standing to attention. They were ringed in the water around the walls and ceiling. From the waterfall, where they stood shoulder to shoulder, the whole width of the waterfall. In the arched ceiling and along the walls. There must have been about 100 of them. All staring with grey, dead malevolent eyes. They were miniature versions of what had attacked them earlier in their journey through the lake. But here they were armed. They held something in their stubby forelimbs. No idea what they were or how they work, but no doubt they would be lethal to Nox and Venandi. The lady of the lake's amphibian guard thought Nox.... Just as at home in the water as they were now, as on the land, which is where they would be, in an instant, coming from all directions – dropping from the ceiling, coming from the walls, the waterfall, if they were so ordered.

Nox checked in with Venandi...*What do you think?*

No idea responded Venandi.

Very helpful thought Nox.

"Clearly and unsurprisingly, we are not trusted, hence this rather ominous looking guard. Yet we will be listened to as no action has been taken against us. So, we still have a little influence in how things proceed from here. The result is by no means certain and by no means out of our hands. How do you want to play it....?" Asked Venandi.

That was indeed a good question. *I guess it all depends on whether the lady of the lake can communicate with me telepathically. If she can, then I'll do the talking, and speak directly to her. If she can't then I guess, I'll have to communicate through you. Fair enough?*

Absolutely responded Venandi – a little relieved.

All we can do now is wait for the lady to put in an appearance, which I don't think will be too long given that her guard is already here,

Nox's definition of time was very different from the lady of the lake. She kept them waiting for 40 Terran minutes. Each second of those minutes the amphibian guard just kept glaring malevolently down at them. They didn't move, other than gentle swaying movements in the water.

Then without fanfare or ceremony, she simply appeared. The lady of the lake was indeed a daunting figure. Rotund, Nox decided politely, tall, regal. She knew who she was and the power she wielded. She had long wavy grey hair. A beautiful, kindly face, with full red lips. Eyes that sparkled. They were the colour of the oceans. Sparkling blue one minute and battleship grey the next. Her eyes reflected her mood. She exuded power and authority. Completely comfortable with her status and her power. No fool. Very intelligent. She allowed Nox to look at her, weigh her up, to assess her. She was doing the same. Her face giving nothing away but secretly marvelling at this beast before her. The magnificence of him. The power he exuded. The intelligence and deep compassion in those beautiful eyes. She could at once sense the terrible strain he was under, the concern he had over the girl citizen … V, that had been brought before her, almost at death's door… She knew who it was that stood before her. Unbeknownst to Nox, when he originally transited from Domus Mundi to Terra, so Servator/Observator Maris (The Sea Watcher on Terra) had also been transported. By direct order of the lady of the lake. The Sea Watcher was one of her most trusted relatives. He had been ordered to watch over Nox, to monitor The Ostium's progress and wherever possible to assist him until Nox was ready to return to Domus with "The One" Vica Pota. The Sea Watcher was to stay behind and do what he could to protect Udal Cuain and the residents: Peter, Isabelle, and the Campbells.

Oh, she knew who Nox was and what he was doing. She knew a lot about Nox. More than he knew himself. One day she would enlighten him. But not today. Today she needed to exercise authority and direction over him. No matter her feelings for him. For she had always loved him. Always would. But that's for another time. Another life. Any memories Nox had of the lady had been wiped clean. Totally and irrevocably.

Nox looked at the lady. He was convinced that he had met her before, that somewhere in his past they had met. He couldn't remember when, or where, but he knew he would. His secondary brain would work on the problem. He would get there in the end. So, he didn't concern himself with the problem any longer.

My lady, can you "hear me?" he thought at her. *My lady, if you can, my name is Nox. Unfortunately, I don't have the power of speech, but I can understand many languages and my best form of communication is through telepathy.*

Nox waited for a response. The lady could of course hear him quite clearly and communicate telepathically very easily indeed. It was second nature to her. It was how she communicated to the subjects of her aquatic kingdom. She just chose to be a little difficult and made him wait a little longer.

So, who do we have here? she asked.

Relieved, Nox heard her soft melodic voice in his mind. It at once struck a familiar chord with him, but again the details evaded him. He parked the query in his second brain, allowing it to work out the details.

My lady, I'm Nox, a stranger to these lands and my companion is Venandi, Ranger of these lands,

"I'm familiar with Venandi's family. One of his kinsmen passed through here a few millennia ago. I remember him well. He did a great deed for us. His family have open access to the lake. Welcome to my lands, Venandi, you and your kinsman are forever friends of the Shila people..." she said to Venandi

"I thank you, My lady. Although I knew my kinsman had transited the lake – details of his, plus every other journey ever taken by my kinsman, are indelibly etched in my DNA. But he would never speak of his journey and he never encouraged any relative to transit this way again. I only do so now out of desperate need. I need to get Nox and his travelling companions – the drones and a young female citizen called V, to The Resistance as quickly as possible. I thank you for allowing me safe passage through your lands"

"Venandi, you are welcome to pass this way whenever you need" She turned her gaze towards Nox. "But you, you are a stranger to this land. Why should I let you pass?"

"Stranger or no, I'm here because I can help rid this land of The Ostium. I'm the protector of Domina Vica Pota – she is the true protector of Domus Mundi and she will be the new leader of this world once The Ostium has been defeated. She will be instrumental in their defeat. Indeed, The Ostium will never be defeated without Vica Pota's help.

Although as her protector, I have failed miserably. She was recently badly hurt, and I beg to ask whether you know where she is. She was badly injured in a bombing raid by what we now know to be an Ostium Stealth drone that we assume had tracked us by our heat signatures, during our submarine voyage through the lake."

"I'm aware of this drone and this attack. I thank you for destroying the drone. But you also killed several of my creatures. That is unforgivable and is punishable by death. The organosuits would have kept you safe. They would not have allowed the Megalodon to have hurt you. Why did you deem it necessary to kill them?"

"My lady, my prime duty is to protect Vica Pota at all times. With my life if necessary. My two drone companions are also sworn to protect her. Contrary to the three laws of robotics, they can kill anything, citizen, Terran or otherwise should they pose a direct or indirect threat to Domina Vica Pota. They are as loyal to her as your amphibian guards are to you. More so. There is nothing they would not do for Vica Pota. Should they deem Vica Pota's life to be in any sort of danger, they are programmed to kill the threat first, without the need of permission, and to defend their course of action afterwards. As you say, the organosuits were indeed protecting us. Unfortunately, the tactics they employed were proving to be lethal to Vica Pota. The G forces involved as they bounced from position to position had made her unconscious and were still climbing. They were fast approaching lethal levels, unless we took action, she would have perished. Both the drones and I sensed this. I was able to telepathically communicate with the organosuits and we all agreed that the best way to protect V was to destroy the attackers. Thus, the drones were released. They killed the attackers before any more harm could come to Vica Pota. I didn't take a unilateral decision to kill the attackers but consulted with Venandi and your organosuits. It was a decision we all took and a course of action that we all agreed upon. We only had one objective. To protect Domina Vica Pota."

The lady of the lake knew all of this. Of course. She was just testing Nox, to see if he was still incapable of lying. It seems that nothing had changed there. He simply couldn't tell a lie.

"Very well Nox. I accept your answer. I accept the reasons why you acted as you did. You will not be punished for killing those creatures."

"I thank you, My lady. Most sincerely. Now please. Do you have any news of Domina Vica Pota."

"Of course, I do Nox. She is here, no more than 10m away from you. We have her under medical supervision. As you say, she was gravely injured in the attack. I'm very aware of the importance of Domina Vica Pota in the fight against this terrible plague, The Ostium. Once the organosuit as you call them, regained consciousness, it relayed her vital signs and condition to my medical team. It was instructed to bounce straight here – we assisted with our submarine tractor beam. On arrival, she was operated on and is now recovering under the care of my medics. We believe she will make a full recovery, but she must awaken first before we can be sure. She is now in an induced coma to allow the swelling on her brain to heal. We are 95% confident that she will be 100% healed.

Nox swooned in relief. "May I see her, my lady? I can't rest until I have seen her,"

"Of course,"

And with that, the guards disappeared, the waterfall opened. And there, V was lying peacefully. Surrounded by medics and machines that were softly buzzing and beeping and medical drones. All watching, monitoring and waiting.

Nox couldn't get there fast enough. The lady of the lake merely smiled to herself. *No*, she thought to herself. *He has not changed a bit.*

CHAPTER EIGHTEEN

Once Nox had satisfied himself that everything that could be done, was being done to help V fully recover, he requested food – an abundance of food and rested. He refused to leave V's side, so the medics had to make a little annex for him right next to V's bed. It was the only way. Nox positively refused to move and no one, not even The lady of the lake herself could persuade him otherwise.

Venandi was given his own quarters – he chose to leave Nox to it. Nothing he could do. So he wandered around for a little, then turned in to get some rest.

Several hours later, Nox's second brain sensed a large contingent of people coming and prodded his main brain awake. Nox was standing and alert by the time the dignitaries arrived. It was the lady. She dismissed her escort, cleared the room of medics and their drones, sat down on a chair next to V's bed and just looked at Nox.

Nox met her stare and looked deeply into her eyes, as she was doing to him. He could sense her trying to probe his mind, he gently resisted refusing to let her in. He didn't invade hers as he felt to do so, would give too much of his abilities away and besides, he didn't feel any threat from the lady, just a willingness to help in any way she could. So he just returned her stare, gently blocking her probing mind and waited.

Eventually, the lady had got what she wanted or had simply had enough of playing a mental fencing match with Nox.

"So," she said. "What are your plans?"

"Plans, My lady? My primary mission was to guard, protect and counsel V. Get her to Domus Mundi, then to The Resistance as quickly as possible. From there, what happened next would be entirely V and Domina Solis Ortus Pota's concern, as would be my role in whatever plans the two of them agreed upon. My plans now? Essentially, they remain the same. To get V to The Resistance as quickly as possible and once there facilitate and help in the planning in any way I can."

"Tell me Nox, what do you think of Venandi?"

Nox looked steadily at the lady of the lake before answering. " My lady, he is a bit of an enigma. At first, I was not sure what to think of him – but the longer we travelled together, the more I was able to understand him, the more I came to listen to him."

"By that you mean the more you were able to penetrate his mind…?"

Nox remained stubbornly quiet.

"Don't be coy Nox. I know your ability to get into people's minds. I will go one step further. I know of your ability to get into any sentient being's mind – be it organic or mechanical, such as a positronic brain. I have yet to meet anyone with a more penetrating, stronger brain than yours Nox. No…don't ask me how I know. Just be assured that I know a lot about you Nox. I also want to thank you for not trying to penetrate my mind when we recently met, although I know you could have easily done so. "

"My lady." Nox looked neither surprised nor curious. He just accepted what The lady had to say and moved on.

- 435 -

"Yes, my lady, the deeper I was able to penetrate his mind, the more I got to understand him. But trust him? He is gaining my trust but he does not have my full trust yet. There is still much I do not understand, such as his fanciful tale about what drove him to come and meet up with us in the first place."

While Nox was saying this, he was looking keenly at the lady of the lake. He thought he detected a little smile, then acquiescence.

"Yes Nox, that was my doing. As you know, I have a history with the rangers, going back some 1,500 years. One of Venandi's distant relatives visited me all those years ago. He did me a tremendous service. In return, I promised to keep watch over his kin. I have been watching over them for millennia. Venandi has been of particular interest to me." Suddenly she looked pained and sad. "Alas, there was nothing I could do to prevent the loss of his wife and daughter, even I have limitations. But I can help him seek the revenge he so desperately craves."

"As soon as I became aware of the increasing strength of The Ostium on Terra and the fact that V was on the cusp of being able to assist in the uprising here on Domus, I too started working on a plan. About a year before your arrival here on Domus I started causing Venandi to have vivid dreams about V, about you – I knew SD59 would be part of the team and I assumed another drone would be bought along as back up. The dreams I implanted in Venandi, were to meet up with you, gain your trust and get him to persuade you to leave your relatively safe, but oh so slow route and to persuade you to take a more dangerous, but much quicker route …through the lake… to me. I can help you and V. I have someone here that can help you. He is incapacitated at present but will be with us in a while. Once you meet him, you will understand why it was necessary to get you here." The lady could feel Nox mind pressuring her into finding out who this individual was. "No Nox. Trust me, please. I can't say any more just now. I have my reasons. Please. Trust me. All will become clear soon. You Nox. You will be delighted." The lady felt the tidal wave of Nox mind recede. "Thank you, Nox." She said, hugely relieved. There was no way she could have withstood Nox. Had he wanted to, he could have quite easily overcome the lady's mind.

The lady waited a minute or two, allowed her mind to recover then went on "Manipulating Venandi's dreams and pressurising him to meet up with you was a fairly easy matter. The problem was, how to gain your trust? Especially as you knew nobody on this planet. I was aware of the holograms left to V. I also knew that Domina Solis Ortus Pota had left a holographic message for V. Not only had she left a message, but SD59 was also partly in the hologram. But the biggest blessing was you Nox. Because you knew her. You trusted her. You knew she was a good person, fighting a losing battle against The Ostium. After all, it was she that was responsible for getting you to V. If you, V and SD59 could somehow receive a message from Domina Solis Ortus Pota stating that she trusted Venandi and that she had sent him to help you, then gaining his trust would be a much easier task."

"After much deliberation, I settled upon the amulet idea. I was able to have the amulet constructed so that it could only be operated by V – coded to her DNA. It could only be worn by Venandi, and, so long as he left it alone, it would not hurt him. But should he try to remove it, or operate it, it would cause him great pain. It would also adhere to his body so that he could not lose it. The only person able to remove it, other than to cut it out of his skin, was V. The recording was a fairly simple matter. I had holographic images of Domina Solis Ortus Pota. It was just a simple matter to manipulate them into saying what I wanted said. Why did I not go straight to Domina Solis Ortus Pota and get her to send me a message that I could use? Two reasons. One, I am not entirely sure everyone in The Resistance is trustworthy – look what happened to you on your return to Terra. You were injected with nanoparticles that would have eventually killed you. No. It's clear The Resistance has been compromised and it's difficult to know who to trust. And two. Simple. I wanted this done in secrecy. Only three people knew of this plan. Me, the person you will meet in a while, who put the whole thing together, and the medium I used to put the amulet around Venandi's neck – and believe me, that was the most difficult part. Finding someone, or something that could sneak up on a ranger and place something around his neck. Under normal circumstances, an impossible task. But I did not use normal circumstances. I thought long and hard and came up with but one solution. Ventus. Or should I say, a relative of Ventus. Yes, the wind. The wind constantly blows, whether as a gentle breeze or as a violent tempest. A ranger would be used to the breeze constantly ruffling around him. Gently teasing him. Always there. Something he was so used to that he virtually ignored it. A simple task for Ventus Vesperi (Evening breeze). The amulet was successfully placed about 6 months ago. Then, nothing to do but wait and get word from Ventus that you had left Terra. Ventus Vesperi then waited for you to emerge from Silbah. He kept me informed of your progress. It was then a simple matter to get Venandi in the right place at the right time. And here you are. The plan worked beautifully – well almost. But V will recover and all will be well."

Silence ensued for a minute or two whilst Nox digested what The lady had said. "We knew there was something wrong with the hologram. It was too…perfect. V worked out what had happened. The only thing she did not know was who had initiated the plan, but she understood that whoever it was, was a friend and on that basis, she allowed Venandi to guide us."

The lady of the lake gave a start of surprise. "Is she that smart?" she asked Nox in wonder.

"My lady, she is the smartest person I have ever met. I never met her parents, but they would be so, so proud of her. She is incredible. She worked out your plan literally within minutes of seeing the hologram."

"So, there is hope that we can defeat The Ostium?" The lady asked breathlessly.

"My lady, with you, Venandi, V and the power of the Resistance behind her, I do not know what V is capable of. But I believe she is the one. The chosen one and so long as she lives, there is every chance that we can defeat The Ostium."

"You are being too modest Nox…" The lady retorted teasingly…

"My lady...?" was all Nox could say, confusion written all over his beautiful face.

"You are forgetting… You. Nox. I think with you and V working together, then anything is possible."

For only the second time in his life, Nox was lost for words.

"Nox, I can help you further. I have communicated the situation to The Resistance – directly to Solis Ortus. She is fully aware of the attack on you and of the injuries sustained by V. She is aware, that at least for now, V can't play any further part in the plotting against The Ostium, but that she should make a full recovery. Our doctors are happier with V's condition and are now convinced she will fully recover. But her recovery will take a little longer than originally thought."

"Given V's condition, Solis Ortus and I felt it best if I continue to provide a safe haven for you, V, Venandi and your drones. V must not be moved and given that The Resistance has to remain fully mobile, it was felt that to place V, in her current condition, in the hands of The Resistance would probably have either ended up killing her or affecting her so badly that she will be of no use. So we agreed that we will meet here. We are now heading to the southern end of the lake. A very small entourage of The Resistance is heading north, to the southern end of the lake. We should meet up in 2 to 3 days. Further, I have agreed that you, Venandi, Nox, your drones, plus the Resistance entourage can remain here, in my kingdom, until such time as V has fully recovered. Then and only then, will you be free to go on your way,"

"Once the Resistance are onboard, we will go to the deepest part of the lake, around 4,000m, sink to the bottom and engage our cloaking device. We will be invisible from all possible predators, be they citizens, animals or Ostium. We shall remain in that state until V is fully recovered. We will then return you to the high watermark at the southern end of the lake and allow you to continue with your quest."

"Thank you, y lady. I say again, that is indeed most generous of you. I hope that one day, I may return the favour."

"Let's not worry about that now Nox. I don't do this for favours, I do it to rid this world of The Ostium. And, to repay a long-overdue debt to V's greatly missed parents – they helped me greatly many thousands of years ago when I was but a girl having just lost my parents. I'm only too pleased to be able to help. I must go. We will meet again before The Resistance board. But worry not. V is in wonderful hands and she will make a full recovery."

"My lady on behalf of myself and V, I thank you. My offer remains. Should you ever need my services, you only have to call. "

The lady just looked at him for several seconds. Then nodded. Summoned her guard, allowed the medics to re-enter the room and left.

Satisfied, Nox had little to do but eat, think and sleep. This he did, ensuring that he ate first, then slept, then started to think. He thought of the conversation he had had with The lady of the lake. Instinctively he knew that something was wrong, terribly wrong. It unnerved him greatly. But, try as he might, he could not understand why he felt this way.

Time passed slowly. Venandi put in an odd appearance. They would sit and talk for a while, then Venandi would leave him to it. Strangely, Nox missed the drones, especially SD59. But the lady had insisted that they remain shut down until they were due to leave. She had been as good as her word. The drones had been fully serviced and rearmed. They were once again, as good as new and ready to go.

Still, this nagging feeling persisted. A conversation that V had had with SD59 - he wasn't privy to it and it was whilst he was recovering at Silbah. But, he had grasped some of what they were saying. He knew it was important, but he just couldn't remember. He passed this problem to his second brain. Nox felt very unsettled, although he had no idea why. Something wasn't right.

Nox didn't move from V's side. He could see that her body was healing. Slowly but surely the odd wire would be removed, then a machine would be switched off and taken away. The worried, strained looks on the medic's faces had been replaced by a more relaxed, untroubled look – even the odd nod and smile as a test result came back. The atmosphere became one of routine rather than crisis management. But still, she hadn't woken. She was sleeping naturally now. Again the medics were untroubled by this – they went as far as to say that this was a huge step forward.

Nox, not being a medic simply looked over their shoulders, getting more morose by the day. Ironic really as the happier the medics got, so the more morose Nox became. Why? Because no matter how hard he looked into V's mind, he couldn't see anything, let alone make contact. He needed some sign from her that all was well, or at least all was on the mend – he knew she was much more complex than the medics realised, especially in all matters relating to her mind. He would only truly begin to relax once her mind had given him an indication as to its true state of health. He needed to communicate with her. He needed to find out what it was that was troubling him.

The minutes drifted into hours and the hours into days. The lady was as good as her word and visited Nox and V on one more occasion before their scheduled rendezvous with The Resistance. She passed pleasantries with Nox, she knew everything about everything and was fully apprised of V's state of health. She was also aware of Nox's troubled and morose state of mind, although she didn't know why he was behaving this way. It didn't help that she couldn't penetrate his mind to find out why. So she waited for Nox to either tell her, or get over whatever it was that was troubling him.

She informed him that The Resistance were running a little behind schedule and that they would have to wait an extra day before they could start their transit through the lake. As to the Palace, it was drifting very slowly towards the meet point. They would arrive within a couple of hours. The Palace would then sink to the bottom of the lake and await the arrival of The Resistance. The lady had watchers in place. The organosuits were already on-site and ready to perform their duties. There wasn't anything more to be done but wait.

Wait. WAIT! That's all that Nox had been doing since V got hurt. He didn't know how much more waiting he could do. But he let none of this show and thanked the lady most deferentially for her visit and for the excellent news she brought. No, he informed her, there wasn't anything else she could do for him. She had done more than enough already and that he was quite fine. Thank you.

The lady excused herself. She, however, saw through Nox's veneer of calmness and patience. But said nothing. She had seen this before and knew what to expect. She knew Nox was much, more powerful this time, both physically and mentally. She hoped that mentally he was able to control his emotions because physically, he would be impossible to stop. Nevertheless, she took what precautions she could. Just in case the same thing happened again. She made sure the medics were surrounded by guards armed with stun guns, that V and her necessary machines were as secure as possible, that other guards were in place not to stop Nox – they couldn't – but just to make sure that no innocent bystanders tried to step in, get in his way, or worse, inadvertently get hurt by the rampaging Nox.

Nox, of course, was tuned into The lady's mind and "heard" every thought. He snorted to himself at the lady's thoughts. There was no way Nox was going to go rogue. He had complete control over himself. So, instead of charging up and down the palace creating havoc and mayhem, he settled himself down and went to sleep.

But sleep didn't come easily. Nox's mind was full of black emptiness. No thoughts, no sensations, no sounds... nothing, like the vacuum of space. Bad analogy Nox corrected himself. Although space is indeed a vacuum. This doesn't mean that space is empty. Nox stopped that thought right there, as he thought that he is beginning to sound like V.

Just as he was drifting off to sleep, his second brain picked up a flash, a dazzling flash of intensely white light from the deep, dark recesses of V's brain. Nox smiled to himself and instantly went to sleep.

Nox was up and about early. Finally, the time had come. The Resistance was but an hour or so away. The Resistance had reached the high-water mark and were preparing to don the organosuits. Nox understood three members of The Resistance were due to board the lady of the lake's palace. Domina Solis Ortus Pota herself and two of her chief aides. But the really good news was that V's mind was healing fast. Nox was able to get deeper and deeper into her mind and to assist with its recovery. But he now knew that she would be entirely healed with absolutely no adverse effects. The lady sensed his change in spirits and was pleased that whatever was bothering him was now no longer. She was even more relieved for the sake of her palace and her citizens. Had Nox rampaged there was no telling how much inadvertent damage he could have done to both!

Nox was wandering around like a child on Christmas morning. He was getting in everyone's way and generally making a charming nuisance of himself. He knew of course that he was distracting everybody he came into contact with, but he simply didn't care. He was just so happy that V was recovering so well and so quickly and that The Resistance were nearly here. Eventually, The lady of the lake had to summon Venandi to have a talk with his friend and ask him to try to keep out of the way. Venandi was a little nervous at this, but did his best and managed, at least for a little while to distract Nox, thereby giving some of the people a brief respite.

The lady of the lake, looking resplendent in a multi-coloured gown made entirely from plants and jewels that littered the bottom of her lake, sat on her throne at the head of the welcoming committee. Just behind her and just in front of the waterfall, were her valued aides and advisors, along with Nox and Venandi. Guards were numerous and resplendent in their dress uniforms. Music sung by the aquatic choir filtered quietly through the room.

Finally, the huge doors at the end of the room opened and there before them stood three tall, and exhausted looking, individuals.

Nox nearly fell over. For there, standing before him, albeit 400m away was a citizen that was pretty much identical to V. Domina Solis Ortus Pota at last. A distant relative, separated by Millennia, but practically identical to V – at least from this distance. In the many years since he had last seen her, just as he was about to be fired to the wormhole that would send him to Terra. She had changed considerably. She resembled V in so many ways. The same poise, the same stature, the same mannerisms. Yet the closer the carpet brought her to him, Nox could begin to make out subtle differences. She was older – an odd thing to say given that V was at least 4,500 years old!! But as far as appearances go, she looked older – in her equivalent of the Terran thirties perhaps? She looked desperately tired and dishevelled. Yet the golden flecks in her eyes were as bright and as intelligent looking as ever. She was a little shorter than V – and V was still growing. Her hair was much longer than V's, much brighter and right now displaying a rainbow of colours. Her figure was much fuller, a beautiful woman. A woman just coming into her prime. It gave Nox some sort of insight as to V's appearance when she reached full womanhood. V was certainly going to be… what's the Terran word he asked himself…? Amazonian? Yes, an Amazonian. Tall, immensely strong, powerful yet strikingly beautiful with an intelligence that would put every other person to shame. Except him of course – sniggered Nox. Which brought him a withering stare from The lady of the lake. It also caused Domina Solis Ortus Pota's eyes to stare right at him. A pair of black and golden lasers, searing straight into his brain. Nox merely looked back. The fear and doubt he had been wrestling with these past three days, was now screaming at him - yet he had no idea why....

"Nox?" she asked quizzically

My lady, Nox thought back at her.

"My. How you have changed. The beast we sent to Earth all those Terran years ago. Look at you now. Welcome back, my friend. I have missed you."

"My lady, it does my heart good to see you. And thank you for your kind words"

"We will chat more later. How is Vica Pota?"

Before he could stop himself, Nox blurted out "Not good, My lady. Her body is healing well. It is her mind that concerns me. I detect no improvement there at all."

The lady of the lake choked back a comment and wiped the look of surprise from her face. She merely looked serenely at Nox and Solis Ortus Pota - her mind shouting questions at Nox - who politely ignored them.

"That is bad news indeed. I had heard that she was going to make a full recovery," replied Solis Ortus Pota.

"Unfortunately, that doesn't look likely, My lady," replied Nox, who then shut up and said no more.

"Welcome Domina Solis Ortus Pota, I wish it were under more pleasant circumstances" boomed the soft, harmonious and gentle words from The lady of the lake, mystified, but willing to play along with Nox. At least for now.

"My lady. Thank you. It is a privilege and pleasure to be here" Bowed Domina Solis Ortus Pota and her two aides, who she introduced as Domina Sapientiae Pota and Dominus Probitatis Viribus.

"You are most welcome; my palace is your palace. You are welcome to stay here for as long as you need," replied the lady.

"We thank you" chorused the three new guests.

"You must be tired and hungry. Come, I have prepared some food for you and quarters have also been prepared. After you have eaten and rested, we will talk. But I must now ensure we depart as quickly as possible for our standby location"

"My lady, if I could…"

"What?" replied the lady.

"Could we first pay our respects to Vica Pota?"

"Of course, how silly of me…Please forgive me."

With that, she rose from her throne, nodded to one of the guards. The waterfall then opened from the middle to reveal Vica Pota lying in her bed. A few medics in attendance, all turned as one and bowed to the lady and her court.

The lady beckoned to Domina Solis Ortus Pota and her aides, who rose as one and stepped forward into V's med suite.

Nox immediately sensed something was wrong. Venandi wasn't far behind him. Nox sensed a threat, ears flat on his head, eyes closed to slits, nostrils fully dilated he looked frightening. The guards who didn't have a clue what was happening merely fell back, suddenly scared.

From the door, something flew in. It took Nox a moment to realise it was H71. He didn't waste time wondering how he came to be there; he simply went into overdrive. He burst through all the guards and put himself between the entourage and the drone. He glanced to his right to ensure that V was as protected as possible, directing Venandi to put himself between V and the drone. He then sprang forward to meet the threat. The drone saw him coming and managed to evade him and headed directly for the med suite. Nox didn't waste a minute, even today people wonder how such a huge animal could move so quickly. Literally within the blink of an eye, Nox was there, between the drone and the entourage. He then leapt. His massive body protecting the entourage, especially V. He leapt just as the drone, the drone that was H71, loyal and trusted servant to V, detonated. Nox took the full force of the explosion. Nox hit the floor next to V's bed, bleeding from every part of his body. His great, massive body bleeding and broken. Great swathes of his flesh and some of his limbs missing. As he fell, his foreleg gently hit V's bed and landed, so, so, softly in the palm of V's upturned hand. Nox was still conscious, saw his hoof in her hand, then felt the unimaginable pain in every part of his body. Just before his second brain shut down, he understood. He knew what it was that had been troubling him. His second brain died. He could feel his eyes shutting down as darkness pooled on the edges of his vision, then come rolling in. The pain ever greater. Just before his eyes closed, he heard the loud, shrieking alarm of V's heart and brain monitors as they flatlined. Then all went silent. Nox knew no more…

AN INTERVIEW WITH THE AUTHOR

Charles Day was born in London and grew up in Hampshire. He was brought up by his mother, and sister, as his mother suffered from Multiple Sclerosis. Leaving home at 17, he went to Bahrain and then started to travel around the world. He lived in South Africa for 10 years, Holland for 2 years and Azerbaijan for a year. Got married (and divorced) twice and picked up five children along the way. He currently lives in a small village in Aberdeenshire, about 20 miles from Aberdeen

What did you do before becoming a writer?
I worked, my entire career, in the oil and gas industry – which satisfied my desire for travel and adventure!

Are you a planner or do you fly by the seat of your pants (a pantser)?!
No, very much a seat of the pants author. Each morning I switch on the computer, a blank page staring back at me, the cursor teasing me and I go where my fingers take me. Believe me writing is an adventure for me as I never quite know where I am going or where the day will end!

What inspired the idea for your book?
A love of science. I wanted to pass on my love of science to kids in the hope that it will spark their interest. I hope that as they read the book, they will learn something, even though they do not realise it!

If you are planning a sequel, can you share a bit about your plans for it?
Absolutely. It is ongoing as we speak. More surprises and you will meet up with some old characters. Perhaps a trilogy, depends on where the sequel takes me, like I said, I only know the start point, the ending? I have no idea!

For more information visit
www.thepotalegacy.com
or contact
Charles@thepotalegacy.com

Printed in Great Britain
by Amazon

24832899R00255